A Part of Me

Also by **Anouska Knight**

SINCE YOU'VE BEEN GONE

Stay in touch with Anouska Knight at:
www.facebook.com/AnouskaKnightAuthor
www.twitter.com/AnouskaKnight

A Part of Me

ANOUSKA KNIGHT

This edition published in Great Britain 2014
by Mills & Boon, an imprint of Harlequin (UK) Limited,
Eton House, 18-24 Paradise Road, Richmond, Surrey, TW9 1SR

ISBN: 978-0-263-24562-2

097-0714

Harlequin (UK) policy is to use papers that are natural, renewable and recyclable products and made from wood grown in sustainable forests. The logging and manufacturing processes conform to the legal environmental regulations of the country of origin.

Printed and bound
by CPI Group (UK) Ltd, Croydon, CR0 4YY

For my sisters, who I love more than Marmite

PROLOGUE

THERE WAS SOMETHING innately foreboding about waking up at an unknown hour in an unfamiliar room. A childlike fear, fortified by pressing shadows and the mysteries they concealed. Revelations better left in the dark.

Against an unexplained sharpness nestled deeply within my throat, I inhaled the softness of my mother's perfume from where she sat motionless beside me. Her presence was little reassurance amidst the thick heavy quiet.

As children, she'd once driven us, weeping, through the night to spend the remaining dark hours in the box room of my grandmother's bungalow. I was reminded now of that long night in the darkness, lying in a bed that did not smell of home, listening to the sounds of my brother's restless sleep from the fold-out bed next to me. I remember being not quite brave enough to risk disturbing so much as the air around me to call out for my mother.

She was here now, but still this felt a lot like that time. The air heavy with a palpable sense of change. The loss of something achingly irreplaceable.

I opened my eyes with another steadying breath. The pinch in my throat cut the action short. Mum shifted beside me.

It was too quiet.

Intuitively, a cool, soft hand tried gently to reassure with soothing motions over the back of my knuckles. The stirring anxiety in my chest blossomed in response. A warm wave of nausea rushed past the scratchiness in my throat then, lacing my mouth with a pitiful flurry of saliva. It hurt when I retched. Across the bleak grey room, the sound was enough to pull the attention of the figure standing quietly there.

I felt my mother's hand close around my own.

'Sweetheart? Try not to move too suddenly.' In the dimness of the nightlight, I couldn't see that she had been crying, but I could hear it, there in the fragile reserve of her voice. Another retch and Mum took back her hand, adeptly lunging forth with a cardboard bowl. The sickness heralded an immediate thumping in one side of my head, forcing closed my eyes again as she wiped the bitter residue from my lips. They hurt too. And my teeth, clenching behind them – sore from the assault of medical intervention. I swallowed to remind myself of it. The pain lessened the further down it travelled. Beyond the neatly folded edges of crisp white hospital bed sheets, pain seemed to disappear altogether.

I couldn't bring myself to look down there.

A faint squeak of shoes on linoleum stirred across the

other side of the room. The sounds grew as their owner began making his way tentatively over. James's hand, heavier than my mother's, ran gently over my head. For a moment, it soothed the angry thump of ache there.

'It's okay, baby,' he whispered. 'Everything's going to be okay.'

There was something fragile in James's voice too, something that didn't belong. He leant in and kissed the straggled brown mess of my hair. His whiskers were long, scratchy, with none of his usual cologne to cocoon me as he closed the distance between us. He smelled the way he sometimes did after his run – of strain and exhaustion. Something in the way he kissed me now paved the way for inevitable memories of the previous morning to filter back home.

The day had begun like any other. The same dull ache I knew would subside from my hips once I was up and showered; enough mischievous nudges to wake me long before my alarm had chance to. And then, the unexpected as I'd pulled back the duvet, revealing that this day would punctuate all others in the last thirty-one weeks.

There hadn't been that much blood at first. During the frantic time that followed, I'd stayed calm – we both had – listening to plans being made as the professionals poked and prodded, recorded and conferred. James had focused on their reassurances, while I'd stacked all my chips on the nudges. That was the practical thing to do. No panicking unless the nudges stopped. All the while I'd kept calm, thinking such practical thoughts, as if thought alone could keep us safely centred in the eye of the storm building around us. Now there was only quiet.

James moved his head beside mine, his breathing shallow against my ear. I listened to it. But there was no relief in him. I knew then. This was the aftermath of that storm. The stillness after the chaos. The changed landscape waiting to be considered. Here in this too-quiet room, the devastation would be met.

Mum took my free hand again, the other engaged in tubing and tape. She was squeezing it tightly now, holding onto it as if one of us might be blown to oblivion otherwise. I lay quite still, suddenly afraid again of disturbing the air around me.

'Amy? Do you know where you are?' James asked quietly, straining to hold the evenness of his voice. He was still holding himself awkwardly beside me, his face hidden from mine. I nodded against him, willing him to stem the rest of his words. He was trembling. 'Amy…We lost him, baby.'

My mother's grip loosened as she broke beneath a subdued shudder of anguish. James's voice cracked against me. 'We'll be okay, baby,' he promised. 'We're gonna be okay.'

CHAPTER 1

Five years later

AS FAR AS uncomfortable experiences went I was pretty good in the saddle, I thought. Calm. Controlled. Cool under fire. And these traits had come in handy over several tumultuous years working within a fast-paced architectural practice. But *this*? This gave a whole new meaning to the term 'pressure'. This whole set-up was geared towards breaking a person. A relentless tap-tap-tapping at the walls of our resolve, thinly veiled attempts to expose our weaknesses so that they could finally tell us what I'd prepared myself to hear all along – that we weren't worthy, that we'd make awful parents, and that this had all been a horrific waste of everybody's time.

A heavy wooden door clattered shut somewhere off the corridor where we sat, fidgeting like apprehended schoolchildren. We both listened to the patter of daintily heeled shoes as they echoed away from us to some other inhospitable depth of the building. I knew it wasn't Anna, she'd been wearing flats when she'd briefed us this morning.

I'd watched her tapping them nervously on our behalf before the panel had called us in, then I'd focused my eyes on the bejewelled toes of those same shoes while James answered the questions each panel member had put to him.

I let out a long silent breath, surprised that I couldn't see a grey plume as it hit the chilly air in this fusty old building. James's knee resumed its impatient bobbing. That James, the epitome of unflappability, was this jumpy only jangled my own nerves.

Every other meeting, interview and session had been conducted in a purpose-built room. A conference suite, an office, our home, even – where there were carpets and coffee and heating. But the Town Hall, this last checkpoint on the home straight, was about as inviting as a Dickensian institution.

I checked my watch. It had been nearly fifteen minutes since the panel had dismissed us to await our fate out here. You could cram an impressive amount of mental self-flagellation into that timeframe, I'd found. I knew James didn't want to hear it, but I needed to blurt out something, and words seemed preferable to anxious blubbing.

'I shouldn't have said we've been looking at bigger houses,' I groaned quietly.

Exasperatedly, James pushed a flop of dark blond hair back from his face and gave his left knee a reprieve from all the jiggling. I'd made him grow his hair out a little after one of the other women on the prep course had said we looked *corporate*. She'd made it sound like a swear word. James couldn't understand why I was taking any sort of advice from a woman who was actually *choosing* single-parenthood. When she'd told us that she was hoping to adopt more than one child by herself, James had whispered that even if she made it to the medical stage, they'd probably find she was certifiably nuts.

I hadn't noticed until just now, but longer hair didn't really suit James.

He turned to face me. 'They didn't ask us anything that they hadn't already read in our report, okay? And there's no rule that says we can't move house one day.' James's right knee took over the bobbing.

I tucked precision-straightened hair neatly behind my ears and began to fiddle with one of the small diamond studs he'd bought me for my twenty-ninth last month. One of the few nights we'd actually gone out together and not fallen out.

'Stability, James. That's what they want to hear, not that we're planning to up sticks and disrupt our home—'

James held a hand aloft to cut me off. 'Amy, forget it. We're not doing this again. We've jumped through every sodding hoop imaginable over the last year just to get to this point. We've just met ten people in there we don't know from Adam, yet they know every last sodding thing there is to know about us.' He was already pointing an accusing finger down the corridor towards the room where the panel were still discussing and dissecting our lives. 'They've been through our income, our childhoods… our sodding body mass indexes, for Christ's sake! If it's all going to come tumbling down now because you said you'd like a bigger garden one day then they can shove it up their pedantic arses.'

'Shh! Someone might hear you!' I sputtered, nervously eyeing both ends of the corridor. James stood. I watched as he moved away from me over to the tired lead window opposite. This journey hadn't been an easy one, but on some level I knew that James had found it harder than I had, and ultimately would find it easier to walk away from, if it was about to come to that.

We're nearly there, I wanted to say to him, but everything about him looked so uneasy. He'd never wear that jumper again. I'd bought it from M&S because walking in wearing his favoured Ralph Lauren might've been read as 'part-time yacht-enthusiast', when what we were aiming for was 'full-time crayon-enthusiast'. I blew out a cheekful of air. Subliminal messages through the medium of casual knitwear – how was *that* for cruising close to certifiable nuttiness?

James shook his head as he looked out onto the dismal March morning. We'd asked for the earliest slot available, I knew I'd be a wreck otherwise. James began jostling the keys in his trouser pocket before turning cool blue eyes on me.

'Anna wouldn't have put us forward to panel if she

didn't think we were ready, you know that. Just… try to relax, okay?' I nodded, reluctantly leaving my earring alone before I pinged it onto the floor again. I decided to chew at my lower lip instead. There was less chance of that ending up on the floor and, unlike diamonds, skin was self-regenerating. Beyond the corner of the corridor, softly striding footsteps were making their way towards us. James's chest rose with a deep intake of breath as he turned back to the window.

The Chair of the panel, a forty-something chap with thinning hair and a name I'd been too flustered to catch, rounded the corner towards us. Awkwardly, I got to my feet and straightened my clothes. I'd gone for a pale blue blouse and pretty cardigan in lavender. Depending on how the next few minutes went, I probably wouldn't wear them again either.

'Miss Alwood, Mr Coffrey. Would you like to come back in?'

I gave a small, unassuming smile and convinced myself he had smiled back. I looked to James for affirmation, but he was steely eyed.

I watched Mr Chair's elbow patches all the way back into the musty room where Anna sat at one of three chairs set in front of the panel. We'd got lucky when Anna was assigned to us. Not everyone liked their social worker but, thankfully, we did. I waited for her to look at us, but only the back of her short blonde ponytail faced our way. My stomach churned. Beyond Anna, the panel of four men and six women looked as though they were sitting at the top table of a wedding reception, with a very small congregation of three with which to share their joy.

I crossed my fingers at my side. *Please, let them be about to share joy.*

'Hey, take a seat,' Anna whispered, gesturing at the chairs we'd sweated out our interrogation on just half an hour ago. I was sure I saw one of the panel members, the adoptee, smile too, but it was so much warmer in here the temperature change was making me feel fuzzy at the edges.

The Chair settled himself into his seat again and fumbled at his papers the way officials with official business like to do. 'Mr Coffrey, Miss Alwood.' A new thudding was taking up residence in my chest. 'We know this can be a rather fraught experience, so we don't wish to subject you to any further unnecessary tension.' James reached over and took my hand assertively in his. *We'll be okay. Whatever happens, we'll work through it.*

'Therefore, we would like to offer you both our congratulations. It is this panel's recommendation that you be approved as joint adoptive parents to a child under the age of four years.'

Thud, thud, thud …

The pulsing inside my chest was the only thing telling me I hadn't keeled over and died on the spot, but even that was beginning to wane. The trembling inside me was being swallowed up by something else, something shocky and numb – a sensation sweeping through my insides chased by a warmer, welcome feeling…

Joy.

Could this really be happening? Finally, were we nearly there? I glanced vacantly through each of the warm expressions of the panel members. Had I correctly understood what had just been said?

I looked at Anna. Her face was rosy with controlled delight, which made something loosen in me, some invisible hawser rope that had kept me steady all these past months, suddenly letting me go enough that I might keel over yet. James nuzzled a kiss against my cheek, his thumb chasing the first wet track as it coursed down my face. He said something to Anna as a broken message began organising itself in my mind.

We're going to have a child. Somewhere out there, our little boy or girl is waiting for us to bring them home.

Skirting along the periphery of my thoughts, I was aware that Anna was saying something in reply to James. She patted my back reassuringly, just a small gesture of comfort but enough to trigger the domino effect. I hadn't meant to dissolve so whole-heartedly in the middle of that room, to be so completely disabled by my own happiness and rendered such a useless blubbering mess, but after twenty-one months of being cool under fire I couldn't keep it inside another second.

There was room for only one thought, one thread of coherence in my mind, and each time it lapped around my

brain, so began a new wave of uncontrollable sobs, muffled only by James's M&S jumper. The jewel-like embel-
lishments on the toes of Anna's shoes shone and danced
like a kaleidoscope refracted through my rather impressive deluge of tears, and then James leant back in to my
hair and said the words. Said them out loud so that we
could hear the truth in them.

'We're going to be parents.'

CHAPTER 2

'WELL, YOU KNOW what they say.' Phil grinned, chocolate eyes peeping from under her blunt designer fringe. All around us, the city's populace of on-trend urbanites basked in the funky basement atmosphere of Rufus's Cocktail Lounge. It had always been our favourite place.

'Go on, Phil, what do *they* say?' I asked, indulging her.

'If your sex-life is crap and you argue all the time, you might as well have kids.' Phil finished her words of encouragement with a blood-red smile and a playful shrug of her shoulders.

'I think you mean *get married*, Phil. If your sex-life is crap and you argue all the time, you might as well *get married*, isn't it?'

Phil hooked a long glossy fingernail around a hair that had affixed itself to her newly reapplied lippy and swept it back in with the others. 'Whatever. They're both bad ideas.' She winked.

'Well, I know which one I'm interested in,' I said, over the mellow beats of Rufus's in-house DJ. 'And it doesn't involve a big white dress.' I smoothed out the creases of my silk pewter vest while Phil let her eyes follow a group of men towards the bar. In the dimness of the club's ambience, her dark brown bob looked closer to black, giving her an air reminiscent of a Japanese doll. Whatever had caught her attention at the bar wasn't enough to hold it there.

'We'll see,' she cooed. 'Once junior arrives, you'll be all loved up and Viv will be banging on about *nuclear families*, and you'll buckle. I'll put money on it. You'll be Mrs Coffrey before the end of next year.'

Phil knew my family too well. Mum had already tried every angle she could to talk me into the virtues of marriage, despite my father having put an abrupt end to theirs after falling for mine and my brother's babysitter. It wasn't that I was against marriage exactly, and in fairness to my father after eighteen years it seemed to be working for him and Petra, but as far as commitment went, I just couldn't see that there was anything more binding than raising a child together.

'Mum just wants the whole wedding faff, Phil. She missed out when my brother married Lauren because Lauren's mum did it all. That's why she's going nuts with this bloody party she's talked us into having. Did I tell you that she's made me order a massive cake for it?'

Phil broke into a husky giggle. 'If she's content with throwing you a mock-wedding reception, Ame, cake and all, take the deal and run.'

'It's not a mock-wedding reception.' I shuddered. At least not outside my mum's head it wasn't. 'It's just a small gathering to celebrate our new status as…' *What were we now, exactly?* '… parents-in-waiting.'

'It's your last chance at a big mash-up before you go all boring on me is what it is. I suppose we've had a good run, though.' Phil sighed. 'You've been pretty good fun, for someone who's already been stuck with the same ball and chain, for-*ever*.'

James wasn't the ball and chain. Ball and chains didn't keep a mental itinerary of all the things we wouldn't be able to do over the next few years. Like skiing holidays, and city-breaks. If anyone was shackling anyone else, Phil probably had it back to front. 'Eight years is hardly for-ever, Phil.' I smiled.

'Sex with the same man for eight years and you're not even thirty yet. It's heartbreaking,' she said absently.

I shook my head, spearing a slice of lemon with my straw. 'You never know, Philippa. You might settle down yourself, one day.'

Phil grimaced at the horror of such a thought. 'And wake up to the same guy for the rest of my days? No. There isn't a man who could swing that deal. I mean, how utterly depressing. No wonder women turn to chips and chocolate once they *settle down*. You'd better buy yourself some loose joggers now, Hon, you've done well to last this long. In fact, I'd been wondering what gift I should bring you guys to your "kissing-our-lives-goodbye" party.

I'll get you his and hers jogging bottoms… with pockets, for your chocolate wrappers.'

Phil smiled while a couple of our remaining cohorts, still lucid enough to follow the conversation, joined in.

'I can't imagine Amy in jogging bottoms,' chirped Hannah, Cyan Architecture & Design's newest office junior. Hannah's wispy blonde hair had become steadily more wispy as we'd worked our way through the cocktails list. 'You're always so… *polished*,' she continued.

Sat beside Hannah, Sadie Espley – niece of Adrian Espley, Cyan's founding architect – looked as though she might actually contribute something for the first time all night. Then her phone flashed again, reeling her face back down behind a curtain of honey-blonde tresses.

'You do know that Amy isn't your boss, right, Hannah?' Phil enquired, drily. 'You haven't *got* to kiss her arse. And before you say it, yes, even though it is indeed a perfectly honed and perky size ten.'

'Twelve now,' I corrected. James had mentioned *Christmas excess* twice since my birthday.

Tom and Alice, Cyan's computer-generated-imagery techie and marketing primo respectively, flopped down onto the right side of the booth, squashing the rest of us four bodies closer to Phil.

'Did I hear something about a perfect arse?' Tom asked, a glaze of dance-induced sweat sticking loose fawny curls to his forehead. 'You talking about my booty again, Philippa?' He never changed out of his hipster jeans and casual shirts, not even for Friday-night cock-tails.

'Not this time, hot stuff,' Phil replied. 'Amy's arse, not yours. Hannah's grown fond of kissing it.'

'Cool it, Phil. Hannah's just being nice. Remember what that feels like? Being *nice*?' I stuck my tongue out playfully and was rewarded with another danger-red grin.

'If you think Phil's got a big mouth, Hannah, wait till you go on a night out with Dana and Marcy,' Alice said glibly. 'You'll think Phil's a pussycat.' Phil blew Alice a kiss. Over the last few years Cyan Architecture & Design had grown enough that the women in the office now loosely formed two groups. Us and Them. Dana and Marcy were definitely thems. Phil said Sadie belonged with them too, and wasn't impressed that I'd asked her out with us tonight. Sadie's relentless preoccupation with her phone wasn't exactly winning her any points. Sadie lifted her head and briefly looked big blue eyes out from trendy rectangular glasses. 'Dana and Marcy are all right, Alice,' she declared.

Phil cocked an unconvinced eyebrow. 'Well, they're not going to be bitchy with you, are they, Sadie? Not with Uncle Adrian paying their wages.'

'I earn my keep, Phil,' Sadie retorted. 'I work all the hours you do.'

'Er, you're in the studio the same amount of hours, Sadie, I'll give you that. But that's not quite the same thing.'

The atmosphere dropped a few centigrade. 'I don't get any special perks, Phil.'

Phil smiled. 'But you don't see Uncle Adrian letting us lot get away with a fumble in the samples library with the lighting rep, Sadie. That poor guy, he only came into the office to show you their new product range.'

Tom began tittering. 'She saw more than that!'

Sadie glared at Phil. 'So who are you, Phil, the sodding fun police?' She tried to meet Phil's glare, then, obviously thinking better of heading further into the argument Phil had started, returned to her text-a-thon. Fortunately, her phone had more life left in it than Leah from reprographics, who'd been face down on the glass-strewn table for at least twenty minutes. Phil stopped glaring at Sadie and muttered something under her breath about dodgy CVs and loose knickers. They'd always jarred. Phil disliked Sadie for the same reasons I couldn't bring myself to – Sadie was twenty-three, with legs up to her eyeballs, and seemed to have way too much fun for just one person. I hoped it would last as long as possible for her. I'd been like Sadie too, once. Phil still was, she just wasn't twenty-three any more and it annoyed her.

Phil shook it off just as a sticky round of Cosmopolitans touched down on the table next to Leah's face.

'So, who's up for going up town?' Alice enthused.

'You guys get stuck into those,' I said, nodding at the drinks. 'I'm just nipping to the Ladies'.' I nudged Tom and Alice so I could wriggle out past them.

A few minutes of peace in the loos and I was glad not to be part of the clubbing debate. By the time I'd re-emerged from my cubicle, I was already flagging. The door into the Ladies' swung open and a familiar head bobbed into view. 'So? We going with them?'

I pulled a face and pumped on the soap dispenser. 'I don't think I'll be out much later, Phil.'

Phil pouted. 'Nah, you're right. I don't think I could listen to Hannah blowing any more smoke up your arse anyway.'

'Give her a break, Phil. She's a nice girl.'

Phil acknowledged me sourly then began retouching her lippy in the vanity mirror. 'I'm a nice girl too, you know,' she huffed indignantly.

'I know! Just… be cool. Give Hannah a chance to know that too.' I finished rinsing the soap from my hands. 'And lay off Sadie. I know you're not keen but she's not so bad. Plus, I don't want to wind Adrian up. He's strung out enough.'

Phil watched me in the mirror. 'Adrian's always strung out. Since when did you roll over for him, anyway?'

I pulled a few paper towels from the dispenser and bent down for a quick cubicle check. 'Since Claire Farrel told him she's taking a partnership with Devlin Raines. She leaves in six weeks.' Devlin Raines were Cyan's main competition in the city. They were a bigger company than us, with offices in several UK cities, and Adrian hated losing anything to them, especially staff.

'Claire's leaving? She kept that quiet. So that's why Adrian's been so uptight.' Phil began tidying her fringe. 'But why does that affect you?'

'Because a few days before Claire gave Adrian notice, he agreed to consider James and I sharing the adoption leave. Claire's leaving has thrown the surveying team up in the air, I don't want him to clamp James down and change his mind about us sharing the time off.'

'How much time is it?'

'A year.'

'A year? Adrian agreed to that? Well, at least now I know why you asked Glitter Knickers to come out tonight. Keep Uncle Adrian on side then, hon.'

'That's not why I invited Sadie, Phil. She's been a little out of kilter lately. I think she's having man trouble.'

'Man trouble? Sadie! You are joking? Jeez, Ame, you are such a sucker. She's been sexting some brain-dead beefcake all night. I bet you any money, she dumps us soon to go cop off with him.'

I watched Phil carefully in the mirror. 'Jealous, much?'

She was trying to keep a straight face. 'You're damned straight, I am,' she conceded, tumbling into husky laughter. 'I could do with a good snog.'

Phil tugged me back out into the throb of Rufus's. Leah from reprographics was now propped up between Tom and Hannah. They were chatting to each other as if it were a bus stop and not a human body sandwiched between them.

'Where're Sadie and Alice?' Phil asked.

'Clubbing's a no-go with this one,' Tom huffed, repositioning Leah's limp arm through his. 'Alice's gone to get a head start on the pizzas and Sadie, er… she left when you guys went to the loos.'

'Sadie left? By herself?' I asked.

Tom shrugged. 'Said she didn't fancy sharing a pizza, or a taxi, with Phil. She said she was going to grab a cab at the rank.' I threw Phil a reproachful look and checked my watch.

'What?'

'Come on, it's one thirty in the morning. We're not leaving her to wait for a cab on her own.'

Phil grimaced again. 'But what about the pizza?'

I narrowed my eyes at her. 'You don't eat pizza, Phil. It's not macrobiotic.'

Phil was better at narrowed-eyes than I was. 'Oh, sod it, Amy. Why do you have to be such a sodding Girl Guide?' she huffed, starting off towards the doors. She waited there impatiently as I said goodbye to the others.

'Come on, then,' Phil called, 'let's go rescue Glitter Knickers.'

*

Ten chilly minutes later, the end of the taxi rank queue snaked into view.

'I don't see her, Phil,' I said, trailing my eyes over the

queue of scantily clad girls and kebab-wielding lads vying for the next available taxi.

'She's a big girl, Ame. She probably got the beefcake to pick her up.'

'And what if she didn't?'

Phil gave the queue a once-over. 'She's not here, Ame.' A commotion broke out in the line, the timeless cocktail of testosterone and alcohol. 'Sod this,' Phil scowled, 'I'm not waiting here with this lot. Work's only five minutes away, let's call a cab from there. Quicker *and* warmer.' As soon as Phil mentioned the cold, I could feel it, seeping in through my jacket.

'We can't, Phil. No unauthorised access at weekends any more. Adrian was pretty clear on that.'

'Again with the Girl Guide thing, Ame! You're such a do-gooder these days.'

I held my hands up. 'Okay, okay! We'll go to the office. But I'm not getting labelled as the Nightshagger, okay? So if we get caught, I'm just gonna flat out say that I know it's you, Phil.'

Phil's face flourished at that. 'Let me tell you now, if I was the one who'd been flushing the un-flushable down the men's loos, I wouldn't risk getting caught there now. The cleaners are on the warpath. Anyway, everyone knows it's Stewart from reprographics, the dirty little monster. No wonder Leah drinks so much, it must be awful working next to Stewie all week.' Phil huddled into me, walking us away from the crowd.

'So Stewart's been slipping into the studios at night! Are you sure?' Honestly, I didn't think he had it in him.

'Yeah, I'm sure. You see, Ame, while you spend your time keeping abreast of promotions, and job restructuring, the rest of us keep track of the important stuff – like who's sneaking into the office at night for a bonk. It would almost be romantic, if the little weasel wasn't married.'

'Stewart's *married*? I've never noticed a ring.'

'That's because he never wears it outside the marital home, the sneaky shit.'

Comical though the saga of the Nightshagger had been, I felt bad for Stewart's wife, whoever she was. I'd seen the flip side of extra-marital fun, and it wasn't much fun at all. Phil shivered as we crossed the deserted courtyard of the immaculately landscaped business square where Cyan Architecture & Design's studios dominated. The studios were housed in part of what was once an old biscuit factory, deep red brickwork dating back to an era when even industrial buildings were beautiful.

We came to a standstill between the two potted box bushes standing sentry at Cyan's sleek glass entrance. Phil was already ordering the taxi by the time I'd silently punched the code into the door keypad, letting us in to the perma-lit reception. It was marginally warmer inside the lobby, but the blast of cold air outside had already highlighted the fact that I was not as sober as I thought.

Phil finished the call as I flopped down into the swivel chair behind Ally's reception desk.

'They said fifteen minutes. We could go and revise a drawing while we wait, if you like?'

I swatted my hand dismissively. Okay, so I'd become a bit of a slave to this place over the last few years, but taken with Phil's abandon it made for a necessary balance within the interiors team.

I began swivelling my chair slowly. 'Why does Ally need so many mini Post-it notes?' I whispered, glancing over the array of neon-coloured squares framing Ally's computer screen.

'Probably so she can tell her arse from her elbow?' Phil leant over my shoulder to read the little memos. 'File nails, stick boobs in Adrian's face, practise counting to ten...'

I pushed her away. 'Don't be mean, Phil. Ally's okay. I like her eyelashes. They're so big, and...' I tried to think past the effects of too many mojitos for the right word '... *lashy.*'

Phil grinned. 'Oh, you like that, do you, Hon? Allow me!' Phil took a luminous-pink Post-it note from the colourful stack of pads beside Ally's keyboard and began fringing it with a pair of scissors from the pencil pot. She leant over the desk and stuck it over my eye. I waited while she did the same to a neon-green Post-it, and slapped it over my other eye. Then she stood back to admire her work. 'How's that for a degree in product design? Give them a whirl, then!'

I began power-blinking and grinning in alcohol-defying unison. It would seem that Phil's cocktail intake was finally taking effect too and an explosion of laughter burst from her throat.

'Ha-HA! That's funny!' she cackled. 'You should defo wear Post-its on party night, Ame, you look *priddy.*'

'BFFs should match, Phillypops. You'll need some too!' I chortled. I held off flapping my new eyewear just long enough to fashion Phil a pair of the same, sticking a set of bright orange paper appendages over her smoky grey eyelids. Once we started laughing again, we were infected. Phil hung over the reception desk in silent convulsion while I threw myself back across the swivel chair, somehow still batting mismatched neon eyelids while struggling for breath.

Had we not finally broken for air, we probably wouldn't have heard it. I caught it first. Somehow managing to hold my snickering long enough to listen a while.

There it was again, someone else's laughter, deep within the design studio. I held my breath and began flapping my hand at Phil, signalling frantically for her to stop giggling.

Phil caught on and shushed. We both heard it this time, a woman's laughter. Definitely.

Slowly, I released my breath and watched Phil's expression sober as she strained to hear. The culprit was already taking shape in Phil's mind, I could tell. 'That randy little sod!' she whispered. 'Come on, let's bust the Nightshagger!'

I was too drunk for this, so was Phil. I could feel that last bout of laughter still sitting high in my chest, threatening to erupt. I watched Phil cock her ear and wait. The giggler had no idea they had company.

'And do what?' I whispered.

'Just bust him! Ame, we'll never have to wait our turn for printouts again, or panic about getting things print-ready before the repro lot clock off! Stewie will do anything to keep this from Adrian! How good's your camera-phone?'

She didn't wait for an answer. Phil grabbed my hand and hoisted me up before we both tried to tack delicately in heels across the reception's polished floor. As we slipped into the darkness of the first studio, whispers at the far end of the office gave way to another ripple of laughter. This time, Stewart joined in with his guest, a muffled masculine growl of a laugh, rising and disappearing in waves as he buried his face somewhere that most likely did not belong to his wife. Whoever did own those places was enjoying his visit. It made the laughter rise in me. I yanked on Phil's hand to slow her Royal Marine-like lead across the darkened office before my lungs erupted into ear-shattering laughter.

What? she mouthed as I held her back. One of Phil's orange non-Marine issue eyelashes was coming unstuck. The grunting was coming from the boardroom, just the other side of a few shafts of moonlight spearing the office windows. Phil yanked us on, passing our own workstations to slump ourselves just the other side of the glass boardroom wall, blinds mercifully shielding us from view.

It probably wasn't the most appropriate time, but the alcohol in me saw fit to roll off a few more comedy blinks. Phil clamped a hand over her mouth, and for a few more moments, we both stayed that way – crouched in darkness and silent hysterics while the grunter grunted on. Over his groaning, Stewie's guest was delivering a running commentary on her talents. Listening to dirty talk was too much. I clamped my fingers and thumb over the end of my nose, trying to hold down the pressure of burning hilarity before it leaked noisily from my face.

Phil was at it too, straining to remain quiet as she leant against the glass wall, but unlike me, Phil was focused – determined to take Stewart down commando style. From behind her makeshift lashes, Phil fixed me with determined eyes. She raised her free hand, aggressively pointing two fingers at her own eyes then mine. Then she signalled the count.

Three fingers…

Two fingers…

One…

We half exploded, half fell into the boardroom. Phil had clearly done this before, going straight for the lights.

'GREEN BERETS! EVERYBODY FREEZE!' she shouted as the half-naked blonde skittered from where she'd been straddling her friend.

The laughter that had been waiting for its escape jumped from my body towards the dazed couple before I could stop it.

For a few seconds, the room became like a vacuum, a spinning black hole sucking away the air. A queasiness immediately filled the void my laughter had left behind. I swayed on my feet.

Sadie looked younger without her glasses.

Disorientated, I watched the groaner lurch from his chair, yanking at his trousers.

'Amy!' James, baffled, running a hand over his muddled blond head. 'Shit! Amy, I can explain…'

CHAPTER 3

'ARE YOU SURE this is what you want to do, honey? Why not leave it a little while, just until you've given yourself a few days to think everything through?' This was the third time Phil had called. It was a rare occasion that saw the softness beneath her prickly veneer, but I guess she thought the situation warranted it. Somewhere in the murky recesses of my mind, I knew it wasn't a good sign.

'All I've done is think, Phil. My head hurts from it. I just…' I watched the rain silently streaming down the windows overlooking the executive homes opposite. So far April had been unseasonably cold. All morning the sky had promised snow, but there was nothing on the horizon now but miserable grey inevitability.

Phil waited for me to get it together, but I'd already forgotten what I was saying.

'You can't just walk, Amy. You've worked too hard at that place. Don't tell Adrian anything, not yet. Just… call in sick. Think about all that later.'

Later? Because *later* would somehow suddenly mean I didn't work at the same company as the man who'd just car-crashed our life? Or the woman he'd chosen to go joyriding with? What could *later* possibly offer? My focus shifted from the streaks of rainwater, breaking my view of the new sandpit in the garden, to the faint reflection I could see of myself in the cold grey glass. I turned away – away from it all, back to the house James hadn't returned to last night. Apparently, he couldn't explain. Other than a flurry of missed calls at 3 a.m. there had been nothing.

'Ame? Are you still there?'

I leant my back against the bookcase and scanned the rest of the lounge. My own home suddenly felt foreign.

'I'm here.'

Anna had advised us to replace the old glass coffee table with this wooden one. Wood was safer, easier to affix corner cushions to. I'd bought those the same day. And the socket covers, the kitchen drawer catches and the fire guard. All deployed and ready for action. We were fully accident-proofed. If you wanted to hurt yourself around here, as in *really* cause yourself gut-wrenching pain, James's idea of love and loyalty was probably going to be your best bet. I tried to shake his name from my head but, from nowhere, the turmoil of the last twelve hours saw its chance and rushed me again. I covered my face with my sweater sleeve, holding the lower part of the phone away so Phil wouldn't hear.

'Why don't I come over?' she tried.

Quietly, I breathed through it. I felt my chest release

again, reluctantly unclenching like an angry fist, and risked a steady lungful of air.

'I can't stay here, Phil. I'm going to Mum's once I've packed some things.'

'Is Viv picking you up, or do you need a ride?' she asked softly.

'No. Thanks. I'll get a cab.' My voice faltered.

'Are you crying? Because if you're crying I'm coming over right now.' A warm rush streaked down either side of my face again. I wiped the tears away, as if that might somehow hide the evidence from my friend.

'Stand down, Phil. I'm not crying,' I lied. 'I have to go. I don't want to be here much longer in case he turns up.'

Phil let out an unappeased breath. 'Okay. Call me, will you?'

I nodded at the phone and set it down on its post before Phil could hear me lose it again.

I hadn't been sure that I couldn't stay here until I'd said it out loud. Now I knew I couldn't. I didn't think he'd have brought her here, but it wasn't impossible. I booked a cab and skipped upstairs, pulling closed the first door I passed. The lingering smell of recent paint was reason enough to shut off that bedroom. James said we should wait, see who we were matched with, but I'd started painting the nursery in neutrals the day we'd returned from panel. Maybe I'd jinxed it. There were superstitions about that kind of thing.

My bedroom felt just as foreign as the rest of the house. I began stuffing a few handfuls of clothing into James's overnight bag before lunging towards my dressing table. The bottom drawer slid out easily, revealing the prettily decorated firebox nestled safely on its cushion of winter sweaters. I couldn't remember where the idea had originated from, my grandmother probably, but I was glad for it now. In the event of a house fire or other major catastrophe, letters, keepsakes – anything of irreplaceable value –would all be to hand in the firebox. All in one place, ready for salvation.

I lifted the découpaged box from the open drawer and regarded it. Dedicated teacher that she was, there wasn't much Mum couldn't achieve with PVA glue and patience. My fingers briefly reacquainted themselves with the delicately placed art nouveau motifs in muted blues and greens, the subtle unevenness of the layered images she'd painstakingly crafted. She'd made the firebox for us that August, busying herself in the kitchen while I'd pretended to sleep up here. James had to return to work eventually, for normality's sake, if nothing else. She'd said such precious things deserved to be kept somewhere nice.

I let my fingers rest on the lip of the firebox. As if I needed to look. As if I didn't know by heart the remembrances kept safely inside. The pitiful testaments to our son's tiny life.

He'd have been at school now. Greenacres Primary in Earleswicke, where his grandmother, headmistress there, could have kept an eye on him for me. Made sure he ate his sandwiches; comforted him if one of the other kids was

mean. Something like anger flared in my stomach. I fed
the firebox gently into James's bag, pulled on my jacket
and skipped out across the landing for the stairs.

Thoughts of Sadie knowing the inside of my home
almost sent me into a delirium. The firebox wasn't the
only thing I couldn't bear her to have been anywhere near.
I padded from the pale stairwell carpet onto the milky
polished tiles of the hallway. We'd spent months fattening
out the file I'd kept safely in the kitchen cupboard. The file
that demonstrated the family we could offer to one of the
thousands of children awaiting a home. Every last detail
of our lives was in there, including our copy of the pros-
pective adopter's report Anna had put together on us. The
PAR was the result of months of countless assessments,
interviews with friends, family, diagrams of our support network, income, medical backgrounds, and it was
not being left here. Sadie probably knew it all anyway,
pillow-talk while I sat at home, oblivious and foolish.
Well, it was all coming with me.

A car horn papped outside as I strode into the white tundra of our clean-lined kitchen. I stood the overnight bag
against the wine fridge and stalked over to the last cupboard at the end run of units.

I yanked open the tall, sleek cupboard door. The door
clattered clumsily, opening only a little way before jarring
back against my fingers, denying me access. The handle
pulled my fingernail with it and a hot pain drew a hiss
from my throat.

I still wasn't used to the cupboard locks, designed to prevent inquisitive little hands from finding their way to trouble. A searing pain flared where I'd snagged my nail. It was already bleeding happily, a burning sensation spreading not just through my fingertip, but it seemed completely through my core, too. I held it up for inspection and found I'd torn the end of it clean off. It was only a fingernail. Anyone looking in would've thought I'd just severed a major artery. I slumped pathetically against the unit doors to the cold tiled floor. Something had been severed, it just wasn't anything that could be tackled with a tourniquet and fast thinking. At the sight of a silly bleeding finger, something tight in my chest, like an over-stretched elastic band, suddenly gave way. I tried not to, but it was futile. It was as if every muscle in my body wanted to cry for itself too. So I let them, right there on the kitchen floor as the taxi papped on outside.

CHAPTER 4

THE WALLS OF my old bedroom weren't magenta any more but an inoffensive cream and peppermint pinstripe where Mum had done away with the bohemian décor of my youth. My once beloved tie-dyed swathes had been replaced with crushed silk drapes in her favourite sage, more befitting of the 1930s home Dad had left us with. For the last week, hiding out here from my life, I'd been fifteen again.

'Sweetheart? Are you coming down? They'll be here soon.' I stopped studying the abstract patterns in Mum's artexed ceiling and rolled over on my pillow. More clattering sounds of saucepans being thrown into service echoed up the stairs.

Mum's Sunday lunch was ritualistic as far as my brother was concerned. Since Lauren had given birth to their second child two months ago, Guy had tried to blag Mum to lay on a regular midweek curry night, too. He'd complained that mealtimes with a mischievous four-year-old had been chaotic enough; add a newborn to the mix and Lauren was beginning to lean towards quicker, easier, less-washing-up meals. Mum hadn't gone for it. She'd told him to be grateful Lauren was still cooking for him at all after delivering two nine-pounders, epidural-free.

'Coming,' I called, stepping out onto the landing. The morning had been fairly sedate, with Mum busying herself with her latest crusade on behalf of the WI and greater good. She'd taken my reluctance to talk about James and my crumbling adoption hopes as her cue to lead the conversation. Earleswicke community centre was soon to be levelled because the parish council shrewdly thought it made more sense to sell the place on than stump up the cash for an upgrade. I was with them on that. The community centre had smelled of damp and lost property when Mum used to drag me off to Brownies there. I was eight at the time and to my knowledge, it hadn't seen a lick of paint since. No doubt I'd hear the whole sorry tale again once Guy and Lauren arrived. I'd use the opportunity to huddle up with Samuel and catch up on all things creepy-crawly and dinosaur. Mum had put them off coming last weekend. A few concerned words from a well-meaning cabbie and Viv had gone on lockdown, prescribing a week of peace so I could lick my wounds. That and endless home-cooking.

The rich homely wafts of roast beef floated up the stairs to greet me. This was how Mum swung into recovery mode, as if food could fix whatever had been broken. She'd launched herself into maniacal cooking when Dad had first left. All of his favourites, every night for weeks, just in case he walked back in through the door. He never did.

'Okay, sweetheart?' She was carrying a tray of tea through to the conservatory as I crossed the kitchen towards her. The conservatory was cooler than the kitchen, the rattan armchair creaking beneath me like a groaning shipwreck as I settled into it. 'How are you feeling today?'

Outside, the garden had held onto the morning's frost, as though the lawn had accepted its abandonment by the sun, stoically contenting itself with ice instead. 'Fine. Thanks. Lunch smells good.' I smiled.

Mum nodded approvingly as she poured a drop of milk into each of the cups. Her hair would redden in the autumn, but until then it would remain nearly as dark as mine, with only the beginnings of grey featuring just where she would clip her corkscrew curls over one ear. Miraculously, I'd dodged the full severity of Mum's curly genes, though I realised now how youthful she still looked because of them.

'A good meal will set you up, sweetheart. Tomorrow isn't going to be easy, but I think you're doing the right thing.'

Thoughts of a Monday-morning showdown with Marcy and Dana heading up the office gossips made my stomach lurch. I'd gone over all the reasons for and against going back there, trying to find a way around it, but the fact was if I just walked out now, I couldn't think how I'd explain my sudden change in circumstances to Anna. Not that job-security alone was going to be enough to dupe her into seeing through our application.

'She should be the one clearing off,' Mum declared, vigorously stirring the tea.

I never thought that James would do this. He'd pleaded for a chance to fix things, to undo the undoable. I'd listened as Phil had coached me through the week on the evils of the unfaithful, but through the malignant mass of bitterness and hurt churning away at my insides, there was something of me that desperately wanted James to fix it all. But we were on social services' schedule, not Relate's. We didn't have time to delve into our brittle relationship and gently nurse what had been broken.

'And should James clear off too, Mum?' I asked.

She tapped her spoon on the rim of her cup, ignoring my accusation of her lopsided justice. 'You know, sweetheart, James has done a terrible thing. But it doesn't make him a terrible person.'

I watched as she set the hot drinks in place between us, then looked away through the glass onto the garden. A little robin flitted down onto the lawn and began pecking away at the grass. Maybe I was the terrible person. Maybe I'd pushed James out, neglected him. There hadn't been much room left for anything that wasn't either work or adoption related for longer than was healthy for anyone.

Mum held her cup to her face and blew over it, settling herself back into her chair. 'He called again this morning.' I carried on watching the determined little bird. James had been calling all week, leaving texts and voicemails, apologising, asking that we talk, offering to take some of his annual leave if that made my returning to work any less humiliating. 'He said he needs to talk to you, sweetheart, before you go back into the office.' I hadn't accepted James's offer but still he'd anticipated I'd go back to Cyan. I hated that I was so predictable.

'Mum, please, don't. I'm not ready to speak to him yet.'

'You can't avoid him for ever, Amy. You need to talk to him. Before the social worker catches wind of all this. Won't you see him in the office tomorrow anyway?'

An unfortunate creature caught the attention of the robin, suddenly transforming it from Christmas icon to ruthless killer. I'd never been great with birds, they seemed all beady eyes and sharp bits to me. 'He has site meetings on Mondays. It'll be easier for me to go back there tomorrow while he's not there.' *While I still have a job.* That's if I didn't lose my bottle first, which was more than possible.

Mum repositioned her glasses on her head. 'For what it's worth, I think you're doing the right thing. I know he's hurt you, sweetheart, but if you're both serious about trying to salvage this, you're going to need to work together. Children need stability, and this situation is far from stable. You need to be very careful you don't jeopardise everything you've achieved over these last months because of one… *indiscretion*.'

Indiscretion. That was one word for it.

'It's not that simple, Mum. He didn't just *slip up*.'

Mum took a sip from her cup. 'James shouldn't have fooled around with that girl, Amy. But men… they *do* slip up, lose their way. Sometimes, sweetheart, they just can't help themselves.'

It was only ever a matter of time before parallels would be drawn between James and my dad. I inhaled deeply and rolled into the inevitable. 'That's just it, Mum, they can help themselves. It's a choice they make.'

'No, not always, Amy. Sometimes they just… they fall into an unexpected situation, and then before they know it they're not sure what they want.'

I wondered if after telling herself the same thing for so long, my mother had somehow erased the basic principles of betrayal from her understanding. Eighteen years on she was still hanging onto the ghost of a notion – that Dad's departure was somehow not of his choosing.

Mum looked out onto the garden. I let my eyes fall to the teacup steaming on the table between us. It felt intrusive somehow to look outside while she did also. She sighed and turned uncertain eyes back to me. 'I'm not trying to be insensitive, Amy. I know how much hurt you must be feeling, I do. But, you and James have been through so much together. Experiences that have bound the two of you. He hasn't led you to believe that he wants a relationship with this woman, has he?' I searched the garden for something to concentrate on. The robin was nowhere, abandoning me to the conversation. The answer to her question was *no*. No, he hadn't. In every one of the messages he'd left these past seven days, James had said that he loved me. He loved me, and that he was sorry.

Mum was still waiting. I shook my head to answer her.

'James knows how complicated things can be, Amy. Hear him out, see what he has to say. Life isn't a walk in the park for anyone, sweetheart. It's complicated and messy and at times, ruddy heart-breaking. But, you have to press on.'

'So what? I should just forget what he's done?'

'No, not forget. James has done wrong, but he *is* trying. Doesn't that count for something?'

It did count for something. Mum had never met another man, waiting for my father to show a fraction of the regret James had shown over this last week. It would be cruel to say to her that it didn't count, I just didn't know whether it counted enough.

'I can't go through with the party, Mum. I'm sorry. Even if we were on speaking terms, I couldn't stand in front our friends and family and… fake it.'

'You haven't got anything to be ashamed of, Amy. Lots of people learn to carry this sort of burden. Relationships are all about accepting each other's imperfections. Goodness knows, we all have those.' I couldn't argue with that. *Imperfections* didn't exactly encompass that which James had accepted in me.

'The party was a nice idea, Mum, but it was your idea. I never wanted a fuss about the adoption, I just wanted the...' I couldn't say the word; it stuck in my throat like a rusty barb. I had to get around this or I'd never make it through a single day at Cyan. I tried to think of something, anything, else, but I was already losing again. I looked outside, hoping the shift in position might slow the inevitable but the tingling was already there behind my eyes.

'Oh, sweetheart. Don't cry. You're tougher than this, I know you are.' Mum leant over and began rubbing my knee reassuringly. I shook my head. I wasn't tough. I couldn't survive a broken fingernail or a mistimed buzzword.

'I'm not, Mum. Guy's tough, not me.' I couldn't recall a time I'd ever seen my brother cry, not even during the catastrophic fallout after he'd walked in on my father and Petra. Guy had glued the three of us together until Mum had finally realised that we didn't need to keep eating Dad's favourites any more.

'Oh, Amy, you're tougher than you think.' She reached for my hand, clasping onto it as she always had whenever I'd brought a crisis home with me.

'What am I going to do, Mum?' I asked steadily, trying not to set myself off again. She was making small circular motions over the back of my thumb.

'Well, first you need to work out what's most important in your life right now, sweetheart.'

'I know what's most important. That part hasn't changed in the last five years.'

'Right. Well, that only leaves one other question. Has James's part in that changed in the last five years?'

James had always been part of that picture, but tensions had been growing lately. Somewhere along the line, we'd stopped laughing and making plans. I realised that there had only been one plan for a long time now, and what had started out as a joint venture had at some point turned James into a back-seat passenger on my much diverted road-trip to parenthood. But never had I imagined him not being there, somewhere, with me. Never had he said he wanted to get off this journey. Or maybe I just hadn't been listening.

A bustling through the front door and my brother's cheerful voice throbbed through the open hallway. 'Hey, hey! Somethin' smells good! Sam… don't *push*! You'll knock somebody over.' Sam scrambled into the kitchen making a beeline for the biscuit jar.

'Oh no you don't,' Mum warned, leaping from her chair to intercept him. A waft of cool air came in with them as Guy plonked Harry's car seat down on Mum's pine kitchen table.

. Lauren followed them all in, rosy cheeked, puffing mousy-brown strands of hair away from her face, arms full of the things Harry couldn't possibly need in just a couple of hours. She dumped her bags and came straight over with an embrace, then reassuringly rubbed my arm. 'Hey. How are we doing?' I smiled crookedly letting her hug me for a second time. 'I'm so sorry, Ame.' I shrugged my shoulders. I was pretty sure I wouldn't blub in front of the kids.

Guy scratched his short-cropped curls and threw me an unimpressed look. I glared back at him, in case he was under any illusion that dealing with Mum's counsel wasn't taxing enough. He arched his eyebrows and held his hands up briefly in submission. He wouldn't say anything about James, for now. I let out a breath as he came over and planted a kiss on my cheek. 'Just say the word,' he said quietly. 'He needs his arse kicking.'

'Samuel Alwood! What on earth have you done to your face?' Sam peered wide brown eyes out at Mum from underneath the hood of his duffel coat, a strange purplish bruise beneath his eye.

Lauren huffed as she pulled him from his coat. 'He stuck a Tic Tac up his nose, didn't you, buddy? Pushed it that far up there, burst a blood vessel.'

Sam grinned at his achievement. 'I made Mummy's legs go funny!' he said triumphantly. Lauren was squeamish, which made it all the more baffling to understand how she'd had not one, but two children with my heathen brother.

I bent down beside Sam. 'Let me see, Curly.' He lifted his chin to allow me a better look. 'Ew, gross. At least you'll have minty fresh nostrils for a while, kiddo.' I stole a kiss before he could make his escape.

'Daddy said I can't put anything else up my nose now, Aunty Ame. Not even my fingers.'

I ran my hand over the softness of his curls. 'Good to know, kid.' I shrugged. 'It's good advice.'

'I've got some advice for you too if you want to hear it?' Guy asked me.

The timer on the oven began bleeping urgently, answered with a grizzled response from the kitchen table. I ignored Guy as Lauren peered into Harry's car seat and groaned. '*Harry!* We can't spend all day in the car! It's not practical.' She began to unclip him from the seat harness as Harry's protestations grew. 'Guy's taken to driving him around the estate to get him off!' she said, scooping him from the chair.

'You'll want to get out of that habit, Guy,' Mum warned, repositioning the oven trays. 'He's got to learn to settle himself sometimes, or he'll grow up expecting the world to do it for him.' She looked over at Lauren peeling Harry like a banana from his snow suit and completely lost track of what she was doing. 'He is scrumptious, though,' she cooed. 'Here, I'll get him off for you.'

Something began boiling over on the hob, sending a crackle of spitting water everywhere. Mum looked over at the veg.

'I'll take him,' I offered. Harry bunched into himself like a hedgehog as Lauren handed him to me. I settled him into my chest and grazed my nose over his downy dark hair. He was going to be curly too. I took the deepest lungful of air I could manage. He still smelled of that something only new babies did. Of softness and milky cotton.

'So? Have you seen him since you moved back?' Guy asked tartly. Harry grunted softly next to my ear. I nuzzled into him, into all that cotton-softness and rocked him gently, unsure as to who was really comforting who.

Mum began mashing the potatoes with unnecessary vigour. 'Have I mentioned the parish meeting at the community centre to you both yet?' It was a transparent attempt to change the subject.

'I haven't moved back, Guy,' I said, rubbing my cheek against my little friend's. 'I just needed some breathing space.' I knew it wasn't me Guy was angry at, but the situation. He was friends with James, he had him down as a good guy too. Guy was always going to struggle with that. He was black and white that way, always had been, but I had other things to consider – a whole spectrum of grey.

I walked away from my brother and lifted Harry's tiny hand to my lips to press a kiss there. There was a reason new babies' hands were sized to match an adult mouth. Kisses were meant for tiny fingers. Tiny, delicate fingers, so perfect it was almost inconceivable that they could be created so easily. So easily for so many. I held Harry's hand against my mouth.

We'd never meant to fall pregnant. I hadn't even missed a pill. It had just happened, and everything had changed, irrevocably. The doctor had told us ours was a determined little egg, the one in a hundred to outwit the advances of contraceptive science and bed down for a chance at life. By some twist of fate, we'd been shown something wonderful, and then, once we'd fallen in love with our tiny stowaway, fate had seen fit to take him away again.

Mum intensified her attack on the spuds. I indulged in another hit of Harry's inimitable scent. 'Come on, handsome.' I clucked, strolling towards the conservatory windows. 'Let's see if we can find that little robin.'

CHAPTER 5

THERE WERE MANY days I'd have rather forgotten during my career as lead designer at Cyan Architecture & Design, but this one was already shaping up to go straight to the top of the leader board. A cyclist with a death wish had just committed the cardinal sin of cutting us up and Mum was still growling at his disappearing reflection in her mirrors. 'Sunshine always brings the idiots out,' she huffed, catching up with the traffic ahead. I was making a point of not looking up there: the city buses were all running the same campaign, posters plastered above their bumpers showing three beautiful children in a tricolour of races, begging the question, *Could you adopt?*

'Stop fiddling with your ear, sweetheart.'

'I'm not fiddling with my ear. Watch the road.'

Mum threw me a sideways glance. 'You're bound to feel nervous, Amy.'

'It's not my first day at school, Mum. *Thank goodness*. Could you have bought a more obscenely coloured car?'

'You're supposed to be a designer – embrace the alternative. Anyway, madam, there's always the bus.'

The bistro-lined streets were already alive with coffee-wielding officebots on their way to work as Mum pulled us over into the bus lane. I eyed the small private car park over by the biscuit factory. James's car wasn't there. Good. Thoughts of what our first encounter might hold had me turning myself in knots. It had been the same for days now, I'd try to work out what I was going to say to him, but even within the controlled parameters of my own mental monologue, it all got messy and jumbled. First the hurt of what he'd done would hit all over again, then the anger at his timing (because if your boyfriend feels the need to bonk one of your colleagues, timing made all the difference, of course). Thinking of James and Sadie together had invariably been enough to trip off further unsightly bouts of snotty crying each time I'd played it through my head. Not being able to remember the last time I'd driven James wild with a single kiss, or was woken in the morning with a kiss of his own, triggered my growing sense of inadequacy just as effectively.

One of the city buses honked and pulled around us into the lane.

'All right, all right. I'm going!' Mum snipped.

I tried not to look at the advertisement plastered across the rear of the bus, but eyes have a habit of seeking out what the mind knows isn't good for it. I'd never been so glad so see an ad for broadband.

I jumped out of Mum's lime-green Honda before I could change my mind. I needed to talk to James, I knew that much. But walking back into the office was a big enough hurdle to deal with today.

'Amy?' She was ducking to better see me as I straightened myself out on the pavement.

'Please, Ma. No more advice.'

'I just wanted to say, good luck. It takes courage to walk in there, Amy. You hold your head up.'

I stopped fussing with my clothes and smiled feebly. 'Let's just see how it goes, Mum.' If I could get this out of the way, anything was possible.

I shut the car door and turned for the courtyard, power-walking towards the cluster of businesses before my feet had a chance to change direction. This did indeed feel like a first day at school. Only worse. The gusto of my power-walk pushed me straight through the glass doors and swiftly across the lobby where two figures loitered at Ally's desk. 'Morning,' Dana called politely. Ally sat open-mouthed.

'Morning,' I called back, rounding the far doors into the offices. I was unwavering in my path.

I shadowed the wall intersecting the office, following it past the first pod of workstations where Alice and her team were already settled into their workload. The marketing lot had a good corner position on the studio floor, made cosy where red bricks remained resolutely exposed before running into the sleek white plasterwork flanking the rest of the studios.

The next group of workstations were all vacant, basking in sun where tall industrial windows stood like a row of guards, flooding the studios with natural light. The view they offered across the courtyard gave my eyes something to focus on while I made it past Sadie's empty desk. I'd nearly traversed the first studio, past the kitchen where more bodies were loitering for morning coffee and gossip. I didn't look inside.

The boardroom lay directly ahead of the interiors team's workstations. I kept on with the power-walk then abruptly veered left, slinking into my chair. My heart was a little racy when I punched the button on my pc.

Not a word from any one of the seven bodies around me to compete with the lethargic hum of my computer. I resisted the urge to fidget. Across the low partition separating our desks, Hannah's face was locked on her monitor. She was being careful not to look at me. Nine days on, it was safe to say even the cleaners knew that Stewart from reprographics was not the Nightshagger.

The other side of Hannah, Phil spun her chair around and sat casually back into it, grinning like a Bond villain. Hers was a unique brand of solidarity, but an effective one. At that predatory smile, a tension eased. *You can do this, Ame. One awkwardness at a time.*

'Amy?' boomed a voice from the office beside the boardroom. 'A word.' My next awkwardness was well over six foot tall and looming in the doorway there. Adrian Espley was an imposing man, with a near-military-grade haircut and the build of a person who had enjoyed rugby in a long forgotten youth, before the Guinness had taken over.

Phil's smile never faltered. *Be cool,* she mouthed, as I waddled past her. There wasn't enough of a distance to deploy the power-walk, damn it.

'Close the door behind you,' Adrian instructed, holding a huge hand out towards the chair beside me. I did as he asked, pulling on the hem of my fitted waistcoat before sitting down in the hot seat. 'I'm not going to dance around, Amy. I'm not happy about this… *situation.*'

My face suddenly felt awkward and rubbery.

'I don't want to know who's done what, all I give a toss about is will it cause me any problems?' My hands felt clammy in my lap.

Be cool. 'Of course not, Adrian.' That was what he wanted to hear, after all. Adrian cleared his throat, a sound I'd come to recognise as his acceptance of a satisfactory outcome.

'Excellent. Right, leave what you're on and get Phil to run you through the Bywater file. New client, just bought a nice place out near Briddleton. Got it for a song, too – the vendors ran out of money before they had to sell up. Managed a nice job on the conversion, very nice, but it's basically a sexy shell, nothing going on inside.' I thought of the comparisons I could draw. 'He's got a fairly healthy budget and the mill would look fantastic in our residential portfolio. I want you to win us this contract, Amy. Get your teeth into it.'

Good. Work was good. I could feel myself relaxing. 'Where are we at with it?'

'He's emailed over a few photos, and a set of AutoCAD plans that the previous architects drew up. He's bringing everything else he's got into the office this morning.' Yes. This was what I needed. 'Right then, I think we're done here. Phil'll get you up to speed.'

And like that, equilibrium resumed in Adrian's company.

Phil was getting one of the architects up to speed on her drawings when I made it out of Adrian's office. I began picking over the papers on her desk. 'Hannah? Have you seen anything for a Mr Bywater? There should be a file?'

Hannah looked sheepishly over her shoulder at me. I sighed quietly. 'Hannah, this morning's awkward enough. I know how the jungle drums work around here, don't worry about it, okay?' Hannah nodded as I took a cursory glance back down the studio.

'She's not in today,' Hannah whispered. 'I heard Dana telling Marcy that Sadie phoned in sick again.'

A slap of papers hit the end of the desk. 'Rohan Bywater. Has Adrian talked you through it, or was he too busy checking the balance of his applecart?' Phil stood leaning with one hand flat on the desk, the other on her hip. 'He's due in this morning, you want me to do the meet-and-greet or—'

'No, I've got it.'

Phil straightened up. 'Is anyone booked into the boardroom? I could talk you through the file, more room to spread out.'

Adrian thudded from his office, shoving balled fists through the sleeves of his jacket. 'Site meeting. I'm on the mobile,' he declared, clumping out of the studio.

'I'll get the coffees,' Phil said, following Adrian out as far as the kitchen. Phil had suggested the boardroom for privacy, not space. I gathered the file and walked through into the boardroom, fighting off the images of James's naked groin in each of the chairs there. To distract myself, I laid out the photos of the Bywater property on the conference table. I still had my snout in the paperwork when the boardroom door clicked closed.

'I've been leaving you messages,' he said, placing the drinks he'd hijacked from Phil down on the long glass table. 'I've been going crazy, Amy. Please, let me talk.'

He wasn't supposed to be here. Funnily enough, that was what I'd thought the last time I'd seen him.

'I can't say anything in my defence, I know, but… it was a stupid mistake. A stupid, one-off mistake.'

'One-off?' I croaked. 'You expect me to believe that?' I choked on my words, an instant trembling firing up in my chest. Already, the conversation wasn't going as I'd imagined it.

'It was never meant to happen, I wish it never had. Please believe me, Amy, I love you. I need to make this right with you. Mum's so excited about flying in—'

'Forget the party, James!' I yelped.

His expression changed. The blue of his eyes growing cooler. 'So what? That's *it* now? Just like that? You're going to throw everything away? *Everything*, Amy?'

My head began to thump. *Me* throw it away? 'You slept with another woman! You watched me go out, like a big idiot, celebrating our plans, and you – *what*? Bumped into her here? It was you she was on the phone to, wasn't it?' The thumping was intensifying.

James's voice lowered. 'I only agreed to meet her because she was going to tell you. She was going to do as much damage as she could. I couldn't let that happen.' I'd played this conversation through my head all week. Pointless preparation. 'I swear, it had only been one time... I told her it was a mistake, and then—'

'And then what?' I snapped. 'You met her to call it all off?'

'Yes!' James exclaimed, circumnavigating the table.

'And what? You accidentally fell into her?'

James darted towards me. I stepped back to accommodate it. 'Amy, shit! I know what I've done is as bad as it gets, but *please*! Let me fix this, we can get over this if you just... *let us*. Please, don't throw away our life together. We're so close to getting what we want, Amy.'

'What *we* want, or what *I* want, James?' The tingling was there again, threatening to render me useless and emotional. He stepped closer.

'I wouldn't be here if I didn't want our life, Amy. You know that.'

I could feel the burn, reaching the edges of my eyes. 'But you betrayed me, James. You slept with her, and now everything's falling apart. They'll never give us our child now—'

'Amy, Anna doesn't need to know about this. Not unless you tell her. I don't want to tell her, I want to make it right.'

Don't cry here. Do not cry here, I warned myself. Somewhere in the back of my brain, I knew that James was playing to my weak spot, but knowing it didn't make the words any less seductive. I grabbed onto the only thing that would keep me steady. The ugly truth.

'How did it start?' I asked, taking a sharp breath. He tried to take my hand but I hadn't offered it. 'Where?'

'Amy, *please.* We don't need to do this.'

'When, and where, James? Has she been in my house?'

Outside, the studio had grown very quiet. A phone rang out, the sound rising above the diminishing volume of the voices around it. He moved over to the glass wall and closed the blinds. I remained where I stood, tense and unyielding.

He pushed both hands through his hair. His was that shade of blond that didn't quite make it through childhood without acquiring a duller, muddier undertone. 'Shit, Amy,' he huffed, looking to his feet. He knew I'd hear it eventually. He approached the table again and idly

moved one of the mill photos around under his finger.

'She started coming on to me a while ago. I laughed it
off, ignored her. And then she turned up at the gym.'

'The *gym*?' I sputtered. 'You haven't used the gym
since your membership expired. That was *before
Christmas!*' I could hear something like hysteria,
sprouting in my voice.

'It wasn't that long ago—'

'Yes it was.' The calculation reran quickly through
my head. 'You stopped going there because of your shin
splints. That's why I paid a fortune for your bloody bike!
So you could exercise without your shins hurting!'

'Amy...'

'You've been seeing her for six months? *Six months!*'
Hysteria was giving way to red rage. All that time, he'd
let me prattle on about us becoming a family.

'She's the reason I stopped going to the gym, Amy! She
was there – and here at work... I couldn't get away from
her! She pursued me. I made one mistake, and I couldn't
shake her off!' I started to feel giddy. 'Amy, listen to me.
I didn't mean to sleep with her—'

'Didn't mean to? *Didn't mean to?*' I growled. Somebody knocked gingerly on the boardroom door. It wasn't
Adrian, he'd have kicked it down if he wanted to.

'How are your shins now, James?' I trembled, a discon-
certing calm settled into my shoulders. *Six months.* Not a
momentary mistake at all. Another rap on the door. 'Did

the bike I spent a month's wages on – while you were at it with Glitter Knickers – did it help ease the pain in your shins?'

Another phone started ringing on the shop floor. No one answered it this time.

'What are you talking about?' James asked as the boardroom door handle began to rattle.

'Your shins, James? How are they shaping up?'

James looked perplexed, so I saved him the hassle of asking again. I launched the toe of my red Mary Jane hard and sure into James's leg. James yelped, grabbing at his assaulted limb. It hurt me, but it hurt him more.

'*AMY*! *What the f*—'

'I'm *sorry*, James!' I retorted mirthfully. 'I didn't mean it! That deliberate, hurtful, action… I *DIDN'T MEAN IT!*'

'Er, sorry to interrupt…' The uncertainty in Phil's voice rendered it almost unrecognisable.

'What?' I growled, the threat of tears driving on my anger. How could he? How could he sit through all of those meetings, the panel hearing, pretending that he wanted a family with me when all the time…?

Phil shifted awkwardly, taking in the spectacle of James sat on the photographs, purple-cheeked and clasping at his leg.

I quickly appraised the dark stranger standing next to Phil. Jeans and T-shirts didn't usually feature this far from Tom's end of the office. Baseball caps didn't feature anywhere at Cyan. 'Can't you take delivery of those, Phil?' I said breathily, nodding at the cardboard tube poking from the stranger's backpack. Drawings were usually emailed in, but occasionally someone paid to have them couriered instead. 'James and I are just... having a meeting.'

The delivery guy considered James, who was trying unsuccessfully not to grimace where he sat. Delivery Guy looked away, the beginnings of a smile eking across his boyish face. 'I think she likes you, mate,' he said, turning strangely pale hazel eyes this way. They were startling next to his dark hair and lightly tanned complexion.

Phil looked at James and began fighting a grin of her own. Delivery Guy pulled his cap from his head, revealing a choppy brunette crop that made his eyes all the more staggering. He instantly looked older. James winced and got to his feet. 'Shin splints,' he volunteered to the other man.

Delivery Guy pouted his acknowledgement. 'Nasty old business, shin splints, my friend. Painful stuff.' He was taller than James. Broader, too – his shoulders wide beneath the black tee, framed by the straps of his backpack. James couldn't make him out either. He looked at me only briefly before hobbling out between the two adults trying to remain straight-faced in the doorway.

Phil moved further into the boardroom. 'Um, Amy?'

I began absently tidying the photos on the table. 'Yep?'

Six months. It was a lot of sex-time. A lot of time for hand-holding and secret-sharing.

'Your next meeting...' Phil said.

I looked up at her. 'Hmm? What about it?' Phil was

smiling awkwardly, trying to convey something in the set of her lips. I frowned. 'My next meeting what? Are these for me?' I said, holding out my hand out for the tube of drawings.

Phil gave up. 'Amy Alwood, Rohan Bywater. Mr Bywater *is* your next meeting. Shall I get Hannah to bring you some fresh coffees?'

I felt the colour drain from my face. Phil shrugged, pairing it with an *I tried* rise of her eyebrows. Mr Bywater sunk hands into his jean pockets and cocked his head, a dazzling smile reaching over his face as I squirmed on the spot. The drawings I'd practically snatched from his hands felt red-hot in mine now.

'Er, Mr Bywater… sorry, come in… take a seat,' I stuttered.

'Should I grab some shin pads first?' he asked, jabbing a thumb at the open doorway. An angry bruise leached purplish-red across his right elbow. I felt my cheeks flush a similar colour. Phil slipped back out of the boardroom leaving me to fend for myself.

'About that, Mr Bywater.' He was smiling. Amused lips, putting me off my already pathetic attempt to redeem myself.

'Call me Rohan.'

'What you just saw, regrettably, was er… not the *norm*, Mr Bywater, I can assure you…' A white peep of teeth slowed me again.

'Call me Rohan.'

'Er…' I nodded to expedite myself back to my point. 'It's no excuse… and I won't bore you with the finer details, but…'

Rohan Bywater moved around the table to look at the stack of photos I'd neatly ordered in front of me. I waited for him to gather them up and take his business elsewhere. Adrian was going to go berserk.

'Have you had a chance to look through these yet?'

'Er, just a quick look,' I bumbled. 'To try to get a feel for the scale of the project.'

'If you want to do that, you'll need to come and see it for yourself.' His skin was the colour of the many contractors I'd worked with – bronzed from daily exposure to the elements. He looked serious now, I wasn't sure I didn't prefer the smiling. I felt the back of my earring give under my fingers.

'So, how does this all work?' he asked, leaning back against the table's edge.

My brain found a foothold. 'Well, we can arrange a site meeting, take a look at the spaces involved. You already have plans and ellies drawn up—'

'Ellies?'

'Sorry, *elevations*. We'll measure up and check them, talk through your requirements, put a fee proposal together for you.' He was listening intently. 'If you're happy with the quote, we'll get a contract of works drawn up for you to sign and then we can get down to the bones of your project.'

'Get down to the bones of it?'

He folded his arms in front of his chest. It was an impressive bruise he had.

'Starting with a meeting so that we can formulate an in-depth design brief together.'

'Together? As in…?'

'As in, yourself and a representative of Cyan's interiors team.'

'Uhuh,' he said, lolling his head again. 'And do all the representatives of Cyan's interiors team wear red heels? I'm just asking because, hey, I like a challenge, but I've seen first-hand how you get down to the *bones* of things around here… as in directly through your friend's trouser leg.' He wore an expression of nonchalance now. He found my discomfort amusing. I found his amusement… annoying.

A knock at the door and Hannah provided a welcome distraction. 'Sorry to interrupt. Can I get anyone any coffees? Teas?'

'Er…' I turned back to face Rohan Bywater.

'No thanks. I have to get going. I'll call the office to arrange a site visit then, Miss Alwood?' He pushed himself off the table and stood before me. 'I'll leave these with you?' He nodded at the papers he'd brought.

'Um, yes. Thank you, Mr Bywater.' I offered my hand to conclude our unorthodox meeting.

'Call me Rohan.' He reached for my hand, but instead of shaking it he turned it over in his, carefully placing my silver stud on my palm. I hadn't even seen him pick it up.

'It's been nice meeting you, Miss Alwood,' he said firmly. 'I'll be in touch.'

I felt my naked earlobe as I watched him follow Hannah out into the office to where James was talking to the marketing team. Rohan Bywater playfully slapped James on the back, pointing to the leg I'd kicked. He laughed, his hand on James's shoulder. James began to laugh too, all boys together. Then Bywater pulled his trouser leg up. It was hard to tell from here, it could've been a birthmark or a graze perhaps, but I reckoned it to be another bruise that engulfed Bywater's knee. Whatever it was, it was large and painful-looking. James stopped laughing, outdone where I hadn't kicked him hard enough for him to compete with the bigger boy's injuries. James looked defeated.

Rohan Bywater put his cap back on and with a parting glance almost caught me watching. He gave James a last friendly slap, then disappeared through the studio doors.

Common assault wasn't what I'd been aiming for, but I'd have taken a sore leg over the sickening weight of revelation. *Six months*. Had they been sleeping together all that time? Or could I cling pathetically to the delusion that they might've been building up to it with a chaste courtship? Yeah, right.

I leant against the door frame, watching James across the office, already flexing his charisma, holding court once more. I must have been mad to think that if I could just stick it here, act normal, things might have a better chance of getting back that way. It hurt just to look at him. The way I'd felt when he'd walked into the boardroom made me wonder whether or not I should just get my things now. But I'd never loved anyone except James. Anna would be contacting us at some point, and I couldn't do any of it without him. I wasn't even sure that I knew who I was without him.

Phil's face bobbed round the boardroom doorway, startling me with an expectant stare.

'What?' I grimaced.

'Oh, I just wanted to say, well done on the *cool*, Ame. You nailed it. You were cooler than cool. *In fact*, I think you might have just knocked The Fonz off the top spot.'

CHAPTER 6

APRIL HAD HAD a change of heart. It had decided it didn't want to be a rubbishy month of late frosts and wet winds any more, it wanted to be daffodils and crocuses and bugs venturing onto the breeze for the first time since last year. I didn't expect the sun would hold, but it was nice to see the lush green of young wheat fields rolling past the window.

I sat in the passenger seat, looking for signs pointing to Briddleton Mill while Hannah hummed along to the tune crackling from the stereo. It was pretty here. Just ten minutes' drive south-west of Earleswicke, I'd enjoyed bike rides with my dad on the public footpaths near here before Jackson's Park had become our agreed rendezvous point on the weekends Petra could spare him.

'Is that it?' Hannah called, slamming her brakes on. I lurched forward, the plush cheeseburger and fries toy dangling from Hannah's rear-view mirror flapped into the side of my head. I batted them aside and read the sign.

'Yeah, that's it. Where the lane forks, we need to take it all the way round to the left, and the mill should be there.'

Trusting Hannah had enough information, I rooted around my bag for my compact. Sleeplessness took its toll on the over twenty-fives and I was starting to look like a panda. I swept a little more powder beneath my eyelids. Warpaint in place, I was ready to pretend to the world that I hadn't stayed up into the early hours this morning, reading and rereading the messages James had sent me before he'd gone to bed. I was also ready to show Rohan Bywater that I really wasn't a complete psycho.

'Wow,' Hannah said bluntly. '*Welcome to my crib, MTV.*'

I clasped shut the compact and slipped it back into my satchel. 'Pretty beautiful,' I agreed, taking in the tree-lined millpond stretching like a mini lake across the foreground. The mill itself, rising from the far edge of the black waters, seemed to double in size as Hannah pulled the car closer to the two VW vans parked out front. One was an old battered orange affair, a campervan like those I'd lusted after in my carefree student days; the other a very sleek and shiny truck you could easily imagine the A-Team exploding from.

'Right then, you ready to measure this place up?' I asked, cranking open the door.

'It's massive!' Hannah laughed. 'We'll be here all night.' Not if I could help it. I still wasn't convinced Bywater wasn't wasting our time but he'd booked the survey anyway, so here we were.

I climbed out of the car and reached for my things. 'You

all set?' I asked, checking Hannah had hold of the drawings. Hannah nodded, agog over the grand design in front of her.

'Okay, let's do it.' I said, slipping into my jacket, pulling my hair free. Dry weather was preferable for the artificially straightened.

Hannah followed me to the only obvious entrance. Further to the right of the door, the original water wheel was turning steadily – fed, I assumed, by the River Earle somewhere over the far side of the mill. We stood there expectantly for a minute or so before I tried the door knocker again.

'They did say ten, right?' Hannah asked, checking her watch.

I knocked again. 'We'll give it a minute, then I'll call the office.' Who was I kidding? That was the last number I wanted to call. I'd thought the sideways glances were bad enough on Monday afternoon, but the whispering had gone into overdrive after a large bouquet had landed on my desk yesterday. Sadie still hadn't shown her face.

'Wait,' Hannah said, 'do you hear that?' I listened for the sounds of somebody approaching the door from the other side. I couldn't hear anything over the gentle gushing sounds of the water wheel. 'They're round the back,' Hannah said. 'I can hear them yelling.' Hannah's bionic hearing led us from the stone path onto the timber walkway reaching out over the millpond where small clouds of insects hung like mist above the water.

We took the timber gangway wrapping itself around the mill's water side, leading us over the pond into a gravelled yard the other side of the mill. I could hear it now: men's voices, laughing from somewhere over the grassy ridge that ran a sweeping line around the yard here.

A crunching on the ground behind us and we both turned to find Rohan Bywater stepping from the mill's rear double doors stained black to match the cedar cladding above them.

He looked less boyish today, pushing navy sweater sleeves up over olive forearms. 'Hey. You found it then?' He was already smiling. Hannah's cheeks seemed to be getting redder. I cleared my throat, striding confidently towards him until I'd made it within hand-shaking distance. There was an approach that went with being female in this industry, forged by enough years of burly builders attempting to make me blush. Phil had never struggled but I'd had to learn how to *show no fear.*

'Hello again, Mr Bywater,' I said, offering my hand. Hannah ambled up behind me, perplexed by my sudden burst across the yard. 'This is Hannah, one of our interns. Shall we get started?'

Bywater looked a little perturbed too. I realised I was probably overusing the power-walk.

'Sure.' He smiled, taking my hand. His skin was rough against mine, not smooth like James's. We broke contact then, him reaching to casually muss the back of his hair. 'Come on in.'

Inside this first room, whatever this room was, it was just as Adrian had described it, well-proportioned and spacious, but with nothing to punctuate the endless wheat tones of newly-plastered surfaces.

'Blank canvas,' Bywater said, walking in after us. His voice lost some of its smoothness as it echoed off the bare concrete floor. Other than protruding cables and the occasional socket fascia hanging off a wire, there was nothing in here to suggest anybody called it home.

'Are all the rooms like this, Mr Bywater? Plastered, wired...?'

He folded his arms and leant back against the door reveal. 'Pretty much.'

'Electrics and plumbing all working?' I asked, taking the papers from Hannah's arms and opening them out on the dusty floor. Mr Bywater nodded. 'Do you know if these drawings are accurate? Just the general layout, I mean.'

He moved to look down at the drawings beneath me. 'They look right. But I'd like this and the next room to be knocked through,' he said, crouching beside me. I followed his finger over the plans. Nearly all of his knuckles were grazed.

'The kitchen is next door?' I asked.

'Yeah, but I'd like to open it out across the back of the building. I have friends over, they eat a lot. Makes sense to make all this back here bigger.' I began scribbling notes on the drawing under us. Bywater watched as I wrote.

I hated that. It always seemed to render my handwriting illegible for some daft reason.

'Nice pen.'

As soon as he spoke, I scrawled *kitten* instead of kitchen.

'Thanks. And upstairs? Are you planning any structural changes up there?'

'I'm leaving the second floor as storage, for now. As you can see on the plan,' I caught a waft of something faintly spiced as he reached across me to the second drawing, 'there are four bedrooms on the first floor. The previous owners intended to make this bedroom the master, overlooking the river on the north side, but I'd like to take the south bedroom, overlooking the millpond. I know I'm spoilt for choice, but that's definitely the best view in the house.'

I glanced over the general layout of the south bedroom. 'Is the existing en suite in there sufficient?'

Bywater straightened up. 'Actually, I've seen something I wanted your opinion on,' he said, pulling a brochure from his back pocket. He began thumbing through it, finding his page then passing it straight over my head to Hannah. 'What do you think?'

Hannah, surprised that he'd addressed her, studied the image. He watched her, expectantly waiting for her feedback. I hadn't worked with very many clients who bothered to include the juniors. Often they simply looked straight through them. 'Well, you're on a private road.'

She shrugged. 'Why not?' She passed me the brochure. The room in the picture was some sort of alpine chalet, doors flung open revealing the snowy vista outside. In the middle of the scene a Nordic beauty lounged in her bathtub, looking out onto the views.

'Showers are for office types. I'm more of a bath guy.' Bywater smiled, burying his hands into his jean pockets. 'So do you think we could do something like this up there?' He lifted his chin towards the exposed beams arching like a ribcage above us.

James was definitely a power-shower kind of person, but I knew he'd drool over a bedroom tub like this. When I thought of bathtubs, I thought of rubber ducks and no-more-tears shampoo, but James was all about the lines. 'I'm sure we could. Are we okay to go take a look?' I asked, getting to my feet.

'Sure. Would you like me to show you around? I can't be in too much danger,' he said, peered down at my shoes. I ignored him. I didn't know why he made me so uncomfortable, other than acting like a total idiot in front of him at Cyan two days ago, which technically was my fault, not his.

It could be worse, I supposed. I could be back at the office.

'That's okay.' I smiled passively. 'We'll come and find you when we've finished measuring up.' Hannah gave him a warmer smile and followed me towards the door.

'I'll be in the back if you need to talk bathtubs,' he called after us.

We'd soon found our way around the upper floors, each room offering its own astounding views over the country-side – the tumbling river, the still millpond and the wood-land encircling much of the property. It was almost impos-sible to resist fantasising about what your life would be like to live in a place like this. Hannah had already given me the lowdown on what her friends would say if the mill were hers; I'd found myself imagining Anna here. Show-ing her around the endless lawns, and the playroom I'd put in next to the kitchen. It was a fantasy all right. Right now, I'd be lucky if I could show her a rational couple manag-ing to stand in the same room as each other. And yet this was the only plan I had – pretending everything was fine, bluffing our way through it long enough to complete the adoption. We could work out all the ugly business after-wards. Simple. I just had to find a way to be around James again without wanting to kick him.

I could not lose another child. Not even a child I didn't know yet.

*

An hour later, in possession of every measurement we could possibly need, Hannah and I stepped out into the back yard. Ahead of us, a grassy bank obscured the source of the commotion we could hear emanating from the other side of the hillock. 'He said he'd be out back. Come on,

I'm curious.' Hannah shrugged, walking up towards the brow of the hill.

The sounds of men messing around grew significantly louder at the grassy summit. 'Bloody hell!' Hannah exclaimed, staring across the meadow. I watched them open-mouthed too, flying up one side of the curved structure, launching themselves into the air before careering back down it again. I counted three men, throwing themselves recklessly up and down the arrangement of ramps. A fourth person, unconcerned by the bikes whizzing past his shaggy head was sitting at the top of one vertical incline, legs hanging over the edge as if he were just perching on a garden wall.

'Go on, Max, I can get more height on my hair than that!' the shaggy one hooted. Max threw himself fiercely into the drop. He made it into the air next to his shaggy friend but miscalculated whatever it is that these guys with no sense of self-preservation are supposed to calculate when gravity yanks them back down to earth. Max left his bike in the air above him, crashing down onto the vertical, sliding all the way back to the bottom of the ramp on his knees. A heartbeat later, the bike followed his slipstream, slumping hard into him.

'That is so dangerous,' I murmured, but he was already scrambling back onto his bike.

'That is so cool!' Hannah yelped, edging closer for a better look. I followed, looking around to see which one of these big kids was Bywater. I knew he'd be one of them, despite his grown-up house, there was something distinctively adolescent about him. It was his eyes that gave him away, piercing beneath the shadow of his black helmet.

'Mr Bywater?'

The shaggy spectator was still yelling his encouragement. Bywater's black helmet whizzed past again. 'Mr Bywater?' I repeated, louder this time. I let him pass twice more before I felt the stirrings of irritation. 'Mr Bywater! Could I just have a quick word, please?' Still nothing. He manoeuvred himself through the air over above the shaggy one's head. I thought I caught him looking my way, but still he didn't stop.

I gave a small discreet sigh. 'Come on, Hannah. We'll wait for him at the mill.' Hannah followed, reluctantly. We hadn't walked far through the spongy grass when there was a sickening clatter behind us.

We both snapped around to see as Rohan Bywater let out a sharp cry.

The biker with the beard yelled something, skidding in on his knees beside his friend. We were still close enough to them that I could see what they were all staring at.

'Oh no,' I panted, hurrying to where Bywater lay writhing on his back. One arm shielded his face while the other grabbed uselessly at his left thigh. I tried to understand which part looked wrong, what it was that my eyes were struggling to process.

Hannah groaned as we came to stand, uselessly, at the

edge of the ramp. The contours of Bywater's left trouser leg suggested something was grossly broken. I followed those lines to his black trainer, realising with sickening clarity that his foot was completely misaligned with his body.

I wasn't as squeamish as my sister-in-law, but this was pushing it. I felt the nausea growing. Blood I was okay with, but tendons and bones…not so much.

Bywater yelped again, skipping my heart along at a quicker rate.

'It's okay, it's okay,' I tried, darting to the floor beside him, but he reminded me of a Barbie doll I'd abused as a child, his leg twisted spitefully past the point of repair.

Bywater began groaning steadily, unearthly sounds emanating from deep within his chest. The ashen expression on each of the other bikers' faces galvanised me. Somebody needed to be in charge here.

'Hannah?' I yelled, turning to find Hannah wide-eyed and quite green beside me. 'Hannah, call an—' A clammy hand grabbed my arm.

'Is it broken?' Bywater demanded, his face filled with panic.

I was suddenly locked by desperate hazel eyes. I could feel the shock etched into my own expression and made a conscious effort to disguise it. 'Just lay still, try to stay calm.' Ignoring me completely, Rohan Bywater began trying to sit up. His foot tugged with the movement like a lifeless strand of flotsam not quite free of its mooring.

I wasn't convinced the nausea wouldn't get the better of me after all.

'*Please!* You need to stay still!'

Rohan looked at the bearded guy in the red helmet. 'Billy, help me,' he pleaded. Billy looked panic-stricken too.

'What do you want me to do, mate? She's right, you need to keep still until we can get you some help.'

Rohan hid his face beneath his arm again. 'Have I broken it, Bill?' Billy cast his eyes over his friend's lower body.

'It's not looking good, mate,' the shaggy spectator offered solemnly. 'Bill, see how bad it is,' he instructed.

Rohan put his other hand over his face too. He was coping remarkably well, considering. His pain threshold was incredible. I tried to second guess what the symptoms of shock were. 'This has happened before,' the shaggy one said calmly, casually nibbling on a stick of liquorice he'd produced from somewhere. I was processing that last statement when Rohan groaned again, clasping at the back of his knee while Billy began to cradle the twisted foot. 'On three?' Billy asked.

Still hidden beneath his arms, Rohan nodded.

I scrambled to my feet. 'Whoa, whoa, whoa! On three, *what*? What are you going to do?'

'Just do it, Billy!' the shaggy guy said. 'He's ready, aren't you, Ro?'

Rohan Bywater nodded again.

Billy took a deep breath. 'One…'

'Wait a minute!' I squeaked. 'What the hell are you doing? He needs an ambulance!'

'Two…'

I looked at Hannah for help of some kind but she was already shielding her eyes. She'd even shuffled back a few paces from the chaos unfurling in front of us.

'Three!' I snapped my head round as Billy sickeningly yanked hard on Rohan's contorted leg. I watched, dumbstruck, as he pulled Rohan's leg completely free of the trousers.

My stomach went into a death-roll. Rohan fell silent. Everything fell silent but the pulsing in my ears. So this was what shock felt like.

'Good news, brother,' Billy said cheerily, examining the contents of his hands. 'You haven't trashed it. But I keep telling you to watch the drops, man. It's gonna hurt if you hyperextend.'

Billy was examining a metal prosthesis in his arms. At one end of it, Rohan's black trainer remained neatly tied to its foot, the laces in a perfect bow. I eyed the scene. Rohan Bywater lay back, casually propped on his elbows. He was smiling at me.

'You've… your leg,' I managed. Hannah remained soundless.

'Surprise.' Rohan smiled.

His left trouser leg lay flat from the knee down. One of the others began to laugh. It was Billy, Bywater's best supporting actor. The shaggy one with his mass of hair and Cat Stevens tee carried on chomping at his liquo-rice stick, Max – all blond and boyish – shook his head, allowing himself a smile. They were all waiting for my response.

I looked down at Bywater and couldn't help myself. 'You jerk.'

Behind me, Hannah gasped. I turned and stormed across the grass to where I'd discarded my satchel, some-where near her feet. 'Come on, Hannah,' I snapped, stalk-ing back towards the bank, trying to outpace the flutter of laughter breaking out behind us. Hannah caught up, laughing nervously beside me.

Bywater's voice followed us over the meadow. 'Oh, come on, don't be mad. I was only pulling your leg!'

'Ignore him,' I instructed. We were nearly at the brow of the ridge.

'At least I didn't play dead!' Bywater added. 'You might have given me the kiss of life!'

He'd be dead a long time before then. I did not need this right now. I did not need joker clients adding to an already tense work situation. *Who even does that? What kind of sicko thinks that's funny?*

'I take it this means we won't be giving him a fee proposal?' Hannah enquired timidly, trying to keep pace with me. The colour had returned to her face. There was a very good chance that mine was somewhere past mid-pink too.

'Oh, he'll be getting one, Hannah.' I was power-walking again. 'First rule of business: if you're client's an asshole and you don't want to work with them,' I said breathily, navigating the soft earth in office shoes, 'you price them out of the game.'

CHAPTER 7

TUCKED AWAY IN the dining room, I didn't hear the front door click to. It wasn't until Mum had put her things down in the kitchen and given James's flowers another approving sniff that I heard her at all. I closed down the stack of tabs where I'd wandered off task and had sporadically trawled the net for anyone else who had set a precedent for sabotaging their own adoption application this far in. Surprise, surprise, I hadn't found anyone that self-destructive. Content that Mum wouldn't stumble across my findings, I checked the time in the corner of my laptop.

'Hey,' I called through, 'I wasn't expecting you home until at least half nine.' I began surveying the information that I was supposed to be concentrating on laid out on the screen in front of me. *Rohan Bywater.* Just reading his name was enough to make my neck bristle.

'Hi, sweetheart. We finished early. Karen and Sue suggested we all get off early so we're full of beans tomorrow evening.' I saved my document and looked over my laptop at her in the dining-room doorway.

'Why? What have the WI got on tomorrow? Fruity calendar shoot, is it?'

Mum shook herself out of her chunky calf-length cardigan and slipped the silk scarf she'd nicked from my room from her neck. 'I wish. I quite fancy myself wearing nothing but a pair of currant buns and a smile. Alas,' she sighed dramatically, 'we're preparing our argument for this ruddy council meeting at the community centre. We've got less than a fortnight and Karen and Sue want to rally as many faces as possible to show the officials that there are people, like us, who really do value the place. The community ruddy values it.' Mum stopped folding her cardigan, an expression of illumination warming her features. 'You should come, sweetheart! We could do with someone there to suggest how to give the place a facelift on a budget. They do it all the time on the telly, everyone coming together and chipping in with a few pots of paint.'

'Earleswicke community centre? Ma, the place doesn't need a facelift, it needs an identity. Or a bulldozer.'

Mum leant on the back of the dining-room chair opposite. 'And where do you think the mother and toddler group is going to convene, young lady, once the council bulldozes it? Or the youth club kids, hmm? Where will they have to go? Or the Macmillan coffee mornings or flower-pressing night? Just because you don't use the centre yourself any more, Amy, doesn't mean that you shouldn't be taking an interest in it.'

'I am interested, Mum.' I probably wasn't that interested. 'But the community needs to come together if they want to hang onto it. A handful of WI members aren't going to cut it. Not unless you go smaller than a current bun.' I swallowed my smile. She didn't look impressed.

'Just remember, Amy, you may have been off enjoying city living these last few years, but Earleswicke is still *your* community. There'll be nothing for anyone here to do if they take the community centre. Well, they can go whistle. They're not having it.' I felt my eyes widen before falling back to the screen and that name again. The WI was supposed to keep Mum out of trouble. Give her some blue face paint and a kilt and she was about ripe to give Mel Gibson a run for his money.

'If it's not viable, Mum, it's not viable. Buildings cost money to run,' I said, reviewing the figures for Bywater's building on screen. The numbers did look a little offensive, but that was the point. There was no way he was going to ask me to work on the mill, not at these fees. *Good*. It wasn't like I didn't have enough on my plate at work.

Mum huffed wearily. 'The council absolutely has the money to run the community centre, Amy.'

'So? What's their issue, then?' I asked, copying Bywater's email address from the papers on the table next to me.

'What do you think? What is *always* the issue, the stingy swines?' Vivian asked.

I gave up concentrating on my task until Braveheart got through with her rabble-rousing. 'They can get more money for it if they just get rid?'

'Bingo. They'll flatten it, and build a car park, or a ruddy pole-dancing club.'

'Probably,' I agreed absently 'Although on the bright side, it'd give you somewhere more lively to hold your WI meetings.'

'You could at least pretend to be interested, Amy. It would be different if it were your gym that was about to close down. You practically live at the place, you'd have something to say then.'

'Not any more,' I reminded myself. James had killed that one for me. I sucked in a deep breath and sank back against the hard dining chair. 'I've got to get through these emails, Mum,' I said, nodding at the screen between us.

She took the hint. 'Right then, I'll leave you to it. Would you like a nice slice of this key lime pie Sue's sent back for you?'

I rubbed a new tension from the side of my head. Did *everyone* know about my failed personal life? 'Not until I'm back at the gym.'

A run-down of all the meals Mum had watched me eat since I'd been staying here flashed through my mind like some sick calorific version of *The Generation Game*. No gym meant I was going to have to start jogging. I hated jogging. Mum lingered in the doorway. 'You know, you don't need to be so controlled all of the time, sweetheart. It's okay to loosen the reins from time to time.' I smiled to pacify her. It was quicker than going into the finer details of my fitness regime and the reasons for it. Mum had gained a little after her menopause, but she'd taken it all in her stride. What my mother constantly seemed to forget though, was that *I* wasn't in my fifties yet. It probably wasn't the best idea I'd had at the time, but I'd immersed myself in the horror stories, endless forum threads, post after post about the average weight gain in that first year after surgery. Twenty to thirty pounds, I'd read. *Twenty to thirty pounds*.

'Have you thought any more about how long you're planning on staying, Amy?'

I shook my head.

'You know you're welcome to stay as long as you wish, darling, and I'll support you in whatever you choose. But it would be good to know what your plans are.'

'My plans aren't really working out at the minute. But I'll let you know if any light bulbs appear over my head.'

'I know, sweetheart. I'm just worried about you. I've been quite excited about having a new grandchild, too, you know. If that's not going to happen, I'd like to know, Amy.'

I was suddenly tempted to go and comfort myself with a huge wedge of Sue Shackleton's key lime pie. Mum had only been home two minutes and I was already in need of a sugar rush. I began pretending to tap out the email

to accompany Bywater's fee proposal, in hopes my bad
influence would finally take her cue and bugger off.

Dear Mr Bywater,
Please find attached quote. Hopefully, by the time
you receive this email, you'll have done yourself a
real injury, and will no longer be in need of our assis-
tance.

I ran back through the text. I *wish*. I sunk my finger into
the delete key and watched the words disappear again.
Mum hadn't moved. I tapped away.

Dear Mr Bywater,
Work for you? I'd rather pull my own eyelids off.

I deleted it again and sneaked a glance at Mum. She was
thinking about leaving me to it, I could tell. Third time
lucky.

Bywater,
I'd love to see someone kick your arse with your own
peg leg.

I bit at the smile forming on my bottom lip and squinted
at his name again.

Mum had just skulked off into the hallway when the
doorbell suddenly echoed to life. She always locked the

door after nine, Guy was probably trying to get in after driving a sleepless Harry around. I listened for the sound of their voices. Then I heard him, asking like some vampire to be invited in.

Mum began dithering in the hallway over her choices. I held my finger on the delete button and cleared my throat. 'It's okay, Mum. He can come in,' I said, apprehensively rising to my feet. James was still in his suit when he appeared in the dining-room doorway, one hand in his pocket, the other fidgeting around his keys. I watched him pull that vulnerable dip of his head, glancing up with uncertain cherubic blue eyes. It didn't have the same effect it used to.

'Can I come in?'

I took a few steps backwards and leant against the radiator on the wall there. James took it as invitation.

'Can we talk?' he said softly. 'Please? Somewhere… private?'

I slid my hands into the back pockets of my jeans. 'Where would you suggest, James? You know all the best spots for privacy. We could go to the gym, or the boardroom, if you like?' I couldn't help myself. This was the stuff we didn't have time to hack our way through on our fast-track to relationship recovery, but I just couldn't help it.

James looked up at the ceiling and sighed. 'Please, Ame. Let's not do this again. I want to make it right. I love you. You know I do.'

'And have you informed Sadie of that too, James? Or are you keeping that option open?' James closed the dining-room doors behind him.

'Sadie's nothing, Amy. I told her that night, that you're the only one. Now you know, she hasn't got anything over me any more. I haven't spoken to her since, I swear it. Not even at work.'

At least that last bit was probably true. Sadie had been off sick most of the week. My stomach tightened thinking about her. James came a little closer. 'I need to be with you, Amy. I need us to be together again. A family.'

James knew how to knock all of the air right out from inside me. The radiator was too hot behind me, but I tried to hold on to it anyway. I needed something to take my focus from James' sugar-coated words. 'I can't talk about this now, James. Not here, like this.'

'So come home. *Please*, Amy. We can work through this, I know we can. We're a team. We've pulled through worse because we stuck together. Come back home with me, Amy, please?' James leant in and cradled my head in his palm. There were lines to his face that hadn't been there when we'd met. He was no less handsome for them. I realised that this was everything Mum had ever hoped for. The man who had wronged her pleading for another chance, promising a lifetime all neatly wrapped up in a white picket fence.

But it felt wrong.

It was going to be hard fighting our way back to okay,

but I realised it was going to be even more difficult pretending we were already there. I gently moved James's hand. 'I need some time, James. I need to be sure of what's happening here. I don't… trust the choices I might make right now.' I'd never been like this, unsure as to what move to make, which path to take for the best solution. I didn't like feeling so out of control, bad things happen when you're out of control.

James held his position. 'That's fair, Amy. It's more than fair. But we don't have time, do we? Anna could call any time now, we both know that. What do you want us to say to her while you're thinking on everything?'

Cool nervousness swept over my neck. James knew he had me in a corner, just as I knew it was the best I could hope for. Bringing our child home was the priority, everything else we could sort through after the adoption was finalised.

James knew what I would say before I said it. 'We say nothing, James. She only wants to arrange a meeting to talk through the matching process.'

'And what if we've already been matched?'

'Matching can take months, James.'

'And sometimes it doesn't. You know that, Amy. They could have had a child in mind for us for months, you know it happens. If Anna turns up with a child's file, are you going to turn around and tell her that you *need time*?'

He was right. These were the thoughts that had been banging around my head when I didn't fill my mind with other things. It had been a month since the panel had approved us, Anna would be in touch any time now. James turned at the movement out in the hallway. We watched my mother's broken silhouette move past the mottled glass. 'Let me make you dinner, tomorrow night?' he said. 'We can talk properly, without company.'

This was what I knew *had* to happen. It had to, or there was no chance of Anna not suspecting something was going on with us. But the offer of dinner nearly had me breaking out in a nervous sweat. My scrawny plan was already falling down. Put a brave face on to the world – yes. Jump back into dinners for two and bed-sharing? I didn't think I was ready to do that. 'No dinner, James. No distractions. Just talk.'

He was watching me, careful blue eyes trained on their target. He seemed more than ready to slide right back into normality. The thought of it made my skin prickle, but that was what we needed, after all. To pretend Sadie had never happened, our family never jeopardised.

James nodded. It was a small victory for him and we both knew it. I felt as though I'd just been handed my own heart to hold. 'I have to get back to this fee proposal, James. I'll come over, but not tomorrow. I'm behind at work, I have contractors waiting on me. After the week- end, things will be quieter.' James nodded again, resum- ing a more rigid posture. He glanced at the papers on the dining table.

'The proposal's not for that tit in the baseball cap, is it?

What was his name?' James began to play with his keys again. He'd achieved his goal.

'Bywater.'

'Bywater? What's a guy like him doing at Cyan anyway?'

Outshining James on the big-boy injuries, if I remembered correctly. I moved past him and opened the dining-room doors. James followed me slowly across the hallway. 'Who wears a baseball cap over the age of fifteen, anyway? Knob.'

I didn't give the obvious answer of James's golfing buddies. Instead, I opened the front door for him and watched him through it.

James turned on the step, his eyes cautious. He was sizing me up, surveying me like one of his buildings, working out where was safe to tread. 'Look, I'm mostly on site for the rest of the week so I won't hassle you, Ame. But we are gonna talk soon, right?' I was still nodding when he leant in unexpectedly and kissed me chastely on the mouth. I watched, rigid and ineffectual as he turned and walked away. James was efficient in the art of closing deals. For some reason, I remembered the time I'd nearly been had by a smarmy car salesman.

I closed the door after him.

'Everything all right, sweetheart? I was just coming to put the kettle on.' Mum was about as subtle as an atom-bomb.

I nodded and passed her into the dining room. She knew

not to ask, leaving me to tidy up my work things in peace. I didn't spend long at my laptop, I didn't even sit. James had thrown my head for the rest of the night, so I fired off Bywater's email and, much to Mum's dismay, headed upstairs.

I was hoping sleep would find me more easily tonight, but the hours soon slipped away as I replayed James's visit through my mind. At least the time issues we were facing with Anna were something we were both aware of. A small voice had been whispering to me that James might take the upheaval of the last couple of weeks as his opportunity to change his mind, to pull out altogether, but he'd sounded genuinely concerned tonight that we be ready for our next meeting with Anna.

I tried to visualise it all being okay, the two of us and the child we didn't yet know, living somewhere picturesque and wholesome, like the mill. Fishing on the riverbank, balloon-adorned birthday parties on the lawns, friends and family coming over with their own kids. We didn't need a super-home. We didn't need anything but the people in that picture, yet still it felt like an unreachable fantasy. And still sleep evaded me.

CHAPTER 8

'ER, HOUSTON? WE have a problem.'

The delicate issue of cohabitation was always going to have to be tackled at some point. This morning, that time had come. With my back to most of the office, I couldn't see Sadie without swivelling my chair, so for nearly three hours, I hadn't, locked in position like a stiff neck. Sadie had proven Phil wrong and had made it past the eleven-thirty benchmark, the time by which Phil had bet a fiver that Sadie would've cried off sick again.

Hannah was admiring a crisp five-pound note, Blu-tacked to her monitor. It was a momentous occasion that saw Phil lose a bet. One small step for Hannah, but a giant leap for office junior-kind.

Phil's chair squeaked again. Hers hadn't stopped swivelling all morning. It wasn't yet noon and so far, her hawkish monitoring of Sadie's end of the office had produced a near constant commentary of whispers and tuts.

'Ame!' she muttered for the umpteenth time. I carried on with the lighting plan the contractors were patiently waiting on. I didn't need to know what Sadie was doing now. 'It's work-related, I promise. You *really* need to deal with this before Adrian does.'

That wasn't necessarily good to hear either. 'Don't tell me the shop-fitters are working from superseded drawings again?' Someone was in trouble if they were. I skipped around the workstation to Phil's desk. Open on the screen was Phil's cc'd copy of the email I'd sent to Rohan Bywater.

'What about it?' I asked. Phil gave me a few more seconds to work out what the problem was. 'I had to give him your details, Phil, because I can't work with him! The guy's a big kid. Please be the point of contact on this if he takes us on?'

Phil pursed her lips as if about to whistle through them. 'Er, I don't think he's going to take us on, Ame.'

Off the back of Phil's expression, I tried to remember the figure I'd ended up quoting him. 'I gave him a second option on the fees.' I shrugged. It wasn't like I'd priced him out of using Cyan completely.

'The fees? Amy! I didn't get as far as the attachments! I've just scrolled down the email to get to them and, and…' Phil actually appeared lost for words. 'Are you mad?' She jabbed a pen at her monitor. 'Read,' she instructed. I skimmed over the email I'd hastily sent the night before, mumbling through the text.

Dear Mr Bywater,
Further to our earlier conversation, please find the

attached fee proposal outlining our costs for the interior redesign of Briddleton Mill House, areas as specified on the accompanying plan. We have drafted two fee options for your consideration, as attached.

If you have any queries, please do not hesitate to contact my colleague, Philippa Penrose, on the above number.

Best Regards,
Amy Alwood

It was only a little buck-passing. It usually took a lot more to get Phil's knickers in a twist. 'I don't see the problem? It's polite, professional…' I joked.

Phil had that rarest of gifts, the ability to bestow a full-bodied smile that held absolutely no warmth to it. 'Scroll down the page, Miss Polite Professional,' she instructed.

I exhaled and began scrolling through the screen. Beneath my message, a large blank space stretched out several lines further down the screen. I carried on moving down through the whiteness, until *that* name appeared again.

Bywater,
I'd love to see someone kick your arse with your own peg leg.

A whoosh of breath rushed into my lungs. It wasn't unlike a scene from *Indiana Jones* when someone opens the crypt and the air gets sucked away before all hell breaks loose. 'Oh shit! *Oh shit, oh shit, oh shit!*'

Phil sat open-mouthed. 'You got that right. Why the hell did you write that on the end of a *client's* email?'

I stared panic-stricken at the screen, willing the words in front of me to change. They didn't. Well, that was that then. I slapped a hand against my stupid forehead. 'Adrian is going to hit the roof. He's going to sack me. I've just given him the perfect excuse to get rid—'

'Calm down,' Phil soothed. 'You didn't copy Adrian in on it. You're just gonna have to call this guy up, quick, and, er…'

'And what, Phil? Apologise for insulting him? Or for being so professionally inept that I didn't check my own email before hitting SEND?' I slumped into the free chair beside Phil, covering my face with my hands. 'I must have pressed the return button, instead of delete. I moved the words out of view,' I said shakily. I began to tap the heels of my hands against my forehead. 'Stupid, stupid, stupid!'

*

My desk phone began ringing out behind us. We all ignored it. All morning I'd wished for something, anything, to take my mind off Sadie sitting a few yards further down the office, flanked by her own team of whispering chair-swivellers. Now I had it. I was going to lose my job. I'd managed to pluck up the guts to come back here, and now I was going to have to explain to Anna anyway that I'd been sacked for abusing a guy with only one leg.

The ringing at my phone cut out, promptly replaced by a tinnier ringing at Hannah's desk.

'Hannah speaking?' Hannah turned in her chair to face me. 'Yep, she's just talking to Phil.' Hannah's eyes widened. 'Hang on a sec.' She covered over the mouthpiece. 'Ally's got Mr Bywater on the reception phone. He's asking to be put through to you.'

I stood bolt upright. 'Now?' I yelped.

'Uh-oh.' Phil grimaced.

Hannah was drawn back to her phone. 'Oh… *okay*.' She covered the mouthpiece again. 'She's putting him through now!' she whispered, thrusting the receiver at arm's length towards me with an apologetic frown. My arms were flapping hysterically, ferociously pointing a finger at Hannah, pleading with her to take the call. *What do I say?* Hannah mouthed, but it was too late. 'Er, hello, Mr Bywater …'

My silent gesticulations continued as Hannah trod water for me. She quickly caught the gist of all the arm-flapping. I was out of the office. No, I was out of the office *ill*. I'd call him back.

'No, Mr Bywater, it's Hannah. We met yesterday. I'm afraid she's not currently in the office, she's… on site.'

Ill, Hannah! You should've said I was ill, with some horrible disease of the mind!

'Can I take a message and get her to call you back as soon as she's in?' I winced at the thought of having to call him eventually. 'Oh,' Hannah said, contemplatively. 'Er, okay?' I watched her return the phone to its base.

Phil looked at me, then Hannah. 'Well? What did he say?'

'Nothing.' Hannah said sheepishly. 'He, er, he didn't say anything.'

'What?' Phil demanded. 'What the hell was he calling for then?'

Hannah began to flush. There was something she wasn't saying. 'What do you mean, he didn't say anything, Hannah?' I asked, already feeling a resurgence of Bywater-related apprehension.

Hannah looked down the office nervously. 'Adrian started talking to him and he ended the call.'

'Rohan Bywater is with Adrian?' I asked, puzzled. 'Adrian Espley?' Hannah looked positively flustered now, darting uncertain eyes to Phil, then back to me again. The flush in her cheeks had deepened to an even cherry-red by the time she looked over to where Adrian's hulking frame loomed into the far end of the studio. At first, I didn't recognise the client beside him. His tan seemed not quite so deep, his shoulders bigger set inside the crisp lines of a slate-grey suit.

'Shit, indeed,' Phil muttered ominously.

Rohan Bywater's dark mussed hair was no different, but teamed with stylish formal wear it came off as a deliberate trend, rather than the messy crop he'd sported yesterday. I felt as though somebody had just plunged a hand into my chest cavity and squeezed what it found lying around in there. Dropping into a crouch wasn't a conscious move, but there I suddenly was, seeking refuge between Hannah and Phil's legs.

'What the hell are you doing?' Phil demanded.

I felt the colour drain from my face. 'Hannah's just told him I'm out of the office!' I cringed.

'You told me to say that!' Hannah whispered defensively.

'I know, I know!'

'Yeah, don't listen to her, Hannah. She kicks people and tells lies,' Phil quipped. I'd have jabbed her in the leg had I not have been in the latter throes of a meltdown. 'Holy hotbuns, Batman!' Phil whispered excitedly. 'He did not look like that when he was last in here.'

'Flipping heck!' Hannah agreed. 'He looks better than he did on his bike too.'

I was about to succumb to a full-on panic attack. 'Phil! What am I gonna do?' Phil cocked an eyebrow and looked down over me. 'Under the desk?' She shrugged. Phil rolled her chair back a little, allowing me the option of shuffling into the alcove. For a second, I actually considered it.

'And here they are!' boomed Adrian, coming to a stand still between the backs of Hannah and Phil's chairs. 'Charlie's Angels.' I scrunched my eyes closed. Adrian could be like an embarrassing uncle at times. Like I needed any help with the embarrassment right now. 'Is that you, down there, Alwood?' he called, a forced joviality in his voice.

Phil cleared her throat. 'You found that earring yet, Ame?' she asked nonchalantly. I quickly pulled the stud from my lobe before wriggling backside first out of my inadequate hidey hole.

'Found it.' I smiled gingerly, holding the stud up in my fingers.

Hannah graduated from cherry-red to scarlet. 'Oh... *there* you are, Amy!' she tried. Phil rolled her eyes.

I tried not to look, but some part of me actually hoped there would be something of Bywater's perpetual smile on his lips. I glanced up at him. His face was more angular when it was serious. His features statuesque and solemn, as if they should be made of marble, not flesh. I think I preferred the smile.

'Amy, do you have a minute? In the boardroom?' Adrian moved off towards the meeting room without my answer. Rohan Bywater watched me get to my feet. 'Local site visit, was it?' He nodded towards the boardroom. 'Shall we?' He didn't wait for my answer either.

The look on Phil's face said it all. *See you on the other side ... maybe.*

Why had I even come back to work again? I mouthed

a few expletives to myself and followed the two men into the boardroom.

Adrian was wrestling with the window blinds, trying to lessen the light streaming into the conference room when I walked in after them. Rohan Bywater moved beside me, the scent of his skin reaching me just before his voice did. 'Cheer up, you look like someone's about to get their arse kicked.'

I swept my skirt underneath myself and slipped into one of the chairs, waiting for the inevitable.

'Right,' Adrian started, 'fantastic news. Mr Bywater is happy with your fee proposal, Amy – thanks for organising that so efficiently – and would like you to get started.'

What?

I checked Adrian's expression. He always exuded elation after securing a new client. Bywater's face was harder to read.

'The *senior* design-led option,' Bywater added. 'That would be you, right?'

I tried not to grimace as I attempted to piece it all together. That email was beyond offensive. 'You're hiring me? As project leader?'

Bywater remained cool in his chair, eyes piercing against his darker features. 'I read through your email last night. Top to bottom,' he added carefully, 'and I can tell I'll be in safe hands.' Bywater watched my hand move up towards my ear. I stopped myself and sat on it instead.

'And you'd be right, Mr Bywater. Amy's one of our best.' Adrian sounded like an over-proud parent.

I tried not to squirm in my seat as Bywater fished to make eye contact. 'I can see why you hold her in such high regard, Adrian. Professional, conscientious... I'm excited to get going,' he said coolly.

'Great!' Adrian approved, clasping his hands together. 'How soon would you like us to get started?' I felt the burn of Bywater's glare, boring into my face. I tried to remain facing him, avoiding his eyes obviously, instead fixing mine on the silky pigeon-blue stripes of his tie.

'Do you like a challenge, Miss Alwood?' Bywater ran his fingers over the tie, stealing it back from me, new grazes gracing a couple of his knuckles.

'Excuse me?' The feebleness in my voice was not lost on anyone.

Bywater's tawny eyes were heavy on me now, daring me to delve into them for the reasons he could possibly want me anywhere near his house.

'Challenges are good, don't you think? It's healthy to push yourself out of your comfort zone, exhilarating even. You strike me as someone who could deal with a few ups and downs and push the mill on for me.' Bywater was almost smiling. For some unsettling reason, I was starting to suspect that his willingness to have me work for him was actually down to the fact that *he* liked a challenge. Worse still, he seemed to like challenging me.

For a second, his smile got the better of him. If he was

looking for a sparring partner, he was going to be disappointed. I wasn't even up to a staring contest.

'I'd like to get the ball rolling as soon as possible, if we can, Adrian?'

'Sure, sure.' Adrian nodded in agreement. 'Amy? How soon can we get up and running?' I was supposed to be starting on a new restaurant next week. I knew then Adrian had seen the fees I'd quoted for this job.

Through a gap in the blinds behind Bywater, I caught sight of James walking resolutely through the office. Sadie glanced up at him as he passed her desk. I shifted in my seat.

Adrian cleared his throat. I reeled my concentration back inside the room. 'Well, ah… when would you like to sit down and work through your needs, Mr Bywater?'

'Monday morning works for me,' he said, looking to his wristwatch.

I glanced sideways. James was hanging over Phil. Phil began pointing over this way.

'Super.' Adrian beamed. 'I'm sure we can get Dana to shift around anything else you've got booked in, Amy.'

I watched James lean in towards Phil, closer than was advisable. She'd been waiting for a chance to let rip but she was listening to him, albeit reluctantly.

'Amy?' Adrian called.

Rohan Bywater's eyes narrowed under darker serious brows. Adrian had adopted a more serious expression too.

'Sorry?'

'Monday,' Adrian repeated. 'You'll be starting at the mill on Monday.' I nodded.

'It's good of you to accommodate me so quickly,' Bywater said, glancing out towards James and Phil. 'I don't want to take up any more of Miss Alwood's time now, though, I'm sure she has other challenges to deal with before we get started next week.' A knot began to form in my stomach. Rohan Bywater set me on edge, but I still owed him a grovelling apology. Something else to dread on an ever-growing list.

'She is a busy girl,' Adrian agreed. 'We can finish up here, Amy. You get on if you wish.' Bywater got up from his chair to shake my hand before I left. I didn't look at him at all now. I left the boardroom to the sound of Adrian asking whether or not Bywater was a rugby man, while I traded one anxiety for another.

*

'What's going on?' I asked James, acutely aware of two things. The first, he had promised to give me space at work, and the second, Sadie was watching the show.

'Anna just called. She wants to make an appointment to come over, to the house.'

'What did you say?' I yelped. 'We can't see her yet!' Social workers were like bloodhounds. She'd know. She'd smell it on us – relationship failure.

'I told her that we're away until next week, to buy us some time. I didn't know what to say, Ame, so she's suggested calling us the week after. I thought she might ring your phone too so I just wanted to make sure we had our stories straight before you dropped us in it.' Phil huffed accusingly. James turned his back to her, shutting her out. I could feel myself getting more flustered at the thought of Anna just turning up. 'We need to sort ourselves out, Ame,' he warned, 'or we're gonna be stuffed.'

I didn't mean to, but the sensation was suddenly there, choking me.

'Amy, please. Don't get upset,' James said, closing in on me.

'That's *your* sodding fault,' Phil snapped at him. I turned away from them, mortified that this might happen here.

Don't you dare, I warned myself, grappling to keep my cool.

'I'm fine, James. Please,' I snipped, pinching the tension over my nose. 'I just need to get back to work.' Because work was going to be just bloody marvellous from Monday onwards.

Keeping my back to the office, to James and Sadie and the rest of them, I stood there like the complete loser I felt, considering all the ways in which my life had so abruptly become this big, ugly catalogue of disasters. I'd thought that I could just press on, one awkwardness at a time, until all the pieces fit again, but I couldn't even make a day without something falling apart in my hands.

If I'd been under any illusion that I could somehow

dupe the rest of the world around me – my boss, my mother, the social worker – into thinking that everything was just hunky dory, it all evaporated into thin air when I saw Rohan Bywater watching me through the boardroom blinds.

CHAPTER 9

'THIS IS SUCH a bad idea,' I groaned, hiding behind my sunglasses as Phil cruised down the lane towards Briddleton Mill.

'Be cool, Ame. This has got to be better than sharing the office with Glitter Knickers and The Snake.'

'Don't call him that, Phil. He's trying.' I should've just let it go. Of all the names she'd bestowed upon James over the last fortnight, The Snake sounded like a term of endearment.

Phil went to say something then changed her mind. She tried again. 'How are you feeling about playing happy families next week?' she asked. 'I thought you said these social workers could sniff out a nervous smoker if the wind's in the right direction?'

'They can,' I said, watching the hedgerows zip past us. 'We'll just have to get through it without her picking up on any tension.' Maybe taking up smoking would help.

Phil eyed our surroundings. 'You do know, Ame, you're like the worst liar I've ever met, right? You start messing with your earrings, then your neck gets redder—'

'Thanks, Phil! I won't be on my own. I'll let James do the talking.' Luckily for us, James wasn't too bad at lying, by all accounts.

'More's the pity,' she muttered, looking out of her window. I could hear the cogs in Phil's head turning over. 'You know, there are worse things than being on your own, Ame. You shouldn't be scared of it. Once you've tasted the heady flavours of freedom again, you'll like them. I know you will.'

'I never said that I was leaving him, Phil.'

'No, you didn't. But you will. He's not right for you, Ame. Honestly, I'm not sure that he ever was.'

I wasn't getting into this. The longest relationship Phil had ever had was with her favourite shade of lipstick. I didn't respond, but Phil carried on undeterred.

'First, you'll fall apart. That's a given,' she said, tilting her head to me. 'Then you'll think that the world is over because you're like your mum, and you can't realise all the plans you made with James in mind. Then you'll come round to the idea that, actually, you used to be pretty kick-ass – *no offence* – the kind of girl who doesn't need to pin all her dreams on another human being, because you're more than capable of going out there and grabbing them by the balls yourself.'

I looked at her, incredulous that she could be so hard-faced.

'What?' she whimpered.

I loved her bones, every last acerbic, un-pc one of them,

but I was not taking relationship advice from Philippa Penrose. We were about as different as we could be on that score. Phil would say that she was independent, but actually she just liked it too much out there, in the game. Phil didn't lust after motherhood or marriage and there was a freedom for her in that, which, damn it, I envied. I used to think that as soon as the right guy, with the right body and the right salary, came along, Phil was as good as cooked, but she was showing no signs of slowing down and I wasn't sure that there was a man on the planet who could reel her in now.

'You'll get back on your feet,' she continued, 'get yourself your own car. Then you'll start looking at finding a place of your own, your own furniture instead of all that artsy glass shit The Snake likes, and then you'll be all set. You know what comes after your own place, right?' she asked, feeding the wheel through her hands as she made the left onto the lane.

'Gin? Cats? Pot Noodles for one?' I asked huffily.

Phil's mobile began buzzing from the back seat. She ignored it. 'Shagging. That's what comes next, Ame. Good, raw, noisy shagging that gets your heart pumping and your toes curling.'

I was beginning to will away this car journey. Arriving at the mill was actually starting to look like the rosier option.

'Probably *the* last thing on my mind right now, Phil.' James had said that it had been the last thing on my mind for months. Probably more months than I'd realised. There was a time we couldn't leave each other alone long enough to eat regularly.

'Then you need to get back in the saddle, hon. Plenty more fish, and all that.'

Nope, I was wrong. Sex wasn't the last thing on my mind. The prospect of ever sitting at a bar making small talk with a stranger was the last thing on my mind. 'And how does that go, Phil? Meeting new *fish*. Remind me.'

Phil glanced over at me suspiciously. 'Drinks, conversation… *fun*.' She said *fun* as if she was teaching me how to pronounce a foreign word.

'Fun,' I mimicked. 'Sorry, but I'm out of practice.'

'It's just dating, Ame. It hasn't changed much since the last time you did it. Think of it as riding a bike. You meet a guy, have a few drinks, tell him a bit about yourself…'

'Ha! Oh yes, Phil… I can just imagine how much fun that would be. *Hi, my name's Amy, I'm twenty-nine, I'm a Pisces and five years ago I had a hysterectomy. Were you planning on ever having children of your own? Mine's a voddy and diet coke.*'

Phil wriggled back into her shoulders a little. 'Wow. It really has been a while since you last rode that bike.'

'The last time I rode *that bike*, Phil, it had more working parts.'

Her eyebrows rose above the rim of her glasses. 'Maybe forget the conversation, just keep it to drinks and fun,' she said sarcastically.

'And what would be the point of that, Phil? It would have to come up at some stage.'

'On a first date?' she questioned. 'Jeez, couldn't you just aim for the usual tonsil tennis and awkward dancing?'

'It's false advertising, Phil! I think a guy has a right to know *before* he starts shelling out for drinks that his *bun* will never rise in my *oven!* I mean, it's kind of a big deal when you're shopping for a sodding life partner.'

My voice was climbing, but the set of Phil's lips instantly made me regret opening mine.

'Not every bloke you meet is going to want kids, Ame,' she said calmly.

'I want kids, Phil! I want them! *Okay*? And at some point in the next couple of weeks, *The Snake* and I are going to be told how, and maybe even when, that's going to happen! And unless I catch him and Sadie at it in the boardroom again, I don't want to hear about the perks of singledom, or dating or sodding *bikes*, all right?'

I didn't look at what she was doing with her lips now. Welding them shut, hopefully. The car fell into silence for a few minutes until a familiar ringtone cut through the awkwardness between us.

'Your phone's ringing again,' I huffed, looking out to where the hedgerows grew steadily less kempt as the lane became the mill's private track.

'Ugh, it'll be Adrian again. I told him I was detouring to the doc's. He'll be wondering how long *women's problems* take to sort out, the impatient git.'

Light-years, was the answer to that one.

'You didn't have to run me in, Phil,' I said, trying to melt some of the ice in my voice.

'Are you kidding?' She smiled. 'I want another look at that body. I've had my fingers crossed all morning Hotbuns isn't dressed when we arrive.'

Hotbuns? Nicknames were the highest accolade Phil bestowed upon any man.

Rohan Bywater's name came crashing into my mind like a raging bull. I looked for a distraction in the scenery whipping past but my brain was suddenly hijacked with unpleasant thoughts of seeing him again, the sickening reminder of the apology I owed him already sending me withering lower into my seat. I don't know why I glanced at Phil then, she wasn't exactly the jollying type. I thought about pleading with her to make an emergency stop while I dreamt up a brilliant excuse not to show, but there was a new energy about her – something excitable and ever-so-slightly sadistic – betrayed by the corner of her mouth and the smile it held there. Phil had ring-side seats and couldn't wait for the show to start. I looked back outside and immediately wanted to sink lower still. We were here.

The morning sun blazed into the clearing ahead, sending the far row of birches into a flickering wall of lime-green leaves. The sweeping barrier of green seemed to be defending the mill from something – the rest of the world, maybe. Despite my mood, I realised again that the photos didn't do the setting justice. Adrian was right, this place was going to look impressive in the company portfolio.

Phil pulled into a spot next to the VW vans. 'Right then. Let's go find Handsome.' She grinned. Reluctantly, I emerged from the passenger side. Phil slammed her door closed and pulled her Anna Wintour sunglasses down her nose. 'Damn, he's got the bod and the house. If he's a lucky boy, he might get to see what I've got,' she purred, before gazing across the water to the ramshackle hut on the bank of the millpond. Two men were balanced precariously on its roof, hammering. The darker of the two looked over at us, exchanged words with his shirtless friend and resumed hammering.

Phil smiled like a predator across the water. 'Heart and toes, honey, heart and toes.'

I took a deep breath and collected my laptop and bag from the back of Phil's car.

'Come on,' I huffed softly. 'Let's get this over with.'

CHAPTER 10

I LOOKED RELUCTANTLY across the millpond towards the long silvered shed and remembered seeing it marked *Boathouse* on the plans. The light glittered on the water beside it, playfully disappearing and reappearing on the surface like one of the whack-a-mole games we used to play in the arcade at Jackson's Park.

Phil was practically skipping her way towards the mill. She was right – technically Rohan Bywater was keeping me out of the office, which was no small mercy. Trouble was, Rohan Bywater wasn't your average client. I'd tasted first hand his idea of funny and could only imagine what lay in store while I was working here. Honestly, the thought of having to deal with another person in my day-to-day who wasn't all they seemed was exhausting. I didn't need it. What I did need, on the other hand, was my job. Like it or not, Bywater had saved my skin with Adrian when anyone else would've had my ass.

Phil was almost at the water, keen to sniff out our host. The little pulses of nervousness in my diaphragm were beginning to group together. *It's only short-term, Ame.* I would keep my head down, get on with it – *not* obsess over the unfathomable reasons Rohan Bywater had come up with to commission me in the first place. I let my lungs fill with the cleansing freshness of waterside air and realised with startling clarity what it was that most troubled me about Rohan Bywater. He was unpredictable.

Unpredictable, uncontrolled, unplanned – these were not my favourite words.

Phil led us eagerly out onto the timber gangway overshooting the water. I counted twelve timber posts as I passed them, each crowned with its own brushed-steel lantern, brand new and modern, chosen by the previous owners before fate had struck and led them on another path away from this beautiful place.

'Shit,' Phil hissed. 'I've only just bought these!' she protested, twisting free her heel from where it had sandwiched itself between two of the deck timbers. I carried on, carefully picking my way to the end of the run without succumbing to the same fate. Once we'd made it to the less perilous gravelled ground on the other side of the mill, I could see that the half-naked man, the shaggy spectator, had already jumped down from the shed roof and was sashaying towards us. He was wearing some kind of cargo trousers and a bulging utility bet, which jostled awkwardly as he walked. Phil lifted her sunglasses just enough to share a disturbed look with me.

'Is that circa 'eighty-one headwear I spy?' she murmured, hiding behind her glasses again. The plume

of mousy-brown fuzz emanating from either side of the
shaggy one's red headband did have a touch of the John
McEnroes about it, while his pointy facial hair was more
musketeer than sporting hero.

'Ladies.' The shaggy one smiled lazily. 'I'm Carter.
Welcome.'

'Carter?' I smiled politely. Carter nodded absently.
Satisfied that acquaintances had been sufficiently met,
he immediately set to giving Phil a brazen top-to-toe
body-scan. Horrified that he would even think he had a
shot at it, Phil's face seemed to fold in on itself, her features contorting like a bad piece of origami you'd inevitably give up on because you hadn't followed the instruc-
tions properly.

'Down this way, are we?' I asked, heading off an
unpleasant incident.

Phil could spring like a spitting cobra, and it was
unlikely Carter would be much of a match for her, even
with the athletic prowess his headband might've projected
back in '81. The three of us began walking towards
the boathouse. Bywater was making his way awkwardly
down off the roof of a second, lower shed I could now
see nestled against the main part of the structure. He
was directly in my eye-line as we followed the path of
balding grass towards him. It felt invasive to watch him
reposition himself carefully, to do with a series of cal-
culated motions that which Carter had probably achieved
with just one, foolhardy lunge. 'Is this a boathouse?' I

asked Carter, trying to distract myself from Bywater's efforts.

Carter scratched at the thin wisps of hair on his honed chest. His was the first tidy body I'd ever seen that Phil had somehow resisted the urge to perv upon. 'Er, yeah. Was. Workshop now. Well, will be when Ro clears all his stuff into the big house,' he said, falling into line at Phil's right side. Phil's shoulders had come in together a little, in that stance old ladies assume when they suspect their handbag's about to be snatched.

Bywater dusted off his hands on work-stained jeans as he steadily walked towards us. I fidgeted with the handle of my laptop-case. In preparation for this morning, I'd run through every wisecrack I could think of on the topic of my relationship with James, and my ineptitude with emails, and my flighty departure from Bywater and his bike ramps last week. Trying to somehow anticipate the trajectories of his jokes before he could roll them out and sting me with them. As we approached each other, I braced myself.

'Morning,' he said, rubbing the back of his wrist across his forehead. 'Glad you could make it.' I waited for the punchline, but it didn't come. No grin. Just the perfectly pleasant whisper of a smile.

Phil stepped forward, reaching out a long, manicured hand. 'Hello, again,' she purred, 'Philippa Penrose. I don't think we were properly introduced, in the flesh.' Bywater took her hand in his much larger, tanned grasp. Blue check suited the olive-skinned.

'Rohan.' He smiled. 'And you've obviously met Isaac Carter here.'

Carter sat his hands on his hips, showcasing the form that went with the name. 'What a beautiful name, Philippa,' Carter added, sweeping a rogue hair from his face. He unclipped a pocket on his belt, retrieved a liquorice stick and slipped it into his mouth. Already I found myself liking him.

I chewed my lip, biting down on a smile, glad that it was Phil, and not me, who would be the first subject of an awkward exchange today. The thought made me glance at Bywater. His eyes met mine, holding me there for a moment before I planted my sights safely on the cycle tracks near my shoes. 'Liquorice, Philippa?' Carter tried innocently.

'No,' Phil said bluntly, her lips settling into a hard line.

'Shall we go up to the mill?' Bywater asked, fighting his own smile. 'I've set up somewhere for you to put your things, make a drink,' he said, looking to me again. 'Just for while you're… doing your thing.'

I regarded him uncertainly. This was the fourth time I'd met with him, and on each occasion he'd thrown me. This time, hospitality seemed to be his chosen means.

'That's very kind of you, Rohan.' Phil smiled sweetly. Someone's phone began buzzing again. Phil turned to retrieve it from the bag slung over her shoulder, startling Carter who had been standing overly close to her. 'Were you just *sniffing* me?' she accused.

Carter slunk back a step like a reprimanded puppy. 'Sorry,' he said, waving the last inches of his liquorice. 'You just… smell nice.'

'Don't,' she said sharply, looking to her phone.

Bywater had given up trying not to smile. 'Carter, why don't you go and see if you can get those last few shingles on? I ran out of nails when you took the belt.'

Phil watched Carter trudge back towards the workshop before turning bee-like eyes back to me.

'I've gotta get back. Adrian's being an arse. He wants me over at the retail park, snagging. I told him to send one of the juniors but…' She trailed off, losing interest in her own conversation. 'You're good, right?' she said with a smile.

My brain was screaming, *No, Phil! I'm not! I am TOTALLY out of my comfort zone with this guy!* 'Yep. Course. Thanks for the ride.'

'Maybe Rohan could drop you home when you're finished? You're only a quick drive away. I'm sure he wouldn't mind seeing my very good friend home safely?' she purred, reaching to shake his hand again. I didn't need to see Phil's eyes to know the delight they held at a second chance to touch him.

'That's okay,' I blurted, considering how best to put the next bit. 'I'll get my mum to pick me up…' My voice trailed off.

Groan.

I knew the exasperation shielded by Phil's glasses, but

she brightened with the opportunity to give Bywater a last departing smile. She threw a goodbye hand into the air and began sauntering back along the pond towards the mill.

Resigned to being left here, stranded, I turned to face my host. A small bump was beginning to form on the inside of my lip, punishment for nipping at it with anxious teeth.

'Coffee?' Rohan Bywater asked. He still hadn't been anything but pleasant. That didn't change the fact that I was all alone with him again, with only pleasantries to cling to.

'Coffee would be great. Thanks.'

'Tea for me,' Carter called, shimmying back up onto the boathouse roof.

Bywater nodded towards the workshop. 'I'll make the drinks here, then we can go on up to the mill.'

He led me through a rickety timber doorway into a surprisingly well-ordered room, an operating theatre for bikes where walls hung with cycle parts and power tools and other things I couldn't identify.

I ambled in, setting my things down on the corner of the workbench there, the only corner not dominated by piles of papers – sketches and scribbled annotation. On top of one of the piles, like some bizarre comedy paperweight, was a foot.

I tried not to stare, but it reminded me of those pretend Prince Charles ears you used to be able to buy from joke shops. Flesh-coloured plastic things, hollowed out that they could sit over what you already had. I let Bywater distract my eyes, following him all the way to the small kitchenette at the far end of the boathouse. 'Make yourself at home,' he called, clanking spoons in cups. I concentrated on looking anywhere but at the foot.

A sofa bed sat outstretched down near where Bywater was fixing the drinks. This place was probably most men's dream hideaway, somewhere to play and tinker then kick back with a beer afterwards. James had never been much of a do-it-yourselfer. He paid for everything that was fixable. Not that everything was. Everything else, he simply replaced.

I pushed James from my head, and wondered where the woman in this picture was. Bywater probably was every bit as attractive as Phil had so vocally pointed out. Some might even say that he was funny, too – when you weren't the target of his humour. 'How do you take it?' he called. 'Or I have chamomile, if you prefer tea?'

'Chamomile?' I smiled, the very word sat juxtaposed with all the metal and mechanics around us.

'For Carter,' he laughed, 'he's the only one who drinks girls' drinks around here.' Carter would have to move onto something stronger if he was going to start tussling with Phil. Protein shakes at least.

'Coffee's great, no sugar thanks.'

Bywater finished the drinks and carried them over to the workbench. 'The milk's full fat, is that okay? Most girls I know like the watery stuff,' he said, passing me mine.

'Full fat's fine, thanks.' James would've had a heart attack at me drinking anything full fat.

'Let me just give this to Cart.'

I smiled gingerly as he ducked back out of the doorway and disappeared around the boathouse wall. Smiles and thank-yous might not be a solid start, but they were a start. I watched the light on the water again and blew the hot aroma from my cup. With the coast clear, my eyes found their way straight back to that foot sitting conspicuously on the workbench. Looking at it felt similar to the time I'd accidentally opened our neighbour's Ann Summers parcel – a privacy breached, never to be reinstated again.

Overhead, the hammering had stopped while Bywater and Carter discussed something in muffled voices. I turned and surveyed the rest of my surroundings. Behind me were more drawings outlining some sort of brace-like contraption alongside what looked to be two or three incomplete prototypes with strapping and Velcro and other plastic appendages. I didn't have Bywater down as a fashion designer, so I reckoned them to be like everything else in here, bike-related.

Without straying too far from where Bywater had left me, I followed the drawings along the wall to a hand-ful of pictures hung haphazardly there and leant in over the worktop for closer inspection. Most of the photos showed BMX bikers mid-air over ramps, much the same as Bywater had set up in the field here. But these pictures hadn't been taken at the mill. The ramps were higher, with crowds of spectators and the bright blare of relentless advertising on helmets and banners. I scanned through a second collection of photos, of Rohan and Carter and other men, sat jubilantly on their bikes with equally enthusiastic women hanging from their necks. Another showed Bywater and a pretty blonde – years earlier I could tell by the subtle differences in a person's face. The blonde featured in three more pictures, larking around with Carter, another sat on Rohan's shoulders on some sun-drenched desert rock, and then the last, holding a birthday cake for Rohan over his hospital bed. In all four photos she was pretty, but seemed less hopeful in this last picture, an expression he shared.

'Shall we go up to the mill?'

The sound made me jump. I spun to face it, knocking a hot splash of my drink over my fingers. Under me, a streak of coffee had spattered over his work.

We both looked at the pools of brown liquid seeping into the drawing. 'I can't believe I've just done that,' I blurted. Bywater watched me set down the offending mug and fish a tissue from my pocket so I could carefully begin dabbing the trail of brown droplets.

'It's okay, don't worry about it, they'll be messed up more than that before the day's out,' he tried, his voice smooth and steady. I continued to fuss, following the trail across the white papers until my tissue found its way to a row of little brown toes. I'd got them with the coffee too, or course. Unsure of the etiquette involved in dry-wiping a person's false foot, I delicately dabbed my tissue over the wet bits. Bywater watched, curiously. All noticeable spills suitably soaked up, I stuffed the soggy tissue back into my pocket, ignoring the burn in my cheeks as Bywater's smile broadened. I looked everywhere except at him, settling instead on making that small bump on my inner lip just a little more pronounced.

Carter's hammering resumed above. Bywater walked towards me, picked up his drink and turned to lean against the bench beside me. I caught something sweeter, more natural than the heavy fragrance of morning coffee. I tried not to look awkward, and shifted awkwardly beside him.

'Do you mind if I just get something out of the way?' he asked, tilting his head to me.

My free hand began fiddling with my jacket button, the other bringing my cup up as a face guard. Bywater repositioned himself slightly and looked through the open door out onto the waters. This was it. This was where he would spell out what a good sport he'd been in the face of my total knobishness and professional ineptitude. And I would agree with him, humbly, because he'd be absolutely right. 'I'm guessing that taking this job on might be… uncomfortable for you, and you should know, you don't need to feel that way while you're here.' I heard him swallow another sip from his cup.

I hadn't expected him to say that... not that I was overly sure what it was he was actually saying – Bravely, I lowered my mug – just enough to look at him properly for the first time since I'd arrived.

'You mean... because you caught me sending totally inappropriate emails to clients and didn't tell on me?' He couldn't see me chewing away at my lip behind my reinstated face guard.

Bywater's eyes held a smile. 'Actually, I was referring to my little joke on the ramps the other day, but you can roll the playground insult about my peg leg into this truce if you like?'

I was already wincing. Even accompanied by his throaty laugh, it sounded even more offensive when he said it out loud. At least he hadn't used the term *disabled*, or I'd have probably frog-marched myself, wrists aloft, to the nearest village stocks right there and then. I owed him an apology. I began gearing up to something I already knew wasn't going to cut it when the true colour of his eyes hooked my attention for a second. They faded to an almost fawn colour at their outer edges, like a mood ring on the cusp of change. My back straightened. 'Ah, I can only... *sincerely* apologise, about... I mean, I... I've never... really, I'm very sorry.' His smiling was making it worse. Why did I always have to be so awkward around this guy? I *was* sorry, for crying out loud, so sorry it was killing my powers of speech. 'Sorry,' I repeated, trying again before my head turned completely scarlet. I hid back inside my mug and looked over its rim only where it was safe to do so, out there onto the twinkling water.

'Forget it.' He shrugged. 'Carter and the boys have thrown around every joke there is. Thought up a few new ones, too. If you really want to insult me, go for my hair.' He was smiling crookedly when I emerged from my cup. Well, I couldn't stay in there for ever. Actually, there was nothing wrong with his hair. But he was right, I had wanted to insult him, and now I couldn't really remember why.

'Actually, I wasn't going to mention the hair,' I quipped, instantly wishing I could gobble the words back up like one of Samuel's Hungry Hippos. Rohan was still smiling. He ran his hand over the ruff of his hair. 'Maybe not as glorious as Shin Splints' golden mane, but you've gotta rock what you've got, right?' he offered, shrugging apologetically.

I felt my head furrow. 'Shin Splints?'

'Yeah, your man with the curtains... and the impressive track record for winding you up.' Thoughts of James made my back stiffen. And *curtains*? Boyzone had curtains. I smiled through the renewed discomfort and pretended there was something of critical significance in my watch face.

'Shall we make a start, Mr Bywater?' I said, waiting for him to exploit the very obvious chink I'd just revealed in my armour. I might as well have pulled out a great big neon arrow and let it flash him towards his next easy joke.

'Rohan. *Please*,' he softly insisted. 'You sound like a doctor when you call me *Mr Bywater*.'

'Sorry, *Rohan*.' I nodded. 'I'm eager to get started if we can.' Rohan pushed himself up from the bench, unsettling more of the subtle fronds of his aftershave. I tried not to inhale another hit of him but he was everywhere.

'Great. Well, I guess you've already seen how it goes around here. We're pretty laid back, so, you know, make yourself at home and, er, don't stress out about splashing hot coffee on anyone's body parts.' He smiled again. 'Not the ones that won't scald, anyway.'

I smiled and tried to think of something to say back.

The hammering above us abruptly stopped again, emphasising that our conversation had stalled. For the first time, I thought I saw him trying to think of something to say too. I suppose that was my cue to drop in with something professional, but I was still busy getting my head around the fact that there was simply no hiding from: Rohan Bywater was being nice to me, and it was completely throwing us both off.

'So, any ideas how long you'll be here for?' he asked, setting his cup down gripping onto the workbench.

'Based on the ideas you touched on with Adrian, I think you're looking at four to six weeks fit-out and decoration.'

'Sounds perfect. There's nothing much happening around here other than a small gathering I'll be having here mid-June, but honestly it wouldn't be the end of the world if there were a few jobs running over.'

'A gathering?'

'Yeah, it's a bit of an old tradition, I guess. I used to

throw a big barbecue, kind of an annual thing with my pals. They all lead pretty hectic lives so it's good when we get together, catch up on what's been happening, who's broken what. I've been moving around, and with one thing and another, it's kinda been on hold the last few years. Carter thought that with this place being fixed up soon, it'd be good to wake an old custom.'

I pulled one of my pads from my bag and began rummaging for a pen.

'Okay, so you need everything finished up early June?' Rohan passed me one of his from the workbench and nodded. I began scribbling. 'Given what you've discussed with Adrian, there aren't that many structural items to tackle. Lead times on finishes are where the issues might be. If we can tie a few suppliers down this week, we should be able to get a better handle on the project, start piecing together a schedule of works.'

He seemed amused again. 'Sure, sounds good. No one really has a set schedule to work around here, usually we just… go with the flow.'

'Go with the flow?'

'Yeah. Why not?' He shrugged.

'I'm more of a planning type of person,' I conceded, returning to my notes. I didn't have much experience of *going with the flow*.

Rohan arched his eyebrows. 'Sounds exhilarating. How's that working out for you?' Not so great, as it happened.

I was chewing my lip again, trying to think of something else to say. 'Should I… get set up here? I can do a lot from the office but some days I'll need to work from site.'

'Actually, I've set you up in one of the mill's bedrooms, if that's all right? Some of my stuff's in there, but there's a desk and a fridge – enough to keep you comfortable.'

'Great. Sounds ideal.'

'Sterling brew, chief,' Carter declared, ambling into the workshop. 'Roof's done. Are we hitting the verts or what?'

Rohan pushed himself up from the bench, stretching through the muscles in his arms. 'I'm just going to go show Amy her new executive office, then I'm going to try,' Rohan leant back to inspect one of the sketches on the wall, 'brace fifteen, but with the extra clip.' Carter meandered past me, perusing the scribbled notes on the wall.

'Can't you get away without it?' he asked, turning to examine the brace contraption on the side.

'It's still moving around too much,' Rohan replied, 'it's nearly there, it just needs a few more tweaks.'

'Did you run this one yesterday?' Carter asked, holding up the brace.

'Uhuh,' Rohan said disinterestedly, 'but the stiffness is still slowing down the line-up. I'm spending valuable seconds looking to see where to plant my foot.'

Carter rolled his head as if stretching through aching

shoulders and pondering the great questions of life all at once. 'So, you going to tinker with it this morning?'

Rohan planted his hands against the workbench next to me and leant forward on them. He had better defined forearms than I'd seen at the gym and I bet he'd never set foot inside one.'

'Uhuh.'

'Cool,' Carter said, seemingly losing interest. 'In that case, I'm gonna go get my yoga on. Give me a holler when you're ready to eat ramp, brother.'

Yoga? It was hard looking at Carter without smiling. Now that I thought about it, he did have something of a hippy guru about him. Rohan's eyes warmed, his features softening with the beginnings of a smile. If nothing else, it probably wasn't going to be dull working here, but there was even less chance of it being easy.

I stood quietly, waiting for Rohan's amusement to subside and for him to take me up to the mill, repeating in my head the only mantra that might see me safely through this project and out the other side.

Go with the flow.

CHAPTER 11

'I'VE HAD AN EPIPHANY!' Phil declared triumphantly, the bustle and thrum of a hair salon clearly audible in the background.

'Where are you, Phil? I thought you were snagging retail displays with the shop-fitters again today?'

'I will be, after I've finished snagging my roots with the colourist. What Adrian doesn't know won't hurt him.' I carried on picking my way over the cobbled street, trying not to wobble where my boot heels hit uneven ground. It wasn't far now to the quaint little shop with the Morris Minor van parked outside. The van was a quirky burgundy thing, with bold gold lettering splashed across its side. Not the obvious choice of vehicle for a fashionable bakery like *Cake*. 'James is on site most of the week, right? So at least you're mostly avoiding him at work. It's Glitter Knickers who's the issue.' I reached the pretty cream shop front and hovered there. I'd already explained to Phil the reasons that I didn't have the luxury of avoiding James, but her replies had consistently involved shovels and patios.

'She's his niece, Phil,' I said, faffing over my watch.

'Yeah, and? She's a gofer, for crying out loud! She doesn't need to work at Cyan with you breathing down her neck.'

I only had half an hour left. Hannah had asked if anyone fancied nipping out of the city to Hunterstone for lunch. As I wasn't working at the mill today, I could either avoid the staff kitchen all lunchtime, again, or come into Hunterstone and cancel the cake for Mum's party. It was a no-brainer.

'He won't get rid of Sadie, Phil.'

'He won't push her off the plank, granted, but if she jumps herself, Adrian won't catch her, Ame, she's too flaky. All we've got to do is *encourage* her to jump.'

Sadie had gone home ill by the time I'd got back to the office yesterday. She hadn't shown at all today.

'Can we talk about it later, Phil? I'm just about to embarrass myself.' I took a deep steadying breath and glanced over the beautiful wedding cakes in the window displays.

'Sure,' Phil answered. 'Where are you?'

'Cake shop.'

'Comfort food?'

'Cancellation.'

'Oh. Party's definitely off, then?'

I tucked the same troublesome lock of hair behind my ear. By force of habit I'd styled myself to perfection this morning, armour firmly in place for another tense day in the office, but despite the promise of yesterday's sunshine and the wonders of expertly applied finishing spray, today's damper air was seducing my inner frizz.

'The party is just a distraction, Phil. We've got bigger things to focus on.' James held too many cards and we both knew it. He'd given me a little space, which I'd appreciated, but Anna's impending visit was looming like a storm on the horizon while I scurried around before she hit, trying to batten down the hatches of a premature reconciliation. But I'd be buggered if I couldn't take control of this one stupid thing – the circus I never wanted.

I waited at the foot of the stone steps leading up to the old-fashioned bakery door, its vintage shop sign swinging overhead, and wondered if they'd have a line in commiseration cakes for the romantically damaged. Mum and I could probably eat a very large one between us. Phil began talking to someone as a hairdryer resumed its assault on her head. 'Ame? I'm going, hon, I can't hear you; I'll call you later.'

My goodbye was futile, drowned out by the hairdryer. I took the steps up to Cake and let myself in through the door. It was warm inside, bursting with the delicious aromas of everything I'd spent the last half a decade abstaining from. Bright and welcoming, it was hard not to feel picked up by the atmosphere in the little shop. The door jangled closed behind me and the pretty young woman behind the counter looked up from her task.

'Hey!' She smiled, warmly.

'Hi.'

'It's… *Amy*, right?' I quickly racked my brain for the cake woman's name, stalling until it presented itself.

'Wow. Do you remember all of your customers' names?' I asked, impressed, and still stalling. When we'd come in to order the cake, we'd only been in the shop for twenty minutes, and Mum had done most of the talking and sampling. She shrugged happily, pushing a few of the loose tendrils from her face. She seemed to have every shade of brown through blonde in her hair, happy enough to let it sit wildly piled at the back of her head.

'I don't know,' the woman smiled, 'some people just stick, I guess. It's getting close now, isn't it? May the…' She began flicking through a diary on the worktop. The first tingle of awkwardness began to rise in my cheeks.

'Actually, I need to er…'

From the room behind the counter, a handsome thirty-something in an open-necked white shirt all too easily created a diversion. He jostled his light-grey suit jacket from one arm to the next. He reminded me a little of James, suave and confident in a way that was more natural gift than conscious effort. There was something different about the way this man held himself, though, more relaxed in the shoulders perhaps. He smiled politely. It was a good smile, but I didn't hold its attention for long.

'I've got to run, Hol,' he said.

My memory clicked.

Holly blushed as the guy leant in and kissed her

tenderly. I watched as he bent down and placed his hands deftly at her waist, laying another, longer kiss on her swollen tummy. 'Right then, young bean, you look after our favourite girl while Daddy thrashes your grandpa over eighteen holes.'

She couldn't be very far off. She was a little bigger than I had been when I'd gone in to the hospital. I turned away to look at the displays of cakes and confection around the room, desperately trying not to feel as though I'd just ram-raided my way into their happiness. Salvation came in the form of my phone, vibrating in my bag. I turned away from them, speaking in hushed tones behind me while I flicked to the message icon. I had two texts, the first from Mum.

I'm not fussing, I'm just checking in. Hope you're surviving another day at the office, my darling, just remember to keep that beautiful head up, and that your mum loves you xxx

I smiled at the screen. I should take a cake back for her. I flicked through to the second message. *JAMES* sat unapologetically centre screen.

This is killing me.
I've left you alone for a week, and it's killing me.
Please come home, baby.
I love you.

Perhaps it was being stood there, a spectator in the middle of someone else's happily-ever-after that caught me off-guard. I glared at the screen, trying not to blink and dislodge the tears that might suddenly be there. Behind me, Holly shooed the man from the shop.

'Sorry about my husband. He's excited.' She smiled as I turned back to face her. She began patting the bump beneath her crimson pinny. It was the same shade as my woollen trench coat. Two women, with only a colour in common. Slipping the phone into my bag, I smiled back at her, but it already felt heavy on my lips.

'Actually,' I said, clearing my throat, 'I'll have to pop back. That was my mum… minor emergency, sorry. I'll call back in the week.' I made it hurriedly to the door. Holly looked on from her counter, almost hiding her bemusement.

'I hope everything's okay,' she called, but I was already on the steps, skipping rapidly down onto the pavement. The frustration bubbled up in me with every strident step forward. Why couldn't my brain just fathom it all out? Override the stabbing I felt in my chest every time I thought of them together? It should be demanding that I go immediately to the house, throw all of James's things into the street and banish him from my life. The life we'd tumbled into together after a one-in-a-hundred fluke. The life that we'd been surviving together ever since.

And then another thought shadowed the last. I wasn't perfect either, and James knew it. And I knew that this was the conclusion everyone but Phil and my brother would eventually come back to, that if James could accept never having his own biological child with me, why couldn't I accept a momentary *indiscretion* by him? A blip. A mistake. It seemed such small sacrifice by comparison.

CHAPTER 12

'ARE YOU LOSING weight, sweetheart?' Mum fretted as we pulled off the main road.

'No, Mum,' I said, pulling down the passenger visor, shielding my eyes from the morning sun. It was always nice here, as if the mill had its own personal reserve of sunshiny skies.

'Is there anything you fancy for tea tonight? I don't want you getting ill.'

'I'm not ill, Mum. Don't fuss. Actually,' I said, waiting for the inevitable murmurs of approval, 'James is coming to pick me up later. I'll probably grab something while I'm out.'

'Oh,' she said, surprised. 'Does that mean you won't be at the house for our brainstorming evening? We're discussing the fundraiser at the community centre, and ideas for recreational clubs we can run there, to bring some money in.'

'I am not ready to join the bloody WI, Mother. Not yet.'

She patted my knee. 'I know, sweetheart. But you need to keep your pecker up.'

The hedgerows broke from view, unveiling the stone and timber mill like theatre curtains drawing before the first act. As anticipated, an *ah* of delight escaped from Viv. Movement from the upper balcony of the mill drew all eyes up there, to the figure standing between the open double doors.

'Is that him? Hotbuns?' Mum asked, peering under her sun visor. I turned around to look at her. 'Phil told me all about him,' she said, nodding knowingly. Why wasn't I surprised? 'She said she can't decide whether he's disabled or not, the funny girl.'

'He's not disabled, Mum. And that guy up there is Carter.' I sighed.

'Carter? Well, what is he doing?' Mum asked, paying less attention to her driving by the second.

'Yoga, I think.'

Carter pulled one foot up into the inside of his other leg and rested it there, his hands slowly rising until they met in an arch over his head. From the waist down, he looked like an Aboriginal on walkabout, the rest of him wouldn't have looked out of place at a *Swan Lake* recital. He even had the chignon, neatly atop his head.

'Do you think *he* might be up for joining the WI?' Viv asked sarcastically. 'We could do with a yoga expert. I think I'll suggest that tonight.'

'Probably,' I mused. Carter would probably do anything for a stick of liquorice.

With Ofsted threatening an inspection, Mum said a

quick goodbye and practically burnt rubber getting back
out onto the lane. I walked the long way around the back
of the mill, so as not to disturb Carter with the annoy-
ances of noisy kitten heels on the gangway beneath him.
He probably wasn't trying to pull a crane pose out of the
bag, but I didn't want to risk throwing him off just in case.

I'd nearly come right up on the mill's kitchen doors
when I noticed the motorbike in the rear yard.

Rohan wanted a simply designed kitchen, freestanding
handcrafted open units that I'd begun planning spatially.
I'd already touched base with three local carpenters to
produce the framework, oak to match the exposed beams
throughout the mill. Each had agreed to come back with
quotes within twenty-four hours of me forwarding them
the drawings, which I would, by Friday, so long as Rohan
agreed the appliances we'd need to fit in there. I opened
my satchel taking the drawings and brochures I'd collected from Cyan's samples library yesterday, and began
walking the balding waterside path towards the boathouse.

A bug flittered around my head as I negotiated my way
across the grass, heels desperate to sink into the still-soft
ground. Today, I realised, felt like the first real nod that
summer was finally on its way. It was the first day I hadn't
bothered with a jacket, warm enough in a cotton shirt and
charcoal wide-leg trousers. I'd bundled my hair up, pinn-
ing loose curls out of the way after spending an irritating
amount of time yesterday tucking it all behind my ears.

The door into the boathouse was closed when I reached it. I raised my knuckles to knock, then held off for a second while I considered the time. It occurred to me for a moment that Rohan might still be sleeping. I'd taken it that he worked from home, but he'd already pointed out that he didn't have a schedule as such to get up for. I was still chewing over that thought when the door swung open. A petite woman with surf-blonde bed-hair stood the other side. I smiled awkwardly, glancing down at the motorcycle helmet in her arms, wondering how it was she could have bed-hair yet perfectly applied eyeliner flicks.

I tried not to look awkward. 'Sorry, is… Rohan in?'

She was appraising me, too. She stepped forward a little as Rohan, still subdued with sleepiness and the exhaustion of other night-time pursuits, came to stand behind her. He ran one hand up the back of his head, the other clamped firmly around the bed-sheet tucked around his waist. It wasn't seeing the flat expanse of his broad chest that made my cheeks burn up, or the way his stomach muscles bunched and relaxed like an undulating river current, but the girl, watching me as I tried to avoid looking at it all.

A small, shrewd smile and she looked just as she had in the photos stuck to the wall behind her.

'Morning,' she said.

'Hi.'

She wriggled out through the doorway past me. Neither Rohan nor the girl said a word to each other before she walked back up the path towards her motorbike.

'Coffee?' he asked, walking further back into the workshop. His voice was still gritty with inertia and other, more vigorous things probably. I bumbled in after him, the woman's accusatory smile still clear in my mind like a strobe of light that doesn't disappear when you close your eyes to it.

As he moved down the boathouse, I caught the whelk of bruising riding bluish purple up over the back of his ribcage. He needed to forget the brace contraption he and Carter were so preoccupied with and start inventing something that would better protect the rest of his body.

'Um, I just wanted to… run through a few things with you,' I said, regarding the papers in my arms, all accurate and comprehensive and crisply folded. I was suddenly conscious that the world was divided into two types of women: the sexy motor-girls with wild hair and feline eye flicks, and the starchy cold-callers with their paperwork and Smeg appliance brochures.

My eyes slid over towards the post-apocalyptic sofa bed. Rohan disappeared behind a makeshift hanging rail the other side of the crime scene. 'Fire away,' he called, his voice steadily coming back to life as he dressed.

I looked back at the door. 'You know, we can do this up at the mill, when you're ready. I'll go and wait for—'

'But you've just walked down here,' he countered. 'Grab a seat, I just need a minute.' I silently puffed out my cheeks a little and gave a parting glance to the boathouse's open door. I opened out a brochure and stared hard into it once Rohan emerged from his modesty screen, still shirtless but thankfully donning a pair of long canvas shorts. 'Let's have us some coffee; I need a coffee.' There was a new inflection to his voice, a detachment I hadn't heard before now.

He moved around the kitchenette while I pretended to study a table of information I already knew by heart. The shorts weren't safe enough for me to look over there, exposing his prosthetic leg below, and naked torso above. I briefly wondered which of these two poles would ultimately hold more sway with Phil, pulling her to her final verdict on Rohan Bywater's physical status. Disabled or Abled? With only a pair of canvas shorts between them. From here, Rohan Bywater very definitely looked able-bodied.

'We need to run through what you'd like in the kitchen, appliances and worktops,' I said, flicking to a page I'd already dog-eared for him. Rohan pushed his head through a baggy red tee. The colour seemed to darken his skin and lighten the brown of his hair, all at once. 'I know they're expensive, but there's a composite in here that I think will be perfect for you. It's incredibly hard-wearing, and we can look at the moulded sinks, which will be more hygienic if you boys are going to be rinsing things like injuries off in there.' Bywater brought two milky drinks over, taking the stool opposite, and began flicking through another of the brochures. 'There's more scope for colour, if you wanted to go with something like Corian, or if you want to remain more neutral, a granite would be another option.' Rohan eyed the notes I'd already made in the margins and gave a long drawn-out whistle.

'Two to seven hundred pounds per linear metre? What's it made from, crack cocaine?' he laughed.

I sat up straighter. Rohan closed the brochure and took a long drink from his mug, pushing the other closer to me. 'I want the mill to look good, for sure, but other than having the place sale-ready, I'm not that precious about what you do here. I trust your…' he began to move his hands flamboyantly, '*vision.*'

I tried not to smile at him mocking my industry. 'Sale-ready? You've only just bought it.'

'I know,' he said matter-of-factly, 'but I get itchy feet, I don't tend to stay in one place for long. In a couple of years, when the time comes, I'm going to want a quick sale.'

Itchy feet? Athlete's foot wouldn't drive me from this place. I'd dreamt of raising a gaggle of children in a home like the mill, who hadn't? Rope swing over the water, family dog frolicking in the river behind… I'd hack off my itching feet with a rusty butter knife before being walked off by them anywhere else.

I picked up my drink. 'So how far are you trusting my vision, Rohan? This house deserves a certain standard of finish. Buyers will expect it.'

'Agreed. But I'm not paying crazy money for worktops. You're right, they look great but if I had money to burn,

I'd probably spend it on another set of ramps, or a new truck – not something that will endure rigorous cucumber slicing for the next billennia.'

I hadn't taken full-fat milk in my drinks for years, but Rohan was awakening my appreciation for frothy coffee. 'You might have a lot of cucumber slicing to do some day,' I offered, taking a sip. 'My mother used to cram the stuff into my school lunchbox, five days a week.'

Rohan smiled. 'You don't like cucumber?'

'Not now,' I said, enjoying the silky smoothness of creamy coffee.

His smile grew into a grin, the first one this morning. 'Maybe you should have asked your dad to pack your lunch, might've got the odd tomato instead?'

I took another satisfying gulp. 'His arms weren't quite long enough to reach all the way back into his murky past to our chopping board, unfortunately.' I smiled.

Rohan nodded to himself, holding his smile out of courtesy, I suspected.

'I don't think I need to worry about school lunches. I'm kind of a one-man band. Carter gets jealous otherwise,' he joked.

I wondered what Carter thought about the blonde who'd just left, before engrossing myself in the five-burner hobs section.

'What?' he said.

'What?'

'The cock of the eyebrow.'

A warmth started to spread across my cheeks, damn it, my eyebrows already trying to cock around again.

'Ah, I get it.'

'Get what?' I replied dubiously.

'The look. I get the look. Megan, who you kinda met just now, she's an old—'

'Honestly, it is *none* of my business.' I didn't mean to cut him off.

He nodded to himself while I progressed to the cooker hoods, wishing I'd have just let him finish. 'So, do you still see your dad?' he finally asked.

His question caught me off guard. 'Um, occasionally. When he's allowed to revisit the inhabitants of his old life.' I smiled, sounding irrefutably like my mother. I was making excuses for my father's lack of interest – I don't think Petra had ever locked him in the wardrobe to stop him coming to see us.

'Maybe he thinks it's better for *you* that he keeps his distance?' And for the second time, Rohan had thrown me off balance.

'What kind of sense does that make?' I asked, taking the bait.

Rohan frowned. 'I'm just saying, maybe he thinks he's not a good enough father to impose himself on you too often?'

I wasn't really sure where we were heading with this, so I decided bowing out was the best option. 'Maybe,' I agreed. 'Parenting is daunting for some, I guess. Complicated.' But the sentiment flopped out of my mouth like a slice of flaccid cucumber.

'Pretty *un*-complicated, if you ask me,' he said, leaning against the workbench. 'If you think you're not going to do a good job of it, why even try when the stakes are so high?'

'Those are fairly ambiguous parameters you're talking about there. Define *not going to do a good job of it.*'

Rohan seemed surprised by me now. 'People are who they are.' He shrugged. 'Some are better at nurturing, some aren't. Some know their own limits and try to work around that. It's no good expecting a person to be something they're not, just because you like the way the idea sounds.'

I wasn't sure I understood. 'So, you're saying it's okay *not* to bother, with your own children even, so long as you're upfront about it?'

'No, I'm just saying it's always better to be upfront. You can't hide from who you are. It's like, I know I'm never going to get a nine-to-five job selling mobile phones. I'm not going to kill myself working in a job I hate so I can pay for a timeshare in Costa del England, and I'm definitely not going to ever settle down and have a bunch of kids to worry about. None of those things are me. None of those things will ever be me,' he added, sinking those last few words into his cup.

It was foolish to feel resentful towards his certainty, but I did. How did he know how he would feel in another ten years' time, when his friends were all enjoying their own families and the right woman came along? I understood the principles of freedom, but to shut any door indefinitely… that I couldn't understand.

'You know, you should never say never. Children change people.'

He shook his head. 'Not all people can be changed, Amy.'

Well, at least he was upfront about it. I decided against adding anything further. Rohan had obviously had enough, too. He gathered up our cups and walked casually away from the workbench. 'It should be harder for people to have children. No one messes up a kid more than a bad parent.'

CHAPTER 13

JAMES HAD PRETENDED not to be impressed by the mill when he picked me up. I'd expected the surveyor in him to wangle a full tour, but he was aloof when Rohan had come to lock the mill up after me. When Carter had complimented him on his new BMW, James was borderline rude.

He hadn't warmed up much on our way here, but then I wasn't exactly chewing his ears off either.

James had accepted the reasons I gave for not wanting to go back to the house with him, I didn't mention the visual reminders of what was at stake if we couldn't make this work again. I knew they'd only confuse the situation. A clear head seemed the best I could offer myself, and as James was reluctant to talk at Mum's, this seemed the obvious choice. Jackson's Park, the perennial middle ground.

The bollards were still down when we reached the car park. Silently James pulled into one of the bays facing the common and shut off the engine. Hazy late-afternoon sun dappled through the greenery onto the cyclists and dog-walkers, still milling around on the network of pathways cutting their patterns across the parkland. I'd rollerbladed every one of these paths. Cycled them, tried out my new Walkman for the first time on them, flown kites and Frisbees, even the all-singing remote-controlled car that Guy had stubbornly never accepted. And they'd been enough for me, trinkets in place of my father's time.

Both Mum and Phil had texted me just before James had picked me up this evening. Both messages were short and to the point. Mum's had read: *Good luck, sweetheart. Love Mum xxx*. Phil's was a slightly more sobering: *Take no shit, hon. Men lie.*

James looked through his window while I watched a grandmother tootling after her charge towards the boat lake and the ducks that had already congregated for them. The grandmother began pointing to the rowing boats so the child could see them all tied together on the water-front barely moving like a line of obedient seaside don-keys, each with their own colour and number. And then the windscreen began to mist over with too much silent contemplation.

'Shall we take a walk?' James asked solemnly.

*

The air outside was a little cooler than it had been this afternoon. James slipped into his jacket and began strolling beside me along the footpath. I'd forgotten how pretty the old Victorian lampposts were along the water-front, strings of lights perpetually suspended between each post in readiness for the festive months.

'Amy?' he said, surveying the land around us. 'I'm not going to keep on telling you that I'm sorry. And I know that you'll think I'm selfish for saying it, but the last few weeks haven't been great for me either.' James always liked to open proceeding with something we could agree on. 'And I don't want to keep bringing it up either, but I promise you, if we can somehow move on from this, if you'll just give me a second chance, I promise that this will never, ever happen again.'

There. Everything I wanted to hear. Now let's kiss, make up and head home. I let out a long release of breath and hoped some of the pressure inside me would eek out along with it. I'd never set out to be an engineer of my own life. I was of the serendipitous line of thinking, right up until it bagged me over the head and left me gasping for air on the floor. I didn't want to be this person, hung up on meticulous planning and perpetual finger-crossing, but there were some things that I simply couldn't walk into now, just hoping for the best. Going home with James was one of them.

'Do you love me, James?' I asked, slowly following the incline of the path up onto the iron bridge. The string of lights broke here, where shorter mounted lamps followed the bridge railings.

'I love you, Amy. But even love has to stand up to change,' he said, resting on the railings. 'I've never met another woman like you, I probably never will. I've been stupid, Amy. I'm not trying to make excuses for myself, but it's been a hard slog, what we've been doing. I'm weaker than you are… I wobbled.' An itinerary of pressures began racking up in my brain. Pressures that I could have better steered us away from, maybe.

'Do you want to be a family, James?' It suddenly occurred to me that this was the first time I'd actually asked him outright.

'I want what you want, Amy. I know we'd be a great family, you'd make us a great family.'

'That's not what I asked. Is it what *you* want, James? Because you can't wobble again when there's a child involved. I want to be a mother, a *good* mother, and part of that is protecting my child. I'm not walking into that situation, dragging a little boy or girl who's already been through the mill into that situation, to find that a few years down the road, we're meeting here for a weekend ice cream and a reminder that we'd messed it all up.' The toddler down by the ducks was shaking the last contents of a spent bread bag, crumbs flying all over her hair as the grandmother chuckled. James was looking at the imposing Victorian townhouses flanking the scenery. Park Lane properties rarely came onto the market, and why would they? With all this on their doorstep? This was where James and I had daydreamed of one day affording. We'd come here one afternoon where, on the advice of his mother, he'd offered me the prospect of a huge engagement ring if I wanted it. I'd said that he could forget the ring, I didn't need any of that, but I'd settle for one of those beautiful old houses to grow old in together.

'Is this what you want, James?' I pressed.

He turned, slipping his fingers through my hair, tucking it away for me. 'It's what I want, Amy.' There was a proviso in his expression. 'But if we're doing this, we need to do it now.'

'What do you mean?'

'Amy, I know how you think. You're wondering whether or not it's feasible to delay the adoption, give ourselves time to get over what I've done. But I can't do that. I can't go through that process again if that's what you're expecting us to do. I'm sorry, baby, but I can't.'

I wasn't actually sure if you could delay the adoption process at this stage, but he was right – I had considered it.

'I don't want to go through all that again either, James.' I didn't have the energy.

'You might think that's me being selfish, but it's not just us I'm thinking about, Amy. We aren't the only ones who've invested ourselves in this. All the interviews, the reports, dragging up everything that happened before – I can't do all of that again. That was why we were having the party, to celebrate the end of all that.'

I felt short-changed that James had seen the party that way. I hadn't wanted a fuss but I'd still thought of it as a celebration of the wonderful thing to come, not of waving goodbye to the hassle of surviving the journey. James lifted his chin to the air and let out a long breath. 'Anyway, that's done now. I've told Mum that we've cancelled, so…' voice trailed off. 'I know I need to make this work, Amy. Get back to how we were, but if we're going through with this adoption, it needs to be now. I'm not trying to force your hand, but I don't want to lie to you about the way I feel on this.'

'You sound as though you want to just get it all over and done with,' I said. 'Like ripping off a big awful plaster.' But I knew I wasn't being completely fair to him. I didn't want to go through the process again either, I really didn't.

'Anna's coming out to the house in ten days, Amy. I know that you'll want to think this all through again, so I'm not going to put any pressure on you to come home if you're not ready. But…' James began bothering at a patch of peeling paint on the old bridge. 'But if we're going to get our heads around this meeting, and the matching process – all of it – if we're going to have this life together, then you need to make a decision, Amy, and soon. We're either going for this, *now*, together… or we're not.'

CHAPTER 14

Everything moves a little slower when you are carless. It was only Thursday and already, particularly on the days I worked at the mill, the lift situation was exhausting the services of Phil, my mum and now Earleswicke Taxis. It was hard enough not being out-cooled around here when everyone who came by could either defy gravity or don a motorbike helmet without it smudging catwalk-standard eyeliner. Having to bum rides off everyone only added to my growing sensations of loserdom.

On the up side, it was quiet. Other than the sounds of a series of perpetual waterfalls tumbling over the wooden wheel outside, there was little to disturb my work. Unless, that was, you opened the windows on the west face of the mill, then you could hear the hoots of thirty-something men larking around on bicycles.

Something of a routine had begun to emerge at the mill, with Rohan spending several hours in the workshop each morning, sliding into the mill around lunchtime for me to fire any queries at him, then the rest of the afternoon out there, finding new ways to bruise himself. This morning

Blonde Biker Chick had dropped in again after breakfast, and Rohan's mood seemed to tip again as a result. He'd given me a set of keys into the mill, so at least I could avoid disturbing them in the boathouse again, although I had caught myself wondering what it was she was hanging around for.

It was obvious really, anyone who could double up as an ad for Gucci boxer shorts wasn't going to be short on the ladies. But this girl wasn't just a pretty face. Twice now she'd come here and riled him somehow. I liked that she challenged the unfluffable Rohan Bywater, but his taking it out on the ramps, and the resulting racket, had necessitated that my bedroom-come-office windows remained closed all morning.

The trouble with too much peace and quiet, though, was that it provided an open playing field for a wandering mind. Mum hadn't grilled me on my time with James yesterday evening, but like James's offer of a little more breathing space, I knew neither reprieve could go on for ever. I did love James, I did. And it may not be as vibrant as it was, or as unblemished, but it was there just the same, asking for a chance to grow again.

I stopped tapping my pen against my lips and let my eyes set on the movement outside the bedroom window where two helmeted heads were rising and falling over the ridge-line in the distance.

The view was slightly different to that back in the studio. Phil had been watching James and Sadie like a hawk, not that I wanted her to. I didn't want to hear it, I was making a concerted effort to keep toxic thoughts out of my head, to focus on the good.

Rohan and co were gathering momentum, flipping their bikes out from underneath themselves. I could imagine theirs was a love started by a first trike at Christmas, or a birthday perhaps, followed by years of fun with their pals. Boys and bikes went together, I guess. It wouldn't be long before Samuel and Harry were tearing off down the street on theirs, Guy in flustered pursuit.

James had kissed the sonographer when she'd told us we were expecting a boy. I didn't want to find out, but James was like a child on Christmas morning, consumed with curious excitement. It had taken us an age to get back out of the hospital. He'd shown the black-and-white images to anyone who would look at them – the strangers queuing at the parking ticket machine, the women in the hospital florist where he'd bought us an *It's a Boy!* balloon to giggle our way home with. He'd looked so goofy as he'd driven us home, enraptured with talk of junior golfing academies and Scalextric.

I don't think either of us had a preference any more. I couldn't recall hearing James mention either sex at any time since we'd made the initial call to social services.

I was still thinking of that enormous balloon when something slammed fiercely into the window beside me.

I counted to ten, twice, before my heart stopped thudding.

Given the near-perfect imprint of a winged creature spread-eagled in dusty silhouette on the window, you didn't need to be an expert on unidentified flying objects to decipher it was a fairly open-and-shut case.

My grandmother had kept a cockatiel, a scrawny bad-tempered creature, in a cage. Its ugly scaly feet had put me off our winged friends for life, but still I found myself baulking at the prospect of anything suffering on the ground outside.

I was hoping a plan might present itself by the time I made it down along the oak-framed stairs. Dealing with suffering animals, that was a boys' job, but all the boys around here were playing in the meadow. I crossed the empty kitchen and walked out into the yard. It was cooler out here, the breeze sweeping up beneath the ponytail I'd tied neatly behind my head. It was easy spotting the little blackbird, dazed on its back against the chalky gravel of the yard. I wasn't entirely sure it was alive until it blinked beseechingly at me.

'I'm not going to eat you, bird.' *I'm not even going to touch you.* Definitely a job for the boys. I began to walk for the brow of the hill when over in the grasses I caught sight of the first cat I'd seen since working here. It was already nosing over towards the mill.

I followed its line of vision to where the blackbird lay prone. 'Oh, come on!' I groaned.

I huffed my way back towards the kamikaze bird, knowing full well that even if there was a box or cloth for me to use inside the mill, that cat wouldn't wait for me to go fetch it.

After banishing all thoughts of Alfred Hitchcock from my imagination, it only took me around ten minutes to pick that blackbird up with my own bare hands. Banishing the sound of my grandmother's voice unfortunately wasn't so easy. *It's more scared of you than you are of it.* I doubted that there was very much in it. On each of my twenty or so attempts to touch it without recoiling, I became more and more aware that I was probably slowly scaring one of us to death. By the time the vacant bird was safely hammocked in my skirt, we were both about ready for a brandy.

Max was glugging from a drinks bottle when I reached them across the meadow. He gave me a friendly nod before pulling a beany on over his mop of blond hair. Carter had said Max was a qualified podiatrist, but he had to be having me on. At the base of the ramp, Rohan was sat on an upturned crate, smoothing down a pressure sock over the top of his exposed thigh. Beside him, one of two prosthetic legs stood propped against the crate, waiting for deployment.

'Have you got a minute?' I asked, trying not to suddenly panic and fling the bird at him with a shudder. Rohan looked down at my legs.

'Sure.'

His forearms flexed as he stretched a second sock over his thigh. There was movement inside my bundled skirt, but I tried hard to ignore it while Rohan pushed himself into the prosthetic socket, securing his limb in place with a series of muffled clicks.

'So, how's it going?' he asked, looking to my skirt again. He moved his hands to unclip the helmet strap underneath his chin, ruffling fingers through richly brown hair where the helmet had tried to flatten it into submission.

'Good. But, I had an issue in the bedroom.'

He smiled cheekily, well-practised laughter lines forming beneath the beginnings of dark stubble. 'And you thought I'd be able to help you out with that?' He lifted one of his eyebrows. 'I'll do my best.'

I rolled my eyes, a new movement in my skirt cutting short the action. Rohan got to his feet and came to stand in front of me. He nodded at my legs. 'The issue?' he asked, a smile in all but his lips. 'Do you want me to… take a peek?'

I held open the fold of powder-blue fabric. There was a cream polka dot on there, but you couldn't see it without paying attention.

Rohan came in closer, the scent of him magnified by his recent exertion.

'Hello, fella,' he said quietly, peering down between us at my feathered refugee.

'It flew into the bedroom window. I didn't know what to do with it, I thought it might get eaten if I left it.'

He looked at me, smiling. 'He should be okay, he's just stunned. He'll be flying around again once he gets his bearings.'

Uhuh. I'd been hoping for something slightly more interventional.

'So… do you want to take it, then?' I asked hopefully, looking up at him.

'Do you want me to take it for you?' He grinned.

Something hard, beak or – I could barely think it – *claw*-like, pressed against my thigh. 'No. No, I'm good,' I lied. 'I'll just set it down over here. In the grass.' *Quickly!*

I moved away from him hurriedly.

'Best to take it back,' he interrupted. 'It's probably got young nearby, so I'd go leave it where you found it. The less intervention the better.'

Right.

I peered down into my skirts. 'I don't believe it,' I groaned, 'it's pooped all over me.' Max began laughing under his breath. *Podiatrist my backside.*

Rohan came back towards me for another look. 'It's supposed to be good luck.' He smiled. 'Anyway, it adds to the polka-dot effect.'

I was thinking of something to say back when the bird suddenly decided to launch itself, flapping and squawking, from its cradle. 'Whoa!' Rohan yelped as the blackbird darted out between us. I seized up with fright. Over a trembling chest I reprimanded myself for trying to do a good deed. Birds were evil, I'd always known it.

'I gotta head off, Ro,' Max called, laughter still affecting him. 'See ya.'

Rohan threw Max a goodbye as he rode away from the far side of the ramps. It wasn't far back to civilisation if you cut over the public footpaths running from here to Earleswicke. I could probably cycle to the mill from Mum's, if I ever really needed to.

The smile had returned to Rohan's features when he turned back to me. I tried not to feel self-conscious about being stood here, covered in bird poo. 'Would you like to give it a whirl?' he asked, gesturing at the bike ramps.

'Excuse me?'

'You can use my bike, if you fancy a crack at it?' he asked earnestly.

'Thanks, but I'll be fine. I've got to get back to work.'

'It'd only take a few minutes, unless you like it, of course. Adrenalin can be addictive.' For some reason, I felt that he was challenging me. Spattered in bird poop with builders turning up in an hour, I was about all challenged-up for one day.

'Honestly, I'm good. I'll catch you later,' I said, turning for the embankment.

'Lots of people are scared at first, it's natural,' he called after me.

I stopped where I stood, and humoured him. 'I'm not *scared,* I just don't see the thrill in throwing myself off a steep incline,' I replied.

'Well, that's because you've never tried it. Come on,

don't worry about the height issue, we can start small. I won't let anything happen to you. Trust me, the worst thing you'll feel is the wind in your hair, I promise.'

'It's not a height issue,' I lied. 'Thanks for the offer, but as it happens I'm not here for… *windy hair*, or to play all day with my mates,' I said, waggling my finger first towards my head then to the bike ramps.

Rohan held his hands up as if warding off any offence. 'Look, it was just a suggestion. I thought you might feel more at ease while you're here if you relaxed a little.'

'I am relaxed!' I said indignantly, my voice heading for the octave higher. *It's you who un-relaxes me,* I wanted to protest.

Rohan shot a look at his feet, hiding another smile. He looked like a naughty school boy, trying not to fire up the school ma'am. It irritated me.

'Thanks for your help with the bird. I've got to get back, I'm walking the builders around the mill after lunch.'

Rohan nodded. 'I'll finish up here and come over, unless you'd rather I kept out of your hair?'

Yes, Bywater. That's exactly what I'd like. I don't need the wind, or you, in my hair.

'No, it would be good for you to say hello to them.'

'Great.' He grinned, clipping his helmet back in place.

'Great. I'll leave you to it then.' I sucked in a deep breath and turned for the mill.

Great.

I'd counted fifteen footsteps over spongy grass before I heard him back on the ramps behind me. The gradual build of his wheels climbing higher, like a pendulum up each side of the curved wood until the breaks in sound told me he was throwing himself effortlessly into the air at each summit.

The wind carried his movements to me, nearly until the top of the ridgeline when the familiar thump of bike and body thudded against the timber slope behind me. I hadn't meant to look back, but suddenly there was too much silence on the breeze. As it turned out, there was a downside to Rohan's affinity for *going with the flow*. It was called gravity.

I scanned the scene, remembering the last time I'd been suckered. He wasn't making a big deal about his fall, and even from here I could see that his prosthetic hadn't disconnected itself from his stump again. But honestly, he had less sense than that daft blackbird. I decided then that Rohan would also be okay, flying around again once he got his bearings, the less intervention the better.

*

The building contractor had shown up at the mill early. It was a good sign. I'd talked him through my intentions with the interiors, content that he'd taken the time to properly get to grips with the project. I was just seeing him off when Carter's campervan pulled into the yard.

'Good arvo,' Carter chirped, wrestling an armful of paint tins from the van.

'Hey, Carter. What are you up to?' I asked, looking over the five tins of exterior emulsion.

'Ro wants to get the boathouse spruced up. I think he's trying to keep me out of your way while you work on this place. That the builder I just passed?' he asked, looking down the lane.

'Maybe,' I said. 'He seems nice, knowledgeable. Just have to see if he comes back with a reasonable quote.' Carter slid the door shut on the van and lifted two of the large tins. 'Do you need some help with those?' I asked, moving towards the paint.

'No, that's okay, don't want you breaking a nail.' He smiled, nodding to the plaster that still sat over my finger. I thought about whipping it off and showing him what a real broken nail looked like. Thanks to the kid-proof door lock on my kitchen cupboard, my finger still throbbed when I got it wet. 'Ro can get the other tins. Where is he?'

I looked across the glistening waters towards the boathouse. The door was still shut. 'I don't think he's been back from the ramps yet. He was supposed to be dropping in to meet with the builder, but I suppose he found something more stimulating to do.'

Carter began walking across the gangway around the mill, swaying with the weight of the canister in each hand. I took one of the paint tins awkwardly in my arms and followed him around the mill wall.

'Who's he over there with?' Carter called over his shoulder, looking to the boathouse.

'Er, Max, earlier,' I replied.

'Good of him to shift all the brambles and weeds over there,' he said, nodding towards the workshop wall. 'The deal was, I get the paint, he cleared the perimeter so we could get started.'

I surveyed the dense pockets of greenery, huddled against the boathouse wall. 'Not all of those are weeds, Carter, most of those plants are rhubarb. I think they like it near to the water. My gran used to grow hers by her pond.'

'Yeah? What, then she used to cook it?'

'Yep. She used to make a serious homemade rhubarb and ginger pie.'

Carter pondered the combination and grimaced.

'You've never eaten a rhubarb pie?'

'Only one of those you can get frozen and whack in the microwave. I wasn't fussed.'

'Well, you should try a homemade one. It's a whole new world. Trust me, add a little ginger in there and it'll blow your mind.'

Carter looked back at the boathouse. 'I'll go rope Maxie in, he can be on rhubarb-picking detail while me and Ro get cracking this arvo.'

'Max left,' I explained, clearing the end of the walkway. 'A couple of hours ago.'

Carter looked towards the ridgeline. 'So who's Ro been riding with?' he asked.

'No one, I don't think,' I said, setting down the paint. It was heavier than it looked.

'For two hours?' Carter asked.

'About two hours.' I was picking up on a shift in him. 'Is that a problem?'

'No, course not. Ro doesn't need a babysitter,' he guffawed, but there was something insincere about it. 'I'm just gonna run down there, drag his ass back up here to give me a hand,' Carter said, setting the tins down at the water's edge.

'Okay… I'll, see you later,' I said, turning for the mill. 'Tell him the builder's coming back on Tuesday, he can meet him then.' *If he can be bothered.* Carter jogged leisurely over the embankment. He raised a thumb in the air and disappeared over the hill.

I wasn't sure why, exactly, but instead of heading back up to the first floor, I hung around downstairs. I scanned the view of the yard outside, the wall of flittering trees beyond the grassy ridge-line, chasing the line of the riverbank I knew lay behind it. I walked back on myself, retracing my steps to the outside doors. I did this twice more, and when Carter appeared on the brow of the hill, a heaviness settled in my stomach.

I watched him hurrying along the path to the boathouse.

He fumbled at the door, disappearing inside. I was walking back out through the double doors into the yard when Carter reappeared on the path holding a set of crutches. He jogged with them in his arms towards me, a new pressure stretching itself out in my chest, inflating like a big black ominous balloon.

'Is everything okay?' I asked timidly.

'Ro's bust his ankle.' Carter grimaced, skipping past me.

'What?' I yipped, falling in beside him.

Carter began climbing the hill in front of us. 'He'll be cool, he's just twisted it. He can't bear his weight on it, though, so he's been kinda… stuck.'

'But—' I quickly ran through all the things I'd done in the time since I'd last seen him. Carter had already run ahead by the time I thought to tell him just how long Rohan had been out there, *stuck.*

I tried telling myself that I didn't know, of course, but the guilt was already colonising the pit of my stomach. Against every instinct to disappear into the mill, I forced myself to wait for them. Fifteen minutes later, Carter pushed Rohan's bike over the bank, a trainer dangling from one handlebar, Rohan's helmet swaying on the other. Behind Carter, a hobbled Rohan, barefoot and fed-up. It made for uncomfortable viewing, Rohan on crutches carefully negotiating his way down the uneven slope.

By the time they finally reached me, the urge to say something was too much. I swept away dark tendrils of hair that had come loose around my face and discreetly cleared my throat. 'Rohan, I… I'm sorry, I didn't real-ise—'

'Are you sure five cans are gonna do it, Cart?' Rohan asked, cutting me off dead.

Carter looked warily from Rohan to me, then on to the tins of paint on the floor. I turned briefly to look at them too. After that, Carter's eyes avoided mine as though he were working something out in his head that he didn't want me to see the answer to. He scratched at his mass of fuzzy hair.

'Er, yeah, my man. I'm hoping to get two coats outta those bad boys.'

Defiantly I fixed my gaze on Rohan. It wasn't my fault he'd cried wolf before. If he was trying to make me feel bad for not dashing to his side à la Florence Nightingale, then he wasn't playing fair. I began shadow-boxing with the idea that he was, in fact, already succeeding in making me feel bad, but when he finally looked at me my resolve completely crumbled. I dug deeper but my inner warrior princess wasn't that convinced with my argument.

'I'm going to turn in. We'll start the painting tomorrow, Cart.'

I was thinking about stating my case when something in his expression changed. Then he looked away – the statu-esque lines of his face pointing off towards the boathouse. I hadn't seen him look that way before. If I didn't know better, I might have said he was embarrassed.

CHAPTER 15

'I DON'T UNDERSTAND. What do you mean, the system's not recognising the postcode? You've picked me up from the same address three times this week already?' I remarked, sitting on the top step of Rohan's staircase. There was nothing elaborate about all the oak around me, but it was beautiful. Simple, clean, as if I'd been shrunk down and popped inside a handcrafted cuckoo clock. Lovely or not, I was still ready to get out of here, and for today, finally, to be over.

This afternoon had been a grueller, helped along just marvellously by my monumental faux pas in the face of injury and basic care-giving. I cast my mind back over the array of badges Mum had stitched to the sleeve of my Brownie uniform. I was pretty sure that along with Friend to Animals, I'd bypassed First Aid and ergo First Aid Advanced, too.

'*I* didn't pick you up personally, sweetie,' the girl on the switchboard managed despite a hefty wodge of bubblegum.

'Well, could you maybe find out who did? Ask *them* to

come and pick me up? Please? What about the other guy who answers the phone, he knows Briddleton Mill.'

'Sorry, sweetie, rules are rules. After seven p.m., if the pick-up is unrecognised, we don't send out. Can you give me another postcode, somewhere nearby that you can walk to?' I looked out at the fading sun laying its last veil over the landscape. Unless the River Earle had its own postcode I was stuffed. 'Never mind,' I said, hanging up the call so I could flick through the rest of my recent calls for Mum's name.

From the gloom of downstairs, one of the rear doors began to rattle, whoever was there bustling noisily through them into the mill.

'Hell-ooo? Anybody home?' echoed a familiar gruff voice. I got to my feet and walked the few stairs down onto the minstrel's gallery. Carter walked out of the kitchen into the open lounge area below me.

'Hey, Carter. Only me, I'm afraid.'

'You working late tonight? I was just coming to check that you'd locked up.'

'No, I'm done now,' I replied. 'I'll make sure everything's secure when I go.'

'You want some pizza? I'm just about to go pick up from Earleswicke. They won't deliver because—'

'Postcode?'

'I know, right?' he said resentfully.

'I don't suppose I could grab a lift with you, could I Carter? It would really help me out.'

'Sure! I've been meaning to tap you for Philippa's likes and dislikes. Come on, you can tell me on the way.'

We locked up and left the mill through the front entrance straight onto the front yard. Over the pond I could see Rohan in the little window of the boathouse, his hands interlocked behind his head. I'd seen from the balcony that he'd been sat in that chair for most of the afternoon.

'Madam, your carriage awaits…' Carter gushed, holding open the passenger side door. Carter skipped around and jumped in beside me. 'How do you like Bertha?' he asked sincerely.

'Bertha?'

'My splitscreen! I named her Bertha,' he declared, gesturing at the vehicle interior. Carter's campervan was pure vintage from its tangerine vinyl seating to the wood-grain Formica cabinetry. It suited him. He looked like he'd driven it into a time portal, some day back in the seventies maybe, and had found himself spat out again here, in the next century. The engine turned out to be vintage too, elongating what was usually a quick journey into twenty-five turbulent minutes, rattling and juddering all the way back to town.

We'd managed to fill a good ten minutes of conversation time with a game of cat-and-mouse. He'd give me a reason why he could be trusted with Phil's address and/or number, I'd give him an example of what she'd probably do to me if I obliged. Finally, he gave up, and I was presented with a new problem, how to avoid asking after Rohan. Carter was blissfully unfazed by long silences, but I always felt a need to fill them.

'So you're into yoga then, Carter? Is it a good workout?' I asked, the greenery outside steadily becoming more interspersed with the grey of pavements, and side streets of Earleswicke's outskirts.

'It's a good workout for mind, body and soul, Amy. That's why the women love it.'

I felt my eyebrows rise. 'They do?'

'Oh yeah. Women like a man who's in touch with his—'

'Toes?' I asked, smiling. Carter waited serenely for me to finish. 'Sorry, you were saying.'

'Inner calm; spiritual contentment; balance – they're all good for the soul.' He let me stew on that a few moments until his voice suddenly climbed to somewhere more upbeat. 'They like a flexible, toned body too, I guess, but it's the philosophy they're drawn to, I think.'

'They are? The *philosophy?* How do you know?' I asked, batting away a mental picture of Carter being *flexible* with a woman, checking the expression beneath his caramel-coloured candy-floss hair to see that he wasn't having me on. Carter's face was a picture of seriousness.

'After I've made love to a woman, I like to offer a demonstration of some of the principal moves. So far, the offer's never been turned down. Although one girl did ask me to put my shorts back on first.'

A bubble of laughter rippled to the surface of my throat. I wasn't sure seeing a physically fit man contorting himself on the floor wasn't more about catching a good show than it was yoga philosophy, but I didn't say so.

James would never gel with a guy like Carter. I suddenly felt a twinge of sadness about that, as if we should've branched out more with our circle of friends. Phil was bonkers, granted, but she was one of very few dazzling stars in our social sky. Carter, I could tell, was a dazzler too.

'I've been trying to talk Ro into joining me, but he works out his endorphins with speed, not serenity.' Mention of Rohan's name brought about a different twinge.

Sod. I couldn't just not ask, it would be churlish. 'How is he?' I asked tentatively. 'Take the next right, then second left onto Stephenson's Road.'

'Who, Ro? Ah, he's fine. Don't worry about him.'

I didn't mean to blurt a reply, but I felt caught out. 'I wasn't worrying about him.'

'No?' Carter said, just as quick over his shoulder. 'You looked pretty wounded earlier when you realised you'd left him in the field. A disabled dude. All alone… injured.'

The guilt that had been gurgling in my stomach all afternoon lurched inside me. 'Is that what Rohan said?' I asked, trying to swallow it away.

Carter laughed. 'Nah, of course not. I'm just playing with you.' He pulled up to a set of lights, the metronomic percussion of the indicator, counting away the seconds.

'So… he's not annoyed that I didn't help him?'

The traffic moved and Carter rolled forward to make the turn. 'Course not. He knows that's how it goes sometimes. No big deal.'

'Are you sure? He seemed pretty fed up when you were helping him back.'

'Yeah, he was. But not with you, he's been kicking stones around since Meg showed up.'

I knew Biker Chick had rattled his mood. 'The girl with the motorbike?' I asked impassively, remembering how Gucci-friendly she was too. 'I think I disturbed them the other morning, I didn't realise he had a girlfriend staying over.'

'Girlfriend?' Carter guffawed. 'Meg's not his girlfriend, not any more. There are enough fireworks exploding between that pair without adding romance.'

'Oh,' I said, relaxing my shoulders, remembering Rohan's state of undress. 'So I didn't interrupt them, you-know…?'

Carter grinned. 'It's possible, but I'd be surprised! It did not end well between those two. You probably interrupted them arguing again.'

'So, they broke up fairly recently, then?' I prodded.

'Hell, no. It's gotta be nearly four years ago. Just after Ro had his accident.' I already disliked her a little bit. If I was being honest, her enviable make-up skills probably hadn't set us off on the best foot. 'Meg's okay, but she's nearly as tough as Ro. They're butting heads but Rohan won't back down, she knows that.'

Asking what they were butting heads over was a question too far. These were the times I wished I had a bit more of Phil about me, and charged ahead regardless of social etiquette. 'So, he's not mad that I didn't help him out today… Well, that's good,' I said, reluctantly steering my curiosity elsewhere.

'Defo. He wouldn't have wanted you to help him anyway. It would've made him feel… y'know.' Carter shrugged.

'Feel what?'

Carter rubbed the back of his shaggy head and looked at me. He had kind eyes, that warm shade of blue like my brother's. Carter smiled and looked ahead at the road. 'As you're gonna be here a while, you might as well know that Ro… likes his independence. It might sound stupid, but he wouldn't have appreciated having to get you to help him back to the boathouse earlier. Even if that meant sitting on his ass for a few hours. I keep telling him to hang onto his phone, but Ro knows best…' He trailed off.

There was light on the horizon, maybe I hadn't cocked up as much as I'd thought. 'So… you're saying he's stubborn?'

'Ro, stubborn?' He laughed breathily. 'Yeah, that would be one word for him.'

'But not so stubborn that he minds *you* helping him?'

'Ro works on a scratch-for-scratch basis. He's got my back covered, and I've got his – so we're straight. It's always been that way. He wasn't mad at you today, he was mad at himself. He's popped that ankle enough times, he knows he's gotta land steady. He was just frustrated.' He shrugged. 'He's over it now.'

Well, bully for him, I'd only been beating myself up about it *all* day. We were only a few miles from home and I spent at least one of them pondering whether I thought of Rohan Bywater as a wounded soldier or a pig-headed heathen. Both, I decided. 'Follow this road all the way onto Victoria Street, then I'm right down the bottom on the left, number seventy-four, thanks.' I sighed. 'So, how long have you two been friends?' I asked in my best chit-chatty, just-making-conversation voice.

'A *long* time,' Carter drawled, stretching the words from his mouth like a piece of chewing gum. 'Ro's the closest thing I've got to a brother.'

'That's nice,' I said earnestly. 'Did you meet at school?'

'Not exactly. Ro was placed with the foster family I was staying with when we were, I dunno, twelve? Thirteen? We just hit it off, I guess because we were the same age and liked the same stuff.'

'You were in care?' I asked, my upper body turning itself completely to face him.

Carter kept looking ahead happily at the road. 'Sure. We both were. Although I was only in foster care while my grandpa was sick. I got into a bit of trouble, and he was ill at the time. He couldn't really cope with me at that age so they wanted him to have some respite. And I guess I needed a bit of time out too. I was back living with him within the year, though, when he got better so…' Carter trailed off as he waited for the traffic at the junction.

'And what about Rohan?' I asked, swallowing at the new dryness in my throat.

'Ro? He was more what you'd call a long-term placement. His mum left him with social services when he was still in primary school. Not really little – he remembers what she looked like and everything. Just left him one day, and didn't really sort herself out enough to go get him back.'

The familiar poplar trees on Victoria Street came into view, and I suddenly felt the urge to deceive Carter and lead him on a few laps of the neighbourhood.

'But you left? The foster home?'

'Uhuh.'

'And Rohan didn't?'

'Not then. He moved onto another placement after that.'

'And you kept in touch?' I asked.

'We were lucky,' he said, glancing at me. 'Lots of foster kids move around. Once they're separated, it's easy to lose touch. And we did for a while, but then by some weird flip of fate, the next foster home Ro went to was Arthur's.'

'Who's Arthur?' I prompted, willing the campervan to slow down.

Carter was already smiling at the recollection, his pointy moustache curling at the edges. 'Arthur was a bearded legend. I liked him because he looked a bit like Chuck Norris. He was the odds-and-sods guy the old locals in our village went to. He had a workshop, and this knack for fixing anything that was taken to him to be fixed. My grandpa took me there one day, I don't know, to knock out a dink in his wheelbarrow or something. He tells me to wait in the car – 'cos he didn't trust me inside probably – and who comes cruising down the street on *the* shiniest electric-blue two-wheeler I ever saw? *Ro*.' Carter shook his head to himself. 'He dropped lucky there, to get a long-term placement with an old gent like Arthur, it doesn't always work out that way. Arthur, what a *ledge*, God rest his soul.'

The campervan was decreasing speed. I was utterly hooked on Carter's story. We'd met some amazing foster carers through our adoption journey, but I knew I couldn't do that. At first, I'd thought it was because I wouldn't be able to let them go again, to love a child only to see them off when it was time for them to move on. But I'd also met with foster parents who'd seen the siblings in their care separated from one another. I'd been told of the difficulties in seeing one sibling adopted, while the other was left behind. I knew such decisions were made to give each child the best chance at finding their forever home, but I couldn't care for two little brothers like Samuel and Harry and then watch as they were parted – I couldn't bear it.

'You said seventy-four, right?' Carter asked, pulling onto the kerb besides my mother's wheelie bin. 'Nice digs.' He was looking past the laurel bushes into the driveway. 'Your car off the road, then?' he asked, looking at Viv's Honda.

'Er, no. That's my mum's car.'

'Just visiting, is she?' he asked.

'No, this is her house. I'm just visiting her, actually, while… my place is decorated.' I mentally kicked myself for lying. Unnecessary lies were the worst offenders. I followed it with a feeble truth. 'It's only short-term.'

I could practically hear the clock counting down to the point where I'd have no decisions left. James wouldn't wait much longer for me to go home, and in many ways over the years, he'd already shown exceptional patience because I'd needed him to. All the waiting and wanting, the preparations we'd anchored, the hopes we'd buoyed – all on the long road to adoption. Our journey to parenthood had not been an easy one, but I'd always found it less arduous than James, to focus on our final destination and keep it in mind. The pressure of having our lives scrutinised pitched against the wonderful promise of our own family had been like two sides of the same coin. By moving back to Mum's, I'd tossed it into the air, and James was still waiting to see if I would catch it, as I wanted to, or let it fall through our fingers.

'Looks like she's been waiting for you to come home,' Carter said, nodding towards my waving mother. She was standing in the open doorway, delighted that Carter was giving her a little wave back.

'Thanks for the lift, Carter. You'd better get going or those pizzas will be cold,' I said, climbing out of his van. Mum was already hoisting a bin bag full of rubbish this way.

'Hi, sweetheart!' she said, waddling over and lifting the lid of the wheelie bin. The bag was too heavy for her, she couldn't swing it in.

'I've got that,' Carter called from the cab behind me. He nipped out of the campervan and rounded the front, whipping the bag from Mum's hands. One swing, and it was in.

Mum looked on approvingly.

'All that yoga's paying off, Carter.' I smiled.

'Yoga?' Mum squeaked. 'Ah, yes! You're the fellow off the balcony, aren't you? I knew I recognised those arms.' I watched curiously as my mother beamed at Carter, somehow managing to hold my eyebrows steady. Beside me, Carter had regressed into a bashful teenage boy. Still, I held onto the eyebrows. 'Do you teach?' she asked hopefully. Carter gave a crooked smile.

'You can't teach yoga, Mrs…'

'Alwood,' Mum cooed. 'But please, call me Vivian.'

'You can't teach yoga, Vivian, you can only instruct,' he said, opening his arms out flamboyantly. Mum nodded, as if some wisdom that had just flown completely over my head had crashed straight into hers, kamikaze-blackbird style.

'And, do you... *instruct?*' she asked, practically elbowing me out of the way to go toe to toe with Carter.

'Not yet,' he said, scratching his head, 'but never say never, right?'

Carter gave my mother a cheeky smile. It felt like cold pond sludge being tipped down my shirt.

'Right,' Mum mimicked. 'Well, I think you could be just the man I've been looking for.' Carter, oblivious to what it was my mum was even considering, looked pleased as punch with himself.

I wondered why there had never been a Brownie badge for eyebrow control.

CHAPTER 16

IT WAS FUNNY how dreading running into a person suddenly helped time to fly right by, not that Rohan, or Carter for that matter, had ventured far from their task all morning. Even from the sundeck of the master bedroom, I could see that the overgrown greenery around the boathouse had all been cleared, and a new skirt of cream paint daubed along the nearside of the building.

My eyes readjusted, falling to the tiny flecks of summer life drifting in the sun-drenched air between the balcony and the millpond, each diffusing the sunlight with the trickery of their wings.

This balcony was possibly the prettiest place I'd ever taken a lunch break, pretty enough that I'd braved the height and hadn't hidden myself away inside all morning while Rohan painted the boathouse out there. He'd held his hand aloft when he saw me arrive earlier, but it was early afternoon and still no words had passed between us. I considered going down there, just to prove to myself that I wasn't being a wimp avoiding him. So far, I hadn't made it.

My phone rudely interrupted the last few minutes of my lunch, buzzing around on the deck next to my feet. I peered down at the screen: Bananarama in their Venus get-up. Originally, Phil's caller id picture had been a lioness, but she'd argued that a man-eater wasn't a man-eater without lippy and great hair.

'Hey,' I said, rising from my deckchair, which had appeared on the balcony overnight.

'I thought you were in the studio today?' Phil questioned.

'I thought I'd work here, instead. Fewer distractions,' I said, watching another run of weatherboard receive its new paint. There was a stiffness to Rohan's movements today, subtle, but it was there.

'You're probably right; it's been a bit *turbulent* around the office this morning.'

'Why, what do you mean?'

'Look, I'm not trying to rock the boat or anything, Ame, but...'

'But what?'

'James and Sadie were having a *really* heated debate earlier. I walked into the Ladies' and—'

'They were in the toilets?' My neck instantly bristled.

I stopped walking my way across Rohan's bedroom to the dying echoes of my heels resonating around the space.

'Yeah,' Phil said quietly. 'I didn't hear much, James sounded really annoyed until I walked in. He said something about drawing a line under it, and everyone moving on? Or maybe something about Sadie moving on? As in, getting another job?'

'Did you hear him say anything else?' I asked apprehensively.

'Yeah. He told her that she was on her own, Ame. And he sounded serious about that.'

I let out the breath I'd been holding. Out in the hallway, the noises of somebody coming through the back doors floated up the mill's open hallway.

'I have to go, Phil.'

'You want me to do any digging?' she asked. 'Dana loves to spill when she thinks she knows something.'

'No, that's okay.' Reconnaissance wasn't going to change anything.

'How about we go for a few drinks tonight? It's been ages,' she piped up enthusiastically.

'I can't. Mum's having another WI meeting at the house. To dodge it, I've told her I have to work late. She'll sulk if I go out on the lash.'

Phil groaned. 'Okay, but I'm starting to wonder if you're not going to end up ditching me for the happy-clapper brigade. We need a girly night, soon, okay?'

'Okay, Phil.'

I said my goodbyes and began walking out across the vast landscape of Rohan's bedroom. Across the landing, the vista of the River Earle welcomed me back into my makeshift office. I slumped into my chair, propped my elbows on the desktop and settled my head briefly in my hands.

Please find somewhere else to work, Sadie.

'Not *still* beating yourself up about yesterday, are ya?' Carter smiled, ambling into the room. He had his toolbelt on again, a new stash of liquorice poking from the top of his pouch. There were flecks of whitish paint spattered in his hair and all across his Joan Baez T-shirt. 'Like I said, don't worry about Ro, he's good. He's had a twenty-four-hour dose of ankle-elevation and frozen peas.'

Carter traipsed over to the boxes stacked against the far wall of the bedroom.

'Glad he's feeling better,' I said absently, trying not to look for an excuse to head straight for Cyan's loos right now. James had said Sadie was on her own. That was good.

'He's getting there. Shouldn't be on that ankle, though. I know it's hurting him,' he said, lifting the lids off a few of the boxes.

My thoughts ferried back over to Rohan. 'So why is he on it, then, Carter? If he should be resting?'

Carter lifted something bulky from one of the boxes and began turning it over in his hands. 'For the same reason Ro does anything he probably shouldn't – to prove a point.'

'Prove a point to who?'

Carter gave the object in his hand a last appraising look. 'Himself, usually,' he mused. I watched as he replaced the lump of wood and started rifling through another box.

'So what brings you up here, Carter. Did you need something?'

'Oh, yeah!' he exclaimed, remembering. 'There's a bearded dude downstairs. Here about the carpentry work.'

'Thanks, Carter,' I huffed, grabbing my phone on my way up from the desk. 'Good job I asked!'

I'd just trudged back out of the bedroom when Carter called after me. 'Yo, Amy?'

I stalled on the landing and peeped back around the open doorway. 'Yep?'

Carter was still hanging over the box he'd been rummaging in.

'There probably is another reason Ro's doing his Universal Soldier impression today,' he said, half of his sandy curls flopping over his face.

'Yeah?' I asked, already preoccupied with the gentleman waiting downstairs.

'I think he could be trying to make *you* feel better. Y'know, in case you were feeling bad or somethin'?'

CHAPTER 17

JOHN HARPER HAD a friendly face framed with a round greying beard, his rural look completed by a waxed flat cap. He was a stocky-looking chap, a man who had clearly spent his life lugging heavy things around with his own bare, gnarly hands. Rohan had been polite and friendly as we'd run through the quote John had put together for us for the carpentry work. He'd offered John the contract immediately, he said because not only was John local, with hands that spoke of their willingness to work, but also because he reminded Rohan of Grizzly Adams.

I'd left Rohan taking his new friend on an hour-long tour of the mill, the boathouse and its surrounding views. The last time I'd glanced outside, Mr Harper had been gesticulating at the battered old rowing boat lying over-grown and abandoned beside the pond.

Since Rohan and Carter had finished the first blotchy coat on the boathouse, the mill seemed to slip into a late-afternoon nap. Rohan had spent the rest of his time inside the boathouse and, dare I say it, taking it easy. The man who never stopped had finally slowed down.

Between his abstinence from the ramps and Carter's mercy run for more bags of frozen veg, it was safe to say that the ankle was not right.

I didn't know if it was guilt that had driven me intermittently back to the balcony, or maybe just the spectacle of seeing Rohan sitting still in the chair beneath the boathouse window, but I'd found myself periodically checking on him. Despite this, I hadn't noticed the vast expanse of sky get so dark until the glare from my laptop screen started to strain my eyes. Fortunately, I'd been organised, and Bryan, the other switchboard operator at Earleswicke Taxis, had already booked me in for a nine-fifteen pick-up.

My head had begun thumping thanks to an afternoon of over-thinking all the possible motives behind several calls I'd received from Sadie. She'd left voicemails after some of them. I'd deleted them all without listening, and then spent all afternoon obsessing about what she might have said. It had not been a productive day.

The only small mercy was that I'd evaded an evening of *jazzing up* recreational programmes for Earleswicke community centre at Mum's. Between her and James, the mill was turning out to be quite the handy refuge.

I saved the documents on my laptop screen and lay back in my chair, stretching the ache from my shoulders. I had twenty-five minutes to kill before going home. My legs appreciated a stretch-out too. The kitten heels had been kicked off hours ago, so I padded barefoot over to the window overlooking the river. In the distance, the faint glow of Earleswicke lay like a dying flame against the smothering darkness of the countryside at night. I checked I'd closed the window properly, then my eyes fell to the cardboard boxes beside me. A couple were still open where Carter had ferreted in them. I ran tired fingers over the nearest box and silently lifted the flap.

The lump of wood was heavy in my hands but I could see now that its design was deliberate. It was an ornament, of sorts, with a small metal plaque at its base, just big enough to catch the light of my dying laptop.

I read the inscription at its centre.

BMX Vert – 2nd Place
Gravity Force International – Vancouver 2009

There used to be a shelf full of the trophies in Guy's old room, but none of them had looked much like this one. I looked back at the doorway. There was no one here now, no sound but the drone of my laptop shutting down and the whispering of my conscience, reminding me that it wasn't polite to go through other people's belongings. I reached to replace the trophy in its box, but the lid lay open, inviting me to peek inside. In the dimness of the room, I could make out at least one more award, this one was more obvious though, cog-like and metal, another inscription at its base.

Gravity Force International – Munich 2010
BMX Park
3rd Place

Beneath it, I made out several more trophies in various forms. My conscience forgot the whispering and cleared its throat. These weren't my things to pry in. I rested the wooden trophy on its metal predecessor and closed the box. I didn't think they were Carter's. He was more adventurous with his yoga than I'd seen him be on the bikes, but something in the back of my mind hoped that they didn't belong to Rohan.

I knew zilch about sports, but I'd heard of Gravity Force. James had flicked the G-Force games on the TV once. Quietly, I'd found myself mesmerised by what the human body could achieve with fearlessness and balance. James had sat through an entire hour's coverage berating the organisers for qualifying a sport *born out of dossing around on public property*. Stamina was the real test of any cycling, he'd said, not acrobatics. It was the Tour de France or nothing.

But even James was a sucker for a trophy. I could imagine Sunday football league. I'd be the one freezing and sodden in the pitch sidelines, but James would be the one at presentation night when junior brought the hardware home.

I left the bedroom and walked barefoot out onto the landing, wondering what James would make of Rohan

Bywater and his unorthodox friends. I couldn't have met a man more different to James if I'd tried. Rohan's bedroom was in a state of dim twilight. I moved carefully across the floor to the balcony doors I'd left ajar earlier. Rohan probably thought I'd gone home hours ago. From outside, the mill would have looked deserted.

I glanced through the crack in the balcony doors to the glow of the boathouse window. Rohan had been sitting at the workbench the last time I'd looked, but I couldn't see him there now.

Downstairs, someone was trying the back doors. I didn't know why they didn't just trust me to lock up myself. With Carter out for the night, I knew it was Rohan. Another shuffling noise and I thought I'd probably better call out to him, before he took me for a cat burglar – or worse, set the alarms with me still inside. I turned to pull to the balcony doors first and just caught movement in the little window of the boathouse.

Rohan sat back down at his workbench.

A second bout of muffled movement coming from the empty kitchen made the hairs on the back of my neck stand. I froze.

There was more than one person down there.

Stay calm, it could be Carter, but there'd been no sign of his spluttering campervan.

I held my breath and patted myself down for my phone, already aware that I'd left it sitting next to the laptop. Quiet and steady, I crept back out into the hall, keeping back from the galleried landing. It was a strange sensation, to have your heart beat so hard you weren't sure whether you were feeling it or hearing it. Without sound, I made it back into the office and quickly flipped open my phone. Downstairs, there was whispering. Not the kind that's controlled for true secrecy, but the kind that's infected with mischief. Two INCORRECT PASSCODEs and a steadying breath and finally I unlocked my phone screen. Downstairs, there was quiet laughter, and high playful voices. Youthful, or girlish… not men, at least.

I swallowed. I could call the police, but what if they struggled with the bloody postcode too? I hit the green phone icon and a list of recent calls flashed up. Earleswicke taxis was at the top of the list, followed by several nameless numbers. All tradesmen. All of absolutely no use to me now. I had less than twenty minutes before the taxi arrived, maybe I could just… sit tight?

A tinny sound, like a stack of hairspray cans rattled across the floor downstairs. I scrolled further through the calls list for more possibilities.

Mum. No. Absolutely not. Viv would freak out, and what could she do anyway?

Phil. Ferocious, yes, but miles away.

Hotbuns Bywater.

Phil had sent me his contact. She'd assigned a picture to it too, but I'd figured out how to get rid. My thumb hovered over his name, then a hissing sound from downstairs stole my attention. The sweet chemical smell of aerosol wafted up over the gallery, already filtering into the bedroom. They were kids. Just kids. But kids could be sodding scary. I couldn't call Rohan up here, not on his own.

I sank my finger onto Carter's name a few spaces below Rohan's. I'd saved his number after he'd insisted on me taking it down for Phil. To my utter relief, Carter answered almost immediately.

'Hello?'

'Carter!' I whispered. 'It's Amy!'

'Hello?' Carter repeated.

'Carter? Can you hear me?' I said urgently.

'Oh, hi!' Carter called, happily. 'How's it goin'?'

'Carter, listen, I think someone's broken in to the mill. They're downstairs now and—'

'Sorry, amigo, but you just fell for one ancient chestnut. Leave a message.'

The long beep of Carter's answer machine kicked in.

Damn it, Carter! I hit the *end call* button, realising I was out of options. Quickly, I dialled again.

*

Eight minutes was a long time hiding beneath a trestle table, but credit to local services they sent two police cars in exceptionally quick time, despite the postcode issue. As soon as I saw the ceiling of the hallway light up in flashing emergency blue, there was a frantic scrambling of bodies downstairs. I didn't think they were quick enough, though. I heard one police car completely round the mill, cutting off the route from the back yard over to the public footpath along the river. The second car remained out front, by Rohan's van.

I climbed out from beneath the table and flipped the bedroom lights on. Somebody in heavy boots and padded clothing was already bustling up the stairs. A female police officer with a short red ponytail and a fringe over her eyes stuck her head around the bedroom door.

'Everyone all right?' she asked, stepping into the room.

'That was quick,' I said, voice thick with relief.

'Are you all right?' she said, looking me over.

'Yeah, I'm fine. I don't think they knew I was up here.'

'Well, you did the right thing staying out of sight. Even kids can up the stakes when they're cornered.'

'I thought it might just be kids, messing around, but I didn't really know what to do about them, so…'

'They were more than messing, I'm afraid, miss. We've got one of them downstairs. The other lad hightailed it over the hill, unfortunately. I'm afraid they've caused some damage to your property.'

She led me onto the gallery. The lounge below was lit now, the artistic talent of the uninvited visitors daubed across the pale canvas of new plaster.

'They did all this?' I gasped. 'In less than ten minutes?'

'Resourceful when they want to be, aren't they? Luckily you're in the process of decorating.'

It was hard not to look at the bright initials dominating the lounge wall as I was led into the kitchen. Two more officers stood beside a young boy, swamped by his oversized hoody. He peered up at me briefly through long scruffy layers of auburn hair. He looked as defiant as he did frightened.

He still had the same pudginess to his face that little Samuel did, it probably hadn't been that long since he was pushing Tic Tacs up his nose too. I was trying to figure out why a kid of ten or so wasn't tucked up at home at this time when the WPC turned gravely to me. 'As you can see, there's been significant criminal damage. We're going to take him in, get hold of his parents—'

'Actually, this isn't my home,' I interrupted.

'No, it's mine,' a stern voice behind me said. Rohan walked in through the kitchen doors. The severity of his piercing eyes made it difficult to look directly at them. He pushed storm-grey sweater sleeves back over his forearms, planting his hands at his waist while the redhead cleared her throat.

'Mr…?'

'Bywater,' Rohan said firmly. Eyes fixed on the young lad.

'Mr Bywater, we've just responded to an emergency call—'

'Made by who?' The question surprised me and the WPC.

I cleared my throat. 'I called them. I was working upstairs when they broke in.'

Rohan looked the full weight of those eyes at me. Actually, *this* was like somebody pouring cold pond scum down my back.

'And how long were you up here, alone with them?' he asked.

Everyone looked at me for the answer. 'Not that long,' I said in a small voice, not sure why I felt like I was being told off. There had been a hardness to the edge of his words.

'Why didn't you call me? I could've been up here in seconds.'

I shifted uneasily. 'I… I didn't—'

'She did the right thing, Mr Bywater,' the redhead said, detaching a notebook from her padded jacket. 'You have a disabled man at the property, is that correct?' she asked, flipping through her notes.

Rohan's glare came sharply back from the boy to the police woman. I watched him stiffen, as if the WPC's words had some medusa-like quality to them. She waited patiently for his answer as I began to break out in a cold sweat. I probably looked guiltier than the kid. I suspected I might actually be in more trouble than he was, too.

'Disabled?' Rohan asked sternly. I expected him to look an accusation at me, but he didn't. He didn't look anywhere near me. 'I guess that would be me,' he said, a sudden calmness in his voice. 'And as you can see, I'm perfectly well.'

The WPC looked uncertainly at me. I was beginning to wish I'd never called them, particularly as I could have probably tackled the intruders myself, scared them off with my debilitating gift of offending people. It was probably my most well-developed muscle.

The officer frowned a little, then scribbled something down.

Rohan looked directly at the boy, petite hands cuffed in front of his NO FEAR hoodie. Rohan's features were calm, but serious. 'So, you've been tagging my house?' he said, fixing hard eyes on the boy's face. If the kid understood him, he wasn't letting on, choosing instead to glare at the floor. 'I can smell it, my man, you've been spraying something. I hope it's good,' Rohan said, moving towards the lounge. He disappeared into the hallway, the house falling into silence again for a few moments before he called back through.

'These walls are paint-eaters, buddy. Fresh plaster will suck the colour straight in. It's too bad we hadn't painted them a few times for you first, or your lines would've been sharper.' The kid let his surprise show only for moment before disappearing again behind his scowl. The police officers looked at each other. 'So where are your friends at?' Rohan said, walking leisurely back into the kitchen, 'They're older, right? Faster on their feet than you, huh?'

'The other kid made a run for it,' the taller of the two male officers said. 'This one's bike is still outside, though, so his mate's probably back in Earleswicke by now if he's on wheels too.'

Rohan looked at the two male offers. 'There are *three* tags in there; three kids' trademark graffiti. So that's *two* kids who managed to give you the slip,' he said, appraising the more portly police officer. The kid smiled at that until Rohan shot him another look. 'I've seen your work on the back of my ramps out there,' Rohan said, pointing his thumb at the kitchen windows. 'You were hanging around here a few weeks back with a couple of bigger lads. They're your crew, I take it?'

It was like we'd all just slipped into the *Twilight Zone*. The kid looked at Rohan and gave a feeble shrug.

'Now would be a good time to name names, my little friend,' the tubbier policeman contributed.

Rohan moved to stand in front of the boy. 'You gonna turn your friends in, buddy?' Rohan asked him. The kid said absolutely nothing.

'Sure he will, when we start talking charges of breaking and entering, and criminal damage over with his parents,' the taller officer added.

Rohan's eyes didn't leave the boy. 'No he won't,' Rohan said to himself. The boy looked straight at him then.

A clattering from the front door knocker ricocheted through the mill. No one said a word at first, just waiting for either Rohan or the boy to break their stare-off.

Rohan shook his head, almost imperceptibly, then

straightened up from the kid. 'Would you excuse me a minute?' he asked to nobody in particular before heading back out of the room.

'That'll be my taxi,' I said quietly to the officers, following Rohan off into the darkened hallway. I was a few paces behind him when he stopped suddenly and planted his arm across the hallway in front of me.

His voice was low and unyielding. 'Disabled?' I'd never heard one word hold so much, like a storm cloud about to burst with thunder.

'Rohan, I—'

'Good to know how you regard me.'

His comment, though justified, took me aback. 'That's not what I meant, I was struggling to speak coherently at the time.'

'Why didn't you call me, then? Instead of the police?' he whispered heatedly.

'I didn't know they were kids! I was… frightened.'

'And you didn't think the disabled man would be any use? Incapable of keeping you safe?'

'That's not what I thought at all.' Actually, his safety had been the snag.

'Then what did you think exactly?'

The door knocker rapped again.

'It was a quick decision, Rohan. No offence intended.'

'This is *my* house, mine to defend. I was in the workshop and you didn't call *me*?' The light from the newly

graffitied lounge filtered through the darkness of the corridor towards us. I watched it pick out the edges of his
features as he spoke, reaching like a new dawn across his
jawline. He'd shaved. The hard line of his mouth unob-
scured. 'I don't need anyone to make my decisions for
me,' he said bitingly.

That caught me off guard too. 'Are you kidding me?' I
snipped, trying to hold ground. 'I didn't decide anything
for you!' It was tiring constantly being on the back foot
with this guy.

'I'm not some invalid who can't take care of his own
home.'

'*What*? That's not how I look at you, at all!'

'No? How about yesterday? Out back with Carter, it
was how you looked at me then.'

The door knocked aggressively. Rohan turned and
yanked it open to a short balding man in a denim jacket,
'One minute, mate,' he demanded.

I felt my eyes narrow. 'You think that was *pity*?' I said,
steeling myself.

'Wasn't it?'

I shook my head and smiled coolly. 'That wasn't pity,
Rohan. I was about to tell you it was your own stupid fault
that you'd been stuck out there on your own in a field
all afternoon. *You're* the one who likes to play games! So
don't sound off at me when they backfire.' Rohan seemed
taken aback by my tone. I was too but it seemed to give
me a second wind. 'And while we're on it, you're missing

far more integral parts than your bloody leg, and I DO pity you for that!'

The look on the cabbie's face said it. He was in the presence of a madwoman, one he probably didn't want in his cab. I'd be on the dole by Wednesday.

I stood there like an idiot, not really sure what to say next. I hadn't flounced out immediately after my rant, and so that ship had sailed. Now where was I? Marooned, that's where, standing uselessly on my metaphorical pier with bugger all else to say.

I caught the cabbie trying to glance down at Rohan's legs. Rohan was too choked with surprise at me to notice. Then, in the dimness of the mill's entrance, he dared to start to smile. 'Like what?' he asked, his tone buoyed with amusement.

I tried to muster more annoyance, but it was already running out on me. 'Like whatever it was that left that big chip on your shoulder,' I said, trying to sound as mad as before. I saw another chance at a big exit, so I launched myself out of the door, storming straight past the cabbie, stopping for nothing until I got into his car.

I waited there, seething a little, for the driver to hurry up. He got in apprehensively after me, the car instantly filling with the smell of someone else's home. 'Lovers' tiff?' he croaked drily. He was watching me in his mirror. 'If looks could kill, eh? No wonder the coppers have turned up,' he chortled.

We drove away from the mill, a pulsing of blue light

throbbing behind us, until finally we were out onto the road. I slunk into the seat, angling myself so that the driver couldn't see my face, and spent the remainder of the journey trying to decide what it was exactly that was making me cry.

CHAPTER 18

I WASN'T BEING a coward, not with a temperature of 39 and a head like a bag of spanners. Okay, so the Lemsip was precautionary, but I knew the onset of something flu-like when it leaked out of my nose.

Mum had left me this morning with two pearls of wisdom. The first, that a third of all sickies are thrown on a Monday, and the second, there wasn't an influenza virus known to man that could stand up to Granny Sylvia's chicken broth. She was detouring to the supermarket on the way home from school. She'd also said that despite my minor concerns regarding a potential brush with bird flu, she thought I was probably just run down, all things considered. I'd told James I didn't want him to catch my bug, which had bought me a little more time here at Mum's.

Phil had decided to bypass the statistical trivia, medicinal recipes and sympathy, and dive straight in with the accusation that actually I was being a coward, avoiding this afternoon's office meeting alongside Sadie et al. She was half right, but the office had slipped to number two in this week's chart of places-to-avoid-at-all-costs.

After a long soak in the tub, and an hour of brain-zapping daytime TV, I found myself flopping downstairs sulkily, shuffling straight to Mum's biscuit jar. The green tyrannosaurus-feet slippers Sam had given her for her birthday were the only things that had taken the chill off my feet. I'd commandeered them for the day, shuffling back into the lounge with the free paper and a steady supply of Maryland cookies. If I was going down for a sick spell in the foreseeable, I was going down with double chocolate-chip.

I snuggled into the sofa and began flicking through the paper. The jobs pages were looking abysmally fruitless as predicted. There were a few part-time positions, and a handful of vacancies doing the ghost shift in a haulage depot. An ad asking for reliable and enthusiastic teenagers for paper-rounds. I wondered how many would apply for that. I couldn't remember being very reliable, or enthusiastic, for most of my teens. I'd better hold off that letter of resignation. I flicked through to the property pages, drawing first blood on the Marylands. I popped a whole cookie straight in, which wasn't very intelligent with a blocked nose. Even around the gasping I couldn't taste it much, but it was still laden with calories so its comfort value hadn't been negated.

I flicked a crumb off the paper in my lap and motioned straight past the modest two and three-bed semis to the killer properties at the back of the section. *Property porn*, James called it, but nosing through pictures of indoor swimming pools and stable blocks was both gratifying and depressing, so I scanned back through the pages to some of the more realistic entries. I nearly lost the half chewed biscuit in my mouth when I saw the photo of the imposing Victorian town house. Stunned, I ran through the particulars beneath the Park Lane property. James had given our details to the local estate agents, stating our interest in the address. It needed work, but it would never have been in our price range otherwise.

My hand went automatically for my phone before the thought struck me – what would I say to James about it? *Look! Our Happily Ever After! When can we get the keys?* A heavy sinking feeling began to bed down. That property was like us, tired and unstable, its delicate potential to be cautiously managed. I lobbed the paper onto the floor and took my frustrations out on another biscuit.

Other than my crunching, the house was utterly quiet. I sent another cookie to meet its maker when a buzzing against my stomach made me jump. In addition to the places-to-avoid-at-all-costs, I also had a list of people-to-avoid-at-all-costs, and numero uno on that list was flashing on my screen.

It wasn't like I hadn't had forewarning.

'Hey, Anna,' I said stiffly.

'Amy! Hi! How are you? It feels like I haven't spoken to you for *ages*!' I already felt clammy and I hadn't even lied to her yet. 'How was the holiday?' she enthused.

Sod! Had James given a destination? I hadn't thought to ask him.

'Good, thanks. Glad to be back into the swing of things, though,' I said vaguely, trying to lead her away from the destination question.

'You must be pooped! How was the party? Did you take lots of pics?'

'Er… not *really*. We were mostly talking and…'

I quickly ran through the minor deceptions we'd laid out in front of her. *Holiday. Party. Happy solid relationship.* Yup, I think that was it.

'You don't sound over-well, Amy. Are you under the weather?' If only she knew, it was highly plausible that I had my very own personal black cloud hovering a foot or so above my fuggy head.

'Not feeling brilliant, unfortunately, Anna. Nothing my mum's home cooking shouldn't sort out though.'

'Oh, I'm sorry to hear that. I won't keep you then, but I think this will definitely lift your spirits. Now that you've got all your celebrating out of the way, I was calling to see if we can get together – I know you're *dying* to hear about matching!' she said, her elation pulling at something floating aimlessly inside my chest. 'Could you both do the eleventh of May? It's a week today?' she asked chirpily.

'A week today?' I sniffed, trying not to sound like I had a coconut stuck up each nostril. 'That sounds great. At your office?' I asked, crossing my fingers.

'No, I'll come to you. You can show me what you've done with the nursery!' she enthused. That thing that had been floating around inside me suddenly felt cast adrift again.

I looked down at myself miserably, and felt my head begin to spin. It could still be bird flu. A pressure was building behind my eye-sockets. I brought my hand up to sooth it, rubbing big circles over them and the bridge of my nose.

'That sounds great,' I said, trying to blot out what the next week was going to entail. 'I can't wait.'

'Great! Shall we say lunchtime again? Makes things a bit easier with your work schedule, yes?'

'Yep. We'll see you at twelve then!' I said, mustering every drop of enthusiasm I had left in me. As if the cloud above me suddenly broke in my favour, Mum's doorbell rang. 'Oh, sorry Anna… I've been waiting for a delivery,' I lied again, 'that's the doorbell now.'

'That's okay! More play equipment for the garden, I suppose?' she laughed. 'Don't worry, I won't tell James you've been spending again, it'll be our secret.'

I feigned a laugh. 'Thanks, Anna. I'll see you next week.'

'Bye for now!' she sang, hanging up the phone.

The doorbell rang again. I got up slowly so my head didn't spin and immediately my nose started running. 'Just a second,' I croaked, fishing for the last scrunched-up Kleenex I'd shoved into my pocket.

I reached the door, considering for a second the state that was about to confront the poor postie, canvasser or feather-duster salesman I would open the door to, deciding quite quickly that I didn't bloody care anyway.

I turned the latch.

He seemed taller in my mother's doorway. Dark jeans sat over sturdy brown leather boots, a battered dark brown leather jacket gaping open over a snugly fitting black tee. It took a few seconds, but my fuggy brain confirmed that it was definitely Rohan Bywater standing there on my mother's doorstep.

I looked him over, trying to make sense of him. He was holding a brown shoebox in one hand. In the other, a well-worn motorcycle helmet.

'I was passing,' he said, glancing back at the chrome and onyx-black motorcycle at the mouth of my mother's drive. 'Your friend Philippa stopped by my place this morning, said you were sick.'

'Umm…' I was getting fuggier by the minute. 'What are you doing here? How did you know…?'

He began mimicking my frown and it threw me. A crooked smile moved over his lips. 'Peace offering,' he said, holding out the shoebox in his hand.

I tried not to look stupid. 'A pair of trainers?'

Rohan smiled awkwardly. 'It was the only box I had.' He shrugged.

Okay. This was officially weird.

'Would, you… like to come in?' I shrugged gawkily. *Please say no. Please say no.*

'Sure. Thanks,' he said, moving past me in the doorway. I closed the door after him and we both stood for a few seconds in Mum's open hallway, him in his James Dean get-up and me looking like a nothing that would feature in a James Dean flick.

'Nice slippers,' he said, beginning to smile. I was definitely going to need something stronger than Lemsip.

'Um, come on in. The kitchen's just through here,' I managed, shuffling off in front of him.

I moved around Mum's island unit to stand behind one of the pine chairs at the kitchen table and watched him follow me in, placing his helmet on the table and the shoebox down on the table top. He pushed the box over to me.

'What is it?' I asked, lifting the lid of the box.

Rohan rubbed his hand up the back of his head. 'I'd like to say it looks like that because of the journey, but that's how it came out of the oven. Pretty much,' he said, a boyish smile reaching over his lips.

I took the bread tin from the shoebox and laid it carefully on Viv's table. '*SORR?*' I asked, reading the scruffy pastry lettering.

Rohan shifted onto one leg and laughed uncomfortably. 'Carter's idea,' he apologised, shaking his head. 'I think he ran out of pastry.'

I inspected the top of the loaf-shaped pie. 'Or maybe

he ran out of room? So, this is *Carter's* peace offering?' I asked quizzically.

Rohan shifted back onto his other leg, scuffed hands braced over the back of one of Mum's chairs.

'Not from Carter, exactly. Carter was only on decoration detail because your girl Philippa kept insisting I show her around. I got it eighty per cent of the way, honest, then Cart took over.'

Rohan's unease was nicely balancing out my burning need to run upstairs and slap some foundation on immediately.

'For someone who doesn't like being helped out, you sure do change the goalposts,' I said bravely.

Rohan nodded, he was going to give me that one. Unceremoniously, my nose began running again. I rummaged around in my sleeve for my tissue.

'I'm sorry I flew off the handle the other night,' he said, a seriousness settling in his features. He leant away from the chair, against the edge of Mum's Welsh dresser. 'I know, I can be…'

'Touchy?' I was a lot braver in my mum's house, it turned out.

'If I blamed it on a dodgy upbringing, would that wash?'

I stopped swabbing my nostrils and thought about it. 'No.'

Rohan nodded to himself again. 'Didn't think so.' He laughed. 'Look, there are guys on site asking me questions I don't know the answers to, and your friend Philippa scares me. So… if I promise to behave myself from now on, will you come back? When you're better, I mean?'

He looked different somehow; it made me want to look at my feet.

'What made you think I wasn't coming back?'

His features grew solemn. It reminded me how he'd looked when the police had arrived. When he'd heard how I'd described him. Labelled him. 'Call it a hunch.'

'I'm sorry I didn't try calling you, Rohan, when the kids got into the mill. I never meant to offend you.'

Rohan's honeyed eyes were still guarded. 'So, you'll come back and save me from your friend?' he asked hopefully. I could only imagine what Phil had been up to. He smiled with me. 'Want to seal the deal with a spoonful of rhubarb pie?' he asked.

'Rhubarb? From your place?' I asked.

'Carter said you liked it, so we saved you some.' I didn't know why he'd gone to the effort, or why I felt so gladdened by it, but I did. I turned away for the spoons in the drawer behind me.

'You first,' I said, passing one to him.

Rohan dug into what looked like a pretty respectable attempt at baking. For the first few chews, he'd kept an even face. I couldn't taste a thing, but he didn't have to know that. I nodded and smiled. 'You'll make a fine husband some day.'

Rohan's eyes began to lose their smile as he chewed.

'Are you okay?' I asked, finishing my mouthful.

'Are you okay?' he choked.

'What's the matter?' I asked, gawping uselessly from my side of the table. 'Er, the bin's in the island unit – under the sink,' I said worriedly, passing him a sheet of kitchen towel. What could they have done between them to make rhubarb so offensive? I was instantly glad for my defective nose.

Rohan turned his back, discreetly ridding himself of what he could of the pie. 'Too much ginger!' he rasped. 'Carter's idea!'

I took a clean spoon from the drawer and dug another small spoonful. Come to think of it, my nose did feel a little breezier for eating it, maybe Carter had just stumbled across a super-food.

'Did he use raw ginger?' I asked, discovering something crunchier than rhubarb.

'How can you keep eating it?' Rohan asked, laughing. 'My throat is on fire!'

It was true, there was a nice warm sensation in my throat too. 'I think this might clear my cold!' I said happily. 'Can I get you a drink?'

'Thanks.' He smiled, slipping out of his jacket. He hung it over the back of the chair. 'You know, if your throat is fire-proofed, you should get a few hot toddies down you. Help clear you up. My foster dad always swore by anything that involved whiskey.'

I pulled the milk from the fridge and poured him out a

glassful. 'And did he also advocate riding high-powered death traps?' I asked, glancing at the motorbike helmet on the table.

Rohan sunk the drink I'd offered him, the sinews of his neck flexing as he swallowed. I waited patiently for him to finish. 'He liked machines. Liked anything with nuts and bolts,' he said, setting the glass down.

I passed him a piece of kitchen towel. 'You have a, er… little milk moustache.'

Rohan laughed, his chin low against his chest as his face blossomed into warmth. I felt something stir in my chest as I watched his rise and fall in soft convulsion.

'So he passed all that on, did he?' I said, distracting myself. 'Knowing your way around bikes, and nuts and bolts, I mean.' I needed to go and get some decent clothes on.

'For sure. He said anyone could break something, but it took a lot more for a person to make something. I guess it stayed with me. He taught me a lot about mechanics, that kind of thing. Arthur used to let me hang out in his workshop, mess around tinkering with stuff while he fixed things up for folks. Let Carter hang around too, which was good, kept us both out of trouble. Art said he'd know I hadn't been in trouble, so long as any new cuts and bruises I came home with were on my legs and elbows.' I watched Rohan bite at his lower lip, shaking his head nostalgically.

I found myself smiling with him.

'So I guess you know what works then, if you ever have boys of your own.'

'Boys?' he blurted. 'As in sons? Like I told you before, parenting's a serious job, not for someone like me.'

'Everyone probably thinks that, though, don't they? Until they are one?' But there was nothing uncertain about him. It was funny how the world worked. Here we were, two people in a suburban kitchen, me desperate to be a parent, and him desperate not to. It didn't seem fair, somehow, to either of us. Rohan might make someone a fine husband one day, but she would have to be nothing like me. 'So does Carter bike like you do? I haven't seen him doing the same kind of crazy moves you and Max go for.'

Rohan's shoulders relaxed again. 'Carter was never really that into getting beat up. You have to take a beating if you're going to give extreme sports a fair go. Cart's more of a physical pacifist than an adrenalin junky, like the rest of us.' He smiled, folding his arms again.

'Carter said that Max is a podiatrist – he's kidding, right?' I frowned.

'No, not kidding. Maxi's a foot man.' His smile broadened. 'I know, he still looks like he's only just started shaving, but I met Max when I was having my rehabilitation. A lot of the guys have *proper* jobs. But they all free up their time for the bikes. You've just gotta be careful what you're doing. Injury can mess up your income if you're expected to clock on somewhere fit as a fiddle on a

Monday morning. Ask Billy how much fun a broken wrist is when you work in a garage.'

'So what about you?' I blurted.

'Me? I was lucky, I guess. My sponsors made sure I was insured up to the hilt, so they paid out big when I had my accident.'

'Sponsors? So, you were a professional BMX rider?' I asked, pretending I hadn't seen the trophies.

'Don't get too excited, I wasn't that good.' He laughed, knocking his prosthetic. 'But they paid up, so I don't have to worry about mortgages, and all that mundane stuff. Got a few fancy prosthetics out of them, too. One for running, one for bathing…'

'Do you miss it?' I asked, certain that someone like him must pine for the arena he'd left behind.

'Yes, and no. I was thirty-one when I last competed, I'd been doing it since I was in my late teens. It was high-octane; some might have thought I was living the dream, I guess. I even had a few supporters who'd follow my progress, y'know? But, I wasn't really breaking through my own expectations, I knew that. I was just starting to think about pursuing other avenues, maybe go back to making stuff, being useful with my hands. I'd already told myself that Munich was going to be my last competitive event when I blew myself out of the running anyway.'

'What happened?'

'I'm not sure. Just landed wrong. It didn't even hurt at first… at *first*. I knew I'd seriously messed up when I saw the bottom of my own trainer. Up here.' he said, lifting his hand to his stomach. I felt mine flop as if I'd just gone over a humpback bridge at speed. 'The whole leg just bent the wrong way. They managed to salvage my knee.'

'Do you really want to talk about this?' I asked, feeling myself turning green.

'I don't mind either way. It's my old life. It's in the past now, probably best left there,' he said, letting go of a deep cavernous breath.

I wondered how we might take the conversation somewhere else. 'What's a tag?' I asked, curious.

The question caught him off guard. 'A tag, as in the kids, the other night?'

I nodded.

'It's like a calling card, every graffiti artist has their own unique mark. That's how I knew it was them who'd been hanging around the ramps too. Their tags need work.' He laughed, shaking his head. 'But they'll get better.'

Rohan hadn't been anything but calm with the kid the other night, at least for the time I was there with them. James would have gone berserk, dragging the boy straight to the nearest detention centre. 'Doesn't that bother you? That there's a gang of kids defacing your property?'

'It bothered me that they got in the house, especially as you were in there at the time, but I don't think that's going to happen again. As for the ramps, they're kids. Lads on bikes. They're gonna be interested. The way I see it, if they're messing around on my ramps when no one's looking, they're not off somewhere else doing something really stupid.'

'Like decorating someone's lounge?' I asked.

'Or worse.' He shrugged, serious now. 'I used to be those kids. Me and Cart, both. We were doing stuff more stupid than that. You know when a kid is really bad news, but the ones that are just being rascals, they just need something to do mostly. And a few ground rules.'

'My mum says the same thing,' I said, looking for tinfoil to wrap the pie in. 'She's trying to secure the Earleswicke community centre for the local *rascals* to have some place to hang out. Them and the flower-arranging posse.'

'The flower-arranging posse? Oh yeah, they definitely need to be kept out of trouble.' He grinned. Rohan had this almost trigger-like quality. When he smiled, he threw everything into it, and inevitably it pulled the same back from me. We held sight of each other for a few seconds across my mum's battered old kitchen table. 'I should be getting going,' he said, lifting his jacket. 'Let you get back to putting your claws up.' He smiled again.

I followed him through the kitchen, out across the hallway, and opened the front door for him. 'Thanks for the pie,' I offered.

'Yeah, go easy on that.' He grinned. 'You might do irreparable damage to your tastebuds.' He slipped his arm through the visor of his helmet and reached forward with the other. I watched his hand go for mine. I wasn't sure why I did it, but I held my hand out for his. Rohan reached past my fingers to the tissue hanging from my jumper sleeve.

'Ooh, that's er…'

'What? Infected with your lurgy? I'm sure I'll survive.' He pulled the tissue free then reached up with the tissue and started to come slowly at me, his hand moving steadily towards my forehead. I followed it until my eyes were too crossed, and Rohan dabbed at me gently with the tissue. 'I've been meaning to get that for you,' he said, passing me the Kleenex.

'Thanks?' I said inanely, taking it from him.

He slipped his head into his helmet. 'I'll see you when you're better.' He smiled.

I smiled back, but his eyes were more startling when framed by the shape of his helmet. There was still a smile in them when he turned and walked away down my mother's driveway.

As soon as I shut the door after him, I felt fluey again. I leant back against the door, and examined the tissue he'd given me. I opened it out and realised why he hadn't bothered over his milk moustache. I'd spent the entirety of our time together with a Maryland chocolate chip stuck to my face.

CHAPTER 19

'A DAMNED E-PETITION! Do they think the likes of Hilda Egginton or Flora Merriweather sit surfing the ruddy net of an evening? Half the people in that meeting thought the internet was something they'd take pond-dipping!' My mother's voice had been steadily climbing since she'd returned from the evening's council meeting.

Phil grinned at me from the other sofa. 'I hope I'm still as spunky when I get to Viv's age,' she mused, popping into her mouth another of the grapes she'd supposedly brought for me.

We listened to the heated conversation Mum was having on the kitchen phone. 'One *thousand* names before they'll even consider it! It's a damned stitch-up, Sue, that's what this is! A bureaucratic stitch-up.'

Phil's eyes widened as if further impressed by my mother's fieriness. Her fringe was always less severe after she'd been for a workout, a lingering glow beneath her porcelain skin only an hour-long spinning class could muster. 'What's she so het up about?' she asked, scooping up another grape.

I wasn't sure exactly. Mum had burst back into the house ten minutes after Phil had arrived, ranting her way straight for the phone. 'I think the council have given them a few hoops to jump through in their quest to rescue the community centre.'

Phil had already lost interest, inspecting the quality of her last manicure. 'Are you taking tomorrow off, hon? Do you need me to cover again? Honestly, I don't mind if you need another day.' She smiled innocently.

Mum huffed her way into the lounge and dropped like a sack of potatoes into the sofa beside me.

'Everything okay, Mum?' I asked, moving my pile of tissues.

'Not bloody really. That useless self-important prig of a councillor, he's underestimated the Earleswicke community, the pompous bugger. He thinks we can't get a thousand people to show an interest in the well-being of our community – well, he's wrong! And I for one will laugh my backside off when we get *more* than one thousand names and he has to…' she searched the air in frustration, 'suck it up!'

'Suck it up, Viv? Did you pick that up in the playground?' Phil teased. 'A thousand names for what, anyway?'

'A thousand names of people who don't want to see the community centre closed,' Mum droned, as if this should be *the* most pressing issue in Phil's universe too. Phil wasn't even from Earleswicke. 'But they can't just be good old-fashioned pen and ink jobbies, oh no. They have to be inputted on the bloody council website.'

'Is that a lot?' Phil asked drily. 'Doesn't sound that many to me.' Maybe not when it came to saving somewhere like Rufus's, or the city gym, but this was a tired old community hall we were talking about. The majority of its services catered for the under-threes and over-sixty-fives, probably not the biggest users of online petitioning systems.

I didn't like to state the obvious but... 'More than a thousand people, Ma? To say that they want to keep the community centre? Isn't that like ten times the amount of people who actually use it each week?'

Mum huffed into her chest. 'That's not the point. It's community spirit, Amy. You'll see. We'll get those names. Blow them, we'll get more than a thousand.' Braveheart was making a comeback.

Phil shifted, repositioning her legs beneath her. She looked even more cat-like snuggled on Mum's red tartan throw. 'And then what? If you get the names? What's their end of the bargain?'

'Then they'll have to reconsider the future of the centre. Because that's what that pompous idiot has said publicly they'll do!'

'If you get over a thousand names?'

'Exactly,' Mum said tartly, sucking her teeth.

The head of Earleswicke parish council was a well-fed hog of a man – I'd had the misfortune of being eyed over by him at a previous community event Viv had dragged me to. For him to state publicly that he'd do anything for those thousand signatures quite clearly suggested what we all already knew. That there wasn't a cat in hell's chance of securing anywhere near that number.

'Well, we'll sign it, won't we, Phil? And we can get everyone at the office, that's another twenty-five, thirty.' I smiled encouragingly.

Mum pushed her glasses back into the mass of curls bunching above her head against the sofa. 'We'll get them. Just you watch. Anyway, they didn't say anything about who could and couldn't sign the bloody thing. Sue made a very good point and has suggested we all phone around family and friends for their names, too. You know how big Granny Sylvia's Catholic side is.'

'Mum, they're not even in England.'

'It's an e-petition, Amy. Geography is no boundary. Names are names.'

'I could ask Hotbuns Bywater for his signature, for you. If I can get him to stand still long enough the next time I see him,' Phil offered, fiddling with one particular nail of interest. 'So do you want me to cover tomorrow, Ame?'

'Hotbuns Bywater? Is that a name you can register on an e-petition?' Mum asked.

'Viv. Let me tell you, that's the name his mother should've registered on the man's birth certificate. I don't think I've ever slept with a disabled guy but I would definitely let him walk me through it.'

Viv sighed. 'If you aren't sure about that, Philippa, you've probably been with too many men.'

'He's good enough to eat, Viv.' She grinned, unperturbed by my mother's tone. 'Solid upper body, bronzed skin, perfect smile. *Great* hair—'

'He's not disabled,' I interrupted. And then couldn't think of anything else to add to that.

Phil stretched two lithe Lycra-clad legs out in front of her. 'Of course he is, Ame, he's only got one leg!'

Mum was all ears, putting her glasses back on her nose as if that would help her hear more clearly.

'Yes, Phil, I know that. But *disabled*, it's hardly a label that suits him.'

'Oh, don't start up one of those dreary political-correctness debates, Amy. We've all got labels.'

'She's right, sweetheart, we do. We give them out, too. I see it every day at school. Spoilt, Bully, Bossy, Nits. And that's just the lunch staff.' She smiled.

'Oh great,' I groaned quietly, 'so what's mine? Failure? Unemployed? Doomed to spinsterhood with strong likelihood of eventual consumption by cats?'

'Actually, sweetheart, I think that one's already taken,' Mum said drily.

Phil stifled a smile. 'Don't be dramatic, Ame. Yours would be… *Transitional*. Mine, on the other hand, would be—'

'That's cheating!' I interrupted. 'You can't choose your own label.'

'Why not?'

'Because you've labelled Rohan as disabled, and I don't think he'd choose it for himself. So why should you get to?'

'Oh, *Rohan* is it now? When did he stop being *That Joker, Bywater*?' Phil asked, watching me. Phil had a laser-like stare that could out glare Superman. I could feel it quite clearly even as she carried on yapping for Mum's benefit. 'They got off on the wrong foot, didn't you, Ame? No pun intended.' I ignored her, and the tingling in my cheeks. 'Despite his utter gorgeousness, I think he might be a decent bloke, you know. He was going somewhere at lunchtime today with a *homemade pie* of all things. I couldn't believe it! On a mercy dash to a friend, I think. I've gotta say, it didn't look the prettiest, and I don't usually go for the goody-goodies, but if the man can cook...'

A voice in my head was already chanting, *Change the subject, CHANGE THE SUBJECT!*

'What's the definition you go by at school, Mum?' I asked, trying to make some general point rather than defending Rohan specifically.

Mum was staring vacantly across the room towards the hearth, plotting Councillor Hog's usurpation, no doubt. 'Definition of what? Disabled? Well, you're disabled if you're unable to do something the way an able-bodied person can.'

I shrugged, content in my reasoning. 'There you go, Phil. That's *definitely* not R…Bywater.'

Phil batted me away. 'Abled, disabled, whatever. Maybe he'll convince me tomorrow, or at least let me take a closer look.' She grinned salaciously.

'Actually, I think I'm going in tomorrow. I left my laptop there on Friday night, so I'll go straight there in the morning. Mum, is there any chance I could borrow your car tomorrow, please? I'll drop you off first?'

'I thought you were ill?'

'I am. But I'm hardly dying.' Actually, I'd felt quite perky this afternoon.

'No, Amy. I'm sorry but you can't. I need my car tomorrow, I have to go to another school in the afternoon. Didn't James say that you could borrow his this week? As he's working from home.'

Phil looked at me disapprovingly. 'You've spoken to James? I thought you were having a time-out from him.'

'A *time-out*?' my mother blurted, 'Philippa, it's been nearly a month; they need to sort themselves out, one way or the other!' Mum settled back into the seat, stretching her legs across the pouffe, filling an otherwise silent lounge with the creaking of leather. Phil munched thoughtfully on another grape.

Mum had been nervy since I'd told her about the call from Anna. 'I am sorting myself out, Mum. I'm just not rushing into anything. Since when was that a bad approach?' I really did not want to get into this but Mum had already jolted around in her seat to face me, her cheeks flushed with sudden frustration.

'Since it risks losing you the one thing you want more than anything, Amy! For goodness' sake, you've got to get yourself sorted out! You do realise what a fine line you're treading here, don't you?' I could see far too much of the whites of Mum's eyes. It had been years since I'd experienced a telling-off in front of a friend, and never before had one been administered with more disorientating vigour.

Phil began unfurling herself from her seat like a mayfly from its cocoon. 'I'm just going to go and put the kettle on,' she said gingerly, heading for the door. I watched her float out of the lounge, aware that Mum was only watching me.

'What was *that*?' I asked, trying not to feel ambushed.

'Amy. You have a week to get you and James back to a point where you can sit through a conversation with your social worker without her pulling the plug on the whole thing! Everything that you've worked so hard for! And you don't seem to be moving any further forward!' Not-so-funnily enough, those had been my thoughts too when I'd called James this afternoon to tell him about Anna. 'What do you want, sweetheart? If James isn't it. What are we aiming for here?'

I felt cornered, harangued. But above all, I felt cheated. 'I want a normal life, Mum!' I hissed under my breath, my mother's emotional ascent sweeping me along with it. 'I want the man in my life to love me enough not to bang one of the office girls just because he can! Or maybe just to have what everyone else seems to get awarded for a quick bloody fumble on a Saturday night!'

The unfairness was suddenly crushing again.

'And you're entitled to want those things, Amy!' Mum said, commandeering my knee. 'But do you want them with *James*? Because like it or not – and I know the timing is awful – you *need* to decide whether you're going back to him or not. Before you don't have that choice!'

I slumped back into the soft corduroy of the sofa and tried not to let the amassing sense of injustice turn to frustrated tears. 'I want… I wa—' I suddenly wasn't sure what I wanted, at least not all of it. Then the tears were there, lining up like a battalion of horses ready to trample me down.

'Don't cry, sweetheart.'

'I'm not crying,' I blubbed, clumsily rubbing either side of my nose.

I just wanted to be a family. A chaotic, noisy, wonderful family where there was love and laughter and tears like anyone else's. And I wanted James to want it too – wanted him to love me enough as I was, to be faithful to me, to love me the way I knew he did once. Maybe I hadn't given him enough attention. Maybe I'd been too desperate to be a mother, but I couldn't help how much I wanted that. To raise a child of my own, to plant a seed of some small part of myself and watch it grow inside them forever and always. A little person, a part of me, who would be better off for having me as their mum and who I would cherish every day in return. I wanted it so much, my bones ached.

The tears that had begun flowing steadily were suddenly slowed again by a thick swelling panic in my throat. It had been hard enough going through it all with someone else, first with our own, and then with the adoption. I couldn't imagine ever doing it alone. A giddying breathlessness kicked in, the thought of it all falling apart like burnt paper, and the stark question that would remain afterwards: how could I have let it?

Mum's expression was pained, as though she'd been watching a terrible picture show play out across my face. I tried to galvanise myself.

'I know I have to sort it out with James, Mum. I just didn't want to have to go back there so soon.' I snivelled. 'I don't want him to think he can treat me that way,' I went on, trying to steady my erratic judders of breath.

'I know, sweetheart. I know,' Mum said, pulling me into her warm embrace. 'But you can work on that, sweetheart, and you will, I know you will. You just can't work on it from *here*.' A few more breaths and I'd almost got my breathing under control, Mum's mass of curls muffling any trailing snivels.

Phil, always intuitive, called through from the kitchen. 'Half-time mouth-swill. Is it safe to come back in there before round two?' Mum wiped my face tenderly and kissed me on the cheek.

'It's safe, bring the biscuits in with you, Phil,' she instructed. I took a deep steadying breath, and hoped Phil wouldn't give me too much stick about the decision that seemed to have just been reached here. Between the things I hadn't said, and those my mother hadn't had to.

Phil padded quietly into the lounge with the tea tray and placed it on the little wooden side table.

'You've forgotten the biscuits,' Mum said, jumping up from the sofa. Phil took mum's seat and watched her leave before fixing warm hazel eyes on me.

'She's beaten you down, then?' she asked, blowing the fringe out of her eyes. I reached up and ran unsure fingers through my own hair. Phil and I were about as different as two friends could get, but we each understood what the other was made of.

'It's such a mess, Phil,' I said. 'But she's right. Nothing's getting fixed while I'm hiding out here, is it? I know how you feel about him, Phil – I hate him too – but put yourself in my shoes. What would you do if you were me?'

Phil watched me intently, none of her usual feistiness to harshen the edges of her face. Other than James and Mum, she was the only person I'd ever shared the firebox with, the only person I'd let share his memory. She knew what was at stake, and why it was so precious. She blew out a cheekful of air and looked down at the rug.

'Well, first of all, I'd never fit in your shoes with these

size sevens,' she said, smiling weakly. 'And second of all,' she shrugged, looking intently at me, 'I'd be asking myself what significance that terrible pie sitting in the kitchen has.'

CHAPTER 20

THERE WERE PERKS to working alongside companies, eager to have us specify their goods on the next chain of hotels or show homes designed by Cyan. Like my kitchen. An arctic tundra of clean lines and minimalist functionality, polished to a mirror-like sheen. James had haggled us the kitchen. It was worth nearly three times what we'd parted with for it. I knew this not because I'd been there when James had gone ahead and chosen it, but because it was a fact he'd enjoyed rolling out each time we'd had dinner guests.

Phil hadn't said much on the way here last night. She'd helped me with a few bags of my things but she hadn't come in, even though James hadn't been here. When he did return home, I didn't ask where he'd been. It had felt good to be held again, arms stronger than my own locked around me. I wanted to believe what he was telling me, that we could get there again, if we worked hard enough. But there was a sense of being like two icebergs, once split from the same glacier, bouncing around each other aimlessly, trying to find how to fit again.

I tried one last sip of my morning brew before making a mental note to buy more milk on the way home later. I tipped away the watery tea James had made me before leaving. He liked to get a couple of hours cycling in on home days. Said it set him up for the day. I wondered how he would take to losing those hours to the morning routine of a toddler, or cope with soggy biscuit marring the flawless lunar landscape of our kitchen.

You have to stop doing this, Amy. Stop looking for cracks.

I wondered how long he'd settle for sleeping on the sofa.

I deposited my cup in the dishwasher, grabbed my bag and favourite blazer and moved into the hallway for his car keys. The oversized circular mirror there told me I probably shouldn't bother asking *who the fairest of them all* was. It sure as hell wasn't me this morning. I found a hairband in the console drawer and pulled my hair back into a ponytail, realising with some disappointment that my nose didn't look any less puffy. The chicken broth had worked wonders, but only on the inside, apparently.

*

The sun was dazzling as I stepped outside, bouncing off James's silver saloon and making our front garden look like the set for some car advert. We could fit four cars on the driveway, but I'd never really needed my own, not with us working at the same practice. I disabled the alarm and slipped into the driver's seat. James's car was yet another immaculate environment, something else he was going to have to learn to flex his exacting standards of tidiness with.

I looked suspiciously at myself in the rear-view. *You're doing it again.*

I hadn't been crying, and yet one of those shuddered breaths took over my chest for a moment. I found myself staring at the steering wheel. *I've made the right decision. This is where I need to be. We're going to get the spark back.* The lady from across the street rushed out of her house, a keyboard under one arm and a large brass instrument under the other, shouting at her kids to get their school bags before they got in the car.

We could make this work, not just for the three of us, whenever that came to be, but for James and me, the couple we used to be.

I cranked up the engine and immediately remembered why James was so fond of the car.

The journey to the mill was quick and smooth. When I pulled into the front yard, something had changed. There was a buzz around the place. A couple of new vans in the yard, the odd tradesman milling around.

I gathered my things and locked James's car, nervously joining John Harper, spectating as an enormous bathtub was winched up to the balcony of Rohan's first-floor bedroom.

'He ordered it then,' I said idly.

John's eyes stayed fixed on the climbing load. 'He's an eager lad.' He smiled. 'Nothing wrong in that.'

I decided to go in through the front entrance. If that thing came down, I didn't really want to be on the gangway beneath it. Across the millpond, two lanky youths were helping Rohan give the boathouse its second coat of paint.

'Who are the kids?' I asked John. He turned slowly, like a ship changing course.

'The one dopey enough to wear a woolly hat in this weather, that's Lee, and the other'n, with the jeans hanging below his arse, that's Tristan. Likes to be called *Stan*,' John said, tapping his finger to his nose. 'So I call him Tristan.'

'Where are they from?' I asked, smiling. 'They don't look very old.'

'Old enough for a good day's hard graft. And a bloody good clip round the ear. If the buggers had broken into my house, it wouldn't be a paintbrush I went at 'em with, that's for sure. There's a third'n, too – young Nathan. He'll be coming after school.'

Neither of the youths was the one I'd seen in Rohan's kitchen. And I didn't think it was the police who'd have set them up in their community service down at the boathouse. Rohan glanced back over his shoulder and saw John and I looking his way. He stopped painting and threw a long tanned arm in the air to wave over to us. I thought to wave back and realised I already was.

John let out a small humph of a laugh next to me. 'You're happy this morning, you don't see many girls turning up to work with a smile like that.' I looked at him, embarrassed. 'Like to see arses hanging out of scruffy jeans, do you?'

'Er, no. Not particularly. I'll see you later, John,' I said, leaving him with a smile too. Lest he think I was particular in who I dished them out to.

After a morning of much activity and a near-calamitous bath delivery, work at the mill was in full swing. I hadn't seen Rohan yet, properly. He'd been busy at the boat-house, but I knew by the fresh garden salad I'd just found in the mini-fridge he'd been up here. I'd tried to ration-alise the small flutter I'd felt when I'd found my lunch waiting for me. He hadn't hand-made it or anything, it was in a deli tub with a use-by date and a barcode, but the slices of cucumber illustrated on the packaging sleeve were notably absent from inside.

'Well, isn't that the bummer?' I heard Carter yell from across the landing. I took the salad and mooched across the upper floor towards Rohan's room, where Carter was appraising the piles of tiles and adhesives covering the balcony. The temporary winch had been used for every-thing once the contractors had realised how much lugging it would save them.

'Hey, Carter, nowhere to pull a lotus flower?' I smiled, digging in for a tomato.

'It's lotus, *just* lotus,' he replied tetchily. I grinned into my salad tub. I moved closer to the doors and stood at Carter's left side. Rohan looked like he was walking alongside the millpond. I wondered if he was going to come and have lunch with us.

'Who are the kids?' I asked Carter, trying not to watch Rohan walk along the entire length of the path. The two lads were pulling chunks out of the battered little rowing boat while John Harper directed their efforts.

'They're the kids who want to ride the ramps every weekend. Ro cut them a deal. No messing around during the week, getting up to no good with the law, and they can use his set-up. Once they've helped him clean up, of course.'

'Are they really going to try to fix up that boat?' I asked, looking at the rickety hull of the little boat.

'Hope not. If they do, I won't be testing it out – not without armbands and a life vest.'

'You can't swim?' I said in surprise. Carter shook his head. I didn't press him on it. 'Did the kids whitewash the lounge, too?'

'Nah, Ro didn't quite trust them that far, but they're doing a pretty good job around the boathouse.'

'Why did he do that? Sounds like they stand to gain more from the arrangement than he does,' I pointed out, watching Rohan disappear beneath the balcony at our feet.

'Probably.' Carter shrugged. 'But what's the alternative?'

I popped another cherry tomato into my mouth as a VW

Beetle of the same colour cruised down the lane towards the mill.

Carter tied his hair up in a knobbly bun on his head, watching the car as it drove into the yard. 'Uh-oh. And it was such a nice morning,' he said, stepping further out onto the balcony. I moved forward a little, just enough to look down through the open doors onto the scene below.

Rohan was standing in the front yard, watching as the blonde pulled up beside his truck, and something in his stance became less friendly. No one said anything as the blonde got out and rounded the car to the rear passenger side. She looked up to the balcony and I nearly jumped backwards. 'Hey, Isaac,' she called, smiling up at Carter. She had a plait made up of a million shades of blonde draped over one shoulder. I was too far away to see if the eye flicks were still perfect.

'Meg.' Carter smiled bashfully. Rohan stood stock still as she opened the back door of the bug, scooping something from the seat there. When Megan moved aside, a miniature version of herself was standing outside the car, blonde hair flopping in every direction over her tiny face. 'Oh, crap,' Carter muttered under his breath. 'You might want to close these doors up,' he said, walking back into the bedroom. I followed him in as the familiar sounds of adult voices forced reluctantly to an even level began sparring in the yard out front.

'Carter? What's the matter?' I asked, looking back towards the balcony.

'Megan's just gate-crashed the last of Rohan's boundaries.'

'Boundaries?'

'Ok, *rules.* Actually, it's just one rule, the one Rohan does not flex on. Ever.' I frowned, waiting for more information to fill in the gaps. 'That he always goes to Lily,' Carter said, as if that explained it.

'Who's Lily?' I asked.

'Lily!' Carter smiled. 'Lily Bywater. Rohan's daughter.'

*

That fuggy feeling I'd had in my head yesterday made an unexpected comeback, sweeping downwards through my stomach and into my shoes. Carter had just stunned me.

'This is not part of the agreement between her mom and him. Ro is going to be seriously pissed off that Meg's just turned up with her.'

'But… I didn't even know he had a child,' I said, dumbfounded. Rohan was not the fathering kind, he'd said so! I hadn't *imagined* it!

'Well, he does. And now she's here. On forbidden ground.' Carter sighed.

'But… he told me that…'

'What? That he *didn't* have a kid?'

I tried to recap our very brief kid conversations. 'No, but… What do you mean, forbidden ground?' For some reason, I felt that Carter was about to burst a bubble, and tell me Rohan was another indifferent father.

'Ro likes to keep Lily settled in her home life. He's never brought her here, or to any of his houses. Too much upheaval for a little kid, he reckons.'

'But he sees her?' I croaked.

'Sure. Every weekend. But only at her place. Only at Megan's. That's his rule.'

I didn't understand it, but then it wasn't taking much to flummox me at the moment. Rohan had a child... who he *did* see... but he *didn't* want to really be a parent to? Or did he just not want to be a parent at his own place? Is that what Carter had just said?

Carter was watching me think it all through.

'But he has all this space? This beautiful place to enjoy.' He also had a beautiful little girl. What Carter was saying did not make sense to me.

'It's just Rohan's way. And Meg knows that. She's been pushing him for weeks to take Lils while she flies out with work. Meg's folks usually stay over when Meg's on an assignment but apparently her mum hasn't been well.'

Assignment. I rolled the word around my head a few times and decided that you had to be both intelligent and engaging to fly out anywhere on an *assignment.* I already had a mental image of Megan seared into my mind, in her denim shorts and khaki vest and beads. In just five minutes, she'd gone from intimidating biker chick to bohemian milf with jet-set lifestyle and great legs. And then there was the beautiful little toddler, stood beside her.

'Why aren't they together?' I blurted.

'Who? Ro and Meg? Why aren't they?'

Had I asked a stupid question? 'I guess it's complicated,' I muttered, trying to undo my intrusion.

'No, not really. It's pretty simple.' Carter scratched his hand over his chest. 'Rohan is a bit of a mixed bag. He'd jump out of a plane just for the thrill; risk life and limb in the pursuit of an adrenalin rush; run into a burning building to save the idiot who started it. He's the bravest guy I know, like that. But no man is without fear of some kind, even Ro. And what's just stepped out of that car down there, well, that's what Rohan is afraid of.'

I didn't follow. No surprise there. Carter read my face perfectly.

'Ro's afraid of two things, only. One, of being relied upon. And two, of relying on somebody else.'

The voices below had settled into an undercurrent of interchanging sounds. Her voice bubbling up here and there, interrupted by excitable squeals from the little girl.

'I'd better go and check they aren't death-staring the hell out of each other,' Carter said, traipsing out of the bedroom. I waited until he was gone before edging back to the doors, stealing a look through the crack at their hinge side.

She had little legs, brown like her mother's, dangling over her father's hip. White sandals were nearly falling from her feet as she huddled into his arms. Rohan was trying to talk around her, but she was trying to put her fingers in his mouth. Megan was less at ease, one hand on her hip, the other flat on her head. They'd reached a stand-off when Carter bobbed out beside them.

I left them then. Whatever this was, it wasn't a spectator sport.

Megan hadn't stayed long afterwards. I assumed that Rohan spent the rest of his day working it out in the meadow. James had offered to cook, so I was making an effort too, and leaving on time.

There was a reassuring rustling in the trees around me when I walked across the yard to James's car. Behind me, I heard a truck door slide open. I hadn't expected to see him again today, he still looked uneasy after Megan's visit. I was probably being paranoid, but he seemed reluctant to stop what he was doing to make conversation with me. I took the hint and began loading my things into the back of the car.

No, I was being paranoid.

I shut the car door and turned around. 'Hey. Busy day baking?' I asked light-heartedly.

He widened his eyes as if surprised that that was the best I had to offer. It made me feel insubstantial. He really was reluctant but now I'd left a conversation hanging in the air. 'I didn't know you had a daughter, Rohan,' I tried softly, sending it with an easy smile.

'I didn't know you had a BMW,' he retorted.

He looked at me, eyes cold with something I wasn't sure I'd earned. I looked behind me, at my reflection in James's passenger window, and felt the whispers of some sort of betrayal I didn't understand.

When I turned back, Rohan was already disappearing around the walkway.

CHAPTER 21

JAMES LOOKED LIKE an Adidas poster boy when I went down for breakfast. I hated his Gore-tex bibtights. I didn't understand their popularity amongst the cycling community, or why nobody had come up with a more flattering design, maybe something with a bum-bag to hide the lumpy bits of the male form. Even so, I probably couldn't blame my unease on James's cyclewear. It was early days, but I still felt like a stranger in my own home, and this morning wasn't bucking the trend any.

'Morning, gorgeous.' James smiled, eager blue eyes happy enough to see me. 'How did you sleep? You were doing a lot of mumbling last night.' He chanced a kiss at the side of my head.

There had been lots of these kisses, gentle repetitive contact. It was good. We were on the right path then. I wondered what I'd been mumbling about, and how it had been loud enough to carry downstairs to him. 'Sorry. Did I wake you?' I said, moving into the kitchen. He'd already laid the table out with an impressive array of freshly squeezed juices, berries and muesli; two places set with our new Vera Wang tableware, a gift from his mother.

'Only when you started yelling.' He flicked his head just enough to shake the blond hair from his eyes. 'Something about not letting her get too close? And *armbands?*' A lightning bolt shot through my recollection. I vaguely remembered dreaming of a large body of ominous black water. It wasn't necessarily the millpond.

'Sorry,' I repeated, taking my place at the table. James brought the cafetiere over, sitting it on a small glass mat. He walked back to the fridge, pulling on its handle when the door jarred defensively against him.

'Damn it, do we have to have these sodding door locks on everything?' he growled. I couldn't blame him, my finger had only just healed over.

'It's not for much longer,' I reassured him. There were still things, lots of ugly things, that we would have to talk though at some point, but not now. Not when we were so nearly there. I got on with pouring the coffees while James busted his way into the fridge. 'Blue top?' he remarked, taking out the milk I'd bought yesterday. 'How can a supermarket run out of milk?'

I waited for him to pour it begrudgingly into the serving jug he had ready on the side. 'They didn't run out. I thought we'd try blue for a while. It tastes better in coffee,' I added, defending my boundary-pushing decision.

'Okay,' he said agreeably, 'but it's easy to forget how

quickly all those added calories add up over a month, Ames.' I watched as he brought the offending milk to the table. 'I have this new app on my phone, it lets you log everything, every last gram of food you consume over a day, offsets it against your exercise log, then gives you your accurate calorific intake. I'll download it onto your phone later, then we'll see how long you're buying blue top.'

James watched me pour twice the usual amount of milk into my cup as the phone began trilling in the hall. 'I'll get it,' I said, grateful for a chance to leave the kitchen. I walked into our hallway, barren except for a few abstract pieces hanging on gallery-white walls. James liked art, liked to collect beautiful things, then keep them all neat and tidy in their place. I picked up the phone from the hall console and checked again in the mirror there that I hadn't made the wrong decision abandoning my hair straighteners this morning.

'Hello?'

'Amy? Hi, it's Anna.'

'Anna?'

'Sorry to ring you early, but I'm going to be in meetings all day.'

I saw my gormless expression gawping back at me in the mirror and promptly turned away from it.

'No, that's okay,' I offered, glad she hadn't caught me at Mum's again.

'It's about our meeting next Monday, I'm really sorry

to do this, you must be on tenterhooks I know, but can we push it back to the Friday? Same time?'

I skimmed through my mental calendar. 'Yeah. Sure. Is everything all right? We haven't forgotten to tick any boxes anywhere, have we?'

'Oh no! Nothing like that. I thought you'd worry, but really no need. This is good news, Amy. I just need a few more days to organise myself before I accost you with any more paperwork.'

James had come to stand in the doorway, listening. I tried not to be distracted by his skin-tight shorts.

'Okay. We'll see you next Friday instead then,' I said for James's benefit.

James folded his arms. 'What box haven't we ticked?'

'None. She just needs to organise more paperwork,' I said, checking the phone was down properly.

'Paperwork? What paperwork? What's the next lot of paperwork about?'

I didn't want to say it out loud in case I jinxed anything.

'You look… *odd*, Ame. Are you okay?'

Maybe. Anna had sounded upbeat, enthused even. I shook my head to relax him, but I found myself wanting to cross the hall and sink myself under his spandex-clad arms. James watched me as the possibility that was taking shape in my mind grew. I mean, it wasn't unheard of to be matched so soon, just as James had already pointed out. Not impossible that Anna had a child in mind for us, and that the paperwork she was referring to was the child's permanence report.

I tried to imagine my hands holding a CPR, the chronicle of his or her life, all neatly collated for us to absorb in rapturous anticipation. It had to be, had to be the reason for the delay.

I really needed to hold onto him while this sank in, but my legs had gone dead. James leant against the bottom of the stairs, studying me. We knew that there were lots of children waiting to be matched, but so many of them had brothers and sisters to consider, sibling groups that absolutely had to be kept together. *Needed* to be. James had been reluctant to adopt more than one child, so we'd agreed it would be a single child that we applied for, however long it would take for us to be matched with one.

I looked at James. A contemplative smile was warming his face. He'd come to the same conclusion, we'd been matched. It was happening! I was smiling now too, and began to move across the hall to him, but James's smile threw me.

'Are you going to work?' he asked, his eyes sloping off to check his watch.

I ground to an abrupt halt. 'What? Yes, why?' I stuttered.

'You're cutting it fine, aren't you? It takes you half an hour to sort your hair.' He smiled. 'It's after eight now.'

I lifted a robotic hand to feel the waves I'd left in my hair tumbling past my shoulders.

James checked his watch again. 'I'd better get a move on, I've got to be back for a call before ten.' He walked over to fish his keys from the key dish on the console table, and laid a chaste kiss on my cheek. 'Have a good day, baby. Don't worry about Anna and her paperwork. Any kid will be lucky to have us, they know it.'

CHAPTER 22

THERE ARE FEW times I enjoy more than sunny lunchtimes in the city. The traffic seems to flow a little slower, the noises of the city are a little quieter, the birdsong a little more harmonic. Everything is hushed down beneath the billowy canopy of sun-infused sycamore leaves lining the avenue across town. We often headed to Marquis Avenue on days like these, there was a spot beside the memorial fountains just perfect for lunch from the deli on warm grass.

I'd spent seven nights back at home. After Megan had turned up with Lily last Tuesday, I'd hardly had any interaction with Rohan. The rest of last week had seen me spend my days wondering how to strike up a comfortable conversation with him, and my nights how to avoid an uncomfortable one with James. Cyan had actually made for a welcome alternative this morning.

'So, how's it all going at Hotbun's place? Has he been rustling up something else for you in the kitchen?'

I pulled my sunglasses out of my hair and slipped them along my nose. Phil had been notably quiet on the mat-

ter all morning. 'He was just being friendly, Phil. No big
deal,' I tried. I had no right to feel hurt that there hadn't
been much friendliness from him since. No daily stocking
of the mini-fridge, no salads, and definitely no pies. He
was busy, with Lily. And I was back home, with James. 'I
expected to see a bit more of you there,' I said, deflecting
her enquiry.

Phil just smiled, lifting her chin to take in the sun on her
face. 'With a kid running wild around the place? I'll pass.
So has she been there every day?'

'Who, Lily?'

'If that's the kid's name,' Phil purred disinterestedly.

The city was alive with other lunchtimers with the same
idea, queues of dressed-down office types in each of the
bistros we passed.

'No. Not every day. I think Rohan goes to her at the
weekends.'

'So what's this Megan doing? Leaving the kid with him
while she goes out partying?'

'No, Megan picks her up every afternoon. Carter says
they're getting Lily used to being at the mill, before
Megan flies out tomorrow and leaves her with Rohan.'

Phil had already scouted a sunny spot and was steering us through the cool air thrown off by the fountains
towards it. 'Flies out where?' she asked, weaving through
the ice-cream-eaters and student tourists snapping each
other on the fountain's ornate plinth.

'Barcelona. She's some sort of photographer. Covers sporting events, or something.' Phil had edged into the lead, eager to stake her claim on a particular patch of grass. She glanced back at me over her shoulder.

'Hate her already. Is she stunning? Of course she's stunning. *He's* stunning. So why isn't she with him? If he's good with the kid and they're all so photogenic?'

I didn't know the answer to that. So I didn't offer one. Phil had already lost interest anyway. We ran a rudimentary inspection for anything sinister lurking on the grass before we sat down, Phil settling gracefully like a swan beside me. Her pink glossy lips drew into a smile, and I realised why she'd wanted this spot.

Phil was smiling a *buongiorno* to the group of olive-skinned lads behind us. She wasn't usually into exchange-students, but Phil was a sucker for an Italian accent and they were chattering away to her obvious delight. 'How old is this kid?' she asked, coming back to me.

'Three.'

'Just what you need with building works going on. Make sure the contractors' liability certificates are all in, hon.'

'I don't think there's much danger of anything happening to Lily, Phil. The way Rohan shadows her, if she tumbled he'd catch her before she made the ground.' I knew this, because I'd found myself mesmerised by them. The way he held her on his shoulders so she could see the fish in the millpond; the way he'd concentrate when he was pulling her hair into a ponytail, careful that he didn't snag. The rough and rugged father and his delicate flower. Phil passed me my sandwich and a small salad bowl. 'Besides, the work's moving along pretty fast,' I added. 'We rejigged the schedule to prioritise upstairs, so Lily has somewhere safe and comfortable to stay.'

'Where's she sleeping, then?'

'In the room next to his. He's had a door knocked through now so he can hear her.'

'Lucky her. Is it all going to be ready in time?' Rohan had asked if I could have Lily's room decked out in her favourite colours. It had been our longest conversation all week.

'Their two bedrooms are finished. All the contractors pulled together for him, and Carter's been helping the kitchen guy out, which has moved things along as well. There's getting less for me to do there now, apart from occasionally keeping a few things on track.'

There was a growing sense of redundancy to my role at the mill. I wasn't sure whether it had come when the work had started moving along, or when Megan had showed up with Lily. I was trying not to examine it.

'That clown? I wouldn't let Carter near anything more complex than a disposable knife and fork. What does he even do?' Phil asked, biting into her ciabatta.

The truth was, I wasn't really sure. 'A bit of everything, I think. I know he helps Rohan out a lot, with maintenance around the place, and in the workshop with the knee thing they're making.'

'Knee thing?'

'I think it's some sort of brace, to reinforce Rohan's leg while he's doing his tricks.'

'Tricks?'

'Tricks, stunts… you know what I mean. Daring feats of acrobatic ability.'

Phil cocked an eyebrow and fished a plastic fork and serviette from their wrapper.

'Okay, so I don't know much about it. But I think he's good, Phil. The way he performs on those ramps… he's talented. No question.' That Rohan managed any of it with only one leg was nothing short of incredible.

Phil frowned. 'You've changed your tune.'

'He's working on some kind of shoe, too. To connect his prosthetic leg better to the pedal. I've seen him trying them out,' I said, digging uselessly with my plastic fork at evasive radicchio leaves.

Phil was making her own attack on a different tasty Italian, sending cow eyes over my shoulder at one of the lads behind us. She set him up with another smile. 'Nice work if you can get it. Playing on bikes all day. Where's his money from?'

'I think he received a pay-out when he had his accident.'

'Don't tell me he's rich, Ame. I've just talked him out of the running for having a kid.'

'I don't think he's rich, Phil. I just think he's paid off what he needs to to be able to do his thing.'

'While the rest of us have to slog it out under a boss's watchful glare. T'rific. You know, Adrian's been a real pain in the arse lately, hovering at his office window.'

Triumphantly, I wangled a sporkful of battered salad into my mouth. 'Actually, I don't think that's meant for us, Phil. James says Sadie's on the way out.'

'Glitter Knickers is? Ha! I knew it! She's been in meeting after meeting with Marcy lately. *Crying* in one of them. I *knew* something was going on.'

Sadie wanted to try sitting in front of an adoption panel. That was enough to make anyone cry. 'I'm not getting my hopes up. Her attendance has obviously improved. She was in before me this morning,' I said begrudgingly.

'She won't keep it up, Ame,' Phil said imperially patting her lips with a serviette. Anyway, I'm not talking about Sadie, Sadie's old news. So, when is this social worker coming out?'

I felt an instant pang in my stomach. 'Friday. Bleurgh.'

'Good and relaxed, then? And how are things going *at home*?'

I tucked my hair behind my ears and let out a long sigh. 'Awkward. He's still on the sofa. But beyond closed doors, who would ever know, right?' *Awkward* wasn't the word for it. *Forced* felt better. I was trying, really trying, not to dwell on anything negative, but James and I didn't even seem to be on the same page any more. How could it have got like this, without me seeing it?

'Whoa, that was a serious sigh,' Phil said, watching me over her glasses.

The Italian lads started chuckling behind us. A ripple of babbled language ensued.

Phil smiled along with them, and the laughter bubbled in response.

'Do you want him to be on the sofa? Does *he* want to be on the sofa?'

'He's started dropping hints, but he was happy enough to keep his distance while I got over my cold. Didn't want to risk catching it.' There I went. Dwell, dwell, dwell.

'He said that? The selfish pig. You'd think he'd be grateful.'

Another snigger behind me and I realised what was so funny. 'Oh, Phil!' I said, quickly hunting for a serviette.

The Italian merriment intensified.

'What is it?' she asked. I reached cautiously to dab at her chocolate-brown bob.

'What is it? Has a bird just crapped on me?' she said, looking accusingly into the trees overhead.

The set of Phil's mouth suggested the Italian globe-trotters had just become a gaggle of undesirable student travellers. She turned a look on them and for the most part, it cooled them off.

'It's supposed to be good luck,' I said unhelpfully recycling Rohan's words from the day of the blackbird.

But Phil was of the thinking that you made your own luck. It did not originate in the backside of any bird.

I tried to control the smile eking across my lips. Under normal circumstances, Phil would've gone straight back to the studio to use the showers there, but she wasn't one for being run off any territory. I knew then our lunch-hour would run as long as was necessary to out-camp the Italian invasion.

'Men are such knobs. Go on, you were saying about James,' she said, offering me a hit of hand sanitiser.

I sighed again. 'Honestly, Phil, I thought it might have been easier than it is, but we seem…' What did we seem? What were we now? 'Stagnant.'

Phil pulled off her glasses and looked straight at me, as if revealing some sort of polygraph technology. 'Have you slept with him? Since all that business, I mean?'

'No.'

'You need to. Get it out of the way. You aren't going to know where you're at until you do, hon. Don't leave it any longer, or you're just gonna build it up until it's an even bigger scarier monster. Like losing your virginity.'

'So what do you suggest, Phil?' Was I honestly this pathetic?

'Dutch courage and a good run-up? You just have to get on with it, hon. Then you'll be able to tell if it's worth sticking with or not.'

If only sex were the yard stick to measure that one out

with. I was sure James would have no problems convincing most. Either way, the thought scared me.

'Maybe next week. We have enough high jumps to get over this week. We just need to keep it together for a few hours on Friday.'

'And then what?'

A new worry twisted in my stomach.

For two years we'd moulded ourselves into the ideal parents material, a desirable home in which to nurture a child. And now I, *me*, who had finely honed and polished every last detail of that picture, was the person questioning its integrity.

'Ame? And then what? If you can get through this meeting?' Phil pressed.

I pushed away the rest of my lunch and took a cautious breath. 'And then we hope it doesn't all fall apart.'

CHAPTER 23

ROHAN AND MEGAN had been upstairs arguing for nearly twenty minutes. Carter had taken Lily down to throw bread to the brood of ducklings he'd discovered over on the far corner of the millpond, leaving John Harper and I conspicuously stuck for reasons to make ourselves scarce too.

'Well, you'll have to cope! How do you think everyone else manages it, Ro?' I stopped readjusting the smaller pieces of lounge furniture and looked up to the galleried landing where all the shouting was coming from. Through the hall, I could see into the kitchen and John, also looking to the commotion above. We exchanged a brief look across the expanse of space between us. John pulled an expression of foreboding then carried on with his task. The lounge had only been a decoration job, but I'd found plenty to keep me busy tucked away in here while the first-floor battle raged on.

'It's not a place for a little girl, Meg! There's the pond, and… power tools everywhere…'

'You're making excuses! We've been over this, now

I'm going to get her things and then I'm leaving, Rohan. You'll just have to deal with it.' A thick silence then Megan walked across the landing. They'd only gone up there to look at Lily's room, then Rohan had lost the plot.

'I'll get her things!' he snapped, overtaking Megan on the gallery. Megan looked down at me, where I was trying uselessly to look busy. I should have offered to hold a hammer or something for John in the kitchen, safety in numbers. Rohan stormed straight across the gallery, irately descending the stairs to where they would spit him out in the hallway. A few seconds later, he swept past the lounge doorway then the front door clattered shut behind him. I'd seen Rohan with Lily, it was obvious that he loved her company. And still, he was so against having her here.

Megan made it across the gallery to the stairs.

Alone again, I surveyed the lounge, wondering if there was anything best put up out of a three-year-old's reach. This was definitely a room for grown-ups. The exposed brick feature wall was a perfect backdrop for the artefacts Rohan had collected on his travels. A set of vintage skis and an old garage sign hung proudly there amongst sepia-toned pictures documenting the lowly bicycle through time. There was nowhere to sit yet, but when the sofas arrived, the browns of the room – the brickwork and the oak floorboards and imposing timber mantel – would be more balanced by the softer masculine tones of deep blues and reds.

'She doesn't need as much as he thinks,' said a honeyed voice, softly from the doorway. I left the ornamental telescope I'd been about to move out of Lily's reach, and faced the woman smiling warmly towards me. She wore a gypsy skirt today, it caught the light like a jewelled veil. 'Is he always so moody, these days?' she asked, moving into the room, her hair a wild mane of blonde.

'Ah, no, not really,' I stammered, trying not to look awkward.

'I bet you hardly see him, right? Always out on the bikes?' she asked, meandering around the perimeter of the lounge. 'I'm Meg, by the way.'

'Amy.' I nodded, trying not to check her out while she looked over the run of pictures hanging on the wall. I looked out through one of the front windows, willing Rohan to hurry up. I could just about see him around the edge of the mill wheel, still busy slamming the doors on Megan's car. 'Have you seen him? Riding, I mean?' she asked, suddenly turning to me.

'Ah, a little. I wasn't really paying attention, though,' I lied.

She laughed softly to herself. 'There are a lot of people who would like to see him compete again. I don't think he realises but he still has supporters, waiting for word of a comeback. Not that Ro was ever a people-person. It's funny, throw a bike in the ring and I've never seen a guy with less fear' she said, continuing around the room. 'But when it comes to people, he's as scared as hell. Always was,' she mused, running a finger along the skis.

'He seems comfortable with your little girl,' I said carefully.

She glanced at me and smiled. 'I know, but until I turned up and pooped his party last week he hasn't had to push himself outside his comfort zone.' She frowned then. 'You're going to be around, for the next couple of weeks, right?' she asked, moving across to the inglenook where I stood. She perched an elbow against the far end of the mantel, bangles falling down her arm. 'Ro said you would be. He also said that you were nice, that Lily would like you, so I was wondering – if you don't mind – could you just keep an eye on her for me? It would make me feel a lot better knowing there's another woman around her?'

She'd caught me off guard. Rohan had said that I was... *nice*? Nice enough that the mother of his child had taken his word for it and was now asking me to play some tiny part in her well-being? My brain was already scrambling to understand where I might rank on Rohan's *nice*ness barometer.

'Er, sure?' I shrugged, sweeping the hair off my face.

'I know he won't let anything catastrophic happen, but maybe you could just check that he's not letting her eat bugs or go swimming with Carter or anything?'

She was smiling at me. I felt like the popular girl had just selected me for the school netball team. 'I don't think Carter can swim.'

'Exactly. But just in case he forgets, or has an attack of confidence?' Meg was even prettier when she smiled. Damn it.

Rohan barged back into the front of the mill, dropping two or three bags in the hallway just outside the lounge. He didn't look at either of us before disappearing outside again.

Megan rolled her eyes. 'He'll calm down.' I looked to the empty door after him, unconvinced. 'This is what Ro does, trust me. He's a commitment-phobe. Frightened to death of another person looking to him for the things *they* might need.'

'Even his own daughter?' I said bravely. It really wasn't my business.

'*Especially* his own daughter. Ro doesn't realise but I'm doing him a favour here. He needs this. I know Ro, and how much he loves Lils, but she deserves to see him more often. They both do.'

The front door went again and Rohan ventured in with a few more things. 'Is that the lot?' he asked curtly.

Megan looked at the small mound of pink bags. 'Did you get the bits out of the back as well?'

'Yeah, it's all out here,' he said, resigning himself to the inevitable. Rohan leant against the door frame and suddenly I realised I was the spare part here. He looked at Megan, then briefly at me, and instantly I felt my cheeks redden.

'Hey hey! We've found them!' Carter boomed from the

direction of the kitchen, stalking into the doorway with Lily on his shoulder. Smiling, she leant down immediately, arms outstretched for her father.

'Hello, baby girl!' Megan cooed, going to them. 'Did you find the ducklings with Uncle Isaac?' Lily nodded, bashful when she saw me in the room with them. 'Mummy's going now, Lils. You're going to have a nice time with Daddy.' Rohan began rubbing Lily's back, soothing over the dark blonde waves cascading down her little white vest. Lily didn't look like she was the one who needed it.

'I'll see you, Amy,' Megan called over her shoulder.

'Let's go wave Mummy off!' Carter called jovially. He and Megan filed out into the hallway, Rohan following on. He turned and looked at me over Lily's shoulder, waiting for Carter and Megan to clear the front of the hall. For the first time in a week, he almost smiled at me.

*

As soon as Megan had left, a new calmness fell over the mill. Or maybe it was just me. I'd already agreed with the tradesman that we were all to be off site by five each afternoon, so that Lily could enjoy a consistent bedtime routine. They hadn't long gone, and I was just getting my things together, checking over John's progress with the kitchen units, when Rohan brought Lily crying across the back yard.

Lily had cried herself pink, cheeks stained with grubby

tears and hair stuck like pondweed to her face. Rohan was cuddling her as they came in through the kitchen doors, reassuring her with soothing words, but Lily meant business. Rohan looked at me, worry stealing some of the tan from his face. 'She fell over, didn't you, baby?' he said into her hair. He sat her on top of one of the appliances, still in its vacuum wrap. Both of Lily's knees were scuffed enough to be spotting with blood. Rohan didn't really seem sure of his next move once he'd got her to the mill and sat down. He looked flustered, scanning the half-finished kitchen for something of use.

'First-aid box?' I suggested. He shook his head. 'Seriously, you lot don't have a first-aid box here anywhere?'

'Can you see us wearing plasters?' he asked, eyes wide with hindsight. It was a fair point. Lily glanced over and saw the blood on her skin, kicking her distress up a notch. Rohan began flapping. 'I don't even have any tissue! Megan said there were plasters in the one of the bags. Where did I put the bags?'

'I have a tissue,' I said calmly, opening my handbag. Surplus from the killer cold James didn't want to be infected with. Rohan looked at the newly installed industrial-grade tap over the sink.

'Was this all plumbed in today?' he said, rubbing Lily's back so much that she was probably in danger of being knocked off the dishwasher. It wasn't allaying her crying any.

'Should have been,' I said, pulling my phone from my

bag. I flicked through to the games folder, opening the paint app Samuel loved. 'Lily? Would you like to play a game?' I asked, offering her my phone. Lily wasn't buying it from me, so I handed it to Rohan. 'Daddy will show you.' Rohan took my phone while I nipped over to rinse two of my pocket tissues under the water. I heard him start to find his way around the first level of the game. I took the tissues back over to where Lily wasn't sure whether to carry on watching me suspiciously or her father shoot a virtual glitter gun.

'I'll do it,' Rohan said, eyeing the tissues in my hands as if I was coming at his child with vinegar and sandpaper.

'Do you want to be the bad guy?' I asked.

I could see the answer in his face.

'Look, Lils. There are cans of spray paint too.'

I bowed down in front of her to take a look. There was a bit of grime to sponge off, but nothing too drastic. I gently pressed the tissue to her little rounded knees. Rohan winced. Other than a small twitch, Lily hardly moved.

I had to admit, I was glad it had gone so smoothly. Rohan let out a breath, his face softening. 'The distraction method. Oldie but goodie.' I smiled.

Lily looked up at her father. There were still the remnants of crying in her voice. 'My legs are sore now, Daddy.'

'I know, baby,' he said, wiping the hair from her streaked face.

I stood, folding up the pink-tinged tissues so Lily couldn't see. 'You are a very brave little girl, Lily. Now you've got knees like Daddy's elbows.' Lily looked up at him again and set to pulling at the neck of Rohan's T-shirt.

'My elbows aren't down there, you loony, those are my shoulders. Here, look.' Rohan pushed aside his sleeve so she could see.

Lily touched the large graze running angrily from Rohan's forearm up over his elbow and grimaced. 'Do you need a plaster, Daddy?'

'Can I have one of yours?'

Lily nodded, turning her attention back to my phone. 'Thanks, baby.' He smiled, kissing her on the top of her head. 'How did you know I'd trashed my elbows?' he asked, cocking his head to one side. He looked more boyish again, now that he wasn't flapping – that infectious smile breaking over his mouth.

'Educated guess.'

My phone started buzzing in Lily's hands. She held it up for Rohan to deal with. Rohan remained perfectly impassive as he turned the face around so I could see *JAMES* centre screen. I flicked it to silent and slipped it into my pocket. One fluid movement.

'Right, Lily. I hope you have a nice night in your brand-new bedroom. And I hope you feel better in the morning,' I said, tucking her hair behind her ear. Lily nodded, sinking herself into her dad's ribs. 'Can I do anything before I go?'

'No, thanks. We're good.' Rohan sighed.

'Do you have everything to hand? In case of any more minor emergencies?' I was swinging into practical mode. Force of habit.

'I'm going to dig the plasters out now.' He smiled. 'They're upstairs somewhere. In one of a hundred bags Meg brought.'

'I could run up for you? It might be easier than you hunting around for them?'

'No, thanks. I've got it. I need to sort through it all anyway.'

I didn't pity him. I'd seen how *lightly* Lauren travelled with the boys' things. Bags galore. 'Do you want to check you have everything? Before I go? Kids come with a *lot* of baggage. Things get forgotten.'

'Amy! Honestly, I can manage. If I need something, I'll sort it myself!' He was smiling, but his demeanour had changed. Almost imperceptibly, but I'd caught it. 'Look, I know you're just trying to help, but I'm not completely incompetent, okay? I can manage to look after my own daughter for a couple of weeks. If I need help, I'll ask for it.'

I wasn't sure where I'd overstepped the mark between helpful and offensive, but clearly I had.

'Sorry,' I said, bemused. 'I didn't mean to say the wrong thing. I just know it can be a bit of a handful some-times.'

Rohan ruffed his hair, glancing up at the ceiling as if

asking to be given strength. It annoyed me. He wasn't the one unfairly being made to feel awkward here.

'Do you? I didn't realise that you had children,' he said. 'I suppose Shin Splints is perfect father material, though.' I felt my back bristle. Whatever winning opinion he might be about to impart, I wasn't sticking around to hear it. I set the soggy tissues down by the sink and collected my things, giving Lily a smile goodbye. Then I left, leaving Rohan, and the awkwardness in the air, behind me.

CHAPTER 24

I DIDN'T KNOW why I felt hurt. I'd seethed all the way back from Briddleton. All the way to Bonza Booze in Earleswicke, then I'd seethed all the way back to the city outskirts and the 'home' I shared with the other seethe-worthy one.

What was Bywater's problem anyway? I mean, the guy ran so hot and cold all the sodding time, there was a serious danger of suffering some form of neural shock just from standing too close. Not that I'd be rushing to make that mistake. Again.

Incompetent? I'd never said that. Or even suggested it. Why would I? He was rude, that's what his problem was. Rude, and suffering the effects of one gargantuan chip on his shoulder. Well, no wonder Megan left him. She was fast becoming a kindred spirit. I might even take to wearing gypsy skirts as a show of solidarity.

I pulled sulkily into my driveway and snapped the keys over to shut the engine off. I got out of the car clumsily with my armful of cheap Chilean red, wondering if Rohan would have been as snippy with her. Of course not. He probably wished every day that she would come back to him, forgive him for being such an obnoxious git.

But then why the reticence about Lily staying over? If he wanted globe-trotting, biker-chick, utterly-likeable Megan back? Who bloody knew what went on in that bloke's head?

I slammed the door and stalked over the block paving, past the ridiculously over-shaped bushes in our 'ornamental' garden. I gave momentary consideration to seething about topiary, too.

James was still working in the study when I dumped my things on the white kitchen sofa. I could see him across the garden in the summer house we'd had converted to an office. I'd wanted to site the sandpit there, so little feet could run along the decking back to the house. James had insisted on a 'sound buffer', so the pit had been relegated to the far corner with the least sun. He'd won that one with some spiel on UV rays. I shook my head to myself. Suckered.

I put the two wine bottles onto the counter and eyed them over with as much reverence as if they were a pair of Ming vases. My invaluable friends for the evening. Phil had suggested Dutch courage – I was going with Chilean. Maybe she was right. Maybe my head wouldn't be so full of distractions if that one piece of the broken pot could be jammed back into place. Brute force, and good glue. I looked across the back garden to James, the difficult piece, lounging back in his desk chair, schmoozing. He'd clock off at 6 p.m. on the nose, giving me less than ten minutes to disappear upstairs for a bath and avoid him for a little while longer.

As I trudged back through the kitchen, it took everything I had not to take one of my Chilean friends up with me.

*

My skin had taken on the texture of a sundried tomato. I hadn't planned on soaking so long but I'd been trying to think of a third reason to leave the sanctity of my airless bathroom, steam hanging heavy like a damp shroud. I was still doing my best when James invited himself in on a current of cool air holding reasons one and two.

'Hey. I've been waiting for you to come home, I didn't hear you get back.' He stepped into the bathroom, chasing the heat away.

His eyes coasted over towards the water, his voice tightening a little as I edged lower beneath the bubbles. 'Tell me which one of these you want to open and I'll get us a glass. I have some news, baby. Really exciting news.' James didn't get excited about anything other than saving a quid or making one.

You're nit-picking again.

I took a deep breath, careful not to send my diaphragm too high above the waterline. 'You pick. I'm not finished yet.' I smiled, looking at my shrivelled toes.

'I just got off the phone to Garnet's.' He grinned.

'Garnet's? The estate agents?'

'Hurry up, and I'll tell you all about it. I've a really good feeling about the next few months, Ame. Come down and we'll crack open one of these.'

Garnet's were marketing the Park Lane property. I waited for a pang of excitement, but it didn't come.

'Don't be too long, baby. You've got goose bumps,' he said, and left me to it.

The bathroom had cleared of any lingering warmth when I finally ventured across the landing's soft sea of beige carpet to my room. Ever the clutter-freak, James had brought my things upstairs and had left them on the chair in the corner. I slumped down at my dressing table and stared at the mirror. Wet brown rat's tails hung limply around my face, helping the blue of my eyes to look colder than usual.

What are you doing, Amy?

The girl staring back at me didn't offer an answer.

I looked back at the hallway stretching ominously towards the stairs and the man waiting down there for me. My eyes hovered over the spare-room door, unopened for nearly a month. Like the sandpit, that little room had become another corner of our home consigned to the shade. Well, I wasn't having it.

I marched out onto the landing and threw open the nursery door, the smell of contained paint immediate. This was a beautiful room – part of my house, not separate to it – perfectly formed with just a few carefully chosen items to welcome a bewildered little soul into their forever home.

I shouldn't have hung the bunting until everything had dried, or the hot air balloon from the ceiling, but I hadn't been able to help myself. The carpet was brand new, woolly under my toes. I walked over it to the built-in wardrobes and reminded myself of the items I'd stocked up on in readiness. New blankets and towels with their kangaroo motif that Mum had swooned over. A few packs of Sam's unused nappies in varying sizes that Lauren had suggested having to hand. The medicine box, stocked and ready on the shelf. And then there was that most conspicuous thing, the emptiness of the hanging rails, waiting for their stash of clothing in colours we couldn't choose yet, and sizes we didn't know.

Mum had bought a beautiful wooden windmill with battery-operated sails to sit on the dresser. I cast a last look over it before wedging the door stop at the base of the bedroom door, and left the room wide open behind me. It would stay wide open until the evening I pulled it to, so little eyes could rest peacefully after their first bedtime story.

My handbag was ringing when I walked back into my room, Mum checking my progress on rounding up more internet-savvy petitioners, no doubt. I found myself hoping for a diversion – anything to keep me from the lounge downstairs.

I slipped my phone from the inside pocket of my bag. I'd got rid of the caller id picture Phil had originally forwarded to me, but I still hadn't changed *Hotbuns Bywater.*

I thought about ignoring it.

'Hello?'

'Amy? It's… Rohan.'

We both already knew that I knew that.

'Hi.'

'I'm sorry to disturb you, but I'm kinda in a fix,' he said reluctantly. The tone of his voice made me feel braver.

'And you're asking *me* for my help? Must be some fix.' Silence at the other end. I wondered if he was rethinking the call. I didn't want him to rethink the call. 'Is Lily okay?' I added.

He let out a breath. 'She's fine. Thanks. Amy, I'm sorry I was rude to you earlier, you didn't deserve it. It was unfair of me. And…I'm sorry.' Something of a pulse had begun jumping in my neck. A silence began to stretch between us.

'Forget it. What's the fix?' I asked, moving over to the bedroom door, softly closing it to.

'Nappies.'

'Nappies? Lily doesn't wear them, does she?'

'Only at night, but… I don't have any. If I do, I can't find where Megan packed them.'

Megan didn't strike me as a mum who would forget the nappies. 'Did you check the bags?'

'All of them. Meg said they were with the bedtime things and medicines but I can't find any of those either. I think I must have left one of the bags in her car,' he huffed. 'Maybe I was supposed to go in the boot? I dunno…'

I started to smile at the thought of Rohan trying to fashion Lily a makeshift nappy in his workshop. 'Well, couldn't you just send Carter out for some?' I suggested.

'He's not here tonight, he's out on some secret date he wouldn't go into.'

I risked a stupid question. 'Can you not go and get them?'

Rohan huffed again quietly. 'I can't. It's not just the bags I'm short. I forgot to get Lily's car seat.'

'She's staying a fortnight and you forgot the car seat?'

'Meg drove off with it in the back of her car! She didn't notice either,' he defended. 'She'll be in the departure lounge now,' he added ruefully.

Ha! Meg hadn't noticed that she was driving off with the *car seat*! Human after all!

'Ah,' I said unhelpfully. 'I guess you are in a fix then. Would you like me to run over with some nappies?'

I could hear Lily playing in the background. Rohan was thinking over his options, I could tell. 'I don't mean to inconvenience you. I know you're probably tucked up for the evening, but I didn't know who else to ask.'

It was only half seven, and he couldn't be further from the truth. 'It's fine, honestly. I'll be there in half an hour.'

He sighed again. 'Thank you, Amy.'

'No worries. I'll see you guys shortly. Bye.'

I clicked off the call. The girl in the mirror across from me looked less cool now, eyes warmer with purpose. I ran a brush through my hair and tied it back, slipping into a pair of jeans and a loose jumper. I didn't need to bother with the supermarket, thanks to Lauren's over-zealous nesting instincts before Harry was born, I already had a mini selection of toiletries and nappies. I moved back into the nursery and began cherry-picking a selection of nappies in various sizes. An unopened bottle of lavender bubble bath, talcum powder, a bottle of Calpol. I stopped myself mid-scramble. Rohan might freak out again if he thought I'd gone on a girly spree for them. Might feel beholden to me and get his knickers in a twist over it. I left the powder and bubbles, but the Calpol was a must. The elixir for everything, Lauren had claimed.

*

James had already started on the red when I got down-stairs. 'Why have you got your shoes on, are you going out?' he asked. 'Are those *nappies*?'

I hadn't intended on misleading him, but once Rohan's name found its way onto my tongue, it felt like a bad move to speak it. 'My brother's just having a crisis,' I bumbled. 'I won't be long.' I smiled apologetically. 'Save me a glass.'

CHAPTER 25

THE THUMPING THING had hardly left me throughout the journey back to the mill. I'd driven most of the way with one hand clamped apprehensively to my neck.

When he opened the door, Lily was wrapped in a bath towel, comfortably perched on her father's side. He'd changed, into a plain blue shirt, rolled up past his elbows. Damp patches showed where Lily's body had pressed against his.

'Hey, Lily.' I smiled, trying to break any residual ice from earlier. Given my record with her father, crampons and a pick might have been advisable.

Lily looked wide-eyed from the door. 'Hello. I've got plasters now.' She hung over Rohan's arm, directing me to her knees.

'I found some in one of the bags. Come on in.' He smiled, stepping aside. I took the bag in past them, the hallway was filled with the delicate aroma of soapy water and shampoo, and the more spiced accents of whatever clung to Rohan's skin. 'Thank you for this, really,' he said, offering to take the bag from me. 'I'm just getting her into her pyjamas, would you like to come up? Unless you need to get back?'

I shook my head. 'No, I'm good for a little while.' I smiled. He smiled too. I tried not to be affected by it.

Rohan held out a hand towards the honeyed-oak staircase. I started up the stairs, realising that the mill felt strangely alien. Not the echoing shell I'd been working in but a home I'd been invited into. Warm and snug and lived in. Rohan followed on with Lily and the bag.

'I don't think I've ever seen you in jeans,' he said, behind me. I should've let him lead, then my backside wouldn't have been so perilously close to his eye level.

'Have you been in a bath, Amy? Your hair is all wet.' I looked down at Lily behind me and smiled.

'Yep. I have. I bet it wasn't as bubbly as yours, though.'

'I got Daddy wet.' She grinned, looking at him for his reaction.

Rohan feigned disapproval and pinched at her tummy. Lily exploded into throaty giggles.

'Did you?' I laughed back. 'Did you like Daddy's new bath? It's a bit like a swimming pool, isn't it?'

Lily nodded enthusiastically enough that the hood of her towel fell back from her head. 'You've got wet hair too!' I exclaimed.

'I don't own a hairdryer,' Rohan noted.

'You should've said, I have a spare,' I said, walking across the gallery. Even the lounge below looked different, more homely. 'Do you have a brush? You should tie her hair back when she's ready for bed. Keep the damp off her pillow.'

Rohan nodded, gesturing for us to walk on through to his room. Like everywhere else, his bedroom had taken on a whole new air, the design scheme we'd rolled out in here suddenly pulled together by the simple but magical act of its being put to use. It still wasn't quite dark outside, but the wreath of pendant lights hanging over the tub and the bedside lamps were all on, throwing warm light onto the stone walls, enriching the tones of the floorboards.

'Excuse the mess,' he said, setting Lily down on already disturbed bedclothes. She looked marooned in the centre of Rohan's bed. I watched her roll over, snuggling into the furred throws there that had already been rolled in before. Rohan began collecting up the line of toys running like a breadcrumb trail to the bathtub in the centre of the room.

'It's not mess, is it, Lily? You're just settling in.' I smiled, watching her wriggle her toes through the mottled brown fur. Rohan, realising he had nowhere to put his armful, lobbed the lot down in the corner next to me. He ran his fingers back and forth through his hair, and yawned.

'Hard work?' I asked, slipping my hands into my back pockets. I wasn't really sure why I was up here.

Rohan laughed softly, looking at Lily then back to me. His eyes held something I thought I'd seen before, when he'd laughed at me for eating Carter's pie. 'I guess she gets that from her dad.' He smiled. 'I don't suppose you know how to do hair?' he asked. 'I have a My Little Pony brush and absolutely no clue.' He looked so hapless I was already grinning as he hunted through the pile, victoriously producing a miniature pink plastic brush.

His hand looked enormous around it, like King Kong wielding an aeroplane. I rolled my eyes and took it from him. 'Lily?' I called, walking over to the bed. 'What does Mummy do to your hair before bedtime?'

Lily held a hand to her head, pudgy white fingers over wet matted hair helping her to think through my question. 'First she dries it with her hairdryer on her bed and then sometimes she makes a plait. Or sometimes she doesn't make a plait.'

I looked at Rohan. *Plait?* he mouthed. It made me smile. 'Okay, sweetie. We'll just put it into a plait for tonight.' Rohan had relaxed his shoulders a little. 'You know my mum has a spare car seat – for my nephew. She hardly uses it. I'm at the office tomorrow so I'll run it over at lunchtime.'

Rohan lolled his head to one side and smiled gratefully. 'Thanks. I bet you think I'm useless, right?' I moved beside Lily and began towelling her hair.

'Lily Bywater! Where are your pyjamas? I can see your tummy!' I squealed. Lily grinned up at me. I pretended to be shocked. Rohan was smiling too. He was such a different creature with her around. 'Rohan, you worry too much. She's clean, and fed – you have fed her, right?' I teased. I sat down beside Lily and started to gently tease out the snags in the ends of her hair. 'You should see my sister-in-law, she's a brilliant mum and half the time, she doesn't know what day of the week it is. She dropped Sam off at nursery last week wearing odd shoes. Him, not her. It happens.'

Rohan picked up a stack of clothing and brought it over to the bed. 'Shall we get your PJs on, Lils? Before Amy plaits your hair?'

'Does she have any hairbands?' I asked.

'Will they sell those where I can get the hairdryer?'

I rolled my eyes, and pulled free the band in my hair while Rohan pulled Lily through her white pyjama top and little pink shorts. He watched with interest as I sat her down on my lap, sectioning off her hair into silky cords, quickly weaving them together. 'I might get Carter to do that,' he said, as I tied my band around Lily's hair. She looked even smaller with her hair all tied down. Ready for a snuggle and a snooze. 'Right then, little lady. We'd better let you get to bed. You've got a busy day shopping tomorrow.'

'You don't have to leave, unless you want to?' Rohan said. 'I plugged the appliances in after you left, brought the kettle and things up from the boathouse. You could make a couple of coffees, if you wanted? While I get her off?'

Lily was rifling through the bag I'd brought. 'Okay?'

We both looked at each other. Rohan rubbed the back of his neck sending a waft of his aftershave my way. 'Don't forget the nappy,' I said, nodding to Lily, stacking them up on the bed. 'Oh, and there's medicine in that bag too. If you wanted to put it up somewhere.'

Rohan nodded. 'Got it.'

I wondered if I was going over the top again, if he thought I was interfering. I decided that was my cue to leave it at that. I got up, wished Lily a good night and walked for the door.

'Amy?' Rohan called after me.

'Yep?'

'Thanks, I appreciate it.'

*

I was admiring John's elegant craftsmanship in the kitchen when Rohan came down twenty minutes later. 'Sorry, I wanted to check that she was sleeping before I left her up there,' he said, padding across newlylaid flagstones to the cooling cup of coffee on the side. 'How much do I owe you?'

'Honestly, it's okay.' I smiled, 'So, Megan's in Barcelona huh? I bet she's missing Lily already.'

Rohan's hair had grown out a little since that day he'd first come into the boardroom. He looked different now in his shirt and jeans, and yet not different at all. Maybe I was different.

'She will be. But Megan's job is important to her.

She still feels the buzz when she goes out covering the games.'

'The games?'

'Gravity Force Games. You probably haven't heard of them.'

I shrugged, letting my shoulders sell the mistruth.

'G Force is an international sporting event. Extreme sports, so you've got your BMXing, motocross, skateboarding. And then there's White G Force, which is the winter equivalent, so snowmobiling, snowboarding, competitive sledding, et cetera.'

Rohan's eyes warmed as he talked now.

'Sounds fun.' I smiled. 'And dangerous.'

He nodded. 'That about covers it.'

'And Megan photographs these events?' No wonder she liked her job.

'Yeah, and she blogs; writes articles, too. Right now she's out there following a Spanish guy, Sebastian Barros. He's pretty prolific in the freestyle motocross. Can you imagine us guys with engines? They are some crazy cats.' Rohan's eyes had that look again.

'You sound like you miss it.'

'I miss the guys. Megan's going to be bumping into old friends I haven't seen, for sure. I miss the thrill of competition; that's just something that's there, in your blood. But no one can compete for ever. You have to find new ways to turn yourself on – adapt or die, I guess.'

Rohan had definitely adapted. My hair was beginning

to frizz, I tucked it away behind my ears, hoping I didn't look like a Def Leppard groupie. 'Where are the games held?'

'All over the world. I've been to some amazing countries.'

'Which was your favourite?'

'Probably Canada. I have a thing for totem poles. I wanted to bring a couple back to the UK, have them standing either side of the ramps, but the shipping costs were... *interesting*.' He grinned.

'Do you ever go and watch the games now?'

'And be a spectator? No. It would drive me nuts. If I had a reason to go out there, work of some kind maybe, but...' He was slipping away somewhere, somewhere frantic and exciting and committed to memory. 'Anyway, like I said: that's my old life.'

I knew that feeling. That constant rolling current between accepting what you've become and mourning what you once were. And then there was the injustice. Of being the unlucky one, blundering obliviously through your own life until *fate* singled you out. A bike stunt gone wrong. A placenta that fails.

'Amy?'

'Hmm?'

'I said you're about to lose your ear— Too late.'

I heard the delicate impact of silver on stone somewhere near my feet. Rohan bent down to retrieve my stud for me. He held it up between his finger and thumb. His eyes moved from the stud to me. My chest tightened as he closed the two or three steps between us.

His voice seemed to have sloped down to somewhere lower when he spoke again. 'You were miles away, just now. What were you thinking about?' He took another step towards me, and I could smell him again.

'Nothing.' I smiled cautiously. 'Old lives.' I watched his hand lift towards my neck, the smell of him filling my senses, locking me to the spot. My hair tickled as I felt him feed his fingers over my shoulder. I swallowed.

'You need this part too, don't you?' he asked, carefully teasing from my hair the tiny silver back to my earring.

I nodded and swallowed again. He leant in to me, and gently pressed the pin of my stud into my ear, his fingers deftly finding their way along the line of my neck to the back of my lobe. When I swallowed again, to my utter embarrassment I knew he'd heard it.

'I'm getting better at the girl stuff,' he said gently, fixing my earring in place.

I wanted to say thank you, to say anything coherently, but I couldn't think of a word short enough to risk speaking. His eyes were glorious, almost unearthly.

Oh no. No, no, no, this was not happening. This could not happen.

'Thanks,' I croaked, my unready voice cracking. 'I… have to be getting home now.'

CHAPTER 26

JAMES RARELY LOST his cool, but there was a tell-tale vein that popped out on his forehead whenever he was that way headed. A fork of lightning pointing down towards his nose and the lines around his mouth that had steadily hardened during the last few miles to work.

'I'll go to five per cent over the asking price. But for that, it needs to be taken off the market today,' he warned, staring out at the road ahead. The man on the other end of the call gave a placatory promise to pass on James's offer and excused himself from the conversation. James hit the button on the steering wheel ending the call.

'Five per cent over? But we agreed last night—'

'It's Park Lane, Amy. This might be our one chance. We have to go in hard.' He'd been so preoccupied with the renovation opportunity that when I'd made it home last night, he hadn't even asked about my time out of the house.

I looked out of the passenger window, the glint of my silver earring in the weak reflection there. I'd practically hot-footed it out of the mill last night. Rohan had been calm while I'd bumbled my excuses and left him watching me drive off the yard from the front door.

Guilt twisted in my stomach. Nothing had happened, but...

I filled my lungs with air and tried to be rational. James was staring at me in between checking for movement in the traffic ahead, waiting for my agreement on the need to *go in hard*. I nodded briefly and looked for something else to watch outside.

'You look tired this morning.' He sighed, pulling off the main street into the biscuit factory car park. 'You were sleep-talking about that plonker Bywater last night. Are you over-working again?'

Adrenalin flared beneath my skin at his name on James's lips.

'No. Actually I was thinking of asking Phil to wrap up there for me. So I can get going on the hotel project Adrian has lined up.' This had been the fruit of my laborious nocturnal thinking. The best and only suggestion I'd managed to come up with. Safe distance.

'You're always thinking about work, Ames,' James said, pulling into one of the reserved bays. 'How are you going to cope with twelve months' adoption leave?'

'I'll cope.' A year away from my life right now sounded like a pleasure cruise.

James turned off the engine and began checking his teeth for muesli in the rear-view mirror. 'So did you sort out your brother's crisis last night?' he asked, moving his inspection to the evenness of his shave.

A burning heat crept over my neck. *Don't be a liar, Ame.*

'Oh! I keep forgetting! Mum was wondering if you'd help out at the fete this weekend? It's at Earleswicke community centre. She needs men to help put the gazebos up for the stalls if you could spare an hour?'

'That place? It's a dump, Amy. What's the point?' he guffawed. A strange affinity for Earleswicke community centre suddenly awoke in me.

'The point is my mum thinks that there's a point. And actually, she's right. The local kids do need somewhere to hang out—'

'Somewhere to hang out!' he scoffed. 'Amy, kids will always hang around in the street causing problems, regardless of what you lay on for them. A derelict community centre won't change that. Right, sorry to kick you out, baby, but I've got a site inspection at nine,' he said, reaching for my bag on the back seat. I put a hand on the door handle and paused, suddenly cemented to the spot. Everything was falling back into the old rhythm. That was the plan, wasn't it? To get back to normal.

Over on the corner, two office types kissed each other tenderly, sharing a goodbye before going their separate ways for the day. She was smiling, gesturing with her wristwatch that she would be late, him more intent on a few extra seconds at her lips. A peck on my cheek diverted my attention.

'Have a good day in the office. Once Anna gets things moving, you'll be a lady of leisure.'

The city was warm outside James's car, just enough of a breeze to sweep a few loose strands of hair over my face. James was already driving away by the time I'd crossed the square to the cluster of trees where Marcy and Tom usually perched for a crafty afternoon smoke. A burst of birdsong in the leaves above me spurred me on into the offices.

I needed to talk to Phil. Anna was coming to go through some serious stuff in two days, I needed to focus and there was too much swimming around my head. Things that didn't belong in there. Phil had to take over at the mill, so everything could calm down again. I strode through the reception lobby with renewed verve, straight through the first office space ablaze with hazy morning light, past Alice hovering over Tom's shoulder and Dom hunched over a greasy café breakfast sandwich, straight to the cluster of desks where Hannah and Philippa sat back to back. Hannah was munching through a breakfast sandwich too – bacon judging by the audible reaction of my stomach. She widened her eyes and bobbed her head in an expression of speechless greeting as a globule of ketchup fell onto her desk. Phil was slowly stirring a spoon around her coffee cup as if winding up the mechanism that would power her movements for the day.

'Phil, I need a favour.'

Phil's shoulders slumped as if I was breaching the universal curfews of favour requests. 'Morning to you too. Can I sink my shitty coffee first?' she asked, slowly spinning her chair. 'What the hell happened to you? You look like you've been shot.'

I followed her eyes to the red spatter across the right shoulder of my blouse. The sinister-looking splodge there was a similar shade to the berries I'd noticed the birds fighting over in the courtyard trees.

'You have got to be kidding me.'

'It's good luck.' Phil grinned, already perkier.

'Ugh. I've got to go sponge this off. Any chance of making me a grim coffee to perk me up?' I asked, turning for the loos.

'Ame?' Phil called. 'Just a heads-up. Sadie's in there. She made a dramatic dash in, about ten minutes ago. Probably building up to another sickie.'

My skin prickled.

'What's wrong with her?' I asked, taking in the streak of bird poo next to my face.

Phil sipped her coffee and grimaced. 'Nothing, probably. Tom asked if anyone wanted a bite of his sausage-and-egg sandwich and she bolted for the toilets. Yesterday it was the smell of Ali's tuna salad. Hard-faced and delicate-stomached, that one.'

'Maybe it's a bug,' Hannah offered. 'She has been sick a lot.'

Phil rolled her eyes. 'It's not a bug, Hannah, or someone else in here would have had it.' She turned back to her desk. 'She's just not a breakfast person. Would rather still be in bed, the slacker. Well, we'd all like to roll in to work at eleven, if we could.'

My skin stopped prickling, turning cold instead.

For five long weeks, James had taken to eating his breakfast at work. Even the smell of the toaster had been enough to trigger the nausea.

Hannah turned back to her breakfast. I could feel myself slipping into some sort of autopilot. Calmly, I turned and walked across the office towards the ladies' toilet. I could hear a pulse inside my ears as I stepped inside, the faint sweet scent of sickness hanging in the air. Sadie turned from where she had been trying to dust more colour over her cheeks. She looked lost, eyes wide and bewildered. I needed to breathe, but my lungs were holding onto their air. Sadie had stopped fussing with her make-up. She opened her mouth and then swallowed the words that never surfaced.

I began to feel giddy. The tremble in my chest pushed its way into my voice.

'Is it James's?'

She was trying to hold herself rigid, but I could already see it in her. A lead weight plummeted inside me, my centre of balance dropping from its rightful position. My heart was fluttering uselessly in my chest, trying to break free like that little blackbird. Sadie's eyes began to glass over.

My voice was suddenly brittle. 'Does he know?'

Sadie's features wrinkled, eyes giving up the tears I knew were there. I watched as her shoulders began shaking around her petite frame.

'He doesn't want to know,' she broke, clamping her hands over her face. 'He's wants me to go to a clinic. He doesn't want us, Amy. He wants you.'

CHAPTER 27

THE SUN WAS beating in through the wooden slats of my lounge blinds, throwing long slivers of light across the buffed floorboards, further warming an already stuffy room. It hadn't taken Anna long before the pleasantries had tailed off into questioning looks.

I kept my sights firmly on the little black buttons of her jacket, so she couldn't see how empty I knew my eyes were. Her drink was sitting forgotten on the new wooden coffee table.

'You've done the right thing, Amy. You're thinking like a parent. Putting the needs of a child before your own,' she said quietly. She had a softness about her. She reminded me of the bereavement counsellor James and I had seen all those years ago.

I'd already removed the kid-proofing from everything. The kitchen door locks had been the first to go, then the corner guards and socket covers. Anna placed her hands lightly in her lap. 'I know that couldn't have been easy for you, Amy. For what it's worth, I'm so sorry.'

Perhaps she thought I would cry. That I needed to. But

there was nothing left. James's callousness had killed it. How could he be so indifferent? After everything we'd endured, how could he be so cruel? This was his own flesh and blood. I didn't need to hear it from his lying mouth, I'd already seen it burnished onto Sadie's face. He'd abandoned them, like they were disposable, beneath him. And then he'd had the gall to pitch that as some twisted testament to his commitment to 'us'. To 'the family we could be'. The pain bit into my chest again. He made me sick.

I'd given myself the rest of Wednesday and all day yesterday to lie in bed, imprisoned by the finality of it all, and now Anna knew the truth too. She was trying to think of something else to carve up the heavy silence in the room. She looked so disappointed. Everything that she'd invested in us, gone. I wondered if she really thought I'd done the right thing, or whether she thought I was just a fool for not doing what so many couples did all the time, and papered over the cracks.

She nimbly slipped the white file she'd pulled from her bag earlier back into its slot. I'd jumped in and told her the gory details, before I lost my nerve – before she had a chance to share a single aspect of the paperwork she'd so eagerly wielded. It was like watching a balloon slip from my fingers, climbing impossibly and irretrievably through the infinite sky. Gone.

I looked at the case on the sofa beside her. 'Was it a boy or a girl?'

Anna shifted uneasily, an apology in her face. 'Amy, I don't think it's going to help to go into it now.'

'You matched us, didn't you? Please, I came this close. Was that their CPR?'

Anna looked stricken with the growing weight of my question. 'Amy, I can't even imagine how you're feeling right now. But given what you've told me, and how your application has been impacted, it would be wrong of me to share with you the contents of that file. I have to protect this child's privacy; above all else, they have to come first. You understand that.'

A new sticky heat flowed under the surface of my skin. Anna looked pained, sorry for me. Sorry for the position I was putting her in. She sighed, pressing her teeth together, her jaw flexing with the movement.

'He's a little boy, Amy. Two years old. He's lovely.'

The heat burnt me up, my windpipe shrinking down to a withered stem.

It's a boy. Again.

I could feel myself shutting down. I couldn't breathe. *Don't ask anything else, Amy, don't ask.* But the questions were already there, jostling for position on my tongue. What colour were his eyes? His hair? How would his features change when he smiled? What would his laughter sound like? The same questions that had plagued me before, years ago, as I'd pretended to sleep in my room while my mother had busied herself in the kitchen.

And then there was the other question. Why did this lit-

tle boy, this lovely two-year-old child, even need somebody to love him? Somebody more worthy than me, who
wouldn't mess it all up so close to the finish line. What
series of events had led him into care? I tried to ask, but
my throat was so tight I couldn't force the sound out.

'Oh, Amy,' Anna soothed, leaping from the sofa and
engulfing me as best she could in her reassuring embrace.
But I was gone. Washed away, drowning in my own living
room.

'Shh,' she soothed. 'It's okay, Amy, it's okay. You'll
work it out. There are other ways. I'll do everything I can
to help you.'

Already, a toddler had taken shape in my mind. A little
boy with a face I'd never know now.

'Will he be okay?' I sobbed into Anna's stumpy blonde
ponytail. 'Will he… have to…wait for… very long…
for another…family now?' I stammered over the judders
in my chest. I knew this feeling. Knew the heavy pull
of grief. Another loss, but this time I could have made
the difference. I'd let this little boy down, taken his forever home from his reach only to send him back like an
unwanted commodity in the front pouch of Anna's bag.

But I wanted him. So much.

Anna was holding my hand and patting my back as best
she could. 'He won't, I don't think, Amy,' she said cautiously. 'There's another couple, a real possibility for him.
They're good people too, Amy. Good people like you.
Now's not the right time for this little boy to come into

another unsettled environment. That's exactly what this child does not need, Amy, and you've protected him from that.'

I nodded against her, trying to resist the desire to beg her to forget all that I'd just said. *How can this be so hard?* Was I unreasonable? Did I want too much? Two parents and a child to love each other – it didn't seem so impossible once.

Anna was still watching me with a pained expression when I emerged from my wad of tissue. I wiped my nose stealthily and smiled my defeat. I knew she probably felt that James was the linchpin missing in action, but strangely I'd felt something like relief ending our relationship. It had felt like finally kicking off a pair of shoes that had been pinching a little, after spending too long convincing myself that tight shoes were better than no shoes at all.

Anna squeezed my hand. 'Amy, I can't even begin to think what it's taken for you to be upfront with me. But you can bounce back from this. There are other ways. You'll be an amazing mother one day, I'm sure of it.'

'When, Anna?' Another breath juddered from my chest. 'When I've found another man who'll accept an adopted child over the biological ones he could have with someone else? Do you know how fragile that plan is?'

'People adopt alone, Amy. There are a lot of children out there waiting for a parent to love and protect them. To give them a home, somewhere that they'll be safe from harm, and nurtured. Where *their* needs will be put *first*,' she said, rubbing my forearm. 'You could provide all of that, Amy, you've just demonstrated that more in this meeting than at any other stage of this process.'

'Do it alone?' I shook my head. I couldn't. It had been hard enough.

'You're from a single-parent family, Amy. You turned out okay.' Anna smiled hopefully. 'Talk to your mum about it. She's got the experience.'

I already knew how hard Mum had found it. She didn't need to tell me, I'd been there. Anna squeezed my hand again, a new determination in her. She stood, rounding over the coffee table, pulling a pen and a small rectangular card from one of her bag's pockets. 'You can't make these sorts of decisions now. You need to take some time, Amy.' She scribbled down a number then came back to sit by me. 'This is my private mobile. Reassess how you feel in a few months and call me on this, any time. I promise, I'll do whatever I can to help. Do you know what you're going to do about your job?' Anna's expression was sisterly, genuine. I slipped the card into my jean pocket.

'I've given notice.'

'Do you know what you're planning on doing then?'

Where did she want to start? New job. New home. New life.

CHAPTER 28

THE ATTIC HADN'T changed much since the last time I'd been here. It still wasn't actually an attic, and it still had the same graffitied NO UNDER 21s sign next to the cavernous entry door. This was the grunge mecca of the city. I watched Phil slipping out of her black mac, revealing yet more vampishness in her black lace bodycon as she paid the girl with the piercings and ice-white hair behind the Perspex kiosk. I felt like a baby sister being dragged out by her funkier, more popular, older sister, because this was Phil's version of *sisterhood*. The boost others tried to provide with cuddles and unfounded optimism, Phil offered gloss-free with tequila and 'screw 'em' philosophy. When she'd stopped by the house earlier this evening, she'd taken one look at me and prescribed a non-negotiable session of sorrow-drowning. Or *celebration*, as she was trying to spin it. Sticky flooring and brick walls enamelled in layers of paint led us along a corridor towards the melodic thrum of something soft and acoustic, beckoning us into the main bar. Phil stalked straight in through the doors like she owned the place, her eyes fixed on the stage, where a pretty brunette with a slender face and tumbling curls sat straddling a harp, cradling her instrument as if one of them were in danger of weeping. An equally beautiful man was accompanying her on the guitar..

'Open mic night?' I asked, taking in the publicity signage. 'Since when?' Despite James's attempts to 're-educate' me, I still liked folk and indie music. Phil, on the other hand, hated anything that wouldn't help a mojito down at an Ibizan sunset party. She ignored me, leading us to an awkward standstill beside an upturned keg barrel littered with empty bottles. I didn't want to come out, I wanted to sit at home with wine and chocolate. All I really cared about tonight was drinking enough cheap spirits to sedate a small shire horse.

'I take it we're hoping to stumble into someone while we're here, then?'

Phil turned sultry eyes on me. 'You need a night out, Ame. By all means, drink yourself into a wailing mess if you'd rather do that than celebrate the back of him but, either way, you're not doing it alone.'

This was not Phil's type of place. It was making me suspicious. 'Phil. Please tell me this isn't your attempt to get me back in the saddle. Because honestly, I'd rather walk.' I began darting eyes warily around us. Phil was in The Attic for a reason, that much was obvious, but the term *double date* had me breaking into a faint sweat.

A petite waitress with a severe fringe squeezed past us with a tray of shots. Drink. That was the answer. And plenty of it. The sooner Phil hooked up with her guy, the sooner I could make my apologies and get back home to obscurity.

'Relax, hon. I haven't set you up. Let's just have a few here. I like this,' she said, bobbing her head towards the band sat beneath the atmospheric effect of some fifty or so hanging light bulbs.

'I'll get the drinks then,' I said, turning to bump straight into another waitress with knobbly pigtails and scarlet lipstick. She began pulling bottles of Corona from the pockets of her waistcoat. I say waistcoat, but it was more of a fisherman's jacket, every pocket crammed with spirits and beers. Phil already had four bottles of Corona in her hands, each stoppered with a slice of lime I was guessing had come from one of the pockets too.

'Saves us going to the bar,' she said, huddling the bottles into her chest while she rooted around for her cash.

'I've got it,' I said, pulling a couple of notes from my purse. The waitress opened out her waistcoat for my change, displaying a line of empty shot glasses like a magazine of bullets. As far as I could see, they all had my name on them.

I nodded at the ready empties. 'What do you have?'

'Tequila… sambuca…'

'Sambuca. Four please.'

'Why don't you just ask for absinthe?' Phil asked, 'Then the Green Fairy could help us hold them.'

I took the first two shots the waitress poured and

downed them. I smiled at Phil, a reminder that it was she who had insisted on making me leave the house. 'Are you going to swap me two of those beers for these, or am I the only one doing shots tonight?' Phil took a little too long to offer me the Coronas, so I downed shot number three.

'Whoa, okay, okay. Here,' she said, swapping for the last shot. She knocked it down, chasing it with a sip from one of the bottles. The waitress sat my change in the palm of my hand and left us to it. 'So drinking yourself until you're a snotty mess on the floor *is* actually the plan, then?' Phil asked, poking a slice of lime further down the bottleneck.

I shrugged. I only had one plan from now on: *no more useless plans.*

'Do you think I'm boring, Phil?' I asked, watching her carefully over the top of my bottle.

Phil's face changed. 'Boring? Course not. You're just… *safe.*'

'Safe as in… boring?'

'No. Safe as in… careful how much control you'll give up.' Background music – more guitars and intense drumming – had begun filling the void between the night's stage acts.

'You think I'm controlling?' I surmised, knocking back another sip.

'No, Ame. I think you're *controlled*. You have been since…'

'Since when? Since when have I been a control-freak, Phil?'

Phil shook her head, turning to face me square on and do what she did best: deliver a blow swift and straight.

'Look. I've never said this to you, Ame, because I know you. Know you don't want to hear it, but… what happened, with Jacob… it was awful, Amy. Unfair. Heartbreaking. I understand why you became so *careful* after that, but you can't factor out bad things from happening in your life, Ame. No matter how meticulously you plan and work and control every last detail, those things are at their own mercy, not yours.'

I hadn't expected to hear his name spoken out loud in this place. The name that stayed safely tucked inside the firebox with his cards and mittens.

'I know.' I smiled, uselessly.

Phil's eyes narrowed as she sized me up.

'You've had a shitty run, Amy. No one could say you haven't. But I worry that… you're so preoccupied with going through the motions, trying to paint your future by numbers, you're going to miss out on the other good stuff that's happening around you.'

Phil had actually been planning this conversation.

'Struggling to see a lot of *good stuff* right now, Phil. Sorry.' The sambuca was beginning to take warming effect, it was also helping me to slide into self-pity territory. 'So, what have I been missing? While my partner of eight years had an affair, trashed our hopes of adopting and got my boss's niece – and fellow happy-camper at the company I've dedicated my entire career to – knocked up?'

There wasn't much coming back from that.

'Rohan Bywater. Now there's something good, right there.'

'*What?*'

'Go on, say you haven't thought about it. I know he's thought about it.'

'Thought what?'

'What, you want me to say it out loud for you? Okay… I've seen the way he looks at you. Trying to work you out. I don't think a guy like that gets intrigued by much, Ame, but he's intrigued by you.'

Phil had just pulled a head-flip on me.

'What do you mean?' I blurted.

'You like him. I know you do. But you won't even consider him because he doesn't conform to your "plan".'

'I've just separated from James, Phil! At least let the bed cool off!' Across the heads bobbing around during the musical interval, an old gent dressed in a white hat and overcoat was weaving through the crowd.

'And do what? Wait around like your mum has? For something to come along and fit the old gap? Amy! Try something new! Would that really be so bad?'

'If you like him so much, why don't *you* make a play for him?' I said, throwing my free hand in the air. The old chap thought I'd signalled him and nodded back at me.

'I thought about it, but then I saw how awkward you were around him that first day I dropped you off. I threw a few comments in the air for you to sweat on, thinking it'd give you a bit of a push or something. But nada. Super controlled, as usual. Even when I tried to push your buttons with the disability thing, you just went on lockdown, Ame. You can't go through your life being so… *careful*.'

'Don't, Phil. We all have different set-ups, okay? And Rohan's…'

'What? Too unconventional for you? How's the conventional route been working out for you, hon? He's gorgeous, funny—'

'We're nothing alike.'

'So?'

'He likes his own company.'

'So?'

'I want a family!'

'He has a daughter.'

'Who he doesn't want to be a full-time parent to!'

'He looks pretty smitten with her to me.'

'He doesn't go in for commitment, Phil. Megan told me as much.'

'And you're taking council from his ex? There are reasons he's reluctant to have Lily more often, Ame.'

'And who are *you* taking council from, Phil? You know a lot about him all of a sudden!'

Phil looked away from me then, at the movement on stage where the next act was being prepared. 'I'm trying something new, Ame. And you know what? I'm having a blast,' she said tartly.

The man in fishmonger gear appeared next to us, waggling his basket of wares. 'Ladies? Anything from the cockle man?' he said with a grin. I wondered if he liked to bite straight into the shells, he was missing enough teeth. I looked down onto the basket of jarred curiosities. I wasn't a shellfish person. Not since a school trip to France in the first year of secondary school when one of the boys had had trouble keeping an oyster down. Three times that thing had slipped back up his throat, only for him to catch it on the shell and try again. My stomach rolled at the memory.

'No thank you,' we both said. The cockle man shrugged and moved on.

'Well, I suppose you won't be seeing that much more of him anyway. How much notice has Adrian said you've got to work out?'

'A month. But I'm owed three weeks' holiday so I'll be finished up at the mill next week. It'll give me time to hunt for more jobs.'

'Well, I hope you find something. York's a long way away, Ame,' she said, her features softening. Claire Farrel didn't think so. She'd nearly worked out her notice period at Cyan and was raring to get started with the rivals over at Devlin Raines. I guess we were both behind enemy lines now. Claire had been there when I'd walked out of the toilets at Cyan. She hadn't said anything to me at the

time but had left me a voicemail that night, telling me that
Devlin's were actively recruiting a new interiors team for
their York practice, too. A hundred and fifty miles away
sounded about perfect.

'I haven't even contacted them yet.'

'But you will. And they'll offer you an interview and
then they'll see your work and fall in love with you, Ame.
It's a done deal.'

'Nothing's a done deal, Phil. Trust me, I know all about
deals falling through at the last minute.' I was out of alcohol.

A new mic stand had found its way centre stage. The
music in the club had started to fade and bodies were once
again turning their focus towards the empty set.

'He's been asking about you,' Phil said, pursing her lips
to one side. 'He said you helped him out the other night,
with Lily. I told him why you weren't at work, Ame.'

'What? Why, Phil?'

She shrugged unapologetically. 'I just thought he
should know what was going on with you.'

'Great, Phil. I still have to work another week there!'
Why the hell had Phil dragged me all the way here to pull
my head to pieces when she could have just done it back
in my lounge? The crowd began whooping, the lights dim-
ming again for the next performer, the compere's voice
echoing over the heads behind me.

Phil looked to the stage. 'Shh. Moan after.' I looked
around the crowd for another stockpiled waitress.

'Ladies and gents, please put your hands together and give a warm welcome to one of The Attic's most loyal talents…The Troubadour With The Tache, The Messy-Haired Minstrel… Isaac Carter!'

CHAPTER 29

I WOKE IN a surrealist landscape of geometric terry towelling. The patchwork of towels draped protectively over my surroundings told me I was in my mother's home. A stabbing, shooting through my head made me shut my eyes quickly again, battening down the hatches before any more daylight could infiltrate my tender brain.

I had the strangest taste in my mouth, salty and oceanic. I flopped a hand around on the bedside table next to me, stumbling across two little capsules. I squinted at them. Mum had a good bedside manner, to a point. You could be forgiven for thinking that the Nurofen were for my benefit, but Viv liked a person good and lucid before she delivered her 'I have no sympathy, it's self-inflicted' speech. I slipped the tablets into my parched briny mouth and sunk the entire contents of the tumbler of water she'd also left there.

Next to my face, PAID had faded to a pale blue inscription on my hand where I'd been stamped by The Attic's doorman. A broken memory of standing centre stage holding somebody's guitar crooning 'I Will Survive' sent my brain back into spasm.

Lying there, I conducted a quick mental rundown of my bodily functions. The headache was a given, but I'd had worse hangovers. Just making it into a new day brought some comfort, at least I wasn't still stuck in yesterday.

The only reason Phil had even talked me into going to The Attic was because she'd turned up at my place just as I was making my way through the bottle of 1988 Krug James had been saving. Phil had only missed James by the time it had taken me to sink a few glasses of his vintage champagne and toast the changes I'd begun making to his favourite crappy artworks with my lipstick. It was childish but I was tipsy and on an adrenalin comedown, so hey ho.

Phil hadn't been there to see James slither home, a look on his face not of someone who felt regret or remorse, for me or our familes – or for Sadie, even – but the look of a tactician, of someone who thought there might still be a deal to be bartered with a weaker opponent.

I'd been mostly sat there on the sofa since Anna had left, the sweet cup of tea she'd made for me cold on the coffee table. I'd been watching the way the sun moved across the garden, how it only just caught the edges of the sandpit in the far corner, waiting for something to suddenly shift and bend the light and finally bathe that area in warmth.

James had moved silently across the lounge to press his shoulder against the French doors. He'd followed my gaze for a moment before clearing his throat, because he would lead this exchange.

'This is such a mess,' he'd quietly said to himself. He'd cleared his throat again as I'd waited for something more substantial. 'She said she'd gone back on the pill, Amy. It might not even be mine.'

When I'd looked at him then, I'd only seen Sadie – remembered the look on her face, the way her eyes had betrayed how James had abandoned her; how he had abandoned us both.

I'd moved Jacob's firebox from my lap then, before the shaking in my chest moved through to my arms and I couldn't be trusted to hold it safely any more.

'And if it is, James?' I'd managed.

His eyes had darted around the room before settling somewhere near my middle. 'Then I'll deal with it. It doesn't need to mean anything for us, Amy. I can talk her around.'

I'd almost heard the last thread binding me to James break then. That last fibre holding us together, giving up.

'*What?* What did you just say?'

James had looked as though it tired him to go through it all again. 'She knows there's no future between us, Amy. If she has that baby, she'll be going it alone.'

I'd moved a cushion over the firebox, burying it behind me. The shaking had advanced to my voice. 'How can you, of all people, be so flippant? So *selfish*?'

James's silhouette had darkened as the sun outside

intensified. 'Flippant? Amy, I've messed up, I get it, and I'm sorry. I should've told you before Sadie did, but I thought—'

'You thought you could contain your own mess, James. Bundle Sadie off for a quick fix before I was any the wiser.' A new growling quality had laced my voice.

'I never said I liked it, Amy. I'm doing this for us, so the panel doesn't retract their approval.'

'You're not doing anything for us, you selfish shit.'

'So what? You'd actually rather she had the kid? That's what you want?'

It might have been different had Anna still have been there. I might still have been the wimp I'd somehow become over those lost years with James and grabbed onto anything he had offered, before Anna had walked out of my house taking my chance of that little boy with her. But that had all gone now, and all there was left was the anger, punching through my chest.

'What I want, James, is to share my life with people who are willing to give as much love as I am! Not flick me a few crumbs from the table and expect me to be grateful for them. Now get out!'

James had dug his heels in. 'Are you serious? I'm not going anywhere, I live here.'

'Get out!' I'd screamed. At some point I'd gotten to my feet, and before I knew what was happening a mug of cold tea had bounced off James's head and exploded against the glazing behind him. There had been large sticky tan droplets slipping off his lying face when he'd brought his hands away again, an angry purple curve over his eye where the rim of the mug had left a smile there for me.

He'd called me a few interesting names as he'd wiped at the tea dripping from his muddy blond hair, bursting into another fit of yelling as he'd ranted his way out of the lounge. He'd shouted something about me stupidly thinking I could do better – control-junkie that I was – with anyone else, as if anyone else would have me. But none of his words had their intended impact. Instead I'd basked in the rosy satisfaction that, for a change, James Coffrey hadn't seen me coming.

I had still been enjoying the aftertaste of my uncharacteristically good aim when James had revisited the lounge doorway, a bag of something frozen held against his eye. He'd hovered there just long enough to suggest I shack up with the *disabled idiot*, seeing as I was such a sucker for a bleeding heart.

'Why don't you go and adopt him? You bloody nutter!'

It had hit me then, like a mug between the eyes, the last line of thought that I was probably ever going to share with this man before we parted forever.

'We're all disabled by something, James.' The real trick was not allowing yourself to be disabled by another person.

But that was yesterday.

Even through the haze of this morning's hangover, through the layers of crap the last few days had heaped on me, I knew that some of the decisions I'd made had been the right ones. It was almost bracing enough to get me out of bed.

'You're up, then?' My mother's disapproving form was looming in the doorway. The weight of my hangover suddenly tipped the balance again. The details of last night were a bit sketchy, not usually a good sign. I didn't even know how I'd got here, and Mum could smell a hangover at a hundred paces. Groan. She was like a scary female prison warden about to ransack my cell for emotional contraband. Dignity, self-respect – the stuff she hoped she'd find in here but, after a night out on the lash with Phil, had absolutely zero chance of discovering.

'Morning, Mum. Don't suppose there's any coffee going?' I croaked, rolling my head over the end of the bed. The sick bowl on the floor didn't look as if it had been entirely redundant through the night. The look on Mum's face told me who'd been swilling it out between deposits for me.

'Yes. There's coffee downstairs, Amy. And I've made you a fried breakfast too.' My stomach baulked. *Don't think about scrambled egg. DON'T THINK ABOUT SCRAMBLED EGG!*

'What time is it?' I asked.

'Ten thirty. Come on, the fete starts in two hours and after keeping me up half the night, the least you can do is come and support.' My body went into a fit of cold shivers. 'Come on,' she demanded. 'Downstairs. Or

I'm coming back up to take photos on my new mobile phone.'

'Ma, I'm sick,' I said pathetically. She was already gliding down the staircase.

'I have no sympathy, Amy,' she called back up to the landing. 'Self-inflicted.'

*

I was still wearing last night's clothes. As if I didn't feel gross enough. My skin wasn't ready for a shower yet, even the gentle pattering of lukewarm water had a very fair chance of sending my fragile body into spasmodic shock. Steadily, I moved down stairs towards the aroma of the freshly brewed coffee.

'Fifty pence a pod, these are,' Mum said, plonking a mug onto the island unit in front of me. 'Make sure you drink it.' She moved over to the oven where something plated and foiled lay in wait.

I picked up my coffee and hovered around the island unit where a montage of faces littered the worktop.

'What are all these?' I asked, picking through the portraits. They were mostly middle-aged, some blond, others brunette, all men. All posing. All posing men.

Mum kept her back to me. 'They're men, sweetheart. Nothing to be alarmed about.'

'I can see that,' I said weakly. 'Why are they all over your kitchen?'

'They're profiles. In between ferrying the contents of

your stomach back and forth to the bathroom last night, I printed off the best of the bunch. I thought you'd like to take a look.'

'Best of what bunch?' I realised my tights were missing. I fought off the panic that someone may have taken me to the loo last night.

'Would you like this now?' she asked, wielding the foiled plate like an assault weapon.

'Best of what bunch, Mum?' I repeated, a growing concern fruiting like a malnourished plant somewhere in the parched landscape of my mind.

'I don't think going out and getting yourself blind drunk is the answer to any of your problems, Amy.'

It was the answer to being sober. I took a deep long breath and waited for the lecture. 'I know. I hardly make a habit of it.'

'I know your circumstances are slightly more… complex, than those between your father and me, but I understand how isolated you must be feeling, sweetheart.'

She said *isolated* like it would be a bad thing. Isolation sounded ace right now.

'What bunch, Mum?'

'I don't want you to be lonely, sweetheart. It can become, well, habitual if you let it. That was my mistake and I don't want you to make the same one. So…' She began faffing with the spotless sink. When she spoke again, she rushed it all out in one go, squashing her words together into one incoherent sound. She didn't need to do that, they were flummoxing enough. 'I've signed you up to Cupid's Cohorts. These are some of them,' she said, holding up a picture of a man I could only deduce had been photoshopped from a knitwear catalogue.

'Mother!'

'It's highly recommended, Amy. I've done my homework. They're all young professionals, like you. Looking for fun and companionship and,' she held up another of the pictures, '*something more serious*,' she read, turning the picture to reveal a short skinhead, a large fish dangling forlornly by its jaw from the end of his finger.

'I don't believe this. If it's not Phil, it's you!' I tried to run my fingers exasperatedly through my hair, unusually voluminous this morning likely thanks to a good splashback of sambuca and a few head-shaky power-ballads.

'Actually, Phil advised against it, if you must know. But then I shouldn't imagine she's ever had to go looking online. She had that lovely Isaac with her last night. They didn't want to leave you alone so they very kindly brought you here for me.'

'Carter was here? With Phil?'

'Of course! Who do you think carried you upstairs? He's very fit, you know. He didn't even drop you when you were sick all over his T-shirt.' I found myself hoping a hangover could be fatal. 'Since when did you eat pickled cockles, Amy?' Mum continued.

I vaguely recalled having a little dance with the cockle

man, and slurring something to Phil about trying something new.

Then it hit.

Luckily, my hand clamped over my mouth buying me enough time to get to the loo under the stairs.

'I'll pop this back in the oven then?' she called after me.

I was too old for this. Too old to behave this way. I needed to grow up, sort my life out. Where to start was a thought almost as nauseating as the sketchy flashbacks of my seafood odyssey.

Content that there wasn't anything else to rid myself of, I flushed the loo and washed my face and hands. Where I'd slept on my arm, several mirrored prints of the word PAID sat in various depths of blue over my cheeks. When the sounds of the flushing died down, I could hear Mum talking to someone at the door. I wiped the streaks of mascara from under my eyes and pleaded with the heavens that it wasn't any of the WI she was showing in.

'No, she's been talking to Ralph on the big white phone. Haven't you, sweetheart?'

I glanced up at the kitchen doorway. It was always open on account of a sticky door frame, as Mum called it. Another job Dad had never done.

A little girl was standing in front of the island, little legs peeking out beneath her pedal pushers and stray curls twisting free of her cycle helmet. The expression on her face made me wish I'd stayed in the loo and spared her the trauma. Rohan had his hand around Lily's shoulder, relaxed and fresh-faced in his open pale blue shirt and battered khaki combats.

'Amy? I said your friend has stopped by to see that you're all right this morning. Isn't that kind?' Mum said. Rohan seemed to be considering the dishevelled mess in front of him. Lily looked like I'd just beamed down from the planet Zog.

I watched Mum walk up to Lily. 'Amy's been a naughty girl,' she said, chewing back a smile. 'She's been out playing and didn't go to bed when she was supposed to.' Rohan seemed particularly impressed by my bed-hair.

'I'll bet you go to bed when you're supposed to, don't you, poppet? So you're nice and fresh for the next day?' Lily began nodding at my mother, responding as all children did to Mrs Alwood. 'Can she have a biscuit, Daddy?' Mum asked Rohan. Lily was chewing her finger, hoping for a yes. Rohan nodded.

'Hey,' I managed feebly, maintaining a safe breath distance. 'What are you doing here?'

'He could ask you the same thing, but we won't go into that,' my mother chimed in as Lily fished in the biscuit jar.

'Lils wanted to say thanks. For the other night.' He turned to check Lily over the other side of the island with Mum. 'Sorry, I'm Rohan. I don't think I said that, at the door.' He smiled, holding out a hand for my mother. The brilliance of Rohan's smile affected her instantly, a blush rising in her cheeks.

'I thought so. I've heard a lot about you, Mr Bywater.

And who's this?' she asked, smuggling Lily another biscuit.

'This is my daughter, Lily,' he said, pride rising in him.

I caught sight of the stack of creepy profile pictures between them. Mum's eyes followed mine. She was about as subtle as an ocean liner, clumsily gathering them together as Rohan watched. He turned back to catch me bulging eyes at my mother.

I smiled meekly. 'How did you know I was—'

'Carter and Phil.' He smiled cautiously.

'You saw them last night?' I asked.

'This morning. Phil stayed over in the boathouse.'

'She did?'

'Yeah, they've been… getting along.'

'Oh,' I exclaimed, still trying to get my head around it.

'Like a moth to a flame.' Rohan smiled.

'Poor Carter,' I acknowledged.

'I was talking about Phil. Carter's got skills, you know.'

'Well, I think he's a splendid chap,' Mum added.

Rohan idly ran his hand through his choppy dark layers. 'We have something for you,' he said, turning for the box behind him. 'Well, Lils picked it out. To say thanks… for coming to our rescue the other night.' He smiled crookedly and let his hand run over to the back of his neck. 'I know it's not what you might have chosen, but when we went for Lil's car seat, we grabbed a few other things and she said you'd like this one.'

Lily, her understandable caution of me allayed with a

chocolate bourbon, toddled round to take the box from her father. She lifted the flaps and pulled out a shiny pink bike helmet.

'Oh! How lovely!' Mum said, stuffing the dating profiles into one of the drawers.

'Do you want to come for a ride with us today, Amy?' Lily asked, holding up the helmet for me.

I tucked clumps of matted hair behind my ears. 'Wow, Lily. Is this for me?' She bobbed her head, her own helmet falling forward on her. 'Thank you, Lily. This is really kind of you.'

'Daddy said you might come if you have a hat for your bike,' she said.

Rohan laughed uneasily. 'It's a beautiful day out there. We were wondering if you'd like to take a ride with us along the footpaths around Briddleton?'

'You've cycled here? With Lily?'

'I bought her a kid seat. It's fixed to Cart's mountain bike. It's pretty good, actually, but er... I'm a bit nervy in case I fall off or something.'

Small electrical impulses were shorting across my body. Maybe my systems were slowly rebooting. 'I've seen what you do on a bike upside down mid-air. I think you'll be okay on a cycle path.' I smiled.

His eyes narrowed a little. 'Thought maybe you could be our wing man?'

Mum was pretending to busy herself over on the back counter. 'I, er...' I looked down at the skirt and top combo

I was still in. 'I haven't showered yet, and... I don't actually think I have anything to change into.' I grimaced.

'You do,' came my mother's chirpy voice. 'You left a pair of jeans here last time you stayed, and you can borrow one of my T-shirts.' I tried not to look at Rohan.

'I thought you wanted me to help at the fete, Mum?'

'Well, why don't you all come?' Mum asked, clasping her hands together. 'There'll be plenty for little Lily, here. Candy floss and a bouncy castle.'

Lily's ears pricked. She turned wide eyes at her father.

'Sounds great to me. But is it far?'

'No! If you're cycling, it's only about ten or fifteen minutes from here. Amy will show you, won't you, sweetheart?'

'But I don't have a bike!' I wasn't even sure I could still ride one.

Mum skipped around the unit. 'I have a bike.'

'You have a bike? Here?' I asked dubiously. I'd never seen my mum on a bike in her life.

'Parisian Day. It was a WI thing, we all cycled down to Jackson's Park for a picnic and a few publicity photos for the Tweeter page Karen wants to set up.'

Tweeter?

'Do you mean *Twitter*, Mum?' I smiled.

She batted her hand at me. 'Tweeter, Twitter – what's the difference? Anyway, we didn't all go. There were a couple of "clicky hips" who opted out, not everyone was game. But I managed to get myself a bike for ten pounds on eBay,' she said flamboyantly. 'It's got a basket on the front, which I'm sure you'll hate, Amy, but it'll give you somewhere to keep your Alka-Seltzers.' She smiled, pushing rogue ringlets from over her eyes.

Rohan had dipped his chin, smiling to himself. 'Does it work? I could take a look at it,' he offered, crossing his arms in front of his chest.

'Amy's brother put two new wheels on it for me. Gave me awful saddle sore but it goes a treat.'

Mum was still looking at Rohan, studying him. His unusual eyes, the perfect line of his profile. She was thinking what I'd been trying not to. That he was probably the most beautiful man that had ever been in this house.

'Should I have a quick shower, then?' I asked quietly, seeing as Mum had it all worked out. Rohan's face softened, his shoulders relaxing a little.

As if I was going to say no.

CHAPTER 30

EARLESWICKE COMMUNITY CENTRE was almost unrecognisable adorned with paper streamers and candy-stripe gazebos, the smell of sugary treats competing on the wind with barbecued meats and real ale. Children were darting haphazardly between the adults and various stalls while some of their more obedient counterparts danced around a maypole to the soundtrack of the afternoon, meted out on an inexhaustible accordion by a chap in Morris dancing get-up.

The journey here had started off a little ropey. My balance wasn't overly reliable at first and Mum had neglected to tell me that the left brake was defunct. When we'd cycled past the hedgerows along the canal footpath I'd definitely swallowed something gnat-like, but otherwise the warm sunshine and fresh air had been just the remedy.

'So, your mum and her friends have organised all this to raise funds?' Rohan asked, leaning the bikes against the railings beside the coconut shy. He reached down to unclip Lily's helmet for her, a flop of blonde hair falling down her back. I'd watched her throughout the ride here, sure that she might fall from her perch, completely at a loss as to what I'd be able to do about it if she did. Thankfully, other than a constant stream of Rohan's body fragrance, the ride had been fairly smooth.

'Er, not funds so much as awareness, I think. This is the only real social hub in Earleswicke. They just don't want it to slip away without doing what they can.'

Rohan walked over to me and reached up to the clasp beneath my chin. My hair had mostly dried in the breeze but there was nothing I could do about the curl now. He lifted my helmet away too, eyes resting on mine. I began babbling. 'The council have said that if the locals can get a thousand signatures on this e-petition they've set up, to keep the community centre open, the council will take it on board and have a rethink.'

Rohan gently placed my helmet in the basket of my bike. He looked at the merriment taking place across the grounds of the community centre.

'There are a few here. That's good.'

I steadied myself after my momentary excitement. 'Uhuh. I just hope they all sign up.' I smiled, watching my mum stride formidably from one person to the next with her clipboard. Lily saw the bouncy castle, squealed and made a dart across the grass beneath the canopy of fluttering bunting. Rohan skipped to catch her up while Mum clocked Lily and Rohan ahead of me and began walking over to the bouncy castle. She was already thrusting her clipboard at him when I reached them, Lily sat yanking at her shoes at the foot of the giant inflatable. I crouched beside her.

'Here, sweetie. Let me undo that for you.' I fiddled with the little denim strap where it fed into the buckle. 'There you go.' I paid the girl for Lily's turn while Mum carried on accosting Rohan.

'And you just put a link on the Tweeter page, and the other Tweeterers can send it out to their friends too?' Mum was asking him.

'Sure. And so your followers can pass it on to their followers, etc. Information moves at a ridiculous rate on sites like Twitter. You should get your friend to put your e-petition up there. It's a good way of racking up a few extra names.'

Mum was nodding emphatically. 'I'll do that. Thank you, Rohan. We definitely need all the help we can get. Going door-to-door is a hassle and some of the women won't go down certain streets on their own.'

Rohan looked around the events taking place in the field. Over by the food tent, a crowd of youths were hanging over their bikes, munching on burgers and other things I still couldn't even think about.

'What if they had chaperones?' Rohan asked, turning back to Mum.

'Chaperones?'

Rohan turned and looked over to the group of youths. I recognised Nathan instantly, the only kid the police had caught that night in the mill. 'Do you know those kids?' Rohan asked my mum.

Mum took them all in as they larked about across the grass. 'I know Nathan. He left us last year. Caspar, his younger brother, is still at Greenacres Primary.'

'You know not to be put off by swagger and attitude, then? Leave it with me, Vivian.' Rohan patted my mum on the arm as he passed her, and walked over the grass to join me at the bouncy castle. A few of the boys called over to him, Rohan throwing his hand in the air back at them.

'Fans of yours?' I said, feeding my hands into my back pockets.

'They're mostly good kids.'

'You have a good way with them, Rohan.'

'Yeah, well… they're lads. They just need a nudge in the right direction.'

I shook my head lightly. 'It's not just because they're lads. You're great with Lily, too.' His chest rose and fell as we watched her from the sideline, his expression warming and cooling with each of her giggles and near-tumbles.

'You're great with her,' he said, tilting his head to me.

I could smell the scent of his skin again, reaching down into my lungs.

'Hey, hey! Who's this, son? It's Aunty Amy!' rumbled an excited voice behind us. Rohan looked back over his shoulder. I stole a few more seconds looking at him.

Samuel was tucking into a pink cloud of candy floss

bigger than his face, Guy clinging to a gourmet burger that required two hands to hold it together. He held it out to me. 'Fancy a bite, sis? Mum said you were feeling delicate today?' I ducked out of his way, unsure how far through my recovery I was. Rohan laughed to himself.

'Rohan, this is my brother Guy. And this is Sam, his better-behaved son.'

Rohan held out a hand for Guy. 'How's it going?' he said, shaking hands. Sam held his hand up to Rohan too. 'Hey, buddy. Nice to meet you. That's quite the sugar rush you've got there.'

'Need our energy, don't we, son? It's the dads and boys obstacle race in five minutes. We want that trophy, don't we, kid?' Sam bobbed his head.

'Dads and boys?' Rohan asked as Lily ran over to him with her shoes. Rohan scooped her up. 'Looks like I dodged that one.'

'Don't I know you, mate?' my brother asked around another mouthful. 'I'm sure I recognise you, where did you say you worked?'

'He didn't, Guy!' I said waspishly, slipping Lily's shoe back over her foot.

Rohan smiled. 'I don't think so, mate. I work from home.'

Someone on a loud speaker announced that all participants should begin making their way to the obstacle course. 'Are you coming to watch *The Machine* go to work?' Guy snorted, flexing his arms.

'Will you come and watch us, Aunty Amy?' Sam asked. 'You have to throw a beanbag, carry a bucket of water without spilling any and then you have to put a hula hoop over your head.'

'Sam, I would love to see your dad trying to get through a hula hoop after that burger.' I smiled. 'It'll be a bit like a magic trick, won't it?'

Rohan sat Lily up on his shoulders, leading us closer to the games track. I could see Mum cooing over Harry, strapped to Lauren's chest. A little further up from them Nathan was stood comforting another little boy, dark hair past his ears. Guy took Sam over to register as entrants while Rohan led us over to the fence.

'Hey,' Rohan called to Nathan. 'What's up with your little friend?'

'Oh, Caspar! Whatever is the matter?' Mum said, following the line of the fence towards us.

'He's all right, Mrs Alwood,' Nathan called. 'He just wanted to go in the race but I've told him he can't.' Caspar didn't look that much older than Sam, seven at most.

'Why can't he go in the race?' I asked, bending down beside the little lad. He had muddy tear tracks down his cheeks. 'Don't cry, sweetie. You can race if you'd like.'

'No he can't. It's for dads and boys and our dad's at the pub. He only likes horse races.' Mum's lips pressed into a long resigned line.

I stood up beside her.

'His father doesn't even turn up to parents' evening.

Caspar's only here because Nathan's looking after him,' she whispered.

'Men and boys! Final call for the obstacle race!' bellowed the man with the speakerphone. Caspar looked utterly deflated.

'Can't he go in with Guy?' I asked. 'Or another adult?'

'Men and boys?' Rohan said, lifting Lily from his shoulders. 'I'll race with you, buddy.' Caspar looked wide-eyed at Rohan. Rohan set his hand on Caspar's shoulder. 'But I have to tell you something before we go out there, my man,' he said, his voice dropping to a whisper. 'I'm *really* fast.' The little boy looked mystified, so did Nathan and Mum. Rohan bent down and began unzipping his trouser leg, turning his combats into shorts. He shuffled free of the right leg, Caspar looking on, then he unzipped the left.

I heard a gasp as Rohan showed the mechanics of his prosthesis off. Mum was trying not to stare, Caspar and Nathan trying to drink in as much of the view as possible.

'*Cool!*' Caspar exclaimed.

'That is so awesome,' Nathan added. Rohan began fiddling with the various metal components of his leg as if tapping at buttons we couldn't see.

He looked up at Caspar, whose mouth still hung open.

'Okay, I've turned the speed down. Transformers always beat humans, we need to give them a chance if we're going to race, don't we, buddy?' he asked. Caspar nodded, agog. 'You ready then?' Caspar nodded again, words evading him.

Mum was smiling goofily at me.

'Will you watch Lily for me?' Rohan asked.

'Sure.' I smiled, picking her up. I felt his hands slip either side of my body, one on my waist, the other on Lily. He leant in and pecked her on the cheek. His eyes lingered on us for a second, then his hands were gone.

Over the sounds of blood rushing through my ears, I could just hear Rohan making robotic noises for Caspar's benefit.

*

It was all over in five minutes. The other dads had been distracted for some reason once Rohan and Caspar had joined the starting line. Guy had struggled with an *unfairly small* hula-hoop, most of the kids were too busy pointing at Caspar's partner and so the chocolate trophy was his.

It had been a good day. A day of lingering looks and light, almost imperceptible, touches, set to the melodious score of Lily's infectious laughter. We were sitting slurping ice creams and cold cans of pop on the bank watching the dying activity of the fete fizzle out around us, Lily blowing bubbles with one of her million lucky dips.

'We missed you last week,' Rohan said, pondering the contents of his drinks can. 'I thought I might have…

overstepped the mark, asking you to come over with the things for Lily.'

I balanced my wrists on my knees and looked across at him. Just thinking about him that night, fixing my earring, made my skin want to ripple with goose bumps. 'Not at all.' I smiled. 'I really like spending time with you and Lily.'

He turned to face me.

'I'm sorry to hear about Shin Splints. It's just my opinion, but you were too good for him anyway,' he said.

Something tightened in my chest. 'Nobody's perfect, I guess. Did Phil mention anything else?' I asked gingerly. Might as well know now.

Rohan surveyed the scene of dismantlement before us.

'She told me about the adoption, and the decision you made yesterday. Must've been rough,' he conceded. Lily was blowing too hard, none of the bubbles were having a chance to form properly. I let out a long breath. 'I didn't realise you were trying for a family, Amy. I'm sorry it didn't work out.'

I smiled and looked down at the grass between my legs.

'Do you think you'll try again?'

'I don't think so. I don't think it's meant to be.' I smiled.

'I thought the same thing,' he said, nodding at Lily. 'But paths change. Even when you don't want them to, sometimes things just take you along a different course.' He was examining his empty can again. 'You know, when we were kids, there was this girl who lived on my street, Cathy Brown – I was crazy about her.'

'Cathy Brown?' I said, arching my brows.

Rohan ducked his head, reading my thoughts. 'She may not sound very hot now, but trust me, this girl had it all going on. Long brown legs, straight black hair down to her ass, the latest Walkman.' I rolled my eyes. 'Anyway, she was a stunner. But it didn't matter what I did to get this girl's attention, she wouldn't even look my way.'

I turned my grin towards Lily, watching her success- fully puff a plume of soapy bubbles into the evening haze.

'Now, I hated school. I never went to a school I didn't hate, and trust me, I moved to a lot of schools, but there was this end-of-term disco and I was desperate for Cathy Brown to be my woman.'

'Your woman?' I smiled. 'How old were you?'

'Thirteen.' He grinned.

I started laughing. 'Okay, so she's thirteen.'

'No, she was fourteen.'

'Oh, an older woman.'

'I was very mature,' he said nonchalantly.

I was trying not to grin so much. 'So… other than your *maturity*, how did you get her to go out with you?'

'I didn't. But I'll get to that point. So Carter and I came up with a brilliant plan. Actually, it was originally Arthur's idea, but we modified it – made it better. Art had told me how he'd got his wife to fall in love with him back in the day. Like Cathy Brown, Arthur's girl had been playing it cool with him, so to get her attention he'd tied a whole bunch of empty cans to the back of his bike and ridden up and down her street until she got sick of the racket.'

'And then what? They fell in love right there on the pavement?' Rohan held up a finger. He wasn't finished yet.

'Art was from another era, so I think flowers featured in there somewhere, a bit of wooing and a lot of handshaking with her father before anyone was falling in love with anyone else. Anyway, Cathy Brown…'

'Ah yes, Cathy.' I smiled.

'So, Carter and I tie on the cans, Carter takes up position across the street from her house so he can see if she's biting or not when I'm riding up and down past her front garden, or if her dad is going to come out and bust my ass for all the noise.'

'You and Carter, aged thirteen? What could possibly go wrong?' I teased. Lily ran up the bank and plonked down in the grass in front of me.

'Hey, it worked. Kinda. So out comes Cathy Brown, in her little roller boots and this yappy little terrier rat dog she had, scurrying beside her down the road. She wasn't really into the whole flower thing, so Carter and I had already decided to up the stakes and fake an accident.'

'An accident? That was your big modification on Arthur's plan?' Lily was plucking daisies from the grass. I began doing the same.

'Sure! And it worked. Carter gave the signal, I threw a

really convincing bunk and played dead on the road. She cruised on over to me, all concerned. I was acting unconscious, thinking she might come in for a little kiss.'

I popped a couple of daisies in Lily's hair. 'And?'

'So I heard her roller-skate over to me, felt her leaning over me, listening for my breath – which I was holding by the way for dramatic authenticity – and then…' Rohan shook his head with renewed disappointment.

'She did not kiss you,' I guffawed. 'No way, no girl is that gullible.' Lily saw what I was doing to her hair and stood up, moving behind me to put a few little flowers in mine.

'Nope. Then her rat dog peed all over my legs.'

I clasped my hands together and threw my head back laughing. Lily jumped. 'Oh, sorry, Lil! That's a classic.' I beamed. He was trying to look hurt, but his eyes held a smile. Lily skipped back off to play with her pile of goodies. 'So you never made it to the disco, then?'

'No. That dog saved me.'

'Saved you?'

'Cathy was going to kiss me that day, I know she was. Right up until I was disgusting and covered in her dog's pee, I was the only thing on her mind. I was a very good kisser. One kiss and it'd have been all over for her. I had a lucky escape.'

'What? But you liked her?' Something tumbled from my hair.

'I know. But if that dog hadn't peed on me, I'd have

taken her to the disco instead of the kid she went with in the end, and it would have been me who got my ass kicked in front of the entire school for stealing a year six meathead's girl. Cathy Brown used that kid to make her boyfriend jealous. I didn't realise it at the time when I was lying on the pavement stinking and wet, but that dog changed my path. For the better.'

Rohan picked up the little daisy head that had fallen from my hair and began spinning it between his finger and thumb. His smile had dipped.

I realised what he was getting at. 'So you're saying James is a yappy rat dog? Who's done me a favour by peeing all over me?'

Rohan shrugged. He turned over on his elbow and gently placed the little flower back into the waves over my ear. He was serious again. 'I'm saying, sometimes you're winning, Amy. Even if you don't see it.'

CHAPTER 31

Mᴜᴍ ʜᴀᴅɴ'ᴛ ꜱᴀɪᴅ anything during the packing of the last three boxes. It was surprisingly easy divvying up the mementos accrued after sharing nearly a decade of life with another human being. The CDs were mainly his, the books mainly mine. Other than clothes, that largely left only furniture. Phil had sent sporadic texts throughout the morning reminding me what I was entitled to half of. The angry sound of gaffer tape being yanked off its reel made me look up at Mum. She stuck another length of silvery tape over another box, huffing with every motion. Any minute now…

'Amy? Don't you think that you need a clear head before you start making any more big decisions? This house is half yours, and you're just walking away from it?'

'This house is half James's too. And I know he'll be wanting to sell it now that he's got his sights on a new property.'

'But what will you do? You know you're welcome to stay but…'

'I'll do what lots of people in my situation do, Mum. I'll

work it out. Start again.' Telling her that I'd emailed my CV to Claire Farrel to pass on might have been a forward step too far for Mum.

'You're handling it all very well, sweetheart.'

'And that's a bad thing because?'

Mum pursed her lips. 'I just wonder if you're distracted at the moment.'

'Distracted by what?'

'By a very pretty little girl and her equally pretty father?'

I began stacking books with less care into the box I was in charge of. 'You were signing me up for dates with bald anglers yesterday morning, Mum,' I said sharply.

'Yes! Dates, with new people, so you didn't feel... adrift. I didn't realise that part of your decision to leave James was because you'd already spotted something that looks like greener grass.' I rolled my eyes and threw more books in. 'Amy, I just want you to be sure of your reasons—'

'I am sure of my reasons! He got another woman pregnant! Then tried to talk her into aborting their child to keep his own life all neat and tidy!'

'And what if she didn't listen to him? You never know, Amy, James might get his head around it and things might work out unexpectedly for you all.'

She did not just say that.

'And do what, Mum? Be *that* woman? Be like Petra? Or do you mean play weekend mum to James's lovechild?'

'Okay then. So what about Rohan's child. Where's her mother in all this?'

'That's different, she doesn't want a relationship with Rohan. She left him!'

'Come on, Amy. You know it's rarely that clean cut.'

Something in those last words resonated with a tiny voice in the back of my head.

'Well, I can check that this afternoon when I go over there, can't I? I was going to take the bike. Get some air.'

Mum left it at that, thankfully. I wasn't really armed with any more answers about Rohan, or Lily, or how clean cut any of it was. I only knew I was looking forward to seeing them, and beyond that…? Well, I wasn't really sure about anything.

*

The public footpath cut a track across several wheat fields towards the winding path of the Earle. The river kept me company as I trundled on towards the mill, taking care not to consume any more suicidal bugs on the way. It felt good to be down here. I'd had a nice weekend, amazingly, compromised only by the haunting thoughts of a faceless little boy spending even longer waiting for somebody to come and love him. I was trying not to think about him – splashing in the bath, playing in the sandpit, snuggling into the warmth of my arms as I read to him. Thoughts like that had almost driven me mad once before.

Carter was sitting in the grass over on the other side of

the ramp when I reached the mill, Lily standing behind him, clipping sparkly hair accessories into his fuzzy mane.

'All clear?' yelled a voice from above me.

'Clear,' Carter replied, holding Lily at her waist.

'Daddy's coming, baby girl!' Rohan launched himself down into the drop. I jumped at the sudden sound and motion beside me. It didn't matter how many times I saw them do this, it was incredible to watch. Rohan was already in the air on the other vertical, flipping his bike out from under his body. His feet found their way home just in time before the bike made contact with the wood again.

'Whoo hoo!' Carter cried. 'Not bad, me old cocker, not bad!' Lily was watching too, shielding the sun from her eyes with a pudgy hand. Rohan moved like a crazy pendulum several more times before completing his run and sliding to a halt next to me. He was panting heavily, beads of moisture glistening on his skin.

'Hey.' He grinned, teeth a perfect ice white against a face too beautiful to risk on bike stunts. I found myself grinning back, the tourist in the pink bulbous helmet.

'No detached legs today, then?' I asked. Rohan reached down and knocked the side of his knee brace.

'Not with this. The holy roller rides again.'

'What does it do?'

'Stops the leg from hyperextending. It's the first knee brace that's been custom made to fix to a prosthetic socket. All I need now is someone who'll manufacture it,' he said, gulping his breath back. 'You next.' He grabbed the front of my bike.

'Me next what?'

He bobbed his head back at the set-up behind him. I looked startled eyes at him. 'You're kidding, right?' Rohan just kept on grinning. 'On this thing? It's a relic.'

'No, on this thing,' he said, gesturing at his bike.

'No way. I can't ride that.'

'I'll ride it, you stand on the pegs.' He tapped the bar poking out from the centre of the back wheel.

I examined the primitive structure he was asking me to balance on. Then I looked up at the timber structure, rising above me like the crest of a frozen wave. 'I'm not good with height. I think I'll pass.' I smiled nervously.

'Go on, Ame!' Carter yelled across. 'He doesn't offer a backy to just anyone!' he said, lifting Lils onto his hip. He started whispering into Lily's ear.

'You go, Amy!' she called, her little voice nearly lost on the breeze.

Rohan knew he'd already won. He slipped his fingers between mine and the rusty handlebars of Mum's bike, letting it fall away from me into the grass. 'I promise I won't take you too high.' He smiled, pulling me over to him.

He ran his thumb over the back of my fingers. I'd probably drop off the very top of the ramp if he asked me to now. Thankfully, he didn't. It still wasn't my most dignified experience. He led my hands onto his shoulders.

I could feel his skin, hot beneath his black tee, hard and rounded muscles flexing under my fingers. Somehow, I managed to clamber up onto the back of his bike, and stand upright on the pegs, holding onto him. Rohan began to ride, gently at first, building height a little at a time. I braced my legs, to avoid any embarrassing knocking of knees.

'Watch her, Ro. She might barf down your back, that one.' The horizon began to fall lower and lower as we climbed the curves. That was the point I closed my eyes.

'Can you feel the wind in your hair yet?' he laughed.

'Yep.'

'Do you still have your eyes open?'

'Nope.'

I felt his shoulders moving with the movement of laughter. 'Can we stop now?' I asked in the bravest voice I could muster. I splayed my fingers out over his chest like a tree frog. It was official. I was a total wuss.

Lily was clapping when Rohan slowed us back down. I had cockle-stomach again. 'Hey, Lils,' I managed, step-ping down off the back of the bike pegs, jelly-legged and light-headed. I sat down beside Lily to let my heart regu-late itself and my legs solidify again.

Lily ducked under my chin, unclipping the helmet she'd picked out for me. She pulled it off and began smoothing my hair with the palm of her hand. I smiled to let her know her reassurance had helped.

'Right, that was entertaining,' Carter chuckled. 'I'm

gonna go help John finish off in the kitchen. It's looking good, Ame. Your design skills are better than your balance.' He laughed, turning for the mill.

'Later, bud,' Rohan called.

Lily was still stroking my hair, helping me back to a more balanced state of being. Rohan kissed her on the head and sat down beside us.

'It's going to be hard when she goes back,' he said quietly, watching her fuss over me. I knew it would be.

'Can I stand on the slide now, Daddy?' Lily asked hopefully.

'Sure, baby. While there are no bikes.' Lily ran off as far up the timber slope as she could before slithering back down it again, giggling.

'When is Meg coming for her?'

'Next Sunday. She'll be finished with Seb Barros, so she'll be taking Lils with her onto Stockholm to watch this year's games. There'll be other families out there too, kids for her to play with while her mum talks shop. We're having this barbecue gathering on Saturday, before Lils goes. You should come.'

'I'd love to.'

Rohan smiled, but there was a sadness to it.

'Maybe Lily could stay over more often? Megan seems keen for you to spend time together.'

Rohan kept his eyes on Lily playing. 'I know. Meg's always had a knack of knowing which way to nudge me.'

I'd found myself trying to dislike Meg, but I had nothing. 'It's a shame it didn't work out for you two.'

'It wasn't really Meg's fault,' he said, eyes heavy with the things he might've done differently. 'I wasn't easy to live with. Meg wanted to take care of me after my accident, I should've let her but… I didn't know how to.'

'That must have been hard for you both.'

'The months after my accident were pretty dark days. I completely lost sense of who I was. What my life was about. Having to learn everything all over again at a snail's pace – it was so frustrating. Meg didn't say that she was pregnant until after she'd moved out. I think she knew that things were muddled enough between us without us trying to convince ourselves that we could be something we weren't. I kinda freaked when she told me. I never planned on being a father, I didn't want to be responsible for another human being. But she wanted to keep the baby, so I said that I would support them, from a distance. I thought it was for the best.'

Rohan wiped his hand over his face, the faint scratchy sound of skin brushing against short whiskers. 'So what changed?' I asked, glad that Meg had made up her own mind.

'I guess I did. I saw Lily, and it was like everything came into sharp focus. That nameless phenomenon when you see your child for the first time. She was the most beautiful thing I'd ever seen. Photos through the post were never going to be enough after that.'

Lily was flopping like a ragdoll as she slipped down the arc. 'So… why only see her every fortnight? Look how much fun she's having with you!'

Rohan slipped his helmet off. 'I didn't say it wasn't tough.'

It didn't seem tough to me. 'So, see her more often. With your schedule, you could see her all the time, surely?'

'That's what's best for me, though. Not necessarily for Lily.' I frowned at him, Happiness was usually a two-way gate. 'Megan's a good mother to Lily. That's all I've ever wanted for my own kid. Meg's not like me, she's reliable, open. I'm not cut out for parenthood. I come from somewhere different than Meg. Her folks gave her a good upbringing, and they dote on Lils. They took care of them both while Megan recovered after her caesarean. Most of the places I grew up, it was every man for himself. It kinda stays with you.'

'But those things don't have to make the wrong kind of difference, Rohan. Not if you don't let them.'

'Don't kid yourself, Amy. Everyone is affected by their childhoods in one way or another. Before I got to Arthur's, I lived at *twenty-three* different addresses. Even now, I don't stay in one place for more than a few years.' He shrugged. 'I guess I don't want Lily to have to deal with that part of me. It's not her fault. I can't drag her around after me every time I get restless.'

'Well, I think you're cutting yourself short,' I said,

watching her have fun in the cradle of the bike ramps, the river trundling through behind her. 'Some things are worth the disruption.'

CHAPTER 32

MY FINAL WEEK of employment at Cyan Architecture
and Design had drawn to an unceremonious end. It hadn't
even felt like a week of work. Everyday we'd had lunch
together, sometimes Carter had joined us but mostly it had
been just Rohan, Lily and me, shooting the breeze over
sandwiches and conversation.

As beautiful as the mill was looking, there was a heavy
sense of finality to what had happened here since I'd first
bumped into its owner six weeks ago. It would be June,
tomorrow. New month, new start. Smarter decisions.

Another firework whistled across the sky, lighting up
the willow trees over by the river. There was still tonight.

Phil was watching Carter, DJ for the night, chunky
headphones clamped either side of his afro as he bobbed
and grooved to the beats emanating from his decks. He'd
rigged up a generator to power the strings of white light
bulbs fanning out all the way from the back of the
mill down to the edge of the millpond and up over the
grassy ridge where twenty or thirty bodies were watching
and cheering over the ramps. We were watching the last

few fireworks explode in the night sky above us. Rohan wanted the display early on, so Lily could sleep after an evening of being proudly shown off by her dad. I hadn't seen them for the last twenty minutes. I'd thought about nothing else for at least ten of those.

Phil's eyes followed a light across the sky, her shoulders bobbing to the catchy beats throbbing in the evening air. 'This place looks stunning, Ame, and those worktops in the kitchen…' I couldn't remember the last time I'd seen Phil in jeans. She was wearing a thin grey T-shirt that slipped off her shoulder, sipping at a bottle of Bud.

'Carter polished them.' I smiled, trying not to giggle his name while she was here. 'Rohan saved a fortune using poured concrete. I didn't think they'd come up looking so good.'

I only recognised a handful of the people here. The guys on the ramps now were hardcore. Strong athletic men, flipping impossibly without pranging into one another as they passed. I wondered if they were from Rohan's old life, or this one, where I lived.

I looked around for him again. I'd already seen how good he looked tonight, in black shirt and casual jeans hanging happily from his hips.

'He's down by the pond,' Phil said drily. 'He was when I went to the loo, anyway.'

'I might just go and get something to eat,' I said, getting to my feet. Phil grinned.

'What?'

'Nothing.'

'Don't think I haven't noticed you slinking off with Carter, Philippa.'

Phil shrugged. 'My chakras respond to him.'

I ignored her and began weaving my way through the strangers, checking their faces as I loosely made my way towards the boathouse. There were some very attractive people here tonight, people always looked more attractive when they were having a good time. I hadn't known anyone congregating around the food and drink in the yard except Lee and Tristan and a few of their teenage friends, who all seemed to be doing their best to demolish the food stocks.

I could see them now, down by the boathouse on the rickety old jetty. Something snagged in my stomach as they sat there, watching the reflection of the fireworks fizzle in the water. Rohan turned to see me coming. He'd declined my earlier offer to help with preparations for the barbecue, so instead I'd played with Lily in the sprinklers, fed the ducklings with her and cut out a few dodgy-looking paper decorations using up the last of Rohan's printer paper. Having seen my issues with balance, Carter had gone up the step ladder to hang mine and Lily's contributions in the trees around the back of the mill. It looked like a snow cannon had gone off once we'd finished sending Carter up and down with them.

Rohan got to his feet as I stepped onto the jetty. Another silver shower flittered over the water.

'Hey.'

'Hey.'

'I wondered where you guys had got to.'

'Lily didn't like the noise. Thought we'd watch them from here, where it's quieter.'

I lifted my chin to take in the colours exploding between the stars in the sky and those on the millpond's surface. 'It's so beautiful,' I said absently, staring up at the riot of colour.

'It is,' Rohan agreed, his eyes as warm on me as the night air.

I resumed sky-gazing, smiling at the stars. The delicate scents of the water played against the smoke of the barbecue and fireworks on the air, then the delicate spice of Rohan's skin when I felt the soft warmth of his fingers find their way into mine. Another explosion of fireworks went off in my chest. Lily looked back over her shoulder at me, at her father's hand around mine. I knew he felt me stiffen.

Rohan held his other hand out for Lily. She came back from the water's edge to stand at my right side, reaching for my hand instead. As soon as she had it, she happily resumed sky-gazing too. We stayed that way for a few minutes, a daisy chain at the water's edge.

Rohan allowed our intertwined hands to coast over to my leg, so he could gently brush his thumb over the white cotton of my dress. 'You look beautiful tonight, Amy.'

'So do you.' I smiled to the sensation of another

flurry of internal pyrotechnics. Something inside my chest began to inflate.

'Yo, RO!' Max called from up by the mill. 'You're up, bud. The guys want to see this new brace of yours, see if you're any slower than usual.' He laughed, his white-blond hair like a beacon to guide us home.

Rohan shook his head, laughing to himself. 'Cheeky blighter. In his *dreams* am I slower than him. Are you coming to watch?' he asked.

'If you promise not to make me join you?' I scowled.

'Scout's promise.' He grinned, leading us off the jetty.

'You were not in the Scouts,' I said dubiously.

'I was, got the badges and everything. Dib dib… dob dob.'

I bounced my hip into him. 'You weren't, were you?' I asked, hoping I wasn't the only one incapable of success-fully earning a full arm of insignias.

'Nah.' He laughed. 'Too busy learning how to break my bones.'

He held onto my hand all the way back up into the yard where dressed-down revellers were helping themselves to beers from the ice buckets and food from the grill. Lily was lagging. Rohan's hand slipped from mine as she ran around me to be carried by her father. We walked on over the embankment, and once again I felt the tenderness of his fingers through mine. He didn't let go of me until we'd made it through those brave enough to dance on the grass, Carter demonstrating his yoga talents watched possessively by Phil, and the bike enthusiasts watching the show.

Lily was yawning when we finally reached the ramps. Only then did Rohan let go of my hand, passing Lily to me so that she snuggled into my shoulder. She was beginning to slump in my arms, tiredness overcoming her.

'Daddy's just going to show them how it's done, baby girl, and then we'll go for a cuddle in bed, okay?'

Lily nodded vacantly. Rohan leant in and laid a kiss on her head, then unexpectedly, his lips chastely pressed a kiss on mine.

That inflated thing inside of me popped like a confetti bomb. Every nerve ending, from my lips to my toes, tingling.

He pulled back, checking my reaction. I reminded myself to breathe again. He smiled that glorious smile beneath hazel eyes, and disappeared into the crowd of bodies.

By the time my brain had regained control of all five senses, Rohan was ready to make his first drop.

I whispered softly against Lily's ear, 'Look, sweetie; look at what your daddy can do.' Rohan threw himself into another crazy display to the whoops and claps of his friends. There was a new fearlessness in him, something released from its tether and allowed to soar. I knew there'd been a sense of triumph in the knee brace he and Carter had finished working on. Nearly every time their paths had crossed around the mill this week, there'd been some flutter of conversation about patents and how they might get the brace out where it could be useful, in rehabilitation centres and military facilities, or even just other sporting arenas where horrific accidents weren't enough to kill the taste these guys had for adrenalin. Rohan hadn't had any injuries for a while now, the knee brace had liberated the way he rode, and he wanted to share that.

Lily wasn't so engrossed with her father's talents and was slipping in and out of sleep. I rocked her slowly, smoothing away the hair from her face, kissing her lightly on the head. I studied her perfect features. Such a precious gift. It was hard to comprehend how so many like her were in need of homes.

'He's back,' purred a honeyed voice, from the crowd behind me. Another appreciative spectator. I kept my eyes trained on him, wondering how many of these people had known Rohan before his accident, and how incredibly gifted he must have been if losing his leg had made him any lesser an athlete.

Something clicked repeatedly near to my right shoulder. I turned and was greeted by a chunky black zoom lens and a scruffy chignon of blonde hair. Megan took a few more action shots before turning her pale blues eyes on me.

'You really did keep an eye on them, didn't you?' She smiled, slipping the camera strap over her arm. She held her hands out to me for her child. I swallowed, knowing that my cheeks were on fire. Lily whimpered as I passed her to her mother, the indentation of my wrinkled dress on her cheek. Megan looked at me as if she could see the imprint Lily had left on me too, and just like that, I was redundant again.

CHAPTER 33

ROHAN HAD BEEN almost as surprised as I had to see Megan there watching him. Actually, that wasn't true. I couldn't have been more surprised if it'd been the cockle man standing next to me, bronzed and bleached by the Spanish sun. I'd managed to stay there next to her until Rohan had finished on the bikes. I'd been hiding out in the yard ever since, behind the trestle-table stacked with cider kegs and burger baps.

Carter had said he could run me home earlier. Trouble was, I hadn't seen either him or Phil for nearly an hour now. For added measure, I'd left my phone upstairs, where Rohan and Megan had disappeared an hour ago.

She hadn't been due until tomorrow. That was the first thing Rohan had said as I stood there, flip-flops glued to the grass while I kept thinking up exit lines.

Megan had been perfectly pleasant throughout. She'd flown in from Barcelona a day early, and wanted to take Lily to see her parents for a couple of nights before they both flew off to Stockholm. Rohan hadn't been ready for Lily to go home, but Megan had pointed out that she was already asleep, and if she took her now, he could enjoy the rest of the night without having to keep the noise down. I hadn't left my spot, they had and had gone off to gather Lily's things together.

'Hey!' someone shouted, jumping up on me from behind. I nearly choked on a piece of bap.

'Phil! Don't do that, jeez.'

'Okay, okay… I'm sorry.'

'Where have you been?'

'Around the front, by the waterwheel. Cart's doing extreme yoga dares round there. He's hilarious. And *very* supple,' she said salaciously.

'Have you been drinking something harder than beer?'

'I had a couple of Carter's shots for him. He's not used to drinking but still, he's pulling some pretty impressive positions. Some of the kids have dared him to down a few shots between each of the poses. That one-legged king pigeon was by far the least expected spectacle of the night.' She grinned.

'Carter's drinking? But we need a ride home.'

'Oh, that's okay. Vicky and Molly are going to drop us.'

'Who are Vicky and Molly?'

'Tall? Friendly? Both kinda Icelandic-looking? I guess you might've noticed them if the *other* blonde hadn't shown up, huh?' I lobbed the rest of the bun in the bin and found one last remaining beer in the ice bucket.

'Sorry, Phil. But I'm having this.'

'That bad?' I pinged the lid off and took my first drink since The Attic. What was I even expecting to happen here? Rohan and I were different in every sense. 'I hate to say it, hon, but that girl is not over him. I think you have a fight on your hands.'

I took a great glug from the bottle. Megan had been territorial tonight. Only a little, but it was there. 'If she's interested, there won't be any fight, Phil. Megan's got it covered here, I think.' I had nothing to compete.

'And what about what you want? Or Rohan?'

'What about what Lily wants?'

'Lily's not your responsibility, Ame. You are.'

'I wonder if Petra's friends said the same thing to her, Phil, before she ran off into the sunset with my father,' I said, shaking my head.

'Petra and your dad are happily married, Ame. It's not neat and tidy, but it's genuine.'

A few people began trickling over the hill towards us. Some of them muttered a friendly 'goodnight' on their way past, then two svelte twenty-something blondes beamed at Phil.

'Are you guys ready?' the one with the band of flower-buds across her forehead asked.

'Ready?' Phil asked me.

'Absolutely,' I said, glugging again. We were crunching a path across the yard towards the timber walkway over the water when a man's voice called down to us from the balcony.

'You running out on me, Cinders?'

The light from the lanterns along the walkway didn't quite reach his face. The two blondes giggled quietly.

'I think he's talking to you,' Phil whispered, loud enough that the people still in the meadow probably heard.

'Er… Micky and Vick—, Vicky and Molly are giving us a ride.' More soft giggling.

'Who? Micky, Vicky, Molly and who?' I could hear the smile in his voice. 'Sounds crowded. Why don't I run you home?'

'Have you been drinking, Juliet?' Phil called up to him, sniggering.

'Not a drop, *Mercutio*. I thought my daughter would be here, so…' His voice turned back to me. 'I'm good and boring if you want that lift.'

In the light of the lanterns, Phil was grinning at me. 'Okay!' she yelped. 'You're right, too crowded. Rohan will take you home. And tell your friend he owes me a ride in his campervan!' she declared, planting a kiss on my cheek and running off along the walkway. Vicky and Molly giggled and followed her, leaving me standing there like a turnip.

An eerie peace settled around me again. His voice cut through it like a sickle. 'Would you like to come up? This is some view up here.'

The moon had burst over the millpond like a radiant pearl, suspended in black water. He'd gone when I looked back up there.

I looked back across the black waters and a shock of goose bumps raced over my skin. Tomorrow would be a new month, I remembered.

*

Inside, the mill was a palette of shadows. I flip-flopped across the hall, finding the chunky newel post with my memory and took the stairs up onto the minstrel's gallery. It was deathly quiet.

I slowed as I crossed the landing, past Lily's abandoned room, tentatively slipping from the darkness into the greyer light of Rohan's bedroom. The balcony doors were wide open, soft light spilling in through them from the lanterns below and moon above. I stepped out onto the balcony, and felt him move behind me.

'Now the work's done, I've been trying to think of another reason to keep you here,' he said quietly, his breath catching on the back of my shoulder.

I swallowed in case I croaked my reply. 'And did you find one?' My heart was palpitating in my ribcage.

He breathed deeply behind me. 'Do I need a reason?' He ran his fingers over the back of my shoulder, a current of goose bumps chasing them down along my arm, around the curve of my elbow.

He held my hand, turning me into him. I could smell him, sweet and male, something faint like fire smoke clinging to his shirt.

'Where have you been?' I whispered.

If he'd been up here necking with Megan, now was the time to say.

'Meg caught me off guard earlier. We had a few things to talk over while I got Lil's things together.' No mention of necking, snogging, and/or heavy petting. Excellent.

He was coming in closer, the broadness of his chest near enough to mine that I could feel his body heat. A rattle of heavy footfall shot over the walkway below us. I tensed. Laughter and more running footsteps followed the first, pattering away towards the boathouse. Rohan looked over the balcony handrail.

'It's just the kids, messing around.' The silhouette of his face was still pointed towards the water.

This time, the noise was more conspicuous. A dull thud and then disturbance on the surface of the pond. Rohan let out a breath. 'Tristan? Whatever you're doing, knock it off. No messing near the water.'

More rumblings of distant laughter.

'It's only me, Ro!' squeaked Carter. His voice carrying through the darkness. Rohan was trying to make him out in the shadows. There was no one on the pale stones of the path.

'Cart?' Rohan called, his voice sharpening.

'It's all right, Ro! John's fixed her up a treat!'

'He's in the boat,' Rohan yelped, darting out past me. I looked out, to the sounds of clumping wood and Carter's giggling. I ran out after Rohan, following him through the dark mill and down towards the jetty. He was there before

I could catch him up, pulling at his shoes, unbuckling his jeans. I could see now, Carter was floating out towards the middle of the millpond, the little boat the lads had helped John refurbish wobbling under him.

'He can't swim, can he?' I asked.

'Like a lead weight,' Rohan said, holding onto the worry in his voice.

'Don't try to stand, Carter!' I cried, watching him fumble to his knees in the moonlight. 'How deep is this?'

Rohan was pulling at his prosthesis, releasing it from its fixing. 'About two of me,' he said, pulling off the lining sock from his stump. I could feel the panic rising.

'What are you going to do?'

'If the oars are in, I'll row him back. If not, I'll have to try to push the boat back with him in it.'

'But what if he doesn't stay in it?' I asked, bewildered.

'Then you're gonna need to call for help. I won't be able to keep him afloat by myself, Amy.' Rohan pushed himself up and wearing only his shirt and briefs dived into the ominous waters. Carter was still rocking the boat – laughing – oblivious to the danger he was in.

I watched Rohan make it steadily across the pond to him, the moonlight sporadically catching his arms as they sliced through the water. I scanned the perimeter for a life ring, or another person. There was nothing. Carter's head popped up from the edge of the rowing boat. He flopped a hand, curiously into the water. Rohan was calling to him in between strokes. Carter was going to go in. Before anyone could get to them, Rohan would be trying to hang onto him, alone.

I could hear the boat rocking clumsily as I scrambled through Rohan's jean pockets for his phone. Nothing. The panic was rising.

I was a strong swimmer, had clocked up hours of lengths at the gym pool. How strong I'd be in a freezing-cold mini-lake, I wasn't sure but I wasn't leaving one or both of them to disappear into these black waters while everyone partied on oblivious in the meadow.

My dress was thin enough, I kicked off my flip-flops and dived in off the jetty.

As soon as my head speared the water, I understood the danger. The cold was like being crushed by a giant hand, my lungs withering down into two shrivelled husks. I gasped against the sensation, breaking into long strides through the water, trying to leave the shock behind me. Rohan had reached the boat, and was pushing Carter back into it.

'What are you doing?' Rohan shouted.

'Helping,' I gasped, trying not to let my teeth chatter. Something reedy tickled my feet. I kicked my legs, trying to climb through the water away from it. 'Let's get this boat back,' I said, swimming around to the other side. Carter flopped back into the boat. Another reed stroked at me. 'Come on,' I yelped. 'Let's go.'

Rohan didn't say another word, moving around to my side where slowly and gradually, between three good legs we somehow began to press the boat through the freezing water. It took at least twice the time to get it back to shore but somehow, silent and shivering, we did it. Rohan crouched awkwardly, panting in the shallow water, trying to wedge the boat safely onto the shore. Eventually, the boat stopped trying to slip free of its stony mattress. We sat there, exhausted, shivering and breathless, beside Carter out cold in his wooden bed.

Rohan's things were still dumped on the jetty. 'I'll tell you what,' he said, finally breaking the sombre silence. His breathing had nearly levelled out. 'You get my leg, then I'll get the towels?' Despite the trauma of the last twenty minutes, I could see his smile in the moonlight. I don't know why, call it the effects of jumping into a freezing millpond and rescuing a berk in a boat, but all the feelings I'd had in my chest tonight suddenly grouped, and erupted as laughter.

*

I'd watched Rohan tending to his friend as I continued to drip from beneath my towel all over the boathouse floor. Finally we squelched in silence back up to the mill, where Rohan had a shirt for me to change into and a hot shower if I wanted it.

Something had hardened in him as he'd pulled Carter from his jeans, wet from being manhandled by a soaked-through friend. I'd tried to hide my shock when I saw Carter's legs, covered in thick angry scarring, the kind anyone would know had been left by horrific burns. Rohan was too busy concentrating on his own thoughts to notice anyway.

He wasn't holding my hand now, as we walked quietly up to the mill.

'Are you okay?' I finally dared.

'Are *you* okay?' he countered.

'I'm fine, Rohan. Just glad our *Baywatch* bit didn't go wrong,' I said, trying to lighten the mood.

'They can't pull that kind of crap without seriously risking something disastrous,' he said sharply. 'Why are kids so stupid?'

We were all guilty of that.

Rohan was still lost in thought as we slipped past the smouldering embers of the barbecues into the darkness of the mill. The music had quietened over the far side of the meadow now. I left my flip-flips at the foot of the staircase and quietly padded up behind him.

He moved off to the concealed dressing area as I ambled over to the balcony doors, to see if it still looked tranquil out there now. It struck me how silly my phobia was. I was fine up here, if I stayed back from the edge, but smaller insignificant heights had my bones turning to rubber. The millpond did look more sinister now as I realised how far into the expanse of water we'd been. I shivered at the thought of those reeds, lassoing my ankles and dragging me to the bottom until the last bubble of life raced from my lips to the surface.

Rohan moved behind me, the towels in his arms only partially preventing the moonlight from catching on some of the contours of his stomach, riding the definition of his neat broad body. He said nothing as he stepped in to me, slipping the damp towel from my shoulders until it fell to my feet.

I waited, nervously now, for him to offer me the towel, but he was transfixed, a look of determination and uncertainty vying for ownership of his features. A flittering sensation crept up my neck. Rohan was too good-looking for just one person, too beautiful, and completely unchartered territory.

He set the towels down on the floor, holding me there with those incredible eyes. I heard myself swallow. I couldn't remember James ever looking at me like that. Thoughts of him hiked up my unease. Rohan was out of my league. What could this utterly intoxicating man want from me that he couldn't get anywhere else? I hadn't been enough for James, how could I possibly be enough for a guy like Rohan?

'You're so beautiful, Amy,' he said quietly, his hand finding its way to the wet cotton clinging to my hip. Stood here, bedraggled in pond water, I almost laughed, but he pulled me into his body, pressing the warmth of his torso against the chill of my wet dress.

My breathing was becoming shallower. He was leaning down towards me. I shouldn't be here, I hardly knew him.

You were with James for nearly nine years. And you hardly knew him. Objection... denied.

I could leave. If I wanted to. Rohan was taking it slow, so I could feel every drop of adrenalin flooding my veins, fight or flight... but his mouth was hovering just over mine. I knew that once he touched down, it was all over for me. A heartbeat passed, and Rohan pressed his mouth to mine. My heart jumped into my throat. I could feel the thudding in his chest as his mouth began to delicately greet mine. I realised that I was kissing him right back. He tasted sweet, new... a new flavour to hold against my lips. Fingers fanned out around my waist as I fell into that kiss, deeply and surely, exploring him with the edge of my tongue. He was waiting, waiting for me to welcome him in. I ran my arms through his, pulling his broad hot back into me. His skin rippled with goose bumps as I pressed more of my wet front against him. He responded, heightening his fervour and forcing his eager mouth deftly over mine.

'I've waited so long for this,' he whispered against my lips. My hand ran up the contour of his back, rising over the breadth of his shoulders, up into all that glorious dark hair for weeks I'd imagined the touch of, the smell of. I let my fingers slip through it, savouring every silky strand.

Rohan bent down and slipped an arm behind my legs, where my flimsy dress clung to my knees. He scooped me up, his lips finding mine again. I wanted to kiss him, and kiss him and never stop finding more of that taste. I was still tasting him when he lowered me down, into the soft furs of his bed throws.

I wanted him. Wanted him with every nerve ending in my body. He knelt down at the edge of the bed beside me, his fingers nimbly following the trail of buttons of my dress. I watched the musculature of his stomach bunch and release in the moonlight as he undid me. I sat up as he neared the end of his task, slipping out of the straps, throwing the wet fabric away to the floor. I couldn't see enough of him, only that which the slivers of the moon allowed. He watched me, I thought, looking down onto my all but naked body. I started to consider what he thought of me – what he thought of the few tiny stretch marks, silvered against my tummy; what he would think when he saw… His hands slipped into a burst of steadied action, pulling at the fly of his jeans. He pushed every-thing down, one merciful shaft of subdued light, stealing my attention from my own imperfections, guiding me to the gift he was about to give me, long and full and ready. I think I'd actually forgotten to breathe. My heart was that little bird again, crazily fluttering against the bars of my ribcage. He leant over me, kissing me deeply again and his hands rounded my thighs sliding fingers over the edge of me. He pulled the last stitch I was wearing down, over my knees, slipping my knickers from my feet.

His hands felt cool, gliding over the swell of my breasts where he next shared the sweetness of his mouth.

He pulled softly at my nipple, gently teasing with his

teeth. I shuddered beneath him. I couldn't wait any longer, pulling him up over me, clamping my thighs around him, wanting him to sink home. Rohan couldn't wait either. I felt the warm press of him against me, against my readiness, a sweet sharp push and…

My breath caught in my chest as Rohan forced himself heavily into me, sliding rhythmically into everything I wanted to share with him. When I could breathe again, I showered his chest with wet kisses, my fingers exploring the lines of his hips, following them down to our most eager parts before they danced over to his back, pulling him into me harder and harder.

Rohan made love to me with the strength and skill I'd seen him apply to everything he did – able and talented, I felt as if sex had been something I might have entirely missed the point of for these last years. Phil was right, hearts and toes… Rohan left everything of me on fire.

*

After we'd laid beside each other awhile, panting and satiated on the expanse of his bed, the first doubts began to creep in. I'd just jumped into bed with another man after a huge emotional trauma. And not just any man. Rohan was a major flight risk, probably not the best person to invest what little trust I had left in me. Well, it wasn't like I was holding out for a big white wedding, at least.

I listened to the differing rhythms of our lungs, trying

to steady themselves, and realised I had to think of something to say to him.

Rohan was already propped on his elbow watching me think. He began to smile, I found myself mimicking him, and then unexpectedly… the giggling erupted. Rohan's bedroom filled with the rapturous sound of childish hysterics.

'Well, well,' he laughed at me.

'Shut up!' I said, whacking him with a pillow.

Giggling turned out to be much more enjoyable than awkward pillow-talk. Giggling, I remembered, I was pretty good at. Rohan pulled the covers up over our bodies, nestling me into the crook of his shoulder. The aftershocks of our laughter made way for a more relaxed silence, as the buzzing in my brain gently subsided.

'What happened to Carter?' I asked, running my fingers idly over the flat of his chest. His burns must have been agonising when he suffered them.

Rohan rolled onto his back beside me. 'He got pissed and let Tristan and the lads talk him into a boat ride.'

'No, I meant to his legs?'

I felt Rohan's chest rise and fall deeply. 'Another case of kids making stupid decisions,' he said wearily. 'He was fooling around, playing with matches in his granddad's garden shed. There was petrol in there, he messed up, tried to put it out.' I winced at the image I'd held on to of those angry pink scars. 'He was just being a boy, I guess, but his grandpa couldn't cope at the time so that's how he came to be at the foster home.'

I looked at the eeriness of the light, falling in through the balcony doors. Tonight was a night for pushing boundaries, being brave. 'And… how did you come to be there?'

Rohan's chest didn't rise so much this time.

'I guess my mum couldn't cope either. I never met my dad, but the guy Mum was living with when they took me away, he wasn't good for us. He liked a drink, could be a mean old bastard. Not to me, but to her. They told her to get rid of him for our good, but she didn't. She kept getting more chances but in the end, they took me. They had to.'

'I'm sorry, Rohan. Did you ever see her again?'

'I tried. Once I'd turned eighteen. Art helped me find a number for her. So I called her, told her I was the kid she hadn't seen for ten years. She agreed to meet me but…'

'She didn't show?' I asked, choked on hope that I was wrong. Rohan gave a small shake of his head. 'Maybe something happened?' I tried. 'Did you call her again?'

'I called her. I called her over and over. I could have gone around to her house, but I didn't want to, you know, pressure her. Then eventually, I received a letter through the post. It said not to contact her again.' My heart sank for him. 'I get the message much quicker these days.' He smiled. 'It doesn't take long for me to stop ringing.'

'Except where's Lily's involved,' I said, trying to put something of warmth back.

Rohan smiled automatically. 'She's changed me,' he said, blown away by the truth of it.

'I did say. Children have the ability to do that. Even after the briefest time.'

Rohan had stopped tracing his fingers over my skin. He took a few strands of my hair between his fingers instead, quietly gathering his thoughts.

'Lil took two days to come out of her mum. Eventually they gave Meg a caesarean,' he said, sweeping his finger through the waves on my pillow. 'Her scar is like yours.'

The instinct was to shift to something else, to play down the significance of that neat line over my groin. Truths were easier to ignore in the dark, after all, like a sandpit tucked away in the shade.

I rolled over, sitting my hands under my cheek so I could see him better.

'I had a little boy,' I said quietly. 'He would have been five years old this August.' I found smiling somehow kept at bay the other things my face might want to do. Rohan remained motionless. 'He was born nine weeks early. I had what the doctors called an abruption. My placenta had come away from the wall of my uterus so he wasn't getting what he needed. He'd been moving around a lot, so I hadn't been that worried,' I added, succumbing to the weight of my ignorance back then. 'They told me afterwards that he was probably moving so much because he was in distress.'

I tried to smile, but the muscles were failing me. I began chewing inside my lip instead.

'I never thought about being a mother until I fell pregnant. At first, I didn't know if I was ready. I was more worried about changing my lifestyle than anything else.' Another ignorance I wish I could go back and change. 'They tried to save him with the section, but—' I still couldn't say it out loud. I took a deep breath as Rohan tried to soothe me with gentle eyes. 'They couldn't stop me bleeding. I lost a lot of blood. They decided to give me the best chance and took my uterus.'

Rohan was silent for a few moments while I relived that night. I'd woken up in a side room, James and my mother stricken with loss.

'What was his name?' Rohan said through the darkness.

I heard myself take a deep breath to help.

'We named him Jacob,' I said shakily.

'*Jacob*. It's a good name, Amy.'

I smiled and nodded, feeling a warm spill run from the corner of my eye onto the pillow. Rohan caught it with his thumb. I laughed then.

'Talk about a party killer!' I said, trying to bat away the feelings brewing in my chest.

Rohan didn't smile, watching me carefully as I regained control. He dried off the wet run over the bridge of my nose.

'I think anyone who adopts a child is an amazing person, Amy.'

'I do too. But it's so tough. Since Jacob, it feels like all I've thought about is being a mother. James isn't all bad; I changed when we tried for the adoption. Do the right thing, say the right thing, live the right way. Now I'm tired out from it. I don't want to pretend I'm someone I'm not any more.'

'So don't. Be yourself. That's enough.' I pulled a deep breath in through my nose. 'It's enough for me,' he added.

He leant forward and kissed me softly on my lips. I watched him as our kiss broke.

'*Enough* has a habit of changing though, Rohan,' I said quietly. 'You didn't want Lily to stay here a couple of weeks ago and tonight you were trying to get Meg to leave her here while she goes to Sweden.'

Rohan's eyes hadn't left mine. 'I guess you're right. Lily has changed me. I do want her here with me, I can't help it. I want to see her wake up groggy-headed in the morning, and when she finds something new she doesn't understand – I want to explain it to her. I want it all. But more than anything, I want her to know what it is to have a stable family life.'

I watched the pieces clicking into place for him as he thought them through. I wanted those things too, but maybe Rohan knew even more than I did just how precious they were.

I slipped my hand over his side, burying my head under his chin, the steady thrum of his heart beating against me. Tonight had been wonderful, a burst of colour amidst some very grey days, but where did I go from here?

'Do you know what I could eat right now?' he asked, stroking a figure of eight over my shoulder.

I stayed where I was, waiting for the answer to vibrate through his chest.

'A knickerbocker glory!' he exclaimed. 'I haven't eaten one of those since I was a kid.'

I smiled against his chest. 'I think they call them sundaes now, but they're never as grand.'

'A knickerbocker glory would rock right now.'

'You know, there's a new parlour, in the city not far from my office. *Old* office. You should take Lily there, she'd love it.'

'How about we try it out first, before Lily gets back from Stockholm? We could even go tomorrow? Just the two of us?'

I rolled away from him to better see his face. 'Like… on a date?' I asked.

Rohan grinned through the twilight. 'Exactly like a date. I'll even pay.'

CHAPTER 34

I awoke to the gentle call of birdsong and the tiny motes of dust, dancing in through the balcony doors, laced in the golden glow of morning sun. Rohan's arm was underneath me, my hair feathered out around us both. I carefully tilted my head to sniff whether it smelled of pondweed or not, but all I could smell was him, in my hair, on the sheets, on my skin.

I tried not to glance at him as if a lingering look might wake him, but I couldn't move my eyes once they'd found him. His eyebrows were softer as he slept, angular and perfect over the closed lids I knew held their own treasures. I followed the straight line of his nose, down past the beginnings of stubble to the contours of his lips – his Cupid's bow that last night had found its mark.

I didn't want to get up, but I was sufficiently out of practice with these kinds of situations that with no make-up, toothbrush or conditioner, slipping away quietly seemed best. I delicately pushed aside the furred throw so as not to wake him and began fishing around on the floor for my underwear. I found my dress hanging over the bath tap, draped across the floor as if I'd been waving it like a white flag last night – *I give up, my life's a mess, but good news! I'm crazy about you!*

I pulled the muddied fabric away, revealing Rohan's prosthetic leg propped up beneath it like a practical joke.

That was new. Knickers, jeans, dress, *leg* – amongst other things strewn across the wide polished floorboards. I looked back at him snoozing, all soft and snug. One prosthetic limb and I was thinking of his body all over again. That perfect, beautiful breath-taking body. It was all I thought about as I dressed, as I found my phone and sneaked downstairs to call my taxi.

*

Mum was flapping.

She hadn't said much when she caught me fishing around beneath the boot-scraper on her doorstep for the spare key, or when I'd bustled in past her for the taxi fare from her money tin. She'd gone to say something when I'd emerged singing from the shower but then had thought better of it and just rolled her eyes instead.

'Can't you just go online, and find out how many names you have?' I asked, sinking my teeth into a second round of buttery toast.

'No, it doesn't tell you that bit until they're all counted,' she said, wrinkling her nose over her glasses at the small telephone screen in front of her.

Today was the last day for her e-petition. Tomorrow the community centre would likely be reclaimed for the suits and the likes of Tristan and Lee would have even more time on their hands. Although once Rohan had dealt with them, something told me they might actually keep their noses clean – at least for a while. Even the reminder of my impromptu moonlight dip couldn't sour my morning's nirvana.

'Mum, you've done all you can. Try to relax.'

'Like you, you mean?' she asked accusingly. 'You've got a spring in your step today.' I knew it wouldn't be long.

'I have a date later. I thought you'd be pleased. No sign-up fee required.' I bit into another triangle.

'With Rohan, I suppose?'

I waited until I'd finished chewing. 'Yes.'

'And will Lily be tagging along?'

'No.'

Her expression softened. 'Just be careful, Amy. Where children are involved, hmm? Petra never gave your father a chance. You're jumping from a long and eventful relationship straight into another… well, *family*, of sorts.'

'I haven't jumped anywhere. In fact, I've been rolling around with stabilisers on for *years*, being careful about everything. I just want to let go a little, leave things to chance for a while. I think it might be *good*.'

'Sweetheart, I want you to have fun. Lord knows you

deserve some. But don't rush into a new relationship. Give yourself some time to find out who you are on your own. Get to know yourself again.'

'I am getting to know myself, Mum! He makes me feel like… pushing my boundaries! Like it doesn't matter if I'm good at my job, or if I don't watch what I eat in case it all piles on, or if I make a complete fool of myself! He's…' I thought about how easy it was with him, despite all the warnings tripping off in my head. 'He's pretty great.'

'Amy, he doesn't know you!'

'He knows enough. He knows I hate cucumber, and that I'm useless with height, and that birds freak me out… *that I can't have children*. He knows all the things I don't want people to know about me, and he still called me this morning.'

'It's not just about him, though, Amy. Or you,' she said, setting her phone down on the counter. 'His child is only young, he and her mother can't have been separated that long!'

'Four years, Mum!'

'Just, give it some time. If it's meant to be, he'll find his way back to you.'

'I don't want to wait for the stars to align for me any more, Mum, it never happens! I just want to have some little snippets of happiness where I can find them. Is that so unreasonable?'

Mum puffed at an auburn corkscrew hanging in front of

her glasses. 'No, sweetheart. It's not.' She reached across and pulled me into a bear hug, rocking me like she did when I was a child. She kissed the side of my head. 'Just… be careful, Amy. I don't think I can bear seeing you hurt any more.'

I squeezed my arms around her. 'Will it make you feel any better if you know we're going to an ice-cream parlour this afternoon? Not a jeweller's?'

She laughed a little. 'Do you want to borrow my car?'

'Are you kidding? It's a first date, I'm trying to look *cool* here, Mum.'

*

Rohan had offered to pick me up, but I wanted to check Carter was okay, and help them with the clean-up operation after last night. I took the same route along the river, cutting across the meadow and the black smouldering patch of earth where the fire had been, following the strings of light bulbs all the way down to the grassy ridge encircling the mill. I left the bike there, walking down the other side across the yard towards the back double doors into the kitchen. They were opened out, and I was just about to step through them when the fervent quacking of ducks on the pond caught my attention. They only came over here when there was food in it for them. I glanced over at the beginnings of the walkway, sweeping around the mill's waterside wall. A piece of bread flew through the air towards several little ducklings, Lily's arm just peeping into view.

I opened my mouth to call out to her, then stopped myself. Megan would be here somewhere too. I heard her voice then, further around along the wooden walkway. I don't know what made me hang back, pondering whether to go back to the river and wait there a while or just burst around the corner with my best 'hello, everyone'.

'Just think about it, Ro. Think about who could see what you've created! All of the key players out there, the people they could put you in touch with!' Megan's voice was imploring, hopeful.

'I haven't been in the game for *four years*, Meg. Most of them won't even remember my name.'

'Of course they will! Ro, I've seen you out there! You've still got it. Think of the publicity you would have, the guy who came back from his injuries, better, *stronger* than before!'

'I don't want to be a poster boy, Meg!'

'Ro… just think about it? For Lily? Look, we don't fly until Tuesday morning; you have your passport, right?' I felt as if I'd just dived into the millpond again, cold and overwhelmed. Megan's voice lowered. 'It would be nice for us to spend some time together too, Ro. Catch up on old times.'

Thud, thud, thud. The sensation in my chest was suddenly so strong I wondered if Lily would hear it.

Rohan's voice dropped too. 'Meg, look… you were right. I do love having Lily around. I do want to see her more, spend much more time together, but—'

'Lily needs more than a part-time father, Ro. We could be a unit, a solid unit if you'd let us.' I heard her feet move, into him probably. Something inside my chest clunked, about to fall off its hinge. 'We could all have the best of both worlds, Ro. Time together and time on our own projects. Look at this place, Lily couldn't want for a more perfect childhood setting. This could be our base. There are good transport links and I've already looked at the local schools. Everything you didn't have, Ro, you can give her now. *We* can give her.'

'And what about us, Meg? You can't just put all of this on the table and think that's all it'll take. Have you forgotten how it was?'

'We've changed, Ro. I know I have, and I *definitely* know that you have. No one else could give her what we could, Ro.'

'We give her everything she needs already, Megan. We've made sure of that.'

'And what about long term, Ro? When her needs change? You know, she's been asking about a baby sister.' Megan laughed, making light of the suggestion. 'Imagine that, Ro, Lils always having someone, like you and Cart.'

I found myself turning slowly, the stone base of the mill cool against my back. Everything felt fuzzy, hot.

I listened to Lily's footsteps hammering along the gangway to her parents as I crossed the yard, knew how perfect they would look standing there together at the water's edge. Lily with her mother's hair and eyes almost as bewitching as her father's. A unit. A family. Everything Rohan wanted for her.

CHAPTER 35

GUY SUNK HIS teeth into another bite of the baguette he'd just constructed after his merciless fridge raid. I couldn't see the point in driving Harry around the neighbourhood to settle him off to sleep with the sorcery of engine vibration, only to bring him here to Mum's once mission had been accomplished. Other than the noises Guy made as he ate and the low drone of the TV, the lounge was subdued, suiting my mood just marvellously.

The news was about as uplifting as usual: death, war, displacement, politics. All the things that should have reminded me to be grateful for my lot. The presenter promised a weather update after the following sports headlines, the screen flashing through to footballers limbering up on a floodlit field.

'How come you're home tonight, anyway? Thought you'd be over at the Bionic Man's,' Guy said, picking a piece of ham off his shirt. Rohan had called yesterday afternoon after I hadn't shown for our ice-cream date. The miserable ride home had given me enough time to prepare a whole speech about why it was better that we were

friends, how I probably shouldn't be rushing into anything new, a handful of other paper-thin reasons that didn't
touch on what I really wanted to say – that I knew what
Megan wanted and that I couldn't blame her for wanting
it; that despite the way my normal faculties seemed to shut
down just by being in the same vicinity as him I couldn't
act on it the way I wanted to; that Lily deserved more than
a fully-fledged attempt from me to steal away her father.

He'd never got to hear a word of it, of course. I'd taken
the coward's way out, again, and had made up an excuse
about helping mum with her e-petition.

'So what is the crack with you and Terminator?' Guy
said, looking at me over his sandwich. 'Mum said you've
been getting it on with him? I like him more than that
knobhead you were stuck with before.' Guy ran the butt
of his baguette around the mess on his plate. 'Who d'you
reckon would win in a fight: knobhead or the Terminator?'

'Do you want another sandwich, Guy?' I asked, thinking of other, more violent ways to occupy his mouth. He
ignored me.

'I like him. Like what he did for the grubby kid at the
fete.'

I felt the murmurings of a sinking feeling. I didn't want
to be reminded of Rohan's virtues right now. They were
already cast into my memory, into every place I'd felt his
touch the night before last. It already seemed a distant
event. The ghost of a sensation ran along my collar bone
as my body remembered his kisses there.

Guy startled me. 'What was his last name again? I swear I know him.'

I rubbed the back of my neck, the television screen flicking through coverage of another sporting event, eager spectators standing in the shadows of huge structures covered in advertising for energy drinks.

'Whose last name?' I mumbled, zapping the channel onto something else, a period drama with not a skate-board, BMX or adrenalin junkie in sight.

'Oi! I was watching that!'

The front door clicked open, echoing through the hall-way, a jovial commotion as Mum stepped into the house laughing and chattering enthusiastically.

'I know! And his face! Did you see it, when they had to read it out themselves?' Mum exclaimed, thrill in her voice.

'I have to say, I was quite surprised, Vivian. I think everyone in that room tonight was!' chuckled her very male companion. Guy and I looked across the lounge at one another, then to the partially open door onto the hall-way. My brother had almost completely stopped chewing as Mum crossed the hallway and popped her head around the lounge door.

'Hello, son. Harry not settling again?' she asked, regarding Guy and his armchair picnic. Harry was still strapped into his car seat, plonked on the carpet beside Guy's feet.

'How did you get on?' I asked, trying to make out

the shape of the shadow hovering in the hallway behind her.

A smile reached across her face before she answered. 'You're not going to believe it, sweetheart. Nearly four *thousand* signatures!'

'What? Four *thousand*? But, there aren't that many people in Earleswicke, are there?'

I heard a small agreeable laugh from somewhere behind Mum.

'We're part of a wider cyber community, sweetheart! Karen said the numbers jumped once she'd put the e-petition on the Twittering thing Rohan was explaining to me.'

There was that name again.

'I said he was a good lad,' came the gruff voice from the hallway.

'Jumped?' Guy guffawed. 'That's one hell of a jump, Mum. What did you do, offer free homemade cake to every signatory?' I sat up in my chair, trying to see the stranger in the hallway. The stranger who knew a *good lad* when he saw one.

Mum was shaking her head in happy disbelief. 'Guy, I couldn't tell you how it worked out to come to such a high number. All I know is, some of the other people on the site Karen put the link on passed the information around their friends and it just… *grew*.'

'And now that old fool and his council cronies have had to swallow their words! They'll lose too much face if they go back on their promises now,' the voice from the hall said.

'Come on in, John,' Mum said, stepping aside. A flat cap popped into view. John Harper looked even more like an off-duty Santa in his berry-red shirt and coffee-coloured corduroy jacket.

'John was at the meeting too,' Mum declared happily. 'All these years living in the same town and we didn't meet properly until I overheard him talking about the work he's been doing down in Briddleton. I thought, Hang on a minute! He must know my beautiful daughter. It's a small world.' She smiled, slipping the scarf from her neck.

'Well, I can see where she gets her looks from,' John said bashfully. 'Hello, young lady.' He tipped his cap.

'Hello, John,' I said, bemused.

'Your mother here tells me you've been having some bother with a sticky door?' Guy still hadn't returned to his sandwich.

'John's going to take a look at it for me,' Mum added, reading the question in Guy's face.

'I'll bet he is,' Guy muttered.

'You'll be in safe hands, Mum. John's an excellent carpenter.' Guy noted my endorsement.

'Why, thank you very much, young lady. The boss has been singing your praises too, you know. You've done a beautiful job of that place, young Bywater's very pleased with you.' John nodded at me.

'Bywater?' Guy said. 'Rohan Bywater… *Rohan Bywater* …' He was like a hound, rolling around the scent of Rohan's name.

'He's been a good lad to work for, too. I've still got a few things to finish off around the place, but he's off tomorrow, so the lad's paid me early. I told him I could wait, but—'

'He's going somewhere?' I asked, that sinking feeling starting to resemble more of a twenty-thousand-leagues-under-the-sea type of sensation.

'Oh, you've missed all the excitement today. Him and his pal with the hair have been scurrying all over the place, getting their things together for some big opportunity with that leg contraption they've been playing with. When I left there earlier, Rohan was loading his cases into his truck.'

Something somewhere between anxiety and nausea rolled inside me. He'd called me this morning, but I didn't trust myself not to make a complete U-turn and ask to meet with him. I hadn't answered the call. An hour later, I'd wimped out again. Then nothing. No more calls after that. I knew he wouldn't keep trying then, it wasn't in him any more to chase the unwilling.

'Would you like something to eat, John? I have a lovely hock of ham? I could do you a bit of salad?'

'That sounds lovely, Vivian. Heckling councillors is hungry work!' John said, led away by my mother.

I sat gazing into the emptiness, trying to find that tiny

speck of relief that somewhere, a right decision had been made. Harry stirred in his seat, his hand rubbing clumsily over his face before sleep sucked him back under.

I'd seen another two buses, this morning, both with the same advertising campaign showing the same faces, asking the same question. I knew the answer to whether I could or not, I just didn't know whether I could do it alone. I'd put my head down, run harder, but like a catchy jingle the question had found its foothold and had stayed with me throughout the day.

I didn't have the luxury of running now.

Guy was studying his phone. I thought about asking him his views on single-parenthood. Anna had said I hadn't turned out too bad from a single-parent upbringing. Guy had turned out better than me. And then there was him. Rohan. Flying the flag for triumph over adversity.

I was pretty sure Rohan would have dragged himself, aching and bruised, through every second it had taken to learn how to walk again, swim again, ride a stunt bike like a professional again. He was fearless that way.

Guy's voice burst through my thoughts. 'Rohan J. Bywater, age: thirty-six; born: Newcastle, UK; height: six foot one inches; weight: one hundred and sixty five pounds; event: Freestyle BMX; medal record: first place Double Vert 2008 G Force Games Madrid; second place Vert 2009 G Force Games Vancouver.' Guy scrolled through the rest of the information on his phone screen, eyes widening. 'I *knew* I knew him. Holy shit, no wonder he whooped my butt, the guy's a machine. Didn't think he had a Geordie accent, though.'

He didn't. His accent could've been from anywhere and nowhere.

'Do you want anything from the kitchen?' I asked, rising from my chair.

'Hang on, don't run off.'

'I'm not running off, Guy,' I said. 'I just don't want to hear your running commentary on a guy you don't really know anything about,' I added, dragging myself across the carpet.

'I know there are a *lot* of people happy to see him back on Twitter,' Guy said, reading his screen. I narrowed my eyes at him. 'Up until last week, his last tweet wasn't since…'

Four years ago.

'…four years ago.'

I left him to it. I'd made a point of not rooting around the net, inputting Rohan's name to find out just how much of a sporting career he'd had before fate had struck. He'd played it down, but I wasn't stupid. He had to have had some serious sponsors to have the sort of insurance pay-out that would have bought the mill and left enough cash to keep him and Carter afloat.

In the kitchen, Mum was chirpily running through all the DIY jobs she'd never got round to around the house while John listened attentively, stopping occasionally to nibble on the platter of food next to him. I tried not to disturb them.

'Would you get that please, sweetheart?' Mum said, turning to John. 'It's probably Lauren, my daughter-in-law, looking for her child,' she tittered.

'Get what?' I asked, just as someone knocked at the front door. I hadn't heard it before. Mum was already back hovering over John's shoulder.

Sure. It was probably Carter and Phil come to announce their unrequited love in an explosion of white doves. *Love birds*. The very term should've forewarned how my romantic life was destined to turn out. A feathery horror show with elements of window-splattering disaster. I pulled open the door, absently thinking such thoughts.

The colour of his eyes never grew any less staggering.

I was gawping, taking in his features, serious and uncertain. It was still like opening the door to a glorious pool of light I couldn't look away from.

Rohan's jaw tightened. 'I just wanted to stop by. See you before I left.'

Still gawping. 'Are you going away?' I asked, feigning my usual ignorance.

He looked at his feet, nodding to himself. 'Just for a couple of weeks,' he said, burying his hands into his jean pockets. 'It's not good timing for me, I had other things I wanted to focus on,' he said, stealing a look at me. I felt my cheeks warm. He looked regretful, as if maybe he wasn't sure about going to Stockholm. His expression changed. 'But something's come up. I wasn't expecting it to, honestly I don't think I'm ready for it, but… it's an opportunity.' I smiled and looked at my feet too. I'd staked my claim on the dino slippers.

'Sounds good. You should go for it.' I smiled, already picturing him and Megan under a Nordic sunset. Rohan wasn't saying anything. 'Well, take care.' I smiled again. 'Travel safely and, er… whatever you get up to, break a leg.' I laughed but it fell flat like a stunned blackbird.

I was still inspecting the edge of the step when the scent of that same spiced soap reached closer to me. I kept my eyes on the floor, at the battered leather boots stood either side of my ridiculous furry dinosaur claws. He ducked down, angling himself so that he just caught the edge of my mouth. That taste again, laced over my lips. I swallowed as he kissed me softly, trying not to lose my nerve and just grab onto him, pull him into me so I could kiss him frenziedly until my air ran out.

And then he broke from me. I heard him swallow before he spoke. 'You know, maybe I could not go tomorrow. Maybe I could stay instead. Go get that ice cream?' I watched him feed his fingers through mine, his thumbs exploring the soft grooves of my hands. But his hands weren't mine to hold.

'No,' I swallowed, 'you go. You should go.' I backed into the doorway. He looked unsure. I'd had no such self-control the last time he'd touched me. He ran a hand up over the back of his neck and nodded, dropping his feet back off the step.

'Can I call you when I get back?' he asked, less sure now.

I pressed my lips together and nodded politely. 'Sure.'

'Sure?' he asked.

I bobbed my head, unable to look at him again. We stood that way for just long enough that both of us knew this silence wasn't going to get any easier.

A new expression washed over him. An understanding.

'I guess I'll see you then, Amy,' he said, turning slowly for the end of the driveway. He gave me enough time to call after him, but thoughts of Lily kept me quiet.

CHAPTER 36

Two weeks of June afternoons sat in Mum's back garden trawling through design agency jobs boards had seen my skin deepen enough shades that my first official fortnight as an unemployed woman could've been spent in the Med.

Phil's skin colour never changed, she was one of those all about the preservation of youth, recoiling at the prospect of wrinkled cleavages and white triangles. I couldn't pick at her logic, she was healthier than I was, as demonstrated by her unchanged breathing into an effortless lap of Jackson's Park. I, on the other hand, had abandoned the gym long enough ago now that I was sure I could taste a little bit of blood in the back of my throat, as per my school days with the PE teacher who was a closet Paula Radcliffe fanatic.

'Claire left on Friday,' Phil breezed, striding along the path like a spring-footed antelope.

There were eight of my strides between the billowy maple trees lining the park footpaths, seven of Phil's I'd noted. I paced my breathing so I could answer without inviting another stitch. 'Yeah, I know. We had lunch last week.'

'I know. She said. When's the big interview?' Phil asked, checking her stats on her wrist watch.

I tried to take a sip from my water bottle but a good eighty per cent of the attempt ended up soaking through my vest. 'Friday. Ten thirty. I won't have too much time to sweat over it. Hopefully.'

'Well, I hope you do, and that you stink when you get in there and they won't even consider hiring you for your lacking personal hygiene.' Phil had rejected the *I'll-try-to-be-happy-for-you* bit and had stayed staunchly with *leave-and-our-friendship-will-never-be-the-same*, instead. Save for a few tears, Mum was trying much harder. I hadn't even had the interview yet.

'I probably won't get it, Phil.' I shrugged, though the movement was lost in my ungraceful jogging.

'Are you kidding? Back-breaking hours, ball-busting clients, and a few well-placed words from their newest partner? This job has your name all over it and we all sodding know it. You'll be shopping for York apartments with somewhere to park your Audi come Saturday morning.'

A little flutter of panic bothered my insides. Devlin Raines were a big deal. This job would be demanding, and difficult and all-consuming. *If* I got it. It would also be my fresh start. In exchange for an attractive package, Devlin Raines would take all of my time, and with it any room for idle reflections of ex pro-bikers, ex-partners and fruitless dreams.

Phil was on the cusp of sulking. 'How're things with Carter?' I asked, changing tack. 'I've missed not seeing him around.'

'Yeah, me too. Him getting hammered at the party gave me an excuse to cool it off for a little while.'

'But he's great, Phil!'

'I know! And I'll call him in a few weeks, we'll hook up. I just need a breather. I got a bit too into him too quickly. It was really freaky, actually,' she said, visibly blown by the effect Carter had had on her.

'I think that's okay, Phil. It's called *liking someone.*'

'I know… I just don't know that I *like* that I like him. I mean,' her voice dropped to a whisper, 'a yoga-loving hippy.' Phil looked genuinely pained. Considering her usual demeanour with men was something akin to that of a partner-munching praying mantis, she was handling her voyage of self-discovery with Carter fairly well. It seemed I was the big fat hussy in this circle. Unlike Phil, I'd already made my ultimate discovery and then had waved it off to Stockholm.

Phil and I had already agreed that Rohan was off con-versational limits until I'd got my head around what had almost happened there.

'I need a breather, Phil. Like right now,' I wheezed, let-ting all the pounding of my body move from my thighs to my lungs. I came to a giddy halt at the foot of one of the park's bridges. Phil, already at its pinnacle, stopped and jogged back down towards me. She began stretching out against the railings.

I took a long refreshing glug of water, eyeing the row of Victorian townhouses across the park. James had told me that he'd bought it, but seeing the SOLD sign hammered it home.

'He is going to be able to buy you out of the house, isn't he? Now that he's taken that on as well,' Phil said, following the direction of my eyes. James hadn't resisted telling the office of his latest bargain.

'He said he would, if it didn't sell. But the agent's already shown a few people around. It's a good family home, in a quiet cul-de-sac. They say it'll shift fairly quickly anyway.'

'Won't you miss it there?' Phil asked, knowing the varied history that went with those walls. The hopes made, and dashed, and made again.

'No. It's better this way, Phil. There's nothing here for me to work towards. The jobs pages are telling me that in clear bold print.'

'But, you've had an interview already.'

'Yes, one, Phil! I found one job that necessitated my qualifications and that was for a job-share at mid-level.'

Phil grimaced. 'Were the hours good?'

'For spending half the week dossing at home on my own? Yeah, the hours were great.'

'Well, it must work for someone, Ame, or there

wouldn't be a job-share, would there? Did they tell you anything about the person you'd be sharing with?'

'She was in the interview. She was lovely, actually. She's separated from her husband and wants to spend more time at home with her little boy. I don't think they'd had many takers for the position, the pay wasn't great. They probably wouldn't have offered it to me on the spot otherwise.'

'Oh, Ame. Of course they would. So I take it you told them to stick it up their bums?'

'Face to face?' Phil knew me better than that. 'Thought I'd see what Devlins come back with first. If it's a no-go, I might need the job-share to tide me over.'

'I'd love to go back to mid-level,' Phil sighed, 'let someone else have all the hassle, leave the work behind when you walk out of the building. Where was it at?'

'Clayton Associates.'

'Where are they?'

'Just on the outskirts of the city.'

'Never heard of them.'

'Exactly.'

Phil skipped past me up over the bridge. 'I'm seizing up; come on, let's walk.' I screwed my drink shut and followed, falling in beside her lithe stride. Sundays in the park were always my favourite. The days where you could see couples on benches, old men reading newspapers, children learning to ride bikes with their parents running anxiously behind.

Phil pulled the band from her hair, ruffling her fringe back into place. 'So, am I at least allowed to ask about the kid?'

'Nope.'

Phil tapped her hands against her thighs. 'I know you miss her.'

'Not talking about it,' I said, repositioning the jacket tied around my waist.

'I was watching you, you know, when you were holding her that night, while he-who-we-shall-not-speak-of was showing off.'

'He wasn't showing off, Phil. He's just—'

'Amazing, I know. I saw.

'You were completely natural with her, Ame. The way I would be with a Gucci puff-sleeve jacket. It was like she just… fit you. And you fitted her, too.'

The endorphins from my run were already starting to wane. I did miss Lily. I missed them both. 'What are you suggesting, Phil? A bit of light abduction?'

'We could probably swing it, but even with Carter's help, Rohan's going be a heavy lift.' I shot a look at her. 'Sorr-ee. I won't mention him again.' We'd fallen into one of those idle walks, more of an amble, where your feet felt heavier with each step.

'Would the job with the split hours really be so bad for you, hon? It wasn't that long ago you were trying to talk Adrian into splitting your leave with James. Now here it is, offered up on a plate.'

I tried not to laugh. 'You're right! But my life is like a Rubik's Cube, Phil. One piece twists into place and three others get messed up. I have no reason to take a part-time job any more. Other than having zero income, and going mad at Mum's.'

'So find a reason.'

'Like what?'

Phil stopped walking, rested her hands lightly on her hips and turned to me.

'Amy, I like my life. Even with that weirdo Carter in it, I like my life – like my freedom. I know that I *don't* want to be a mum. Ever. I like being able to lavish all of my money on myself, on indulgences like expensive cosmetics that I can leave out next to my pill, because some kid who's nearly as demanding as I am isn't going to wake up before I do and eat them. I am just not meant to be that woman, Ame. But… that isn't you. You *are* meant for it.'

Other than peripheral updates on the adoption that never was, we did not do the kiddie talk. Any strand of conversation even remotely linked to the subject of child-rearing was nearly always administered by Phil with a short sharp scratch. She lifted her hands and let them slap noisily against her thighs. 'Ame, you're meant to be a mother. And there's a kid out there who's waiting for you to go and be their mum. I can feel it, Amy. I believe it. You can think I'm just trying to make you stay, and you can go all the way to York if you want to, but you're going to find exactly the same truth up there.'

The park was so pretty, dappled in sunlight and shade.
'I don't think it's meant to be, Phil.'

'Bullshit,' she snapped. 'You've done it before and you
could do it again, if you wanted to. It wasn't James driving
everything on the last time, Ame, it was you. It was always
you. They're going to offer you that job on Friday, Ame,
and you can think that I'm being selfish, because I don't
want you to move away, but I'm telling you, there isn't a
job out there that's going to fill that hole for you. There
just isn't.'

'Go through it all again? Apply to be a single parent?'

'Just *a parent*, Ame. Why put any more labels on it than
that? In an ideal world, we'd all have someone to hold our
hands but sometimes we've just got to take a bloody big
breath, be brave, and dive in.'

'Phil, you've got Carter just waiting for the chance to
hold your hand, and I don't see you diving in! You've
blown him off!'

'I didn't blow him off, I just cooled it for a few weeks.
Blowing him off would have been turning him away on
my mum's doorstep when he's about to leave the country.'

'I'm not talking about him!'

'Why not? Anyone could see that Rohan's into you.
Why just let him go off with his ex, if he's asking
you to talk him out of it? What else has the guy gotta
do?'

'Nothing. He hasn't got to do anything. He should just… get on with doing his thing.'

'And what if his *thing* is you?'

'Phil!' I said in exasperation. 'I'm not it! His *thing* is his daughter… and his sport. That's why he's out there with Megan, in Stockholm, and I'm here. We have nothing in common! You've seen his lifestyle, Phil, he was a professional sportsman. He's got thousands of followers online, people who are like him, into the same things he's into.' People like the mother of his child. 'It would never have worked out anyway.'

I started walking again.

'Thousands of followers, huh? You've been stalking him, then?' she said, reaching a hand onto my shoulder.

I stopped moving and let out a long breath. 'No… my brother has.'

'Well, let's have a look, then,' she declared, ripping her phone from its strapping around her arm.

'Phil, I don't—'

'So don't. I will.' She began tapping the screen. '*H-o-t-b-u-n-s*… I'm kidding,' she teased. I stood there, conspicuously silent as Phil rifled through the internet pages. 'Ah. Here we go…Bloody hell, nineteen thousand followers. He is a popular fella. No wonder Viv hit her petition figures, Rohan put a call out to all his biker disciples,' she said, her thumbs making light work of the information in front of her.

'Rohan did what?'

Phil's eyebrow twitched, happy that she'd hooked me. 'He offered up one of his old bikes for anyone who signed and forwarded the link for the petition. I guess that makes him a nice guy.' She carried on scanning through the phone screen, looking for more proof that I should've pulled him into Mum's house that night and locked the door behind him.

'Damn, Ame, he looks good in a suit. These photos are recent – wanna see?'

I shook my head, dawdling beside her, trying to occupy myself with the other activity in the park and purge him from my head. Megan probably took those pictures. I did not need to think about any of it – *see* any of it.

'Looks like he's been a busy boy. He's doing a lot of handshaking with other guys who *don't* look so good in suits. They don't look very Swedish, either.'

'I don't think everyone in Sweden necessarily looks like Sven and Ulrika, Phil.'

'Okay, so how many of them have names like…' She peered closer at her phone. 'David Green and Roger Phillips? Of *Liverpool*-based global non-invasive ortho-paedics company Ortho-Ped Technologies?' Phil's voice lilted with the same confusion that was starting to fuzz my own head.

'What?'

'That's what it says. That he's been in meetings with these guys, some sort of manufacturing deal with this Ortho-Ped place. *Ortho-Ped Technologies are market leaders in the development, manufacture and supply of prosthetics, bracing and support products—'*

I interrupted Phil's spiel relay. 'Rohan's in Liverpool? As in England?'

Phil peered at me over the top of her phone. 'Now I'm no Judith Chalmers, Ame, but I'm pretty sure there isn't a Liverpool in Sweden.'

I pulled the phone from her hands, fingers hungrily whipping through the pictures on Rohan's profile. She was right. He did look good in a suit, but then we already knew that. There were entries, too, Rohan's updates on the meetings he'd had, the potential for his knee brace. I scrolled through them impatiently. For every snippet of information he'd posted, flurries of followers had replied to the thread, encouraging, congratulating... asking when they'd see him return to competitive sport.

'He never left the UK, hon.'

'But, she said... going to the games would open doors for him...'

'I guess not everyone's into the sassy photographer types?' Phil smiled, folding her arms in satisfaction. 'Looks like he didn't want to go through the doors Miss Thing might open for him when he could kick a few down by himself over here.'

I looked through the blurb at the top of Rohan's profile. There was a photo of him, his silhouette upside-down over a bike ramp against a setting sun. Beneath the picture simply read:

Ro Bywater
G-Force Gold Medallist
Beating my own path somewhere, probably on two wheels.

CHAPTER 37

I'D MISSED FOUR calls from Mum. I was just flicking through the times each had been made when her name appeared centre screen.

'Hi, Ma.'

I could already hear the impatience mixing with the hesitation. 'So? How do you think it went?'

I smiled at the phone, minding the tram tracks as I skipped across city square. Devlin Raines had been as thorough in their interview assault as I'd expected. Usually I might have felt more intimidated during the experience, but since last weekend's discovery that Rohan hadn't loped off into the sunset with Megan, I seemed to have this invisible cloak of indifference about me, impermeable to the effects of normal everyday concerns.

'Good. I think. They're going to let me know,' I answered. Rohan had to be back by now. I'd tried to think of reasons to just *stumble* past the mill but other than a well-timed river accident involving a canoe I didn't own, I was all out of light bulbs. I wasn't sure that he would save me now anyway.

'Oh,' Mum said. Even in her silence I could hear her mood dip.

Clinging to my portfolio and phone, I fed my way into the pedestrians on the pavement. The lunchtime bistro rush reminding me that as the only full-time option that didn't involve tele-sales, I did actually need this job.

'Mum, nothing's set in stone,' I reassured her. 'Even if they do offer it to me, I've got a lot to think about before I make any decisions,' I lied. My things were mostly still in boxes, awaiting their final destination. James and I had accepted an offer on the house and as soon as the conveyancing was complete, I'd have enough for a good deposit to put down on my own place before the job, if I got it, started in September.

'You mean like leaving your family and friends? Don't forget, you do have another option. It might be a lesser role, sweetheart, but the last interview you had offered far more flexibility for families.'

'But I don't have my own family, Mum.'

'No, and if you move away, sweetheart, you're going to be saying goodbye to the chance. Putting those hopes to bed for good. You'll have no support network up there.'

Mum had dropped a few well-placed hints over the last few weeks, how single parenthood might be nightmarish at times, but the rewards joyful enough that she couldn't regret a single day of raising us alone. Since James had emailed through details of the offer on the house, Mum had turned into Loyd Grossman and had been online and through the virtual keyhole of every three-bed semi in Greenacres Primary's catchment.

I stopped fussing with my earring, trying to hang on to the small semblance of something normal that the interview had at least given me. Rohan hadn't gone to Stockholm, but Megan wouldn't stay there for ever. 'I know, Mum. Look, I'll see you later, okay?'

There was an eruption of school children's laughter in the background, and I knew I was saved. Mum quickly said goodbye.

I knew I was causing her worry. Had been for years. That something had lifted in her since she'd been spending time with John might make York that tiny bit less painful for her. He'd volunteered to do a little remedial work here and there at the community centre, while Mum and her cohorts directed the rest of the voluntary task force. I'd never seen her so buoyant as she had been lately, a balloon bobbing on its ribbon, anchored to the earth only by the possibility of her daughter moving away. I didn't want her to be distracted from her fun, I wanted her to float away on it.

The only curse of being a parent is the constant worry you have for your child, she'd said. She deserved a bit of respite.

Past the main cluster of eateries, the pavement traffic thinned out enough to reveal the rows of shop fronts lining the square. Metal buckets filled with bright blooms drew my eye to the quaint little row of shops I could see running off the cobbled row further ahead. Mum loved flowers.

I made the hundred yards or so past a handful of rustic gift shops to the flower displays outside The Midnight Garden. The sunflowers were sumptuous beside paler, dusky pink peonies. I scanned them all, my eyes wandering too far and catching on the window display next door.

A little wooden windmill stood behind the glass, calico sails and the same pale mauve base as the one left behind in the spare room of my old house. Mum said she'd found it in town. I idled over to look at the other things on display with it. The toes of two little flip-flops peeking from beneath the brim of a sunhat, a toddler's T-shirt bearing the slogan 'I still live with my parents'.

I was poring over the delights of other items when the shop door rattled open. She was carrying too much in her hands, two of her bags slipping from her fingers onto the shop step. She let go of a small yip, and through the rest of her bags I caught a glimpse of a neat little bump beneath her dress.

'I've got it!' I called. A few of the baby clothes had nearly tumbled from one of the bags. I picked them all up, reading the words next to The Beatles logo on the little stripy Babygro.

'*All you need is love.* That's cute,' I said, slipping it back into the paper bag.

I straightened up to hand the things back to her. She looked like a rabbit in the headlights. I suppose we both did.

'Thanks,' she said timidly. I was still holding onto the bags, Sadie not sure enough to reach for them.

The pulse in my neck started to jump. *Why didn't you just go in the flower shop?*

I held the bags out for her.

She smiled, unsure where to direct her eyes.

I was trying not to look for that little round tummy again. I was literally blocking her path, suddenly embarrassed that I'd been caught gazing in, hankering like a child through a chocolate-shop window.

'How far along are you now?' I asked, trying to take some of the acidity out of this unfortunate crossing of paths. I didn't know where to look either, my smile falling flat.

Sadie cleared her throat. 'Twenty-two weeks.'

Phil hadn't even tried to update me on the office situation. I'd been blissfully unaware of Sadie's progress until a minute ago. She had that glow about her that only pregnancy seemed to bring.

'Do you know what you're having?' I asked, surprised at my own forwardness.

Sadie looked just as surprised, shaking her head and smiling weakly. 'I think she's a girl, but my mum says boy.'

'Twenty-two weeks… you'll find out soon enough.'

'Look, Amy, I—'

'It's okay, Sadie. He and I... it wasn't right, anyway.'

'It wasn't right between him and me either,' Sadie said, tucking the hair behind her ear. 'We haven't spoken for weeks.' She smiled, but hers fell flat too.

I didn't know why I felt empathy for her. 'Sadie, James can be...'

'A selfish pig? I know. But we don't need him. If he doesn't want to play a part in this little one's life, then we'll be just fine on our own.' The determination in her eyes was soft at the edges. Of all the women in the office, bar Phil, Sadie was the last one I'd have imagined walking straight into parenthood alone.

'Aren't you scared?' I asked.

She looked older since the last time we'd seen each other in the loos at Cyan. More weathered. We both were. 'Of having this baby alone? I'm petrified. I suppose you think I deserve it. You were always kind to me, you deserved better than I gave you back.' The shop door rattled behind her as another shopper left the shop, smiling as she squeezed past us. Sadie had done me a favour. It hadn't been the easiest mercy, or the most painless, but it was still a mercy of sorts.

'I don't think you deserve it, Sadie. I think James has a problem valuing the things he's got. Will you have anyone to help you?'

Sadie let out a long breath. 'My mum's going to be

around. She'll help me in the birth... but I don't want her to do everything or I'll be reliant on her. This is *my* child. Mine, to protect and take care of all by myself. Because I'm going to be her only parent, at the end of the day.'

The softness in her expression had nearly completely left her now. Sadie was resolute again. My phone began to buzz from within my bag.

'Good luck, Sadie. I hope everything goes well for you.' I meant it.

She blew a small puff of air from her lips. 'Thanks, but luck's overrated. All you need is love, right?'

I found myself nodding softly. Sadie gave me a last acknowledging smile, then slipped out from the shop entrance, leaving me there. I could see the windmill again in the shop window, still turning away the seconds unaffected by the changes in the world beyond the glass. Time would pass regardless. Sadie would have her baby, and if fate was kind to her, she would see her child through sleepless nights and chickenpox; first days at nursery, school, her first job interview. And she'd do it all alone if she had to.

My phone stopped buzzing, the noise replaced with a bleep alerting me to my voicemail. I swiped open the screen and retrieved my messages.

Hi, Amy. Phil Jenson here.

I know we said we'd be in touch over the next week or so, but I'm afraid as you're actively seeking employ-

ment, we didn't want to run the risk of you being snapped up.

Amy, we'd be delighted to offer you the position up in York. It would be great if you could give us a call at the office once you've picked up your messages.

CHAPTER 38

Mum set down her Tupperware tub of homemade iced buns in the foyer and ushered me excitedly into the main sports hall. Paint fumes hung heavy in the air, diluted with the sweeter flavour of newly sawn timber.

'Well? What do you think? Not bad, hey, for a bunch of grandmas and a tribe of uncouth youths?'

'And one grandfather!' John mumbled, walking in behind us, flecks of icing clinging to his moustache.

'They were for the boys, cheeky,' Mum chided, clearing the debris from John's mouth with her thumb. 'Come on, I'll show you what they've done to the smaller rooms.'

The basics of the hall were as I remembered, but I'd forgotten how impressive the effects a good clean-out and a thrifty facelift could have.

'It looks great, guys,' I agreed, squeaking across the newly buffed floor towards the secondary rooms at the back of the hall. 'I can't believe you've managed to do all this in just a couple of weeks!'

We'd just reached the far doors when Tristan and Lee burst through them, jostling each other for ownership of a basketball.

'We've had help.' Mum frowned, moving out of their way. 'Slow down, boys! Don't break anything before our grand reopening! I hope you've finished cutting that grass.' Her voice dropped to a whisper. 'They're good boys really, I couldn't believe it when they walked some of the girls round with their petitions. Karen's taken two of them on to keep her garden for her.'

I held the door open for Mum and John, leaving the boys to their squeaky scuffling on the floor behind us. 'Still looks like you've had your hands full.'

John took the door from me. 'Not us, the new *recreation coordinator* has been in charge of the youngsters. He's had 'em cracking on, too.'

We moved into the next room, brightly painted with crafting tables and a whole library of toys and playthings. It made sense to have the toddler group housed next to the kitchen where mums could replenish themselves with caffeine and sugar. 'Coordinator? The council have taken someone on?' I asked, following Mum through to the next room.

'Only part time. He's very good with the kids, he's had them footballing outside, volley-balling, roller-derbying – which I'm not so sure we'll stick with for health and safety reasons. But his main class has already seen enough people sign up that he'll be instructing here most days. He's just finishing up a taster class now so…' She held a finger over her lips.

John held the door open as we slipped through it. This was the room in which I used to have to suffer the injustice of watching my fellow Brownies receive their illustrious badges. It was cleaner now, newly painted in muted tones. As we rounded the wall, several pairs of jogging bottom-clad legs peeped into view, toes ceiling-bound, splayed out on their rectangular mats like fumigated bugs.

'And just bring your attention back to the present … focus upon the third eye… and continue… to breathe…'

I knew that gentle voice.

Carter caught sight of us as we hung back in the corner of the room. His face burst with a smile, his hand throwing a silent wave to me.

'Take your time… but when you're ready to get up… stretch, and slowly rise again.' Gradually, one by one, each of the bodies in the room came back to life.

I hadn't seen Carter for weeks, I wasn't sure that Phil had either, we'd maintained our pact of silence on each other's love lives.

'Hey, stranger!' he beamed, crossing the floor to us. He scooped me up for a hug. 'How's it going? We've missed you!'

Mum was smiling suspiciously. She hadn't said a word about Carter working at the centre. I wasn't sure why but I had a feeling she was up to no good.

'Good thanks, Cart. How are you? You've landed your dream job!' I grinned. It really was good to see him.

'Ah, well… the WI girls took a shine, talked me into the position with a promise of low pay and regular home baking.'

Mum gasped indignantly. 'And what else?'

'Oh yeah,' he said, smoothing the hair around his hairband, 'they reckon if I can keep the kids occupied a few evenings a week at youth club, I'll go to heaven, too.'

'And you're worth every sticky bun I've made you so far, Isaac,' Mum assured him. The dozen or so pensioners in Carter's class had mostly got back to their feet, huddling in smaller pockets of conversational groups as Carter led us over towards the firedoors. As soon as he pushed them open, a current of summer breeze swept into the room.

'It's been easy work for him since that monstrosity turned up,' John said, pointing to the ramps outside on the community centre's field. A swarm of kids were already careering over them on skateboards and scooters.

Carter released his hair from its band, ruffling it all free. 'Ro's reward for the kids, they've been busting a gut to get this place shipshape.'

His name was enough to make my skin tingle, I turned to see if Mum or John had caught it but they'd silently slunk off somewhere.

It was good to see the kids playing, but another thought twigged as I watched them.

'Is he moving away again already?' I asked jokily. Rohan couldn't be planning on spending much time at the mill without his beloved ramps. Megan might've talked him round, a fresh start somewhere.

Carter hung his head and laughed to himself. 'Ro hasn't got time to move house. He's been playing with the big boys, he's found a prosthetics company to work with him on the braces. They've given us a sweet new set of ramps to test ride them on.'

I kept pace with him as he stepped out further into the sunshine on the playing field. I'd been trying my best not to check in on Rohan's progress online. It hadn't been easy.

'That's great, Carter. I'm really thrilled for him. For both of you.'

Carter smiled, lifting his face to the sunshine. 'He tried to call you, you know.'

I sighed, giving the sun my face too. 'I know.'

'It threw him, not knowing whether to keep trying or not.' The guilt swelled inside me again, just as it had that last night on Mum's doorstep and most days since.

I gave up on the sun. 'It was difficult, Carter. He had other things going on, I didn't want to… complicate anything for him.'

Carter turned to me, his warm blue eyes knowing and intent. 'Ro's a complicated character. It's kinda his charm.' I couldn't argue with that. 'Even I haven't worked him out completely. I've never heard him talking about putting down roots before.' He shrugged. 'But after talking it all through with Meg, he's got it all planned out.'

My heart sank.

This was what I wanted for him, and Lily, but that didn't take the sting out of it. I smiled over the sensation of a complete body blow.

'That's good. I'm glad they've worked it out.'

'Yeah, me too. Meg's been really understanding, considering. I think she was hoping for more but they're working together for Lils.' Carter had turned back to the sunrays.

I tried to keep the puzzlement from seeping into my voice. 'Working together?'

Carter didn't move. 'Yeah. They've agreed to share Lily's care, so Meg can travel with work and Ro can do what he needs for the manufacturing bods at Ortho-Ped. Meg's looking for somewhere local to buy so Lils has less upheaval. They're talking about starting Lily at Greenacres nursery after the summer. Your mum looked surprised too when I told her yesterday, you kinda look like her a little now.'

I understood now why Mum had suddenly seen fit to thrust me and Carter together, a last-ditch effort at keeping me down here, with my family and friends, and him. I gave up on my voice. 'But... I thought...'

'Like I said. Complicated characters.'

A hot tingling was reaching up my neck. Carter began yelling over to the skateboarders, 'Oi! Clever lad – no helmet no play.' One of the other kids pinched his nose at Carter, motioning his hand like the waves of the sea. Then he lost his balance and slipped onto his backside. Carter rippled with chesty laughter. 'Little buggers, teach them to take the mick out of non-swimmers,' he tittered.

I knew my mother too well. She'd been screening Carter, working out when it was good for me to bump into him. It might've annoyed me but thoughts of Rohan were already heavy in my head, and other places. There wasn't room in my brain to make sense of what I thought about his and Megan's unexpected arrangement.

'They've done a good job with the paintwork, Carter,' I blurted, trying to force a change in brain activity. I was moving away in a matter of weeks, I needed a job, a purpose – none of which I had here.

'They're all right. It's a shame you're not moving anywhere closer, they could've come and splashed a bit of paint around for you, too. York, is it? Philippa said you haven't found anywhere yet.'

'You've seen Phil?'

A healthy glow tinged Carters cheeks. 'Hey, yoga brings people together.' He shrugged. I laughed quietly at my feet. It was a strange thought – Phil getting past her reservations and enjoying the company of a man like Carter for a change. It made me glad; he'd be good for her. Hopefully, she'd be good for him, too. 'So you're still at Vivian's for now? he asked.

'For now. I need to find somewhere soon, I start my job in September.'

'Yeah, congratulations on the big job.'

'Thanks.' It sounded hollow, even to me.

'Philippa's worried that you're going to be lonely up there.'

I smiled. 'I won't have enough time for loneliness, Carter. The job's pretty full-on. Anyway, I thought I'd try independent living for a change. Cut my own path.'

Carter looked over his shoulder at me. 'I know someone else who lives by that code.'

I moved over to Carter and reached up to peck his bristly face. The house-hunting wasn't going to do itself, no good would come of putting more of Rohan into my head than was already there. 'Say hey to him for me, Carter.'

'I will.'

'And don't let Phil boss you around too much.'

CHAPTER 39

'AND THEN, AUNTY Amy, the treeannysaurus rex comes in the room and bites the raptors so the people can exscape and the treeannysaurus rex ROARRRS!'

'It did? So the *treeannysaurus* saved the people?' I asked, trying to match Sam's wide eyes. Sam gave me a toothy grin and nodded his head emphatically. I feigned a look of deep-seated concern.

'Don't worry, Aunty Amy, I'm not afraid of dinosaurs. I can karate chop them if any come to Nanny's house.'

'I hope there aren't any coming to Nanny's house!' Mum called through from the kitchen. She went back to humming over John's cherry pies.

I gave a huge sigh of relief. 'Phew. Thanks, buster. I feel much safer having you here to look after us.' I smiled. 'Do you know that palaeontologists, those are the people who know lots of stuff about dinosaurs, think that dinosaurs turned into birds?' Explained a lot, I thought. Sam looked puzzled. I tried something easier. 'Does Mummy know that Daddy's been letting you watch *Jurassic Park*?'

'She does now,' Lauren grumbled, stepping into the

sunny room. 'That explains all the roaring at six o'clock this morning. Come on, Sam, Aunty Amy's busy on her laptop.'

'No, it's okay,' I said, Sam already fleeing from the conservatory to re-enact the T-rex's closing scene in the garden. 'Dinosaurs are more entertaining than…' I peered at the bottom of the screen, 'page seventeen of two-bed flats with no parking.'

'That bad, huh?' Lauren asked, soothing Harry over her shoulder. 'Wowsers. They aren't cheap up there, are they? You're going to need that salary.'

She was right, I could have a three-bed semi here for that, with a garden and parking. I puffed my cheeks out as a feeble mewling sound suggested Harry either agreed with us on the state of house prices or had smelled the Sunday lunch leftovers.

Lauren planted a kiss on him. 'Yes, young man. You cry. I want you nice and hungry.' Harry was onto something and stepped it up a gear.

'Still won't take the bottle?' I asked.

'It took me half an hour to express four measly ounces this morning. I bet he won't have it. He hates it!' At the sound of his mother's voice, Harry raised the stakes, breaking into a throaty protestation. 'Sorry,' Lauren winced, 'do you mind having him while I go and warm it up? Guy's already snoring in the lounge.'

'Sure. I've been waiting for a turn,' I beamed, seizing my chance at a snuggle.

'Hello, little boy! Are you giving your mummy a hard time?' I grinned. Harry stopped crying, watching me making daft gooey faces at him.

'Oh, crap and sod!' Lauren groaned. A growing circular damp patch had appeared over each of her breasts.

'Every time he cries, I bloody leak! Are you okay if I go and change, first?' I nodded, awed by the reaction of Lauren's body to Harry's voice alone. My milk had come in a few days after Jacob, but there was no bleating voice calling for it. 'I don't know how single parents do all this on their own. I honestly don't. I want my body back!' Lauren huffed. I smiled, nuzzling my face into Harry's downy hair. Outside, Sam was roaring at a butterfly. He caught me watching him and growled back across the garden at us.

I was going to miss them.

Somewhere in the distance over Mum's garden fence, the tinny melody of an ice-cream van was making his approach onto Victoria Street. Sam stood bolt upright in the garden, paralysed as he tried to pinpoint the source of the sound.

'The ice-cream man! THE ICE-CREAM MAN! Nannn-neeeeee!'

'Here you go, Sam!' I laughed. 'I've got some pennies here!'

Mum stepped into the conservatory. 'Did you say you had some cash?'

I rose from the rattan sofa, pulling a fiver from my back pocket.

'Whoops, you've just dropped something, sweetheart.' Mum bent down to retrieve a small white card. She scanned it, then swapped it swiftly for the five-pound note. 'Right, come on then, Samuel. Let's see what they've got.'

I turned the card over in my fingers. Anna's phone number sat scribbled over her social services contact details.

'How have you managed to keep him quiet?' Lauren asked, Harry's bottle warming in the jug she held. 'You've got the gift, Amy,' she said, reaching for him. 'Hey, maybe you could try him with the bottle?'

Anna's card was hot in my hand still. I slipped it back into my pocket. 'Actually, Lauren, staring at the laptop's given me a bit of a headache. I'm just going to have ten minutes upstairs,' I said, passing Harry to her.

'Oh, okay. Can I get you anything?' Harry's mood was beginning to freefall. He wasn't the only one.

'No, thanks,' I called from the kitchen. 'I'll be good in a few minutes.'

*

A few minutes turned into twenty, studying the artexed ceiling and Anna's penmanship. Downstairs was mostly quiet, Guy had stopped snoring, Harry was indisposed with his mother's milk and Samuel with the frozen counterpart.

I should've been back down there, spending as much time with them all as I could, but a heaviness in my chest had me pinned on my bed. Sadie had popped into my head, the image of her manhandling her bags alone, defiant that she was better off without an unwilling co-parent. I'd never asked Anna to talk me through single-parent applications. I'd dismissed the idea before even giving it a chance. I carried on studying the swirls in the artex, looking for the right path to present itself.

Outside the front of the house, it sounded as though somebody was moving their recycling bin, the sounds of empty cans rattling against each other along the pavement outside Mum's laurel bushes. I listened as the sound grew closer, then disappeared further up the road. I'd been looking at Anna's card long enough that I knew her number by heart now. I tried to think what I could ask her. What I would want her to say. It was too soon. I needed to reassess, like she said. But even I had to admit it, Mum was right. Once I left for York, I'd be putting those dreams to bed.

The nomadic recycler had doubled back on themselves, the clanging of metal growing louder again back down the street. I listening to this up and down the road twice more before Mum called up to ask if I could see who was making all the racket from my bedroom window. I pushed myself up and slumped over to the bay window, waiting for the noise to return to our part of the street again. I let out my window all the way. His red tee made him completely unmissable as he rode slowly past the mouth of the driveway, a few feet behind him, a bunch of cans strung to the back of his bike danced noisily over the tarmac. If I hadn't still heard the commotion, I might've thought I'd imagined him. A few thudding heartbeats later and he cruised past again, this time kneeling on his seat with his other leg outstretched behind him. A giggle bubbled up in me.

'Amy!' Guy bellowed upstairs. 'Your biker buddy—'

'I know!' I yelped, dancing out onto the hallway. My feet sounded clumsy on the stairs, my breathing suddenly laboured.

'Do you want me to go chase him off?' Guy teased.

'In your dreams, bro. He'd run rings around you.' I grinned, nipping out through the front door. When I reached the laurel hedge, I couldn't see him at first, the rattling cans had stopped. I stepped out, so I could see around the post box, to the heap that was lying in the road. His bike wheel was still spinning, the only motion as I stepped closer.

I had to admit, he played dead convincingly. It struck me then how foolish Cathy Brown had been to miss her chance.

'You appear to have had an unfortunate accident,' I said passively, coming to stand beside the spinning wheel. Nothing. I laughed a little and checked the street for cars, for a second considering whether he could have actually fallen for real. The street was quiet, thank goodness, this was my first body in the road.

'Okay, I'm checking your pulse now,' I declared,

crouching beside him. Still nothing. I realised I didn't actually know how to check a pulse anyway, although that wasn't the thing most concerning me – Rohan didn't appear to be breathing. At the risk of being completely suckered again like a total nitwit, I couldn't help but let the worry bubble up a tiny bit.

I leant in, to feel for any air over his lips. 'Rohan? Are you okay?' A hand wrapped around my wrist and two glorious hazel eyes opened at me. Something fluttered inside my ribs. He didn't have to reach far, closing the inches between us until I felt the warm welcome press of his mouth on mine. It was like another realm opening out beneath me. Something wonderful and delicious to topple into, where my vertigo left me to happily plummet. Everything else fell away with me. Thoughts of new jobs and old dreams, for one precious minute, freeing me of their binds.

'Are *you* okay?' came a breathy voice. I hadn't realised we'd stopped kissing. 'You haven't got a dog, have you?' He smiled, his face bursting into warmth. I heard tittering coming back from Mum's drive, Mum, Guy and Lauren all poking their heads around the bushes. Sam burst out, growling, with his claws held up.

I tried to still the fluttering in my chest before Rohan heard it. 'No, just the T-rex.'

Rohan took them all in, completely unfazed by the spectacle of them, or us, here in the street. 'They're not the most conventional bunch, are they?' he asked.

'Nope.' I smiled. 'They're pretty wonderful, though.'

Warm fingers slipped between mine. 'Unconventional is good.' He smiled, still lying there. 'I hear you're set on beating your own path?'

The heavy feeling was back, the binds finding their way back to me like the reeds in the millpond. It was difficult to look at him then, that softness in his expression I'd seen him reserve for Lily.

Rohan was studying my expression too. 'I thought maybe we could try a new path, together?'

A million what-ifs exploded behind my eyes like fireworks, chased by the sweeter sensation of Rohan's hand pressing against my back. He pulled me into him, his lips finding mine, and I was freefalling again.

CHAPTER 40

TARDINESS WAS NOT a good start. Parking had been a nightmare in a city plagued by roadworks. I'd lost one earring in the foot well of my car, the other deposited in my purse for safekeeping while I honked at the traffic. I'd had three separate offers of lifts to avoid this exact scenario, but no – I was doing my independence bit. That was the whole point, after all, to beat my own path.

It had only been ten minutes. I'd stopped pacing after five, sitting instead, watching the blossom drifting past the grand lead windows like spring snowfall. A support crew would be great right now, but I needed to do this on my own.

'Miss Alwood? Would you like to come back in?' Mr Healy was an urban planner by trade. A lofty man with a kindly face who'd already been through our mutual acquaintances in a bid to dejangle any nerves. It had almost worked. I followed him back into the meeting room.

Anna was sitting in the same position she had been two years ago, her hair longer now, hanging over her shoulder blades. Just as before, she didn't turn to look at me until I'd taken my seat. The chair, Dr Collins, was herself an adoptive parent of three boys – most likely with a much bigger garden than mine and hired help if she needed it. Despite the softness in her smile, my stomach was already churning.

'Miss Alwood, you've been on quite the journey in your efforts to adopt. I don't believe we've ever heard a social worker speak so highly on behalf of an applicant.' *Thud, thud, thud* … My heart seemed to think I was in the middle of *The Krypton Factor*. 'I have to commend you on your determination, and your integrity.'

But… I could hear it in the back of her throat. I forced my hand back down from my naked earlobe and slipped it under my thighs.

Dr Collins looked at her fellow panel members then came back to me. 'We'd like to offer you our congratulations, Amy. We will be forwarding our recommendation to the Local Authority for their approval. We think you'll make for a marvellous candidate to parent a sibling group of up to two children under the ages of five years.'

Thud, thud, thud. I swallowed as I tried to un-jumble what I'd just heard.

'Congratulations!' came a whisper beside me.

Anna tried to wipe her face discreetly before pulling my hand from under my leg and squeezing it earnestly. Dr Collins spoke again, but I only caught parts of it in my delirium. Something about being satisfied that Clayton Associates were an accommodating employer, and that my part-time voluntary work at Greenacres Primary had equipped me for most of the hurdles that lay ahead.

I tried to take it all in. Suddenly I had a better understanding of what it must've felt like for each of the birds that had collided with Ro's bedroom window over the last couple of years. Right now, I couldn't have been more shocked if I'd have flown nose-first into someone's double glazing.

'And how lovely that your mother is headmistress at the primary school your children will attend.'

What I'd just heard was like a bucket of cold water in the face, bringing me round.

Your children.

The words punched through the air like a scud missile. That's what she'd just said to me. *My children.*

I managed to hold it together while another of the panel members reminded me that the senior official at the local authority still had to review all of the paperwork including the recommendation of the panel before the absolute decision was made. Dr Collins impressed on me that it wasn't unheard of for the senior official to go against the panel's suggestion, but such incidences were very rare.

But there was no room for fear in me. I was all full up.

Anna had quickly closed the pleasantries with the panel, ushering me out through the maze of corridors to the huge entrance vestibule of the Town Hall, I think so she could finally free herself of her professional constraints and bear hug me with abandon as we snivelled into one another's hair.

'I can't believe it, Anna. I just… it's happening. It's really going to happen now.'

Because no one else was responsible for this, no one could walk out on me or change their mind or let me down, and it have any bearing on my application to be an adoptive mum.

'I told you!' she squealed. 'I told you you would do it, Amy! What will you do now? You can't drive anywhere yet, you're shaking like a leaf. Will you call Rohan?' His name still made my tummy flip. I looked at my watch.

'No, he'll be taking Lily to her after-school swimming lesson now.'

'Oh,' Anna said forlornly. Rohan had this effect on most women. I couldn't blame her, I was still trying to manage my own swooning tendencies when he was around. 'It's a shame he couldn't be here,' she mused.

A smile broke over me as I remembered him standing completely naked in the tub trying to pull off one of Carter's more advanced yoga positions this morning. He'd said a morning soak would help relax me. The endorphins after half an hour of belly laughs had definitely helped.

'He wanted to, but Lily's mum's away with her boyfriend this weekend so he's having Lily tonight, and I... well, you know. Didn't want a fuss if things didn't go well.'

'Well, it's still a shame. He was telling me how much he's looking forward to Lily having a little brother or sister to enjoy the rope swing with. She might get both, now! If you get a sibling group!'

I smiled with her – the thought was intoxicating – although I didn't think we'd be trying out the rope swing over the millpond until everyone had their swimming proficiency, Carter included.

'Rohan's a great guy, Amy. Us social workers have a nose for these things. I could see it by how much he really wanted this to work out for you, even though he says it will mean you won't move in with him for a while yet.'

It was the only downside. The only one. But no matter how much pleading Rohan had got Lily to do on his behalf, it was too important that I do this right. That any child I might have to love would feel secure and safe in our home, without the risk of any unsettling changes. I didn't think Rohan was going anywhere, even Carter had said it, with Lily over for half the week and a rolling contract with Ortho-Ped, Rohan's foot had finally stopped itching. And me? I knew I wasn't going anywhere, and so there was no rush. That was the next adventure to look forward to, the next path we would beat together, as an extended, unconventional and, if fate was kind to us, *happy* family.

Anna wiped the residual mascara from under her eyes and took a deep satisfying breath. 'So, can you grab a quick coffee before you shoot off and share your news? I could do with someone to limit the amount of grasshopper pie I keep buying at Gino's Caffe. I am… eating for two now.'

I snapped my head around at her, open mouthed.

'Anna! That's amazing! Congratulations!' The tears were there again, erupting in a state of shared happiness. Anna giggled, her emotions getting the better of her, too. 'I'm so happy for you, Anna, that's just… What an amazing day,' I said, wiping the deluge from my face.

'So you've got half an hour to share a few rounds of grasshopper pie?' she asked, laughing.

'Absolutely.'

We probably looked like two escapee pandas when we pushed through the decorative doors of the Town Hall together. We were both giggling like children as we took the stone steps down onto the small paved square, dotted with planter beds and flurries of white blossoms. Anna was reminding me of the ills of morning sickness when a block of orange caught my eye at the roadside.

Carter and Phil were haggling with a parking warden, Phil gesticulating over towards the Town Hall while Carter pulled idly at a curly strand of hair. Rohan straightened up from where he'd been leaning against Bertha, Lily still in her school uniform on his hip.

'Looks like someone couldn't keep away,' Anna gleamed.

Lily waved, her blonde plaits just clinging together after a hard day's play at Greenacres. I could see her leaning to be allowed to run over to us, but Rohan was holding her, unsure. Carter tugged on Phil's jean pocket and they both forgot about the warden and looked over too.

I could see the question in Rohan's eyes as we walked

quietly over the square towards them, blossom flittering through the air like paper snow all around us. I must be mad not moving in with him, I could barely stop myself from running across the paving stones and launching myself through the air at him. He set Lily down with a few words whispered in her ear, and ran a hand up the back of his neck.

I could feel the smile, leaching into my features. He smiled back, those perfect lines of his mouth, the warmth in eyes still waiting for their answer. I nodded softly.

Rohan's eyebrows lifted, inviting me to confirm what he thought I'd just told him. My mouth broke into a grin, laughter escaping me as I nodded again and held up two fingers, clearly enough that they could all see it. Anna squeezed my arm, Rohan, Phil and Carter all exploded into rapturous whooping, and Lily burst into tears at the sudden commotion behind her. She ran away from it all, until she'd made it safely to my legs. I lifted her up, into me, burying my new tears in the softness of her blonde plaits.

'It's okay, sweetie. Everybody is just so excited.' I laughed, through the escalating efforts of more tears. I seemed to be suddenly made of water. If Mum could have been here with us instead of being stuck preparing for the good, the bad and the ugly of parents' evening, Carter might've needed armbands. Anna stepped away as Rohan fed his arms around us, pressing a kiss onto my lips. I wanted him to squeeze me tighter in his arms, this was my favourite place.

He moved his mouth to my ear. 'Well done, Mama Bear. We're going to have some fun now,' he whispered, sitting another kiss on mine and Lily's cheeks. 'I hope they like bikes.' He grinned. Carter and Phil caught up, the traffic warden berating them as he followed them over. Carter seemed to have heard my wishes, and clamped his arms around us all, locking Phil, Rohan, me and Lily in my arms, together.

'Are you crying, Phil?' Rohan laughed.

'No!'

'I am,' Carter squeaked, burying his head into Phil's shoulder.

'Oh bugger it, I am too,' Phil sniffled.

Beyond our circle, there in the middle of Town Hall's remembrance gardens, Anna was sniffling again. I looked to check she was okay when Rohan reached an arm around her too, pulling her into the fold.

But there was a grey cloud trying to edge in. 'If you don't shift it, *now*, I'm going to ticket you,' boomed a disgruntled voice. Carter reached out, an invitation for one more in our cuddle puddle. The warden batted his hand and stropped off in Bertha's direction.

As nice as it felt to be there, in my cluster of support and affection, the air was starting to get a little thin wedged between so many bodies.

'So, does anyone else fancy grasshopper pie?' Anna asked in a small voice. I couldn't even see her face.

'Grasshopper pie? Has that got liquorice in it?'

'No, Carter.' I smiled.

'Rhubarb or ginger?'

'No, Rohan.'

'Calories?'

'Phil, seriously.'

'I can help you work those off, Philippa.'

Carter yelped.

'I meant with yoga!'

'Oh, sorry.'

'Does grasshopper pie have grasshoppers in it, Amy?'

'I don't think so, baby,' I said. 'Let's go and find out.'

The city felt different as our unlikely rabble made their way to Gino's Caffe. The pavements could've been made of clouds for the lightness I felt inside myself. Nothing would ever replace Jacob, or the life that should've been his, but Jacob wasn't all that had slipped away that night in the hospital. I'd lost a part of me, a part of who I was. And now, sat here in the warm atmosphere of a little bistro on one of the city's side-streets, surrounded by laughter and conversation and grasshopper pie, I finally felt as if I had it back.

* * * * *

ACKNOWLEDGEMENTS

First and foremost, I have to thank Anna Scott, ITV producer extraordinaire, blonde bombshell and all-round good egg. No, you didn't have a hand in this book; however, in my typical buffoonery I neglected to thank you in the last and, after all the laughs and fabulousness you brought with you, a thank you was the very least I owed you. Thank you!

As always, gargantuan thanks galore to my rip-roaring ever-enthusiastic, ever-encouraging editor Donna–The Don–Hillyer. I couldn't possibly bust through the pain barrier without you. Well, you and an endless supply of chocolate-dipped confections and caffeine. The power of three, right there, folks.

Huge thanks also to the powerhouse of office ninjas at Mills & Boon/Harlequin UK for your massive support throughout the last twelve wonderful months. I must've caused at least one of you an epic headache so, to that person in particular, a very hefty thank you. And soz! I'm going to roll the lovely lot at Cherish PR into that too. Thanks gang! Aspirins are in the post.

To my agent Madeleine Milburn, thank you for coming aboard. It feels good already, Agent Milburn! (You might want to get some aspirins in too.)

Jim, thank you for always deserving a thank you, and thanks too for shrugging it off when you didn't hear one as often as you should have.

To my other brilliant boys, Bodhi and Wolf, for letting me slip away quietly into my room and regress into grimy student-esque habits without raising too many complaints about missed bedtime stories and school projects, thanks, fellas–you're more awesome than I know how to write.

Mena, thanks, kid, for lending me your ears and telling me which ideas are really too naff to write about. Taz, thanks for lending me your home so I have somewhere else I can shuffle my grimy student-esque habits around. I'll replace the chocolate-dipped stuff...and the coffee. Mum, thanks for telling me that I can do it. And then telling me again.

Last but definitely not least, an enormous thanks to Clare and Podge. Clare, for helping me to understand a journey that has to be heard, not researched, and Podge for the memory of school-trip oysters, a trauma burned into my psyche. You both rock.

Look out for Anouska Knight's next book,
coming in 2015.

Alex Foster lives a quiet life—single, working at the food
bank…avoiding the home she hasn't visited in eight years.
Then her sister Jaime calls. Their mother is sick and Alex
must return home. Suddenly she's plunged back into the
past she's been trying to escape.

Returning to her home town, memories of the tragic
accident that has haunted her and her family are impossible to ignore. Alex still blames herself for what happened
to her brother. It's soon clear that her father blames her
too—as well as also blaming Joseph Finn, her former boyfriend. Alex struggles to deal with the past, her guilt, and
her undeniable feelings for Finn—will she ever escape the
ghosts of the past?

Turn the page to enjoy
an exclusive extract

PROLOGUE

Five generations of Fosters have lived in Eilidh Falls.
Four of them without incident. Blythe Foster had never
really counted the awkward birth of her third and final
child as trauma enough to break the disaster-free run of
the Foster lineage, but her husband Ted had never completely managed to forgive the staff of Kerring General
for young Dillon Foster's 'sleepy' arm.

Dill's arm wasn't that sleepy. Alex and Jem were
always catching their little brother putting that arm to
more than effective use when mischief demanded it.
Alex thought that it made their father quietly glad each
time Dill got into a scrape, as if that somehow confirmed that it was going to take a damned sight more
than a little nerve damage to slow a Foster lad down,
thank you very much. This morning, however, Blythe
Foster wanted nothing more than for her nine-year-old
son to do just that. She'd offered a friendly, informal,

nothing-too-fancy get-together to a family she'd often felt might benefit from a little neighbourliness and now she only had seven hours left to pull off the perfect Ideal Home-standard soirée. An informal soirée, mind. Only with her best bone china.

Blythe had watched Joseph Finn walking up the long garden track towards the Fosters' house, out on the edge of town. She'd allowed herself a smile as she'd heard her daughter exchanging quiet greetings with him at the door before leading him into the kitchen.

'Good morning, Mrs Foster,' Finn had offered. Blythe hadn't had a chance to return the courtesy when Dill burst back into the kitchen for the umpteenth time, aggressively wielding the new bow and arrows his father had given to him the day before.

'Holy cow! It's the buck-toothed assassin!' Alex had joked. Dill loosened his stance just long enough to give his biggest sister one of those wonky smiles of his. Alex affectionately ruffled Dill's mop of sandy hair and grinned as Dill flashed her an unapologetic toothy smile. He was at that stage where baby teeth had been ousted for big grown-up teeth that didn't quite fit him yet, but he was no less the charmer because of them.

'Dillon Arthur Foster, I've told you, not in the house. Those things are sharp and dangerous!' Blythe warned sternly.

'But dad said this would be good exercise for making my arm stronger!' Dill had protested. Another look from his mother and Dill's shoulders slumped.

It had been Joseph Finn's idea. Not the soirée, absolutely not—Finn was the last person who wanted to sit making chit-chat around a dining table under the watch-ful scrutiny of his girlfriend's family, Edward Foster in particular—but it was Finn's suggestion to forego a few hours out in the sun with Alex and take Dill off Blythe's hands instead. Blythe had almost hugged him to death when he'd offered. Joseph Finn, she'd realised then, wasn't quite as scrawny as he'd been just a year or two ago when Alex had first brought him to her mother's attention. He was now a young man of eighteen, with broadening shoulders to go with the harder angles of his face the passing years had blessed him with. Blythe had hurriedly thrown a few sandwiches into a bag for them, offering several still-warm blueberry muffins if Finn would take Rodolfo along with them for some much overdue exercise. Basset hounds were notably lethargic, but Rodolfo didn't even bark at strangers in his yard, he was that idle.

'I'll stay here then, Mum,' Alex had offered, warily regarding her brother and the way his face lapsed into vacancy as he sneakily raised his bow and arrow again, taking aim at the picture of Jem, his less tolerant sister, on the kitchen windowsill. 'I'll wash up or something… while Finn takes Hyper Robin Hood and Lazy Dog for some fresh air.'

Blythe had tried not to watch as Alex and Joseph Finn had traded conciliatory looks while Dill sprang about the kitchen, perfecting his aim again. Yes, Blythe liked Joseph Finn, she'd decided. And she would tell her husband later on what a lovely boy he was for their daughter. What a nice man she thought he'd make and that Ted should be friendly towards him when

Joseph brought his mother over for dinner later. Maybe she wouldn't tell Ted everything she liked about Joseph Finn, like the way she'd seen him looking at her Alexandra—as if he'd will the rest of the world to fall away to nothingness so that he could absorb every last molecule of her without distraction. Alexandra. Her beautiful, clever girl, on the edge of womanhood and all the excitement and heartache and wonder it had in store for her. Ted had already told his wife that she probably spent too long listening to too many bloody operas about all-enduring love neither time nor obstacle could prevent. He'd also said that no daughter of his was yet old enough to have a serious boyfriend, that Alexandra would have her romance now and then forget all about the Finn boy once she eventually went off to university.

We'll see, Edward Foster, Blythe had thought to herself and then, in case Ted wanted to add anything further, she'd turned up *The Magic Flute*.

Summer's grip seemed tighter still down by the river. 'The Old Girl', the locals called it. Generations of parents had taught their children to be mindful of the river's moods, that she could change and you'd be sorry if she caught you out. It was only early September, but Alex had already noted that even the new college term hadn't curtailed the feeling that Eilidh Falls was still in the bosom of long, hazy days and short shadows. 'Don't come home wet!' Blythe had warned Dill, as they'd left the house. This was an afternoon perfect for paddling around in the plunge pool up by the succession of gentle waterfalls from which the town took its name. To manage the temptation, Alex and Finn had agreed to avoid the falls and head further downriver, where the water was too fast for paddling.

Finn had asked what everyone wanted to do. Dill wanted somewhere to hang his archery target, Rodolfo wanted to collapse and walk no more and Finn himself wanted to sketch out a few scenes of the local landscape for his final-year college art project. Alex simply wanted this, right here, exactly as it was, but she didn't say so, of course. That wasn't the cool thing to say, even to Joseph Finn, who didn't much care about *cool* anyway.

An hour had already passed; Dill was on his third attempt to successfully sink home one of his missiles into the cork target hanging against the alder tree. His fingers were sore, so periodically he'd slumped forlornly into the grass beside his sister as she watched Finn's drawings of the riverside come to life on the page before him. Each time Dill had taken a break, Alex had cheered her brother with a hearty dose of slobbery raspberries blown into his neck. Once she had him giggling, his gangly limbs overtaken with the weaknesses of laughter, he was easy enough to pin down. And then he'd go and gather his arrows and try again.

'You just moved again!' Finn accused.

'I did not!'

'Trust me, I am paying very close attention, Miss Foster. And you just moved, again. The shadow beneath your lips has changed.'

'Are you drawing my lips?' Alex murmured, suddenly self-conscious that she was guiding even more attention to them by speaking. She didn't think she had particularly sketch-worthy lips. Her nose was too straight too, like her dad's, and she knew her eyes were utterly unexceptional. 'Sorry, hang on a sec…' she said, desperate to steal her own face back for a moment. She flicked her head around to check that Dill was still behind her, trying again with his sleepy arm to pull the bow-string back with enough vigour that just one of his arrows might have enough gusto to make it as far as the target. Alex's eyes fell to the litter of spent arrows on the ground between Dill's feet and the alder tree. Lying there, they didn't look sharp or dangerous at all. 'Do you want to try standing a little closer, Dill Pickle?' Alex asked gently.

Dill didn't even turn around, his right arm jutting awkwardly out at an angle to his body. 'Nah. I'll get a good one in a minute,' he sighed, stretching back the bow-string until his elbow began to shake with the effort. Dill's fingers released the string and the very definite sound of taut, twanging cord cut through the air. Even Rodolfo raised his melancholy face to follow the arrow cutting its wobbled path straight over the top of the target and into the far branches overhanging the water.

'Ah, man! I missed,' Dill exclaimed, his arrow hanging precariously from its leafy cradle.

'Dill, that was a great shot!' Finn shouted, jumping to his feet. 'Quick, grab another arrow and try again. While you're still motoring.'

Alex was on her feet too, smoothing the flecks of grass from where they clung to her bare legs. Dill tried again, concentrating hard enough that he didn't appear to be breathing. Or maybe she was imagining it.

Concentration.

The arrow twanged through the air, thudding home into the outer band of the target.

'Dill! You hit it!' Alex yelped, leaping towards her brother. Rodolfo seemed sufficiently stirred by Dill's achievement to wriggle unexpectedly from where he'd been sprawled out on the earth, just as Alex was trying to skip around him. For a moment there was a scrambling of toffee-coloured fur and long tanned legs, and then those same legs found themselves tumbling into a patch of stinging nettles by the riverbank.

Dill burst into a fit of throaty laughter as Finn kicked through the stingers after Alex.

'Ouch,' Alex whimpered, as two big hands pulled her to her feet. Dill stopped laughing now that he could see his sister's reddened legs. The rash on her skin had risen as quickly as the nettle stems had again, after being temporarily flattened by clumsy limbs. Finn surveyed their hostile environment. Alex saw that his legs were getting stung too. Finn wasn't like the other boys his age in town. He didn't buy his clothes from the same shops they all seemed to; in fact he always seemed most comfortable when he was wearing something spattered in oil paint, or clay or whatever medium he'd been working in.

'Alex, climb up on to my back. I'll carry you out.'

'But…then you'll get stung again.'

Finn turned soft green eyes on her. 'And?' He smiled. 'You're my girl, Alex. I'll carry you.' Alex might have melted right then; melting was perfectly acceptable at seventeen, she felt, but Dill had started making theatrical retching sounds behind them at the romance taking place over in the nettle patch.

Finn didn't seem to notice the nettles after that. He gently scooped her up and waded back out of the stingers, gently setting Alex down beside his pencil tin and paper pad, and began scouring the grasses around them. Dill had already lost interest and had taken to scratching something into the tree bark with one of the arrowheads.

'What are you looking for?' Alex asked, still a little aflutter at Finn's gesture of moderate heroism.

'Dock leaves. I saw some as we were walking in off the path. I'll be back in a minute.' Alex had sat there like a good patient, being patient, as Finn went off to ramble through the undergrowth. Dill was still battling on with what looked like the beginnings of a letter 'D' against the tree trunk. The fluttering had abated now and Alex's legs had begun to tingle and itch.

'I'm just going to see if I can help Finn find those dock leaves any quicker, Dill. Don't move, OK?' It looked as though Dill would be there a while; he wasn't even on the 'I' yet. 'Maybe just do your initials, hey, kid?' she suggested, as Dill called a preoccupied reply. 'I'll be one minute.'

Alex found Finn further into the thicket than she'd expected, with an armful of scraggy leaves. 'Do we need all of those?' she asked, rubbing at the discomfort along the backs of her legs. Finn crouched down, scrunching up one of the healthier-looking leaves in his hands and then gently rubbing it along the clusters of pale blisters colonising her skin.

'I got extra in case Dill decides to roll around in there too, before we get him home safe and sound,' he smiled. 'At least we'll have something to talk about over dinner later. I don't know much about mechanics.'

Alex realised then, Finn was actually nervous about the dinner Blythe had been planning. Nervous about eating with her father. She couldn't help but smile.

'He's not as bad as he likes to make out, Finn. Honestly. He's a big softy,' she said, touching him lightly on the shoulder.

Finn got back to his feet. 'Your dad? You sure? I think he blows up the tyres on people's cars with his own mouth. He sure doesn't seem overly *soft* towards me.' Finn reached his hand forwards, taking the edges of Alex's fingers in his. She was fluttering again, way before he leant in, laying the smallest kiss at the edge of her lips.

Alex swallowed, trying to speak past the hammering in her chest. 'Trust me. My dad's bark is a *lot* worse than his bite,' she managed. 'He's just protective of us kids.'

It was at that moment Alex's words seem to spring to life, taking the form of urgent, echoing barks rising into the air somewhere back over by the riverbank. Alex saw the look of her own surprise reflected in Finn's face. They both hurried the hundred or so yards back through the thicket and grasses to where the alder tree hung mournfully over the water's edge, Rodolfo's fervent barking enough to jostle his stout body around on the spot as his urgency towards the river grew.

'Where's Dill? *Where's Dill?*' Alex allowed her eyes to sweep first left, then right along the grassy riverbank. She was still screaming Dill's name when Joseph Finn shouted something and jumped into The Old Girl. Alex could see now, Finn was following the arrow already floating away downriver.

If you enjoyed **A Part of Me**,
why not share your thoughts with
hundreds of other Anouska Knight
fans and post a review at:

Also by Anouska Knight

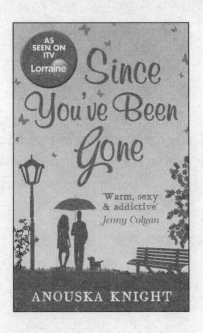

Make it a summer to remember with the fantastic new book from Sarah Morgan

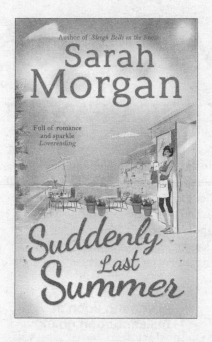

Fiery French chef Elise Philippe has just heard that the delectable Sean O'Neil is back in town. After their electrifying night together last summer, can she stick to her one-night rule?

Coming soon at millsandboon.co.uk

There's a first time for everything...

V!RG!N

RADHIKA SANGHANI

Ellie has never considered her lack of sexual
experience a problem—until her doctor effectively
calls her a binge-drinking virgin. Now she's on a
mission to pop her twenty-one-year-old cherry.
Can she overcome a domineering mother, brave
the waxing salons of London, avoid having her
heart broken and shed her V-plates once
and for all?

**Coming soon at
millsandboon.co.uk**

Discover more romance at

www.millsandboon.co.uk

❤ WIN great prizes in our exclusive
competitions

❤ BUY new titles before they hit the shops

❤ BROWSE new books and REVIEW
your favourites

❤ SAVE on new books with the
Mills & Boon® Bookclub™

❤ DISCOVER new authors

PLUS, to chat about your favourite reads,
get the latest news and find special offers:

🔲 Find us on facebook.com/millsandboon
🐦 Follow us on twitter.com/millsandboonuk
❤ Sign up to our newsletter at millsandboon.co.uk